CLASSIC ADVENTURES ACCORDING TO SPIKE MILLIGAN

Other titles by the same author:

Fiction
THE MURPHY

Children's fiction and poetry
A CHILDREN'S TREASURY OF MILLIGAN – CLASSIC
   STORIES AND POEMS
BADJELLY THE WITCH – A FAIRY STORY

Non-fiction
THE FAMILY ALBUM – AN ILLUSTRATED AUTOBIOGRAPHY

Poetry
A MAD MEDLEY OF MILLIGAN

Other related titles
SPIKE MILLIGAN – A CELEBRATION
THE GOONS – THE STORY

CLASSIC ADVENTURES ACCORDING TO SPIKE MILLIGAN

First published in 2002 by
Virgin Books Ltd
Thames Wharf Studios
Rainville Road
London W6 9HA

Black Beauty According to Spike Milligan first published in
Great Britain in 1996 by Virgin Publishing Ltd
Frankenstein According to Spike Milligan first published in
Great Britain in 1997 by Virgin Publishing Ltd
The Hound of the Baskervilles According to Spike Milligan first
published in Great Britain in 1998 by Virgin Publishing Ltd
Robin Hood According to Spike Milligan first published in
Great Britain in 1998 by Virgin Publishing Ltd
Treasure Island According to Spike Milligan first published in
Great Britain in 2000 by Virgin Publishing Ltd

Illustrations by Rob Seabury

A catalogue record for this book is available from the British
Library.

ISBN 1 85227 963 X

Typeset by TW Typesetting, Plymouth, Devon

Printed and bound in Great Britain by CPD Wales

CONTENTS

BLACK BEAUTY
ACCORDING TO
SPIKE MILLIGAN

There once was a horse called Black Beauty
He was well bred and always did his duty
He came from very good stock
He had a lovely body with a huge cock
His mother was lovely with a wonderful tail
Which dragged behind her like the Holy Grail
His father died, a handsome dude
And he ended up as dog food
Black Beauty would lead a long life
A mixture of Peace, Tranquillity and Strife.

1. MY EARLY HOME

I will always remember my early stable
We think of it when we are able
My mother was a horse
And, so was I, of course
I always stayed close to my mother
Because of horses, there were no other
I drank my mother's milk I recall
Otherwise I would have got bugger all
Oh yes, I remember when I was young
Grassy meadows, flowers and dung.

The first place that I can well remember was a large pleasant meadow with a pond of clear water full of frog spawn in which I nearly drowned. It would have been the first case of a horse drowned in frogs' spawn. Over the hedge on one side we looked on to a ploughed field where a woman was pulling a plough with a man steering it, occasionally striking the woman with a whip. It was a typical rural scene mixed with wife-beating. On the other side, we looked over a gate at my master's house. If you stood the other side, you could see us looking at our master's house. At the bottom, a steep bank overhung a running brook. Girls with babies born out of wedlock used to throw the babies in there to drown them.

Whilst I was young I lived on my mother's milk because I could not eat grass. In the daytime I ran by her side, and at night I lay down close by her side. When it was hot, we used to stand by the pond in the shade, watching the children fall in and drown. When it was cold, we had a nice warm shed.

As soon as I was old enough to eat grass, my mother used to stuff it down my throat until it kept coming out the back. I went six times that day. She was a police horse and used to go to riots and her master would bash people over their heads. I was so proud, I couldn't wait for the day when I had a rider who would bash people over the head.

I used to run with the young colts. We would frequently bite and kick.

One day there was a great deal of kicking, one or two horses were kicked unconscious. My mother whinnied to me and, as I had just been kicked unconscious as well, she ran toward me.

'Pay attention to what I am going to say'; so I paid attention. 'The colts who live here are cart-horses, and of course they have no manners. You have been well bred and well born; your father had a great name in these parts. I hope you will grow up gentle and good, lift your feet up when you trot, and never bite or kick.'

I have never forgotten my mother's advice; I knew she was a wise old horse, and our master thought a great deal of her. He thought of her when he was in the garden, he thought of her when he was in bed, and he thought of her when he was in the kitchen. He never thought of her when he was in the loo. Strange that. Her name was Duchess.

Our master was a good man, sometimes he was a good woman. Strange that. He went to church every Sunday and lit candles. Not much happened, except the church burnt down. When she saw him at the gate, she would neigh with joy, and trot up to him. He would pat and stroke her and say, 'How is your little Darkie?' I was a dull black. He would give me a piece of dry bread, the mean bugger, and sometimes he brought a carrot for my mother. Why did she do this grovelling for a bloody carrot? My mother always took him to the town on market day in a little gig.

There was a ploughboy called Dick who sometimes came into our field to pluck blackberries. When he had eaten all he wanted, he would have 'fun' with the colts, throwing stones, bricks and sticks to make them gallop. We did not much mind him, for we could gallop off; but sometimes a stone would hit and hurt us.

One day, he had just thrown a brick at my head; the master was in the next field watching, and catching Dick by the arm and his private parts, he gave him such a box on the ear and a kick up the arse. We never saw Dick any more but we heard that he joined the French Foreign Legion and was killed by an Arab who threw a brick at him. Old Daniel, who looked after the horses, was just as gentle as our master, so we were well-off.

2. THE HUNT

One day a hunt galloped thru
That is a thing they used to do
As the hunt galloped by
'Get the bastard,' was their cry
Who the bastard was they did not say
And we never found out to this very day
In fact they were chasing a hare
The trouble was, it wasn't there
Frustrated, they chased a rat
But they didn't even catch that.

Before I was two years old, something happened which I have never forgot. It was early in the spring; there must have been a little frost in the night and a light mist still hung over the plantation and meadows and hung over the house. We were feeding in the part of the field where the mist hung overhead. In the distance we heard what sounded like a cry of dogs. The oldest colt raised his head. He said, 'There are the hounds!' With the mist hanging over them we could only see their legs. We cantered off to the upper part of the field, where we could look over the hedge and see the other side. My mother and a very old riding horse in a wheel chair were standing near.

'They have found a hare,' said my mother, 'and if they come this way, we shall see the hunt.'

And soon we could only see the legs of the dogs in the mist. They were tearing down the field of young wheat next to ours. They did not bark nor howl nor whine, but kept on a 'yo! yo, o, o! yo! yo, o, o!' at the tops of their voices. Dogs who say 'yo! yo, o, o! yo! yo, o, o!' are very hard to find. Then came a number of men in green coats on horseback, all galloping as fast as they could. Some were doing 100 miles per hour and soon they were away into the fields lower down; then they seemed to lose the scent and the dogs left off yo-yoing and ran about in every direction, mostly away.

'They have lost the scent,' said the old horse, 'perhaps the hare will get off.'

'What hare?' I said.

'How do I know what bloody hare? Likely enough it may be one of our own hares; any hare will do for the dogs and men.'

And before long the dogs began their 'yo! yo, o, o!' again, and back they came, all together at full speed, making straight for the wrong way, to the part where the high bank and hedge overhung the brook.

'Now we shall see the hare,' said my mother, and just then, a hare, wild with fright, rushed by. Six or eight men leaped their horses clean over the hedge, close to the dogs. The hare tried to get through the hedge; it was too thick, and she turned sharp round to make for the road, but it was too late; the dogs were upon her with their wild cries; we heard one shriek and that was the end of her. 'Heel!' said the master of hounds, and blew his horn. The hounds did not heel, seemed not to hear, and went on tearing the hare to pieces. 'Heel!' he shouted again, but they did not hear. He whipped-off the dogs, who turned on him and tore him to pieces. These were called 'sportsmen' and they were all upper class; the Prince of Wales was one of them.

Then there was a sad sight – two fine horses were down. One was struggling in the stream, and the other was groaning on the grass. One of the riders was getting out of the water covered with frog spawn and mud, the other lay quite still.

'His neck is broken,' said my mother.

'And serve him right too,' said one of the colts.

I thought the same, but my mother did not join with us.

'Well! No,' she said, 'you must not say that. Although, I never could make out why men are so fond of this sport; they often hurt themselves, they get covered in mud, they fall off and break their necks, often spoil good horses and tear up the fields, and all for a hare or a fox or a stag or an elephant, when they could get one more easily, pre-prepared and oven ready, from the butcher's.'

Whilst my mother was saying this, we stood and looked on. Many of the riders had gone to the young man, but my master, who had been watching, was the first to raise him. His head fell back and his arms hung down, his legs shot up and everyone looked very serious, especially the one with his head hanging down. There was no noise now; even the dogs were quiet, and seemed to know that something was wrong. They carried him to our master's house. It was young George Gordon, the Squire's only son, a fine, tall young man, a cruel bastard, and the pride of his family, with his head hanging down.

They were now riding off in all directions, in fact two riders rode off in the opposite directions, to the doctor's, to the farrier's, to the butcher's, to the baker's, and no doubt to Squire Gordon's to let him know his son had snuffed it. When Mr Bond, the farrier, came to look at the black horse that lay groaning on the grass, he felt him all over, and shook his head; one of his legs was broken. Then someone ran to our master's house and came back with a gun. Presently, there was a loud bang and a dreadful shriek; Mr Bond had shot himself. And then a humanitarian put the horse down, and then all was still; the black horse moved no more.

My mother seemed much troubled. She said she had known that horse for many years. His name was Big Dick Rasputin. He was a good, bold horse, and there was no vice in him; he occasionally screwed a brood mare, that was all. She never would go to that part of the field afterwards.

Not many days after, we heard the church bell tolling for a long time. Looking over the gate, we saw a long, strange black coach that was covered with black cloth and was drawn by black horses; this was for the stiff. It was carrying young Gordon to the churchyard, to bury him. That's what happens when you die, you never ride again. What they did with Big Dick Rasputin I never knew; he was sold as dog food.

Oh terrible ending as dog food in a tin
It doesn't encourage a racehorse to win
Fancy the Derby winner
Ending up as a dog's dinner.

3. MY BREAKING IN

Oh! terrible breaking in!
It should be considered a sin
I had to gallop, walk and trot
I thought that was the lot
I was taught to go fast or slow
To stop, start and then go
A man would sit on your back
I'd take him there and bring him back

The man was Squire Gordon by name
I kicked him in the balls whenever he came
They each swole up like a marrow
He had to wheel them round on a barrow.

I was now beginning to grow handsome; some people grew up, but I grew handsome. My coat was coal black; at night people used to walk into me. Mind you, I still looked like a horse. When I was four years old, Squire Gordon came to look at me. He examined my eyes, mouth and legs. He felt them all the way down, because that's where they were. Then I had to walk and trot and gallop before him. He seemed to like me and said, 'I seem to like you. When he is broken in he will do well.' My master said he would break me in himself, to save the expense of hiring a groom, the mean bastard! The next day he began.

Everyone may not know what breaking in is. It means you have a bloody awful time. You have to wear a saddle and carry on your back a man, woman, child, or a hundredweight sack of potatoes; or, in times of war, you have to carry a cannon. You have to learn to wear a collar. You have to be able to have a cart or a chaise fixed behind you, so that you can hardly walk without dragging it after you. It's hell I tell you. Many horses have gotten a hernia trying to pull them. You must go fast or slow, start or stop, as the driver wishes; you have no bloody choice at all. You must not speak to other horses nor bite nor kick nor crap nor have any will of your own. You might as well be bloody dead. You must do your master's will even though you may be very tired or hungry, but you can report him to the RSPCA. When the harness is once on, you may neither jump for joy nor lie down for weariness. It's a complete loss of freedom.

I had, of course, long been used to a halter and a headstall – that's a stall I sleep in with my head – and was then led about in the field and lanes, even if I didn't want to go. For those who have never had a bit in their mouths (most men have had a bit on the side), it is held fast by straps over your head, under your throat, round your nose, and under your chin, everywhere except behind your arse; so that no way in the world can you get rid of the nasty hard thing; it is very bad! Yes, very bad! But with the nice oats, and what with my master's pats, kind words, and gentle ways, I got used to wearing my bit and bridle, but it was still bloody terrible.

Next came the saddle, but that was not half so bad; they put it on my back, very gently, and my master got on. I immediately bolted and threw him. It certainly felt queer, but I felt rather proud to have thrown my master. However, he continued to ride me a little every day, and I would throw him every day. I soon became accustomed to it, and so did he.

Next was putting on iron shoes. The blacksmith took my feet in his hands, one after the other, and cut away some of the hoof. I stood still on three legs, sometimes two, or even one, till he had done them all. Then he clapped on a piece of iron the shape of my foot and drove some nails through the shoe into my hoof, so that the shoe was firmly on. My feet felt very stiff and heavy, but in time I got used to it.

Next was to break me to harness. First, a stiff heavy collar just on my neck. (The things they were putting on me made me weigh twelve stone more than I really was.) It was a bridle with great side-pieces against my eyes called blinkers. I could not see on either side, but only straight ahead; I kept crashing into things each side of me, one was an old lady. Next there was a small saddle strap that went under my tail; that was the crapper. I hated it; it stopped me having a crap. I never felt more like kicking, so I kicked him in the goolies and they swelled up like water melons. He had to put the harness on me while balancing his balls with one hand, and he could only move very slowly. In time I got used to everything – and he got used to swollen balls – and I could do my work as well as my mother. I used to wash up after dinner. Yes, I was a very good horse.

I must not forget to mention one part of my training. My master sent me for a fortnight to a neighbouring farm with a meadow which was skirted by railway lines. Here were some sheep and cows, and I was turned in amongst them. I couldn't help treading in it.

I shall never forget the first train. I was feeding quietly near the pales, which separated the meadow from the railway, when I heard a strange sound at a distance, and before I knew whence it came – with a rush and a clatter, and a puffing out of smoke, a long black train of something* flew by, and was gone almost before I could draw my breath. I turned, and galloped like fuck to the further side of the meadow as fast as I could go, and stood there snorting with astonishment and fear. In the course of the day many other trains went by, some more slowly; these drew up at the station close by, and sometimes made an awful shriek and groan before they stopped. They had run over a passenger.

For a few days I could not feed in peace, as passenger after passenger was run over. I began to disregard it, and very soon I got used to the sound of the train stopping and the passengers being thrown off. Now, no railway stations frighten me – not Cannon Street, Paddington or Euston.

'But,' said my mother, 'there are many kinds of men; there are good, thoughtful men like our master, who, thanks to you, has swollen balls.' She said there are many foolish men who are ignorant, who couldn't spell influenza even though they had got it. Some men were awful* and they spoiled horses; in fact, strewn all round where we lived there were spoiled horses lying in the fields. Some men used to deliver coal and some would fall down the coal hole and were never seen again. 'Now don't forget son,' said my mother, 'do your best wherever it is, and keep up your good name.' I did, but when I felt like it I kicked them in the balls. The only respect I ever got was from men I had kicked in the balls.

---

* Carriages.

4. BIRTWICK PARK

I was to work for a new master
To me, it was a disaster
In new stables I had to pass
A horse with an enormous fat arse
Ginger was his name
Alas, that's what he eventually became.

It was early in May, when there came a man from Squire Gordon's who took me away to the Hall. My master said to me, 'Good-bye, Darkie, be a good horse and always do your best; and stop kicking people in the balls.' I could not say good-bye, so I put my nose in his hand and bit off a finger. I left my first home, and as I lived some years with Squire Gordon, I may as well tell something about the place.

It was mortgaged up to the hilt. Squire Gordon's Park skirted the village of Birtwick. It was entered by a large, rusty iron gate, at which stood the first lodge, and then you trotted along on a smooth road between clumps of large old trees; then another lodge and another gate, which brought you to the house and gardens. Beyond this lay the home paddock, the old orchard, and the stables. There was accommodation for many horses and carriages and there were good stalls, large and square, each with a low rack for hay or porridge or pâté de foie gras, they were called loose boxes because, in fact, they were falling to pieces.

Into one such fine box the groom put me. He patted me, then went away. Wow, read all about it, groom pats horse and goes away! When I had eaten my corn I looked round – it must have been that bloody corn I'd eaten. Next to me was a horse with a thick mane and tail, and a pretty head.

I put my head up to the iron rails and said, 'I say, horse, pray tell me, what is your name?'

He turned round and said, 'My name is Merrylegs: I am very handsome, carry the young ladies on my back, and sometimes I take our mistress out in the low chair. They think a great deal of me, and so does James.' The bigheaded little creep! 'Are you going to live in the next box?' he asked.

I said, 'Yes.' There are fields and meadows all round but these bastards make me live in a box.

A horse's head looked over from the stall beyond.

'So it's you who has turned me out of my box; it's an outrage for a colt like you to come and turn a horse out of his own home.'

'The thing is this,' said Merrylegs, 'Ginger has the habit of biting and snapping and kicking people in the balls: that is why they call him Ginger. One day he bit James in the arm and made it bleed.' Good. 'Miss Flora and Miss Jessie, who are very fond of me, were afraid to come into the stable for fear of being kicked and bitten. They used to bring me nice things to eat – steak and chips and spaghetti Neapolitan.'

I told him I never bit anything but grass, hay, corn and people.

'Well,' said Merrylegs, 'I don't think he does find pleasure in it.'

'Nonsense,' I said, 'there is no greater pleasure than biting and kicking people.'

'John is the best groom that ever was; he tries to please Ginger. He plays him Schumann's Violin Concerto. He has been here fourteen years and he is still as simple as when he started. He says his brain hurts if he thinks. And you never saw such a kind boy as James is; so it's all Ginger's own fault that he did not stay in that box.'

5. A FAIR START

One morning, after a grooming by John
The Squire asked him to take me on
He put on a saddle and rode very slow
So I threw him off and I jolly well did go
I galloped everywhere
But didn't seem to get anywhere
Finally knackered, I was just able
To crawl back to the stable
The stableboy James was always around
Sometimes, for fun, I would trample him into the ground
But after three weeks in hospital 'tis true
He came back, good as new.

The name of the coachman was John Manly; the name of his coach was Percy; he had a wife and one little child, and they lived in the coachman's cottage.

The next morning, he took me into the yard and gave me a good grooming, and just as I was going into my box with my coat soft and bright, the Squire came in to look at me, and seemed pleased.

'John,' he said, 'I meant to have tried the new horse this morning, but I have other business. You may as well take him a round after breakfast; go by the common and the Highwood, and back by the water mill and the river, through Swansea and Kent; that will show his paces.'

'I will, sir,' said John.

After breakfast he came and fitted me with a bridle. Then he brought the saddle, which was not broad enough for my back; he saw it in a minute, and in another minute went for a bigger one, which fitted nicely. He rode me slowly at first, then a trot, then a canter, and when we were on the common, he gave me a light touch with his whip, and we had a splendid gallop at 100 miles per hour.

'Ho, ho! my boy,' he said, as he pulled me up with that powerful wrist, 'you would like to follow the hounds, I think.' The fool! I never want to follow hounds.

As we came back through the Park we met the Squire and Mrs Gordon, walking; they stopped, and John jumped off and fractured his ankle.

'Well, John, how does he go?'

'He is as fleet as a deer, and has a fine spirit too; the lightest touch of the rein will guide him but don't stand behind him or he'll kick your balls. Down at the end of the common they were shooting rabbits near the Highwood – people rarely see horses shooting rabbits. A gun went off close by so he pulled up a little and looked; it was another horse shooting rabbits. I just held the rein steady and did not hurry him, and it's my opinion he has not been frightened or ill-used while he was young.'

'That's well,' said the Squire, 'I will try him myself tomorrow.'

The next day I was brought up for my master. I remembered my mother's counsel, and my good old master's, and I tried to do exactly what he wanted me to do. I found he was a very good rider; once or twice I threw him; landing on his head, he became an imbecile. And thoughtful for his horse too; we didn't use the crapper, so I could crap. When we came home, the lady was at the hall door as he rode up.

'Well, my dear,' she said, 'how do you like him?'

'Der he trew me on my hed,' he replied; 'pleasanter creature I never wished to mount. What shall we call him?'

'Would you like Nigger?' said she. 'He is as black as a nigger.'

'I think it is a very good name. If anyone says it, we could take them to a race relations board.'

When John went into the stable, he told James that master and mistress had chosen a good sensible English name for me: Nigger, because I was black. They both laughed, and James said, 'If it was not for bringing back the past, I should have named him Big Dick Rasputin, for I never saw two horses more alike.'

'That's no wonder,' said John, 'didn't you know that farmer Grey's old Duchess was the mother of them both?'

I had never heard that before. So poor Big Dick Rasputin, who was killed at that hunt, was my brother!

John seemed very proud of me: he used to make my mane and tail almost as smooth as a baby's bum, and he would talk to me a great deal, 'Keep still you bastard.' I grew very fond of him, he was so gentle and kind, 'Keep still you bastard'; he wanted me to keep still.

James Howard, the stable boy, was just as gentle and pleasant in his way – 'Keep still you bastard' – so I thought myself well-off, but sometimes I would trample him into the ground. There was another man who helped in the yard sweeping up the horse dung. I didn't like him, so I did as much of it as I could.

A few days after this, I had to go out with Ginger in the carriage. I wondered how we should get on together; but except for laying his ears back and biting the driver, he behaved very well. He did his work honestly, and did his full share, usually in the middle of the road — a street cleaner used to clear it and sell it to rose growers — and I never wish to have a better partner in double harness. When we came to a hill, instead of slackening his pace, he would throw his weight right into the collar, the silly little fool, and pull away. So I let him — I just sat next to the driver. John had oftener to hold him in than to urge him forward; he never had to use the whip with either of us.

As for Merrylegs, he and I soon became great friends: we went out drinking together at the City Hall trough; he used to let me ride him. He was a favourite with everyone, except King Edward, and especially with Miss Jessie and Miss Flora, who used to ride him about in the orchard. He used to run under low branches so they would get knocked off; they had fine games with him and their little dog Frisky. He used to trample it into the mud and fracture its skull.

Our master had two other horses that stood in another stable, one on top of the other. One was Justice, a roan cob, used for riding, or for the luggage cart; the other was a very old brown hunter, named Sir Oliver, who was past it now, but was a great favourite with the master, who helped him stagger through the Park. He sometimes did a little light carting on the estate, but regularly collapsed, for he was very weak. He could be trusted with a child as long as it wasn't older than three, otherwise his legs collapsed under him; as it was, he had a pacemaker. The cob was a strong, well-made, good-tempered horse, and we sometimes had a little chat in the paddock.

'How are you?' I asked.

'I'm very well,' he answered, 'piss off, Nigger.'

6. LIBERTY

John took me out to exercise
He gripped me fast with his thighs
But I gave a huge cough
That threw him off
It gave him a shock
As he split his head open on a rock
But after three weeks in hospital 'tis true
He came back, as good as new.

I was quite happy in my new place, and all who had to do with me were good and bloody boring, forever patting me and giving me apples, and I had a light airy stable and the best of food. What more could I want? Why, liberty! For three years and a half of my life I had had all the liberty I could wish for; but now, week after week, month after month and, no doubt, year after year, I must stand up in a stable night and day except when I am wanted; sometimes I lay down which is like standing, only lower down; and then I must be just as steady and quiet as any old horse who has worked twenty years and been shot for dog food. Straps here and straps there and a thing under my arse so I couldn't shit, a bit in my mouth, and blinkers over my eyes.

Now, I am not complaining for I know it must be so. I only mean to say that for a young horse full of strength and spirits who has been used to some large field or plain, where he can fling up his head, and toss up his tail, crap and gallop away at full speed leaving the field full of horse dung, then round and back again with a snort to his companions – we all like to snort a joint – I say it is hard, never to have a bit more liberty to do as you like. Sometimes, when I had had less exercise than usual, I felt so full of life and spring, that when John took me out to exercise, I really could not keep quiet; I did fifty press-ups and fifty sit-ups; do what I would, it seemed as if I must jump, or dance – I would do the fox-trot – or prance; and many a good shake I know I must have given him; every now and then he would fall off, specially at the first; but he was always good and patient.

'Steady, steady, for Christ's sake steady, my boy,' he would say. 'Wait a bit and we'll have a good swing, and soon get the tickle out of your feet.' What was the bloody fool talking about? I didn't have any tickle in my feet, I haven't got feet! Then, as soon as we were out of the village, he would give me a few miles at a spanking trot, and then bring me back as fresh as before, only clear of the fidgets, as he called them. Spirited horses, when not enough exercised, are often called skittish when it is only play, and some grooms will punish them, but our John did not. I would come to a halt and catapult him over my head; he knew it was only high spirits. Still, he had his own ways of making me understand by the tone of his voice – 'Keep still you bastard' – or by the touch of the rein. If he was very serious and quite determined, I always knew it by his voice, 'keep bloody still', and that had more power with me than anything else, even King George V, for I was very fond of him.

I ought to say that, sometimes, we had our liberty for a few hours; this used to be on fine Sundays in the summertime. The carriage never went out on Sundays, because the church was now a Buddhist temple.

It was a great treat for us to be turned out into the Home Paddock or the old orchard. The grass was so cool and soft to our feet, the air was so sweet, and the freedom to do as we liked was so pleasant; to gallop, to lie down, to climb a tree, and to roll over on our backs, squashing the apples. The groom had to work hard to scrape and hose them off. This was a very good time for talking. One day I said to Ginger, 'How are you getting on you old poof?' and Ginger replied, 'Not very good – I am still a bloody horse.'

7. GINGER

One day, Ginger was standing in the stable
Something which I did, when I was able
'No one,' said Ginger, 'horse, man or frog was kind to me'
I said, 'Patience, why don't you wait and see?'
I would have to bloody wait for eternity
Now Ginger wasn't very clever
He had a noisy hacking cough
Why didn't he just fuck off.

One day, when Ginger and I were standing alone in the shade, still being horses, we had a great deal of talk: he wanted to know all about my bringing up and breaking in, and I told him I'd never done a break-in.

'You see,' said Ginger, 'I was taken from my mother as soon as I was weaned and put in with a lot of other young colts: none of them cared for me and I cared for none of them, fuck 'em. There was no kind master to bring me nice things to eat like sausage and mash. The man in care of me never gave me a kind word. He didn't even say, "fish, cupboard or teeth", or any other words that would have been acceptable, like elephant, pudding, etc.

'A footpath ran through our field, and often boys would fling stones at us. I was never hit, but one young colt was badly cut. We settled in our minds that these boys were our enemies. We waited till they were not looking, and we rushed and then kicked them all to the death.

'We had great fun in the free meadows, galloping up and down and kicking boys to death. But when it came to breaking in, that was a bad time: several men came to catch me, and when at last they were all on my back, one caught me by the forelock and another caught me by the nose, and held it so tight that I could hardly draw my breath; yet another took my under jaw in his hard hand and wrenched my mouth open; I bit his fingers off and spat them out; and so, by force, they got the halter on and put the bar into my mouth; then, one dragged me along by the halter while another flogged my arse, and this was the first experience I had of man's unkindness.

'There was one – the old master, Mr Ryder – who I think could have brought me round when I was unconscious, and he could have done anything with me; he could have taught me petit point, chair caning and cooking. His son was called Sampson and he boasted he never found a horse that could throw him, so I did; I threw him in the river. I threw him again and again, trampling on his head till it lost its shape.

'I think he drank a great deal – he leaked – and I am quite sure that the oftener he drank, the more he leaked; he flooded the stables. One day, he worked me hard in every way, digging ditches, chopping trees and mowing the grass. I was tired and miserable and angry. Next day, he mounted me in a temper. I threw him off and rendered him unconscious by landing him on his head. He recovered consciousness, remounted me and seemed determined to stay in the saddle as he used super glue on the seat of his trousers; but I threw him, leaving the seat of his trousers on the saddle.

'At last, as the sun went down, I saw the old master coming out with a sieve in his hand. He was a very fine old gentleman with a sieve in his hand. He had white hair, and his voice had white hair. I should have known him amongst one thousand. Unfortunately he was not standing in the middle of a thousand people, so I didn't know him right away. "Come along, lassie, come along, come along," but I didn't come along lassie. What did he think I was, a dog? And hadn't he seen the size of my tackle? No, I let him come along to me. He led me back to the stable; as we arrived, there was the bastard Sampson. I snapped at him and bit his ear off. "Stand back," said the master, "you've not learned your trade yet, Sampson." His trade was, in fact, a stone mason. Why an apprentice stone mason wanted to learn to ride a horse seemed pretty pointless to me. In my stall, the old master mixed up a brandy and coke for me, which restored me no end. To Sampson he said, "If you don't break this horse in by fair means, she will never be good for anything except a hotel porter." '

8. GINGER'S STORY CONTINUED

The next time Ginger and I were in the paddock
We had been sharing a six pound haddock
He had been sold to a cruel man
A real shit called Sadistic Stan
To Ginger he was very cruel
He treated him like a mule
So Ginger started to try and bray
Day, after day, after day
It was a very good impression and eventually
Ginger kicked him in the face
And bits of him went all over the place

Ginger was a chestnut horse and he told me that a dealer had wanted another chestnut horse to match him, but the only horse they had was white, so they painted it with three coats of chestnut emulsion.

'I had been driven with a bearing rein by the dealer, and I hated it. I liked to toss my head about; I would toss it in the air and catch it as it came down. I hated to stand waiting by the hour for our mistress at some grand party or entertainment; they wouldn't let us sit down or lean against a lamp post.'

'Did not your mistress take any thought for you?' I asked. 'I mean, didn't she send out a drink and sandwiches?'

'After this, I was sent to Tattersall's to be sold; I had a label on me saying "Horse for Sale". A dealer tried me in all kinds of ways – sitting on me, standing on me, laying on me. At last they sold me for £3.00 to a gentleman in the country. His groom was hard tempered and hard handed. If I did not move in the stall when he wanted me to, he would hit me with his stable broom or feather duster, whichever came to hand. He wanted me to be afraid of him, and so he wore a series of devil masks. I bit a lump out of his arse. I made up my mind: men were natural enemies and I must defend myself, even if that meant hiring a solicitor.'

'I think it would be a real shame if you were to bite or kick John or James or the King of England.'

'I don't mean to,' he said. 'I did bite James once pretty sharp – I took three fingers off him – but John said "try him with kindness". So, instead of punishing me, James came to me with his arm in a sling and served me a whisky and soda with some little cheesy biscuits on a silver tray. I have never snapped at him since.'

Master noticed the change in Ginger – his paint was wearing off. One day, he came to speak to us, as he often did, and gave each of us a beautiful glass of Chablis.

'Aye, aye, Jim, 'tis the Birtwick balls,' said John. 'He'll be as good as Nigger by and by; kindness is all the physic he wants. All he needs is an occasional glass of Chablis.'

'Yes, sir, he's wonderfully improved, he's not the same creature that he was; he's somebody else. It's the Birtwick balls, sir,' said John, laughing.

Until then, I never knew we had Birtwick balls.

This was a little joke of John's; he used to say that a regular course of the Birtwick horse balls would cure him and any vicious horse. Where did they get a supply of Birtwick balls? The thought of grooms going round horse boxes with a pair of garden shears removing the testicles for future use is terrible. These balls, he said, were made up of patience and gentleness, firmness and petting.*

9. MERRYLEGS

The children with Merrylegs used to play
Whether he liked it, he did not say
But he often said back in the stable
'I'd strangle them if I was able'
When he couldn't stand any more
He trampled them all over the floor
The father said, 'You'll pay for this, you'll see'
Said Merrylegs, 'No, I did it all for free.'

---

* A cover up for the act of castration.

Mr Blomefield, the Vicar, had a large family of boys and girls; he used to fuck like a rabbit. When the children came, there was plenty of work for Merrylegs, and nothing pleased them so much as getting on him by turns and riding him all about the orchard and the home paddock, and this they would do hour after hour.

One afternoon, he had been out with them a long time, and James brought him in.

'What have you been doing, Merrylegs?' I asked.

'Oh!' said he, tossing his little head, 'I have only been giving those young people a lesson. They did not know when I had had enough, so I just pitched them off backwards; that was the only thing they could understand.'

The house, by now, was full of crippled children.

'What,' said I, 'you threw the children off? I thought you knew better than that. Did you throw Miss Jessie or Miss Flora?'

'Yes, yes. In fact, I threw them further than anybody else. I am as careful of the young ladies as the master could be, and as for the little ones, when they seemed frightened, I kicked them off. I am their best friend but sadly they don't seem to know when I have had enough, so I have to hurl them off. Each one of the children had a riding whip; I took it in good part but, Christ, it hurt. I didn't wish to be cruel, but I'm afraid some of them I put in the hospital. Besides,' he went on, 'if I took to kicking then where should I be?' I don't know but I know where they would be – in the hospital with swollen balls.

10. A TALK IN THE ORCHARD

Ginger and I were not of the carriage breed
We were built for speed
I had racehorse blood in my veins
And five pints of it
I was happy with my mistress on my back
But, alas, I didn't know the way back
I don't know which way we went
We must have driven via Surrey, Sussex and Kent.

Ginger and I were not of the regular tall carriage horse breed, we had racing blood; I had a bottle of about twelve pints in my stable. We stood about fifteen and a half hands high, but if we stood on a chair we were even taller. We were just as good for riding as we were for driving or standing on chairs. Our master used to say he disliked either horse or man who could do but one thing, like play the trombone. He would mount a horse and play the trombone. It was a spectacular sight to see him at full gallop playing 'The Flight of the Bumble Bee'. Mind you, he preferred to play it after dark, and consequently, at full gallop, he, horse and trombone went through many a plate-glass window. Our favourite practice was for me to saddle Ginger and then mount him, then put a saddle on my back and our mistress would ride on that. She could see for miles.

My mouth was so tender and my teeth had not been spoiled or hardened with McLean's toothpaste. I always used a good mouthwash after a meal – it was three-year-old Malt Whisky. Ginger did not like the bit, and Sir Oliver would say, 'There, there, don't vex yourself.' Now Ginger never vexed himself – he got another horse to do it for him.

I wondered how Sir Oliver had such a short tail. Was it an accident?

'Accident?' he snorted. 'Some cruel boys tied me up and cut off my long beautiful tail, through the flesh, and through the bone, and took it away.'

What he had left looked like a feather duster protruding from his bum. 'How,' said Oliver, 'can I ever brush flies, mice, grasshoppers, or elephants off my sides?'

'What did they do it for?' asked Ginger.

'Thieves would wear it as a disguise; they would fashion my tail into wigs and beards and rob a bank. Just fancy, somewhere in London my tail might be doing a robbery.'

Sir Oliver was a fiery old fellow; smoke used to sometimes exude from his bottom. Of course there were some nervous horses who, having been frightened, would let go a lot of dung.

'I have never let go a lot of dung,' said Sir Oliver. 'I remember one dark night, just by farmer Sparrow's house where the pond is close to the road, a hearse bearing a coffin overturned into the water. Both horses were drowned, the corpse floated away and was never seen again. Of course, after this accident, a stout white rail was put up that might be easily seen. However, a second hearse crashed through the rails, the horses were drowned, and the stiff floated away like the first one.'

When our master's carriage was overturned he said that if the lamp on the left side had not gone out, John would have seen the enormous hole the road makers left: his carriage disappeared down it and, to this day, he has never been seen again.

11. PLAIN SPEAKING

A pony was being whipped by a man
Master said, 'I'll stop him if I can
Sawyer, you shit, that pony's made of flesh and blood'
'He's no good, sir, he be a dud'
Sawyer the shit took up the reins
And my master blew out his brains

And they buried him in the garden
Where the praties grow.

The mistress was good and kind and had a large bank overdraft. She was kind to everybody, not only men and women but also horses and donkeys, dogs and cats, cattle and birds, kangaroos, buffalo and wart hogs. If any of the children in the village were known to treat any creature cruelly, she would beat them with an iron bar and hang them upside down outside for the whole day. And if somebody didn't find favour with her, she would tell her husband, and he would blow their brains out and bury them in the garden where the praties grow. Sometimes, our master weighed very heavy. Sometimes he weighed fifteen stone, and when riding me gave me curvature of the spine.

One day, he saw Sawyer ill-treating a pony. 'Sawyer, you shit!' he cried in a stern voice. 'Is that pony not made of flesh and blood?'

'Flesh and blood and temper,' said the shit.

'And do you think, you shit,' asked master firmly, 'that treatment like this will make him fond of your will?'

'I haven't made out a will yet,' said the shit.

Mr Sawyer, the shit, did not react, so my master took out a blunderbuss, blew his brains out and buried him in the garden where there was becoming less and less room. The master was much grieved by the loss of the shit. He broke down and said, 'Oh, deary me.'

One day, when he had stopped saying 'oh, deary me,' we met Captain Langley, a friend of our master's. He was driving a splendid pair of greys in a kind of brake. What kind I could not say. The master backed me a little, so as to get a good view of them.

'They are uncommonly like my wife, a very handsome pair,' he said. 'I see you have got hold of a bearing rein.'

'Yes,' said the captain. 'I like to see my horses hold their heads up.'

'You shit,' said the master, 'I think every horse should have a free head. They should be sent by parcel post to the horse in question.'

'I'll think about it,' said the captain, but as he drove away, my master took careful aim and blew the captain's brains out, and we had another grave to leap over.

12. A STORMY DAY

Oh, terrible night of storm and wind
As though the storm fiend grinned
Master had to go away
So I was in the dogcart that day
When we reached the tollgate it wasn't surprising

The tollman said the river was rising
We drove thru the water to the other side
Mostly I was under water, and nearly died
On the way back we went through a wood
'I don't think,' said John, 'we should'
Then a tearing, an oak tree crashed on the road
It missed us but hit a toad
We returned by the flooded bridge over the river
The thought made me shiver
The tollman said, 'Stop, the bridge is washed away'
'Thank god,' said John, Hip, Hip, Hooray.

One day in autumn, he called it Wednesday because that's what it was, the master had a long journey on business. I was put into the dogcart, and John went with his master. We went merrily along until we came to the tollbar, and the low wooden bridge. The river banks were rather high, and the bridge, instead of rising, went across just level, so that in the middle, if the river was full, the water would be nearly up to the woodwork and planks. However, as there were good substantial rails on each side, people did not mind it. My master's business engaged him a long time. I saw her wave him good-bye from the bedroom window.

A great rush of wind blew up and removed the seat of my master's trousers. The wind was blowing a gale against me, and I had to take two paces backward for every one forward. By the light of dawn, we arrived back.

The mistress ran out, 'Are you really safe my dear?'

'Yes, absolutely safe.'

They gave me a good feed that night; they gave me a grog of Best and a bottle of Moet et Chandon with an ice bucket.

13. THE DEVIL'S TRADE MARK

One day, John and I saw hence
A boy forcing a horse to jump a fence
He was giving the horse a thrashing
John wanted me to go and give him a bashing
Just then the horse threw him off her back
And he hit the ground with a thwack
He tried to grasp the horse's reins
But my master came and blew out his brains.

One day, John and I had been out on some business of our master's – we were buying shares in Woolworths – and we were returning gently, flat broke, on a long straight road. It must have been a Roman road. At some distance, we saw a boy try to leap a pony over a gate. The pony would not take the leap, so the boy jumped it for him to show him the way. Then the boy tried again, and hit the pony with a whip, but he only turned off on one side, scratching the boy's leg. He whipped him again, the pony turned, and scratched his other leg. Then the boy got off and gave the pony a hard thrashing. When we reached the spot, the pony put his head down, threw up his heels, and hurled the boy neatly into a hedge of nettles and, with the rein dangling from his head, he set off at a full gallop.

'Oh! oh! oh!' cried the boy, as he struggled about among the nettles, 'I say, do come and help me out.'

Then my Master rode up, dismounted, picked up his blunderbuss, and blew the boy's brains out.

'Thank ye,' said John. 'I think you are in quite the right place, and maybe a little scratching will teach him not to leap the pony over a gate that is too high for him.'

The farmer was hurrying out into the road, and his wife was standing at the gate looking frightened.

'Have you seen my boy?' said Mr Bushby as we came up. 'He went out an hour ago on my black pony.'

'Oh yes, he fell off,' said the master, 'and to put him out of his misery, I blew his brains out.'

'What do you mean?' asked the farmer.

'Well, sir, I saw your son whipping and kicking the pony, so I took careful aim and blew his brains out. It seemed to calm him, and your son is now sleeping in my garden.'

The mother began to cry, 'Oh! I must go and see my boy.'

'You will have to dig six feet down,' said John, 'that's where he is.'

We went on home, John chuckling all the way. He told James about it who laughed and said, 'Serve him right. I knew that boy at school: he took great airs on himself because he was a farmer's son; he used to swagger about and bully the little boys; of course, we elder ones would not have any of that nonsense and let him know that, in the school and playground, farmers' sons and labourers' sons were all alike, so we beat the shit out of him. I found him at a large window catching flies and pulling off their wings, so I am glad you blew his brains out.'

John said, 'There is no religion without love, and people may talk as much as they like about their religion, but if it does not teach them to be good and kind to man and beast, it is all a sham – all a sham, James, and it won't stand when things come to be turned inside out and put down for what they are.'

I personally have never had my things turned inside out, so I didn't know what he meant.

14. JAMES HOWARD

One morning, across came the master
At two miles per hour he couldn't go any faster
In his hand he held a letter
I suppose he couldn't find anything better
It was from Sir Clifford at Clifford Hall
Which, to me, meant fuck all
Sir Cliff wanted to replace his Coachman Fred
Primarily because he was dead
No one volunteered for the job
Except a bisexual called Rob.

One morning in December, John let me into my box after my daily exercise – twenty press-ups and twenty sit-ups. He was just strapping my cloth on, and James was coming in from the corn chamber with some oats, when the master came into the stable. He looked rather serious, and held an open letter in his hand. John fastened the door of my box, touched his cap, and waited for orders.

'Good morning, John,' said the master, 'I want to know if you have any complaint of James?'

'Complaint, sir? No, sir.'

'Is he industrious in his work, and respectful to you?'

'Yes, sir, always.'

'You never see him do a pee when your back is turned?'

'That, sir, I cannot swear.'

'When he goes out with the horses to exercise them, does he stop about talking to his acquaintances, or go into houses where he has no business, leaving the horses outside?'

'No, sir, he always takes the horses in with him. I will say this, sir, that a steadier, pleasanter, honester, smarter young fellow I never had. I can trust his word, and I can trust his work. Perhaps he does do a pee when I'm not looking, I know those people in laced hats and liveries, but whoever wants a character of James Howard, let them come to John Manly.'

He really was an arse licker. The old bastard had tried to find out if the young lad had ever committed something unusual, like wanking.

'James, my lad, set down the oats and come here.' So he set down the oats and came there. 'John's opinion of your character agrees so exactly with my own. John is a cautious man, when you pee against a wall he never looks. I have a letter from my brother-in-law, Sir Clifford Williams, of Clifford Hall. His old coachman, who has lived with him for twenty years, is getting feeble; his legs have dropped off and he wants a man to work with him to get into his ways, like robbing banks and interfering with little girls.'

So he would take on James.

It was settled that James should go to Clifford Hall. I never knew the carriage to go out so often before; after yes, but never before. When the mistress did not go out, she stayed in. The master drove himself in the two-wheeled chaise. But now, whether it was the master or the young ladies, or only an errand for the master's pile ointment, Ginger and I were put into the carriage, and James drove us. At first, John rode with him on the box, telling him this and that, and after that, James drove alone.

Then, it was wonderful what a number of places the master would go to in the city on Saturdays, and what queer streets we were driven through. Every second person, in fact, was queer. He was sure to go to the railway station just as the train was coming in, and cabs and carriages, carts and omnibuses were all trying to get over the bridge together; that bridge wouldn't hold them all, for it was narrow, and many fell off. And there was a very sharp turn up to the station, where it would not have been at all difficult for people to run into each other; and so they did if they did not look sharp and keep their wits about them.

15. THE OLD OSTLER

My master wanted to visit friends forty-six miles away
That would take all bloody day
Next morning I was in harness, master took the rein
We grabbed a little rest on the way there
And we had to grab a little on the way back again
Master drove fast and slow
Then, to cap it all, it started to snow
When we got back I was frozen of course
And I thought, 'bugger being a horse.'

We were to visit some friends who lived forty-six miles from our home. The first day we travelled thirty-two miles; there were some long heavy hills, but James drove so carefully and thoughtfully that we were not at all harassed. He never forgot to put on the drag as we went downhill – he looked lovely in it and did not forget to take it off at night. He kept our feet on the smoothest part of the road, and if the uphill was very long, he set the carriage wheels a little across the road, so as not to run back, and gave us a breathing space. All these things help a horse very much, particularly if there are kind words in the bargain like 'Lovely, lovely, good boy, nicely,' etc.

We stopped at the principal hotel. Two ostlers came to take us out. The head ostler was a pleasant, active little man with a crooked leg. He used to play hockey with it. The man unbuckled the harness with a pat and a good word – 'fish.'

I never was cleaned so lightly and quickly as by that little old man. When he had done, James stepped up and felt me – it was lovely.

'Give me the handling of a horse for twenty minutes, and I will tell you what sort of groom he has had,' said the crooked little ostler. So they gave him a horse, but after twenty minutes he had to give up. 'I'm sorry, I have no idea what kind of a groom he had.'

16. THE FIRE

Oh, one terrible dark night I suddenly awoke
And the stable was full of the dreaded smoke
I started to choke and perspire
My arse had caught fire
When we got outside it was amazing
For the whole stable was blazing
I was lucky, I nearly died
Many were trapped who ended up fried
They ended as a hamburger on a plate
Oh, dearie me, what a terrible fate

Later in the evening, a traveller's horse was brought in by the second ostler, and whilst he was cleaning him, a young man with a pipe in his mouth lounged into the stable.

'I say, Towler,' said the ostler, 'just run up the ladder into the loft and put some hay down into this horse's rack, will you? Only lay down your pipe first.'

'All right,' said the other, and went up through the trap door; I heard him step across the floor overhead and put down the hay. James came in to look at us the last thing, and then shut the door behind him.

I cannot say how long I slept, nor what time in the night it was, but I woke up very uncomfortable, though I hardly knew why. I got up. The air seemed all thick and choking. I heard Ginger coughing and choking; I could see nothing, but the stable was very full of smoke.

I heard a soft rushing sort of noise; I discovered it was coming out of me. And then I heard a low crackling and snapping. I did not know what it was, but a horse doesn't know everything. A horse does not know that Leonidas and his Spartans held the pass at Thermopylae against the Persian hordes.

At last I heard steps, and the ostler burst into the stable; it went all over the floor. He began to untie the horses and tried to lead them out, but he seemed in such a hurry, and so frightened himself, that he was in constant need of fresh air. The first horse would not go with him; he tried the second and third; they too would not stir. He came to me and tried to drag me out by force; of course, that was no use. He tried us all by turns and then left the stable shouting, 'All right, burn you bastards, burn!'

No doubt we were very foolish, but danger seemed to be all round, and there was nobody we knew to trust in, and all was strange and uncertain. The fresh air that had come in through the open door made it easier to breathe, but the rushing sound overhead grew louder, and as I looked upward, through the bars of my empty rack, I saw a red light flickering on the wall. Then I heard a cry of 'Fire!' outside; it wasn't outside – it was in here! The old ostler quietly and quickly came in; he got one horse out, and went to another, but the flames were playing round the trap door, and the roaring overhead was dreadful.

The next thing I heard was James's voice, quiet and cheery, as it always was.

'Come, Beauty, on with your bridle, my boy, we'll soon be out of this smother.'

It was on in no time; then he took the scarf off his neck, and tied it lightly over my eyes. The fool – I immediately walked into the wall. He led me out of the stable, crashing into everything. Safe in the yard, he slipped the scarf off my eyes, and shouted, 'Here, somebody! Take this horse while I go back for the other.'

A tall, broad man stepped forward and took me, and James darted back into the stable. I set up a shrill whinny as I saw him go. 'Ah, shut up,' said the tall, broad man.

On the other side of the yard, windows were thrown up, and people were shouting all sorts of things: 'Land ahoy!' 'God save the Queen.' A lot of good that did. Then came a cry:

'James Howard! James Howard! Are you there?'

Well, he wasn't. I heard the crash of something falling in the stable, and the next moment I gave a loud joyful neigh. 'Shut up!' said the tall, broad man. Then I saw James coming through the smoke leading Ginger. He was coughing violently and wasn't able to speak.

'My brave lad!' said the master, laying his hand on his shoulder. 'Are you hurt?'

James shook his head, for he could not speak.

'Aye,' said the big man who held me, 'he is a brave lad, and no mistake.'

I pulled myself free of the big man I didn't like him; I bit his nose off. He put it in a handkerchief and took it away.

' 'Tis the fire engine! The fire engine!' shouted two or three voices. 'Stand back, make way!' My master didn't stand back and the fire engines ran over him. James helped him to his feet but he was covered with muck and dung and embers from his smouldering trousers. The fireman put the hose on him, and blew him out the door.

There was a dreadful sound; it was that of the horses falling from the top floor. We were taken in and well done by, with firemen playing their hoses on us all night.

The next morning, the master came to see how we were; we were soaked. James looked very happy after a visit to his mistress. His mistress was much alarmed in the night with James climbing into bed with her. Then the under ostler – there was one under ostler and one on top – said he had asked Dick go up the ladder to put down some hay, but told him to lay down his pipe first. Dick denied that his pipe had started the fire.

Two poor horses that couldn't get out were cooked to a nicety, and then exported to some French restaurants.

17. JOHN MANLY'S TALE

We went to visit a friend
Whose life was reaching its end
Master came to say good-bye
And advised him to try and not die
His doctor had said he would live for twenty years
So he need have no fears
So he got out of his bed
And stood on his head
But the blood burst a vessel in his brain
And he immediately died yet again.

The rest of our journey was very easy – we got a lift on a wagon. A little after sunset, we reached the house of my master's friend. We were taken into a clean, snug stable and a kind coachman made us very comfortable. He had put in armchairs and curtains.

'Your horses know who they can trust.'

'Yes, they could trust Queen Victoria and her ghillie John Brown who was giving it to her,' said James. 'The hardest thing in the world is to get horses out of the stable when there is a fire, flood, earthquake, hurricane, thunderstorm, plague, leprosy and toothache.'

We stopped two or three days at this place, and the stable girls gave us a relief massage. Before James left us for the night he said, 'I wonder who is coming in my place.'

'Little Joe Green at the Lodge,' said John.

'Little Joe Green! Why he's a child!'

'He is fourteen and a half,' said John, 'he is small, quick, and willing as well, and you don't tread on him. He is kindhearted too, his kidneys are kindhearted, and he has a kindhearted liver too. We were agreeable to try him for six weeks.'

'Just six weeks?' said James. 'He won't even grow an inch in that time.'

'I was never afraid of work yet,' said John, 'yet I am afraid of lions.'

'I'm frightened of ducks,' said James, 'but I'm not afraid of lions, not as long as they stay in Africa.'

'I'll just tell you how I look on these things. I was just as old as Joseph when my father and mother died of the fever, within ten days of each other.

We laid odds on them as to who would go first. My father did, and I won £5.00. Then I was left with my crippled sister Nelly. Alone in the world, without a relation; I was a farmer's boy not earning enough to keep myself, much less the both of us. But our mistress (Nelly calls her an angel, and she has good right to do so), went and hired a room for her with old widow Mallet, and she gave her knitting and needlework. She taught her plumbing and made her re-plumb the house. The trouble was, when we turned the gas taps on, we got fountains of water, but out of the water tap we got gas, so we used to cook on that upside down. The master took me to the house where I had my food, my bed in the loft, a suit of clothes and three shillings a week so that I could help Nelly. Nelly couldn't help me, so I pushed her over a cliff. Nelly, who had climbed back up the cliff, was as happy as a bird. So you see, James, I'm not the man that should turn up his nose at a little boy. If you did, he would be able to see up it.'

'Then,' said James, 'you don't hold with that saying: "Everybody look after himself?" '

'Yes,' he said, 'fuck everyone else.'

James laughed at this, then he said, 'You have been my best friend, except for my mother; I hope you won't forget me.'

'No, lad, no!' said John, 'and if ever I can do you a good turn, I hope you won't forget me.'

'No, no, no, what's your name again?'

The next day Joe came to the stables to learn all he could before James left. He learned to sweep the stable and to bring in the straw and hay; he began to clean the harness, and helped to wash the carriage. As he was too short to do anything in the way of grooming, he walked underneath the horses and did what he could there.

'You see,' James said to John, 'I am leaving a great deal behind; my mother and Betsy, and you, and a good master and "mistress".' The mistress would certainly miss him. 'I will be able to help my mother much better with a new wooden leg.'

Merrylegs pined after him and went off his food. John took him out several mornings with a leading rein. He also exercised me – doing somersaults, the pole-vault, the long jump and the one hundred metres breast stroke.

Joe's father would often come in and do bugger all. He understood the work, and refused to do it.

18. GOING FOR THE DOCTOR

Oh, I was called out one early morn
Just as the day was about to dawn
Mistress kept having to go

Seventeen times an hour, she had filled the poe
Get the doctor in a hurry
And while you are out, get a takeaway curry
We all galloped like hell
When we got there, we rang the bell
'Do you know what the time is?' the doctor said
'We're all in bed'
There we were covered in mud and grime
And all he wanted to know was the bloody time
We told him our mistress was ill
Time after time the poe she would fill
The doctor attended her and I could hear him speaking
'I'm afraid, sir, your wife is leaking.'

I had eaten my hay and was lying down in my straw, fast asleep, when suddenly I was awakened by the stable bell ringing, and I heard feet running up the hall. John called out, 'Wake up, Nigger, you must go well now, if ever you did.'

'Now, John,' said the Squire, 'ride for your life; she's had an attack on her water works. She's filled the poe seven times in the last hour.'

I galloped as fast as I could lay my feet to the ground.

When we came to the bridge, John pulled me up a little and patted my neck. 'Well done, Nigger! Good old fellow,' he said. He would have let me go slower, but my spirit was up, and I was off again as fast as before. My legs were a blur; I had never had blurred legs before. It was all quiet – everybody was asleep.

As we drew up at Dr White's, John rang the bell twice and then knocked at the door like thunder. The window was thrown up, and Dr White, in his nightcap, put his head out and said, 'What do you want?'

'Our mistress is very ill, come quickly.'

'Do you know what time it is?' asked the doctor. Here we had galloped eight miles, and all he wanted to know was the time. 'Wait,' he said, 'I will come.'

His horse was ill, so they decided to ride me. So the doctor rode off with me, leaving John with an eight hour walk ahead of him.

Soon we were at the master's house. He stood in the door with a blank cheque made out to the doctor. He had sent his son to the village to kill the money lender. I was now very ill; I must have caught something off the doctor while he was riding me.

One day, my master came to see me. 'My poor Beauty,' he said, 'you saved your mistress's life and saved us all from drowning.' Yes, I had done it for the mistress, but never again! Next time, she would have to die.

19. ONLY IGNORANCE

Oh, deary me, I have become very ill
The vet has brought me a pill
It is the size of a tennis ball
And I have to swallow it all
They started to bleed me, they took plenty
When it was finished, I was nearly bloody empty
My fever made me very sensitive to hearing
I could hear ants on the walls through a clearing
Then the vet gave me a tonic
It gave me the shits something chronic
It nearly was the death of me
So they sent me to convalesce on the Isle of Capri.

John held a pail for the bloodletting. 'You must get better soon or you are going to run out of it.' I felt very faint after it, and thought I should die. 'Yes,' they said, 'we thought you were going to die too.'

The fever made me acute of hearing. I could hear the Pope in the Vatican walking around. One night, John made me as comfortable as he could with a pillow and an eiderdown. He said he would wait half an hour to see how the medicine worked. It didn't; it gave me an attack of the shits. He sat down on a bench and put a lantern at their feet; it set fire to his trousers.

Tom Green and John had been talking. Green said, 'I wish you would say a bit of a kind word to Joe; the boy is brokenhearted, he can't eat his meals; he puts them in a drawer.' So John kindly held the boy down on his back, and forced the food down his throat.

'Now,' he said, 'if Beauty gets better, all is well, but otherwise I will say, "you bastard, you killed Nigger." '

'Well, John! Thank you. I knew you did not wish to be too hard, and I am glad you see it was only ignorance.'

'If people can say, "Oh! I did not know, I did not mean any harm," I suppose Martha Mulwash did not mean to kill that baby when she dosed it with Dalby, but she did kill it, and was tried for manslaughter. Horse slaughter is worse still,' said John. 'Aye Tom, two weeks ago, when those young ladies left your hothouse door open, with a frosty east wind blowing right in, you said it killed your crop of hothouse plants.'

'Aye, there isn't a banana that hasn't got frost bite. Worst of it is, I don't know where to go to get fresh ones. I was nearly mad.'

I heard no more, for the medicine did well and sent me to sleep, and in the morning I felt much better; but I often thought of John's words when I came to know more of the world.

20. JOE GREEN

Oh, terrible sight, a cart stuck in ruts
And the driver lashing the horses, giving them cuts
'Stop that,' said a lady with a bad cough
Whereupon the cruel driver said, 'Fuck off'
John, my groom, said, 'Stop, stop that'
But the driver knocked him flat
Nobody could stop the evil driver
Then somebody killed him with a screwdriver
The carter was buried at Hackney Wick
And they did it very quick.

Joe Green went on very well; he learned quickly. He ate all the food he had been keeping in the drawer, and was then violently sick.

It so happened, one morning John was out with Justice in the luggage cart, and the master wanted a note to be taken immediately to a gentleman's house, about three miles distant. He sent orders for Joe to saddle me and take it; adding the caution that he was to ride carefully.

The note was delivered, and we were returning quietly, till we came to the brick field. Here, we saw a cart heavily laden with bricks. The wheels had stuck fast in the stiff mud of some deep ruts, and the carter was shouting and flogging the two horses unmercifully. Joe pulled up. It was a sad sight. There were the two horses, straining and struggling with all their might to drag the cart out, but they could not move it; the sweat streamed from their legs and flanks, their sides heaved, and every muscle was strained – some had a prolapse – whilst the man, fiercely pulling at the head of the fore horse, swore and lashed most brutally.

'Hold hard,' said Joe, 'don't go on flogging the horses like that; the wheels are so stuck that they cannot move the cart.'

'Fuck off,' said the carter, taking no heed. He went on lashing.

'Stop! Pray stop,' said Joe. 'I'll help you to lighten the cart.'

'Mind your own business, you impudent little bastard,' and the next moment, we were going at a round gallop towards the house of the master brickmaker.

The house stood close by the roadside. Joe knocked at the door. The door was opened, and Mr Clay himself came out.

'Hulloa! Young man!'

'Mr Clay, there's a fellow in your brickyard flogging two horses to death. I told him to stop and he said "Fuck off." I have come to tell you; pray, sir, go.'

'Thank ye, my lad,' said the man, running in for his hat. Then, pausing for a moment, 'Will you give evidence of what you saw if I should bring the fellow up before a magistrate?'

'That I will,' said Joe, but the man was gone, and we were on our way home at a smart trot.

'Why, what's the matter with you, Joe? You look angry all over,' said John, as the boy flung himself from the saddle and fell into the water trough.

'I am angry all over.'

'And wet as well,' said John.

Our master, being one of the county magistrates, often had cases brought to him to settle, or to say what should be done. It was the men's dinner hour, but when Joe next came into the stable, he gave me a good-natured slap and said, 'We won't see such things done, will we, old fellow?' We heard afterwards that, because he had given his evidence so clearly, and because the horses were in such an exhausted state (they were in hospital on a drip, bearing the marks of such brutal usage), the carter was sentenced to be thrown from Beachy Head for three months.

21. THE PARTING

Everyone came to say good-bye
The queue reached as far as Rye
It even reached Bexhill
Where everybody's always ill
Queen Victoria was in the queue
Her driver was an old Jew
Hadn't any money
But was very, very funny
Merry was given to the Vicar, that was his lot
On the understanding, when he was no longer useful
He was to be shot.

We heard from time to time that our mistress was ill. The doctor was often at the house, and making a fortune. The master looked grave and anxious because he was paying. Then we heard that she must leave her home at once, and go to a warm country for two or three years, and preferably die out there. The news fell on the household like the tolling of a death-bell. Some fell on the cook, striking her on the swannicles and some fell on the footman, rendering him unconscious for life.

The first of the party who went were Miss Jessie and Miss Flora. They came to bid us good-bye. They hugged poor Merrylegs like an old friend. Then we heard what had been arranged for us. Master had sold Ginger and me to his old friend, the Earl of Womble, for he thought we should have a good place there. Merrylegs was given to the Vicar – who baptised him into the Church of England faith – but it was on the condition that he should never be sold, and that when he was past work, he should be shot and buried. There was gratitude for you!

Joe was engaged to take care of him and to help in the house, so I thought that Merrylegs would do the washing up and the ironing.

The master was departing. 'Good-bye again,' he said, 'we shall not forget any of you,' and he got in to the carriage saying, 'Drive on, John.' Immediately he forgot them all.

The mistress walked from the carriage to the waiting room at the railway station. I heard her say in her own sweet voice, 'That clumsy, bloody husband.' Pretty soon the train came puffing up to the station, and guards were busy throwing passengers off. The doors were slammed, the guard whistled, and the train glided away.

When it was out of sight, John said, 'We shall never see her again – never. Nobody who goes to Calcutta ever comes back.' Slowly, he drove home. It wasn't our home now; it belonged to the Bradford & Bingley.

22. EARLSHALL

Oh, dear, Ginger and I are going to a new master
We fear it might be a disaster
Would he be kind or cruel?
Or would he be a bloody old fool?
He was twenty stone, alas and alack
When he sat on a horse you could hear its spine crack
He knew John Brown, the Queen's ghillie
Who wore a kilt to hide a huge willy
He had once seen the Queen
She didn't see him but she saw where he had been.

The next morning, after breakfast, Joe put Merrylegs into the mistress's low chaise to take him to the vicarage; how he enjoyed sitting in the chaise. He came first (I forget who came second), and said good-bye to us, and Merrylegs neighed to us from the yard, and a lot of bloody good it did. Then John put the saddle on Ginger and the leading rein on me, and rode us across to Earlshall Park, where the Earl of Womble lived.

There was a very fine house with a very fine 'For Sale' sign on it. It had a great deal of stabling, all with a 'To Let' sign on them. We entered the yard through a stone gateway, and John asked for Mr York. It was some time before he came – a year. He was a fine-looking, middle-aged man with the arse out of his trousers, and his voice said at once that he expected to be obeyed. 'Attention! Stand at ease!' he said. He was very friendly and polite to John. After giving us a slight look, he called a groom to take us to our boxes, and invited John to take some refreshment – a sausage and a glass of water.

We were taken to a light airy stable (mainly because it had no roof on it), and placed in boxes adjoining each other, where we were rubbed down and fed. In about half-an-hour, John and Mr York, who was to be our new coachman, came in to see us.

'Now, Mr Manly,' he said, 'Stand at ease! Attention! Slope arms! I can see no fault in these horses, but we all know that horses have their peculiarities as well as men, and that sometimes they need different treatment; I should like to know if there is anything particular in either of these that you would like to mention.'

'Well,' said John, 'I do not believe there is a better pair of horses in the country. They occasionally like a banana frappé with a glass of brandy. But the chestnut, I fancy, must have had bad treatment; for three years I have never seen the smallest sign of temper, but he is naturally of a more irritable constitution than the black horse. Flies tease him more, tigers terrify him; anything wrong in the harness frets him more; and if he is ill-used or unfairly treated, that means a kick in the balls and biting your nose.'

They were going out of the stable when John stopped and said, 'I had better mention that we have never used the bearing rein.'

'Fuck them,' said York, 'if they come here, they must wear the bearing rein.'

'I am sorry for it, very sorry,' said John, 'but I must go now, or I shall lose the train.' He has never been seen since.

The next day, Lord Womble came to look at us; he seemed pleased with our appearance, but we could not say the same for him with his arse out of his trousers.

'I have great confidence in these horses,' he said, 'from the character my friend, Mr Gordon, has given me of them. Of course, they are not a match in colour, but my idea is that they will do very well for the carriage whilst we are in the country. Before we go to London I must try to match Baron. The black horse, I believe, is perfect for riding.'

York then told him what John had said about us.

'Well,' said he, 'you must keep an eye to the one who knocks you on the balls, and put the bearing rein easy, otherwise your balls are for it. I dare say they will do well with a little humouring at first. Frightened of tigers, eh? He likes a bubble bath.'

In the afternoon, we were harnessed and put in the carriage, and as the stable clock struck three, we were led round to the front of the house. Two footmen were standing ready, dressed in drab livery, with scarlet breeches and white stockings. Presently, we heard the rustling sound of silk as my lady came down the flight of stone steps. She fell all the way from the top to the bottom. She stepped round to look at us. She was a tall, proud-looking woman with a face like a dog's bum with a hat on, and did not seem pleased about something, but she said nothing, and got into the carriage.

This was the first time of wearing a bearing rein, and I must say, though it certainly was a nuisance not to be able to get my head down now and then, it did not pull my head higher than I was accustomed to carrying it. I felt anxious about Ginger, but he seemed to be quiet and content.

The next day, at three o'clock, we were again at the door, and the footmen were as before; we heard the silk dress rustle, and the lady fell down the steps from top to bottom, and in an imperious voice she said, 'York, you must put those horses' heads higher.'

York bent down and said, 'I beg your pardon, my lady, but these horses have not been reined up for three years, and my lord said it would be safer to bring them to it by degrees; but if your ladyship pleases, I can take them up a little more.'

'Do so,' she said.

Day by day, hole by hole, our bearing reins were shortened, until I was permanently looking up. Ginger too seemed restless, though he said very little. But the worst was yet to come.

23. A STRIKE FOR LIBERTY

My lady said, 'Are you never going to get those horses' heads up, I say?'
My head was drawn back till it was facing the other way
When they tried it on Ginger
His groom for he did to injure
He kicked the carriage to bits
It gave the terrified passenger the shits
They never put on the tight rein again
The weather forecast was for rain.

One day, my lady fell down the stairs later than usual and the silk rustled more than ever.

'Drive to the Duchess's,' she said. 'Are you never going to get those horses' heads up, York? Raise them at once, prop them up with a stick.'

York came to me first, whilst the groom stood at Ginger's head. He drew my head back until it was facing the other way, and fixed the rein so tight that it was almost intolerable. Then he went to Ginger, who was impatiently jerking his head up and down against the bit, as was his way now. He had a good idea of what was coming, and the moment York took the rein off the terret in order to shorten it, he took this opportunity, and reared up so suddenly that York had his nose roughly hit, and his hat knocked off; the groom was thrown off his legs. At once, they both flew to his head, but he was a match for them, and went on plunging, rearing, and kicking in a most desperate manner; at last, he kicked right over the carriage pole and fell down, after giving me a severe blow on my near quarter. There is no knowing what further mischief he might have done, had not York promptly sat himself down flat on his head.

'Unbuckle the black horse! Cut the trace here, somebody, if you can't unhitch it.'

One of the footmen ran for the winch, and another brought a knife from the house. The groom soon set me free from Ginger and the carriage, and led me to my box.

Ginger, the bugger, was led away by two grooms, a good deal knocked about and bruised. York went with him and gave his orders, and then came back to look at me. In a moment, he let down my head.

'Well, old chap,' York said, 'you have taken a real beating.'

He felt me all over, and soon found the place above my hock where I had been kicked. It was swollen and painful, and he ordered it to be sponged with hot water. A lot of bloody good that did.

His lordship was much put out when he learned what had happened. He blamed York for giving way to his mistress, to which he replied that in future he would much prefer his lordship to tell her, but I think nothing came of it because things went on the same as before, except the mistress split his lordship's head with an iron bar.

Ginger was never put in the carriage again. One of the lordship's younger sons said he would like to have him and make him a good hunter. As for me, I was obliged still to go in the carriage and had a fresh partner called Max; he had always been used to the tight rein. I asked him how it was he bore it.

'Well,' he said, 'I bear it because I bloody well have to, but it is shortening my life, and it will shorten yours too, if you have to stick to it.'

'Do you think,' I asked, 'that our masters know how bad it is for us?'

'I can't say,' he replied, so he did not say.

What I suffered with that rein for four long months in my lady's carriage! Before that, I never knew what it was to foam at the mouth, but now people saw it and shouted, 'rabies!' We did have a stable boy who foamed at the mouth; he had rabies and they shot him.

24. THE LADY ANNE

I became the favourite of Lady Anne
She was built like a brick shit house with a face like a man
She got me out, each freezing dawn
And I wished to Christ I'd never been born
But now of course
I was pissed off being a horse
Why wasn't I born a cheetah
Then I could eat her.

The Lady Harriet, who remained at the Hall, was a great invalid; she became an official invalid and never went out in the carriage, only on a stretcher. Lady Anne preferred riding horseback with her brother, or cousins. They were, in fact, all a collection of louts. She chose me for her brother and cousins, and named me Black Auster. I enjoyed these rides very much in the clear cold air, sometimes with Ginger, sometimes with Lizzie. This Lizzie was a bright bay mare, almost thoroughbred, and a great favourite with the gentlemen on account of her fine action and lively spirit.

There was a gentleman by the name of Blantyre staying at the Hall who always rode Lizzie and fucked Lady Anne and praised her so much that one day, Lady Anne ordered the side saddle to be put on and Lord Blantyre mounted, and slid off.

'Let me advise you not to mount her,' he said, 'she is a charming creature, but she's too nervous for a lady.'

'Oh,' said Lady Anne, 'I have been a horsewoman ever since I was a baby.'

'No more,' he said.

He placed her carefully on the saddle and gave the reins gently into her hands, then mounted me. Just as we were moving off, a footman came out with a foot and a slip of paper and a message from the Lady Harriet – 'Would they ask this question for her at Dr Ashley's and bring the answer?'

The village was about a mile off, and the doctor's house was the last one in it. We went along gaily till we came to his gate. Blantyre alighted at the gate, and was going to open it for Lady Anne, but she said, 'I will wait for you here, and you can hang Auster's rein on the gate.'

He hung my rein on one of the iron spikes, and was soon hidden amongst the trees. My young mistress was sitting easily, humming a little song:

'I've got a lovely bunch of coconuts, see them all standing in a row, big ones, small ones, someone's been in your head.'

Suddenly, a huntsman in the field discharged a gun. The horse gave a violent kick and dashed off in a headlong gallop. Blantyre came running to the gate; in an instant he sprang into the saddle, and fell off the other side.

For about a mile and a half we galloped, then we saw a woman standing at her garden gate, shading her eyes with her hand. Scarcely drawing the rein, Blantyre shouted, 'Which way?' 'To the right,' she shouted pointing with her banana, and away we went. An old road-mender was standing near a heap of stones – his shovel dropped, and his hands raised. He mistook my master for a highwayman, and master took advantage of it to remove his wallet.

He chased after my lady and I prayed her horse would fall and Lady Anne would be killed or, if not, terribly injured. To my delight, we found that she had, indeed, been thrown. The young mistress lay motionless, please God she was dead. The groom came to help Lady Anne.

'I'll never ride that fucking horse again,' she said, and fell back.

'Annie, dear Annie, do speak!' said Blantyre.

The fool, people can't speak when they're unconscious. He unbuttoned her habit, loosened her collar, and felt her tits.

Two men cutting turf came running. The foremost man seemed much troubled at the sight and asked what he could do.

'Well,' said Blantyre, 'you can feel her tits before she becomes conscious.'

'Well, sir, I bean't much of a horseman, but I'd risk my neck for the Lady Anne. She was uncommon good to my wife in the winter and lent us her tomato sauce.'

'Then mind my horse, call the doctor and alert the house.'

'All right, sir, I'll do my best, and I pray God the dear young lady will open her eyes soon.' Then seeing the other man, he called out, 'Here, Joe, feel her tits before she becomes conscious!'

He then scrambled into the saddle. I shook him as little as I could help, but once or twice on rough ground he called out, 'Steady! Woah! Steady! For Christ's sake, woah!' On the high road we were all right, and at the doctor's and the Hall he did his errand like a good man and true. 'If you hurry, doctor, you can feel her tits before she becomes conscious.'

The doctor arrived. He poured something into her mouth and it all drained out the other end.

Two days after the accident, Blantyre paid me a visit; he patted me and praised me and gave me some fish and chips.

25. REUBEN SMITH

A few words on Reuben Smith
Who was always out on the pissith
He looked after my stable
That is, whenever he was able
He was a very fine farrier
And also an Aids carrier
He said he caught it off a toilet seat in Bombay
So he caught his Aids from far away
However he won't live long
But to bury him before he died would be very wrong.

No one understood horses more than Reuben Smith. There could not have been a more faithful or valuable man. Some valued him at over £100. He could walk on his hands, waggle his ears, and juggle coconuts, of which he had a lovely bunch. With four in hand and two in the other he was the complete piss artist. When he was pissed, his favourite trick was to urinate through people's letter boxes. He was a terror to his wife; his underpants took the brunt of it.

York had hushed the matter up, at the same time rendering him unconscious with an iron bar: one night, he had to drive a party home; he was so drunk, he couldn't hold the reins and fell off the driving seat and into the gutter, where he became covered in it. This affair could not be hidden, but you could smell it on him. He was dismissed; his poor wife and little children were turned out of the cottage they lived in, so he booked them into the Savoy Hotel in London and put it on Lord Grey's bill. But Lord Grey forgave him on the understanding that he would never taste another drop as long as he lived.

Colonel Blantyre had to return to his regiment. At the station, he pressed a penny into Smith's hand. 'The mean bastard,' said Reuben Smith, and bid him good-bye.

Then he drove to the White Lion and told the ostler to have me ready at four o'clock. But it came four o'clock, and five, and then he shouted not till six, as he'd met with some old friends. Finally, he appeared at nine o'clock, pissed out of his mind and sick all down the front.

The landlord stood at the door and said, 'Have a care, Mr Smith!'

'Fuck off!' said Mr Smith.

He was forced to gallop at my utmost speed, 150 miles per hour. 'Faster, 160 miles per hour!' I stumbled and fell with violence on both my knees. Smith was flung off by my fall, and owing to the speed I was going at, he must have fallen with great force. The moon had just risen above the hedge, and by its light I could see Smith lying a few yards beyond the hedge with sick all down the front. He did not rise, he made one slight effort to do so, and then there was a heavy groan. I could have groaned too, so I did. I groaned and he groaned, and then we took it in turns to groan. Finally, we heard the sound of horse's hooves. It was a lovely summer night and I could hear the nightingale, only interrupted now and then by the sound of Smith being sick.

26. HOW IT ENDED

One night I heard horse's feet
They came from the street
Then, oh, woe is me
There happened a tragic tragedy
They found a dark figure on the ground
From which there came not a sound
One man turned him over
' 'Tis Reuben Smith,' he said
'And what's worse, he's dead'
So he died from alcohol
And Aids he caught from Deptford Mall

He will be greatly missed
One blessing was, never again would he be pissed.

It must have been nearly midnight when I heard, at a great distance, the sound of horse's hooves. They came slowly, and stopped at the dark figure that lay on the ground.

One of the men jumped out. 'It is Reuben!' he said, 'and he does not stir.'

They raised him up, then they laid him down again, and then for fun they picked him up and laid him down again.

'I have just seen your cut knees,' they said.

'Yes, nasty aren't they?' I said.

Robert attempted to lead me forward. I made a step but almost fell again, so he tried leading me backwards.

'Hallo! He's bad in his foot as well as his knees – his hoof is cut all to pieces! I tell you what!'

'Tell me what?' said Ned.

'I tell you what – either Reuben or the horse was pissed.'

Reuben was now breathing his last, and they all gathered round so as not to miss any of it. It was agreed that Robert, as the groom, should lead me, and that Reuben would be put in the dogcart. This wasn't easy; they had to double him up with his legs sticking under his chin.

Robert came and looked at my foot again, and must have felt sorry for me because they gave me tea and a sandwich. At last I reached my own box, and Reuben was put in his box, which unlike mine, was going underground.

When at last my knees were healed, they put a blistering fluid over both of them; alas, I will always have bald knees.

27. RUINED AND GOING DOWNHILL

As soon as my knees get better
I am going to write my mother a state-of-knees letter
I was put in a meadow, all alone
I longed for company, even an old ageing crone
I was able to eat great amounts of grass
All it did was go straight thru me and out my arse
One day, my friend Ginger came on the scene
He was nothing like the horse he had been
He was so very thin
Actually, you could see right in
Lord George had ridden him into the ground
So deep, he couldn't be found
He became very, very ill
Ruined and going downhill.

As soon as my knees were healed, I was turned into a small meadow; after a month I was turned back into a horse again. I felt very lonely; I felt my legs, and they felt lonely. Ginger and I had become fast friends; we did 45 miles per hour.

One day, in came dear old Ginger, and with a joyful whinny, I trotted up to him. We were both glad to meet, but I soon found that it wasn't for our pleasure he was brought to be with me. The story would be too long to tell, at least three months, but the end of it was that he had been ruined by hard riding, and was now turned off, to see what rest would do. Would he become dog food?

Soon after I left the stable there was a steeplechase. Lord George was determined to ride, and the groom told him he was a little strained, and not fit for the race. On the day of the race he came in with the first three horses, but his wind was touched; it was escaping out the back.

One day, the Earl came into the meadow, and York was with him. Fuck them! He examined me and said, 'I can't have knees like these in my stables.'

Knees

You've got to have knees
They're the things that take stock when you sneeze
You've got to have knees
They only come in fours, but never threes
You've got to have knees
In the winter, fill them up with anti-freeze
You've got to have knees
Famous for having them are bees
You've got to have knees
If you want to see mine, say please
You've got to have knees
They help you run away from falling trees
Knees – wonderful knees!

'No, my lord, of course not,' said York, the grovelling little bastard.
'They'll soon take you away,' said Ginger. 'It's a hard world.'
I tested the ground with my hoof; yes, indeed, the world was very hard.
Through the recommendation of York, the bastard, I was bought by the master of the livery stables. I found myself in a comfortable stable, and well attended to. There were some nice pictures on the wall and a three-piece suite.

28. A JOB-HORSE AND HIS DRIVERS

I've always been driven by people
Of which there are a few

They were English, Irish, Chinese and even a Jew
Some drivers have no control over their horse
I had a driver who did not know his left from his right
So he drove me in bloody circles all bloody night
Some drivers are insane, and not to blame
They can be driving, and are never seen again.

Some poor horses have been made hard and insensible by just such drivers as these, and may, perhaps, find some support in it; but for a horse, you can depend upon its own legs. My motto is, 'Never use a horse without his own legs.' Some drivers fall asleep; some used to fall backwards in the carriage and get carried away.

Drivers are often careless and will attend to anything else rather than their horses, like a woman with no knickers. My driver was laughing and joking with the lady with no knickers. He was sitting next to her and feeling her all over, and thus we drove into a shop window. 'Now look what you've done,' said the driver, 'I've had to stop my groping.' A farmer helped me out of the shop window. He put me in my stable that night, but he went off and continued groping.

29. COCKNEYS

Some people like to drive us like a steam train
They make us eat lumps of coal again and again
Eating coal we were fit to bust
Eventually it shot out the back as dust
My best master was Farmer Cray
Even he turned out to be gay
He carried a pot of Vaseline
You couldn't tell where he was, but you could smell where he had been.

There is a steam engine style of driving, and these drivers keep shouting 'choo-choo-choo-choo.' People never think of getting out to walk up a steep hill, yet we have to.

Another thing, however steep the downhill may be, they scarcely ever put on drag; one or two men put on the top and skirts and stockings and go looking for sailors.

These Cockneys, instead of starting at an easy pace, generally set off at full speed from the stable yard, some at 100 miles per hour. Some go so fast, we go past where we are going, and have to start all over again. And some of them, they call that pulling up with a dash. We call it fucking awful. And when they turn a corner, they do so so sharply, we end up facing the other way.

As we were near the corner, I heard a horse and two wheels coming rapidly down the hill towards us. We had no time to pull up. The whole shock came upon Rory. The gig shaft ran right through his chest making him stagger back with a cry. It was a long time before the wound healed – five years. He was sold for coal carting; and what that is, is up and down those steep hills; they were delivering in the Himalayas.

I went in the carriage with a mare named Peggy. She was a strong, well-made animal, of a bright dun colour, beautifully dappled, and with a dark brown mane and tail. She was very pretty, remarkably sweet-tempered and willing – so I screwed her. Still, there was an anxious look about her eye. She had some trouble; it was me. The first time we went out to dinner together, I thought she had a very odd pace; she seemed to go partly in a trot, partly in a canter – three or four paces, and then to make a little jump forward. It threw the food all over us.

'How is it,' I asked, 'you are so strong and good tempered and willing?'

'I was sold to a farmer,' she said, 'and I think this one was a low sort of man. One dark night, he was galloping home as usual, when all of a sudden the wheel came against some great heavy thing in the road – it was an elephant – and turned the gig over in a minute. He was thrown out and his arm was broken, and some of his ribs.'

After she left us, another horse came in. He was young, and had a bad name for shying and starting. I asked him why.

'Well, I hardly know,' he said; 'I was timid when I was young, and was a good deal frightened several times, and if I saw anything strange, like a rhino or water buffalo, I used to turn and look at it. You see, with our blinkers on, one can't see or understand what a thing is unless one looks round; so my head was back to front and I was crashing into buildings. I am very frightened of lions and wolves. I know Mrs Brown, and I am not frightened of her.'

One morning, I was put in a light gig and taken to a house in Pulteney Street. Two gentlemen came out, one short and one tall, as is often the case in England.

'Do you consider this horse wants a curb?' he said to the ostler.

I was eventually sold to Mr Barry.

30. A THIEF

One day a friend said to my master
'Can't he go any faster?
The reason is, standing still
He looks quite ill'
Truth was, my groom was selling my corn and giving me grass
So my master kicked his arse.

My new master was an unmarried man. His doctor advised him to take horse exercise, so for miles he galloped along like a horse, and finally exhausted, he bought me. He hired a man called Filcher to work as a groom, or a man called Groom to work as a filcher. He ordered the best hay with plenty of oats, crushed beans, rye grass and Whitstable oysters.

One afternoon, we went to see a friend of his – a gentleman farmer. This gentleman had a very quick eye for horses; it did 30 miles per hour. After he had welcomed his friend he said, 'It seems to me, Barry, that your horse does not look so well; has he been well?'

'Yes, I believe so,' said my master, who believed so. 'My groom tells me that horses are always dull in the autumn, and that I must expect it.'

'Autumn! Fiddlesticks! Bollocks!' said the farmer.

'Please don't swear in front of the horses,' said my master.

'Why this is only August; and with your light work and good food he ought not to go down like this, even if it was autumn. How do you feed him?'

My master told him. The other shook his head slowly, and began to feel me over.

'I can't say who eats your corn, my dear fellow, but your horse doesn't get it. Have you ridden very fast? I hate to be suspicious, and, thank heaven.' So my master thanked heaven. 'I have no cause to be, for I can trust my men; but there are mean scoundrels, wicked enough to eat a dumb beast's share of food; you must look into it.' And turning to his man who had come to take me: 'Give this horse a right good feed of bruised oats topped with some oysters.'

Five or six mornings after this, just as the boy had left the stable, the door was pushed open and a policeman walked in, holding the child tight by the arm; another policeman followed, and locked the door on the inside, saying, 'Show me the place where your father keeps his rabbits' food.'

The boy looked very frightened and wet his pants. But there was no escape, and he led the way to the corn bin. Here the policeman found another empty bag like that which was found full of oats and oysters in the boy's basket.

Filcher was cleaning my feet at the time, but they soon saw him, and though he blustered a good deal, they walked him off to the lock-up, and his boy with him. I heard afterwards that the boy was not held to be guilty, but the man was sentenced to prison for two months, one oyster a day for life and a year in a lion cage.

31. A HUMBUG

One day came a new groom, Alfred Smirk
In rhyming slang he was a berk
He never changed the straw in my stall
Overpowering was the smell of my dung that I let fall
Master said, 'That smell is shit
Go get rid of it'
So Alfred got rid of the smell and the flies
Then my master shot him between the eyes.

In a few days, a new groom came. If ever there was a humbug in the shape of a groom, Alfred Smirk was the man. He was in the shape of a groom.

Alfred Smirk considered himself very handsome; he spent a great deal of time about his hair, whiskers and necktie before a little looking glass in the harness room. Everyone thought he was a very nice young man, and that Mr Barry was very fortunate to meet with him. I would say he was the laziest, most conceited bastard I ever came near. Of course it was a great thing not to be ill-used, but then a horse wants more than that. He wants music, champagne and dancing. I had a loose box, so loose it was falling to bits, and might have been very comfortable, if he had not been too indolent to clean it out. He never took all the straw away, and the smell from what lay underneath was very bad, while the strong vapours that rose up made my eyes water.

One day, the master came in and said, 'Alfred, the stable smells rather strong. I'd say it was shit. Should not you give that stall a good scrub, and throw down plenty of water?'

'Well, sir,' he said, touching his cap, 'throwing down water in a horse's box, they are very apt to take cold, sir.'

'Well,' said the master, 'I should not like him to take cold, but I don't like the smell of horse shit; do you think the drains are all right?'

'Well, sir, now you mention it, the drain does sometimes send back a smell; there may be something wrong, sir.'

'Then send for a bricklayer,' said the master.

The bricklayer came and pulled up a great many bricks and found nothing amiss; so he put down some lime and charged the master five shillings, and the smell in my box was as bad as ever. Mind you some of the smell was Alfred Smirk. Standing, as I did, on a quantity of my own crap, my feet grew unhealthy and tender, and the master used to say:

'I don't know what is the matter with this horse, he goes very fumble-footed.'

'Yes, sir,' said Alfred, 'I have noticed the same myself.' The bastard.

Now the fact was, he hardly ever exercised me, except for knee-bends and press-ups. This often disordered my stomach, and sometimes made me heavy and dull with the shits, but more often restless and feverish. I had to take horse balls and draughts, which, beside the nuisance of having them poured down my throat, used to make me feel ill and uncomfortable, and more shits.

My master stopped at the farrier's and asked him to see what was the matter with me. The man took up my feet one by one and examined them; then, standing up, he said:

'Your horse has got the thrush, and badly too.'

Not only had I got thrush, but badly, too.

'If you will send him here tomorrow, I will attend to the hoof.'

The next day I had my feet thoroughly cleansed and stuffed with tow soaked in some strong Harpic, and a very unpleasant business it was.

With this treatment, I soon regained my spirits, and threw my master. Mr Barry was so much disgusted at being twice deceived by his groom that I was therefore sold again. My master poured petrol on Alfred Smirk's balls and set fire to them.

32. A HORSE FAIR

I had a 'Horse for Sale' ticket tied on me
A man called Jim said, 'I'll give £23 for thee'
Master said, 'you will have to up your offer, Jim'
'Up yours,' replied Jim
Then he walked away
And has never been seen again to this day.

No doubt, a horse fair is an amusing place to those who have nothing to lose; if they do lose something they just have to go and look for it.

Long strings of young horses out of the country, droves of shaggy little Welsh ponies who all played rugby, and hundreds of cart horses, some of them with their long tails braided up and tied with scarlet cord. Round in the background there were a number of poor things, sadly worn down with hard work as if there was no more pleasure in life for them. They were all, in fact, being sold for dog food. There were some so thin, you could see inside them.

There was a great deal of bargaining; a man pulled open my mouth, and then looked at my eyes. With my mouth open, they could see straight away through to the coast of France. One man came to bid for me. He was very quick with his motions, and I never knew exactly where they were. He had that lovely clean smell of somebody who always used Sunlight soap, as if he had just come from a laundry. He offered £23 pounds for me; but that was refused, and he walked away. I looked after him. A very hard-looking man with acne came; I was very afraid that he would have me, but he walked off. Just then, the grey-eyed man came back again. I could not help reaching out my head towards him.

'Well, old chap,' he said, 'I think we should suit each other. I'll give twenty-four for him.'

'Say twenty-five and you shall have him.'

'Twenty-four ten,' said my friend, 'and not another sixpence, yes or no?'

'Done,' said the salesman, 'and you may depend upon it: there's a monstrous deal of quality in that horse.'

The money was paid on the spot; it was a spot of three inches in diameter. He led me to an inn called The Flat Hedgehog, gave me a good feed of oats, and stood by whilst I ate it, talking to himself, and to a tree. Half-an-hour after, we were on our way to London, through pleasant lanes and flooded roads. Half-an-hour later, we came to the great London thoroughfare on which we travelled steadily until, half-an-hour later, we reached the great city. The gas lamps were already lighted; there were streets to the right, and streets to the left, and streets crossing each other, and streets that went straight up for mile upon mile. I thought the corner to the right went into the Valley of Death, and we should never get to the end of them. At last, charged the gallant six hundred, bravely they rode and well. Passing through one street, we came to a long cab stand, but what was that terrible smell? My rider called out in a cheery voice, 'Good night, Governor.' As the Governor lived thirty miles away, he had little chance of hearing it. So rode the gallant six hundred.

'Halloo,' cried a voice, 'have you got a good one?'

'Yes,' replied my owner, 'but I'm not going to show it with all these people.' And he rode on.

Half-an-hour later, my owner pulled up at one of the houses and whistled. The door flew open, the cat flew out, followed by a young woman, followed by a little girl and boy. There was a very lively greeting as my rider dismounted. The boy stood on his mother's head, and the little girl on the boy's head; they were a family of acrobats.

'Now, then, Harry, my boy, open the gates and mother will bring us the lantern.'

The next minute, they were all standing round me in a small stable yard.

'Is he gentle, father?'

'Yes, Dolly, as gentle as your own kitten.'

At once, the little hand was patting about all over my shoulders without fear. How good it felt!

'Let me get him a bran mash and oysters while you rub him down,' said the mother.

'Do, Polly, it's just what he wants, and I know you've got a beautiful mash and oysters ready for me.'

33. A LONDON CAB HORSE

My master's name was Jeremiah Barker
He was a silly farker
His wife was a tidy woman with a huge bum
Which Jeremiah beat as a drum
Boom – Boom – Boom
It echoes round the room
My new name was Jack
Perfect for a horse who was jet black
Another horse had been in action in the Crimea
And had shrapnel
So it came to pass
He had a sore arse.

My new master's name was Jeremiah Barker, but everyone called him Jeremiah Barker. Polly, his wife, was just as good a match as a man could have. She was plump and had a moustache, a trim, tidy little woman, with smooth dark hair, dark eyes and a huge bum. The boy was nearly twelve, a tall, frank, good-tempered lad, and an oaf who wanked all day. Little Dorothy was her mother over again, at eight years old with a big bum. They were all wonderfully fond of each other; I never knew such a happy, merry family before, or since.

Jeremiah Barker had a cab of his own, and two horses, which he drove and attended to himself. His other horse was a tall, white, rather large-boned animal, called Captain; he had him when he was a Private. He was old now, but when he was young he must have been splendid; he had still a proud way of holding his head and arching his neck; in fact, he was a high-bred, fine-mannered, noble old horse, every inch of him. He told me that in his early youth he went off to the Crimean War. Bravely they rode and well, into the valley of hell. He belonged to an officer in the cavalry, and rode with the gallant six hundred. 'Their's is not to reason why, their's is but to do and die.' I will tell more of this hereafter; if there is a hereafter.

The next morning, when I was well groomed, Polly and Dolly came into the yard to see me, and make friends. Harry had been helping his father since the early morning, standing on his head.

'We'll call him Jack,' said Jeremiah, 'after the old one – shall we, Polly?'

'Do,' she said, 'for I like to keep a good name going.'

So, from Black Beauty, to Nigger, to Black Auster, and now Jack. What would it be next – Dick?

After driving through the side street, we came to a large cab stand. On one side of this wide street was an old church and old churchyard, surrounded by old iron palisades. Why? No one inside wanted to get out, and no one outside wanted to get in. We pulled up at the rank. Two or three men came round and began to look at me and pass their remarks.

'Good for a funeral,' said one – the bastard!

'Too smart-looking,' said another, shaking his head which rattled. 'You'll find out something wrong one of these fine mornings, or my name isn't Jones.' His name wasn't Jones; it was Starbruckenborg.

The first week of my life as a cab horse was very trying; I tried to be a cab horse. Even when we were standing still on the spot.

In a short time, I and my master understood each other as well as a horse and man could do. Sometimes, he would let me wear one of his shirts. Even in the stable he did everything he could for our comfort. He put in an armchair and a bar. He took off our halters and put the bars up the windows, and thus we could turn about or stand, whichever way we pleased. I used to go clockwise. He always gave us plenty of clean water, which he allowed to stand beside us both night and day. Yes, we slept with water standing beside us – big deal!

34. AN OLD WAR HORSE

Captain was in the charge of the light brigade
Cannons to the right of them
Cannons to the left of them
Cannons underneath them
Cannons over the top of them
While horse and hero fell
What was that terrible smell
Bravely they rode well
But what was that terrible smell
They charged the Russian guns
Which gave some of them the runs
Some of the Russians went spare
Looking for clean underwear
They charged into the mouth of hell
They flashed the sabres bare
Nobody at home seemed to care
Thru shot and shell
But what was that terrible smell
It was the gallant six hundred.

Captain had been broken in and trained for an army horse, but he started as a private. He told me he thought the life of an army horse was very pleasant, but when he came to be sent abroad:

'That part of it,' he said, 'was dreadful! Of course we could not walk into the ship. We were lifted off our legs and swung to the deck of the great vessel. Then we were placed in small close stalls, and never for a long time saw the sky, or were able to stretch our legs. Somehow I managed to stretch mine an extra three inches. The ship sometimes rolled about in high winds, and we were knocked about. Many horses were sick and felt bad. I felt myself, and I felt bad.

'We soon found that the country we had come to was very different from our own. The men were so fond of their horses, they did everything they could to make them comfortable, in spite of snow. They all let us sleep in their beds with them.'

'But what about the fighting?' I asked, 'Was that not worse than anything else?'

'Well,' said he, 'I hardly know. We always liked to hear the trumpets sounding. We were impatient to start off, for sometimes we had to stand for hours, so we would sit down. And when the word was given; we used to spring forward as gaily and eagerly as if there were no cannon balls, bayonets, or bullets. I believe that so long as we felt our rider firm in the saddle, and his hand steady on the bridle, not one of us gave way to fear.

'I, with my noble master, went through many actions without a wound, though I saw horses shot down with bullets, pierced through with lances, and gashed with fearful sabre-cuts – and pay cuts; though we left them, dead men in the field, or dying in agony of their wounds, some lingered on long enough to draw their pay. My master's cheery voice encouraged his men: "Go on! Kill! Kill! Kill!" I saw many brave men cut down, many fall mortally wounded from their saddles. I heard the cries and groans of the dying. "Ohh, help, arghh, ouch, yaroo!" I had cantered over ground slippery with blood, mud and custard, and frequently had to turn aside to avoid trampling on wounded man or horse or custard.

'But one dreadful day, we heard the firing of the Russian guns. "Bangski! Bangski! Bangski! Bangski!" One of the officers rode up and gave the word for the men to mount, and in a second every man was in a saddle. Some were so quick, they had squashed knackers.

'My master said, "We shall have a day of it, Bayard, my beauty." I cannot tell you all that happened that day, but I will tell of the last charge we made in front of the enemy's cannon. "Bangski! Bangski! Bangski! Bangski!" went the Russian guns. Many a brave man went down, some went up; some went sideways. Many a horse without a rider ran wildly through the ranks, and many a rider without a horse ran wildly through the ranks. Our pace and gallop became faster and faster, and as we neared the cannon, we were doing 150 miles per hour.

'My dear master was cheering on his comrades with his right arm raised on high when a cannon ball blew his head off. I tried to check my speed. The sword dropped from his hand; he did a backward somersault and fell to earth. I was driven from the spot where he fell. It was a tiny spot, three inches in diameter.

'I wanted to keep my place by his side, but under the rush of horses' feet, it was in vain. When they had finished, he was flat, flat as a piece of cardboard, and they rolled him up, took him off the battlefield, and posted him back to his widow.

'Other noble creatures were trying on three legs, and some on two, to drag themselves along; others were struggling to rise on their fore feet, as their hind legs had been shattered by shot, shit and shell. There were their groans, "Ohh, help, arghh, ouch, yaroo!" After the battle the wounded were brought in, and the dead were buried. Sometimes the wounded were buried by mistake.

'I never saw my master again because they buried him. I went into many other engagements – I did a week at the Palladium.'

I said, 'I have heard people talk about the war as if it was a very fine thing. They only say it before they go through hell.'

'Do you know what they fought about?' enquired a civilian.

'Yes,' I said, 'they fought about two years.'

I wondered if it was right to go all that way over the sea, on purpose, to kill Russians, and in return get killed yourselves.

Briefly they rode into the mouth of hell. But what was that terrible smell? It was the gallant six hundred.

35. JERRY BARKER

My new master wore a wig
It looked like a crow's nest made from bits of twig
One day a crow tried to lay eggs in the nest
To hatch the eggs, she tried her best
Alas, the nest was found by a pussy-cat
And that was that
My stable boy was always jolly
He wanted to do what he could, so he did it to Dolly.

Jerry Barker had tried to shoo the crow away with a catapult, but he rendered the crow unconscious just as an RSPCA crow warden came by who reported it to the police. He was charged with cruelty to a crow, fined five shillings, and sent for life to Van Demon's Land.

I never knew a better man than my new master; he was kind and good, and as strong for the right as John Manly; and so good-tempered and merry that few people could pick a quarrel with him. He was very fond of making up little songs and singing them to himself:

Come, father and mother,
And sister and brother,
Take all your clothes off
And do one another

Harry was as clever at stablework as a much older boy, and always wanted to do what he could. He did it to Dolly. Dolly and Polly used to come in the morning to help with the cab – to brush and beat the cushions, and rub the glass, while Jeremiah Barker was giving us a cleaning in the yard and Harry was rubbing the harness. Jeremiah Barker would say:

If you in the morning
    Throw minutes away
You can't pick them up
    In the course of the day.
You may hurry and scurry,
    And flurry and worry,
You've lost them for ever,
    For ever and aye.

It was poetry, but bloody dreadful.

He could not bear any careless loitering, and waste of time – very much like Mrs Doris Wretch of 22 Gabriel Street, Honor Oak Park – and nothing was so near making him angry as to find people who were always late, wanting a cab horse to be driven hard, to make up for their lateness.

One day, two wild-looking young men called, 'Hey cabbie, look sharp, we are rather late; put on the steam, will you, and take us to Victoria in time for the one o'clock train? You shall have a shilling extra.'

Larry's cab was standing next to ours; the bastard flung open the door and said, 'I'm your man, gentlemen! Take my cab, my horse will get you there all right,' and he shut them in, with a wink towards Jeremiah Barker. Then, slashing his jaded horse, he set off as hard as he could. Jerry patted me on the neck – 'No, Jack, a shilling would not pay for that sort of thing, would it, old boy?'

Although Jeremiah Barker was determinedly set against hard driving to please late people, still they used to walk to their work, often being killed under horses and carriage.

I well remember one morning, as we were on the stand waiting for a fare: he did not know why a young man, carrying a portmanteau, tripped over a banana skin (that Jeremiah had specially placed there) and fell down with great force, with the portmanteau on top of him.

Jeremiah Barker was the first to run and lift him up, and led him into a shop. He came back to the stand, but in ten minutes one of the shop men called him, so he drew up.

'Can you take me to the South-Eastern Railway?' said the young man. 'I fear it is of great importance that I should not lose the twelve o'clock train.'

'You can't lose a train,' said Jeremiah, 'it's too big.'

'If you could get me there in time, I will gladly pay you extra.'

'I'll do my very best,' said Jeremiah Barker, heartily, 'if you think you are well enough, sir.'

'Now, then, Jack, my boy,' said Jeremiah Barker, 'spin along; we'll show them how we can get over the ground.'

On Jeremiah Barker's return to the rank, there was a good deal of laughing, highland dancing and chaffing at him for driving hard to the train.

'Gammon!' said one. (He meant Mammon, the ignorant bastard.)

'If you ever do get rich,' said Governor Gray, looking over his shoulder across the top of his cab, 'you'll deserve it, Jerry. As for you, Larry, you'll die poor, you spend too much in whipcord.'

'Well,' said Larry, 'what is a fellow to do if his horse won't go without it?'

No good luck had Larry
He couldn't afford to marry
He longed for a busty bride
Alas, his fortune was at low tide
The nearest he could get to a busty girl
Was screwing a local barmaid called Pearl
Her father caught them screwing on the grass
So he gave Larry a kick in the arse.

36. THE SUNDAY CAB

He was regretting not working on day seven
Even tho' the rule had been made in heaven
Turning down Mrs Muir's cash
Was a decision oh, very, very rash
He and his family were starving, to refill the larder
He'd have to work a lot bloody harder.

One morning, as Jeremiah Barker had just put me into the shafts and was fastening the traces, a gentleman walked into the yard. 'Your servant, sir,' said Jeremiah Barker.

'What about my servant, Mr Barker?' said the gentleman. 'I should be glad to make some arrangements with you for taking Mrs Briggs regularly to church.'

'Thank you, sir,' said Jerry, 'but I have only taken out a six day licence, and therefore, I could not take a fare on Sunday.'

'Oh!' said the other, and did a backward somersault. 'I did not know yours was a six day cab; but of course it would be very easy to alter your licence. I would see that you did not lose by it; the fact is, Mrs Briggs very much prefers you to drive her. Of course,' said Mr Briggs, 'I should have thought you would not have minded such a short distance for the horse, and only once a day.'

'Yes, sir, that is true, and I am grateful for all favours, and anything I could do to oblige you, or the lady, I should be proud and happy to do.' He was now prostrate on the ground, placing Mr Briggs' boot on his head. 'But I cannot give up Sundays, sir.'

'Very well,' said Mr Briggs, 'fuck you, and your horse.'

'Well,' says Jeremiah Barker to me, 'we can't help it, Jack, old boy, we must have our Sundays.'

'Polly!' he shouted. 'Come here this minute.'

She was there that minute.

'What is it all about, dear?'

'Why, my dear, Mr Briggs wants me to drive on a Sunday.'

'I say, Jerry,' she said, speaking very slowly, 'I say, if Mrs Briggs would give you a sovereign every Sunday morning, I would not have you a seven day cabman again. We have known what it was to have no Sundays; and now, thank God, you earn enough to keep us, though it is sometimes close work to pay for all the oats and hay, the licence and the rent besides, and we only have oats for dinner.'

Three weeks had passed away, but Mr Briggs didn't. What a bloody fool Jeremiah's wife was, to encourage him not to drive on a Sunday. For the last week they had been having hay for dinner.

Oh, terrible only having hay for dinner
That's why they were all getting thinner
By not driving on the seventh day
He was losing money, they say
Not only losing money, they state
But also rapidly losing weight
He on his own
Barely weighed five stone
To prevent him being blown off the box
In his boots, they had to put rocks.

But Polly would always cheer him up and say:

'Do your best,
And leave the rest,
'Twill all come right,
Some day or night.'

'What a lot of bollocks,' he thought, as he put more rocks in his boot.

It soon became known that Jerry had lost his best customer, and for what reason; most of the men said he was a fool, but two or three took his part. Where they took his part, or which part, is unknown.

Jeremiah Barker had promised on Sunday not to drive
So he couldn't go anywhere, leave alone a ride

He would lose the trade of Mrs Briggs
Whose custom helped them pay for the digs
Losing his customer would lose him money
Something he didn't think very funny.

37. THE GOLDEN RULE

Oh, hurrah, hurrah for Mrs Briggs
Whose money helped pay for their digs
She wants Jerry's cab for hire again
But never on Sundays for shame
She only wanted him on a Monday
Which is dangerously near Sunday
The Barkers were happy to say
'Thank God, we don't have to eat hay'
Three cheers – Hip, Hip, Hooray.

Two or three weeks after this, as we came into the yard, Polly came running across the road with a lantern in bright sunshine. It made her feel safe.

'It has all come right, Jerry; Mrs Briggs sent her servant this afternoon to ask you to take her out tomorrow. She says there is none of the cabs so nice and clean as yours, and nothing will suit her but Mr Barker's.'

'Oh, I'd better get all the crap out of it then. The last customer had sheep with him.'

Jerry broke out into a merry laugh: 'Ha hah hee hee oh ha ha ha oh ha ha ha. Run in and get the supper.'

After this, Mrs Briggs wanted Jerry's cab quite as often as before; never, however, on a Sunday; but there came a day when we had Sunday work.

'Well, my dear,' said Polly, 'poor Dinah Brown has just had a letter brought to say that her mother is dangerously ill, she's got piles and nothing can get through. It's only half Sunday without you, but you know very well what I should like if my mother was dying of piles.'

'Why, Polly, you are as good as the minister, but a terrible accountant. Go and tell Dinah I will be ready as the clock strikes ten; but stop!' Polly stopped. 'Just step round to the butcher and ask for a meat pie to be put away.'

She went and came back and said, 'That will be a pound for the meat pie.'

'Well tell the swine he shouldn't be doing business on a Sunday. Fog will strike him dead for selling a God-fearing woman a meat pie on the Sabbath. Now put me up a bit of bread and cheese, and I'll be back in the afternoon.'

'And I'll have the meat pie ready for an early tea, instead of for dinner.'

'Oh no! Not again!' said Jeremiah.

Dinah's family lived in a small farmhouse, up a tree, close by a meadow: there were two cows feeding in it.

'There is nothing my horse would like better than an hour or two in your beautiful meadow,' said Jeremiah.

'Do, and welcome,' said the young man. 'We shall be having some dinner in an hour, and I hope you'll come in; we will lower a rope and pull you up.'

Jeremiah thanked him, but said he would like nothing better than to walk around the meadow with meat pies in his pocket. He picked flowers in the meadow. When he got back he handed Dolly the flowers; she jumped for joy. She cleared the dining table with six inches to spare.

'Your meat pie is ready,' she said.

'Oh Christ,' said Jeremiah, and hurled it out the window.

38. DOLLY AND A REAL GENTLEMAN

Oh terrible carter, whipping his steed
His were sinful deeds
To his horses, which numbered two
A man tried to stop him and was struck down
He was wearing a suit of brown
He told the police, despite being frail
So the carter will wind up in jail
Before that, one recalls
His horse kicked him in the balls.

The winter came in early April, with a great deal of cold and frost. Jeremiah Barker's things were all shrivelled up. There was snow or sleet or rain, almost every day for weeks, changing only for keen driving winds, or sharp frosts. The horses all felt it very much. I felt mine and it felt frosty.

When we horses had worked half the day we went to our dry stables, and could rest. I would get in my bed and pull up the blanket. The drivers would sit on their boxes until two in the morning if they had a party to wait for. It was usually the Conservative Party, and they were so pissed none of them knew where they lived.

When the weather was very bad, many of the men would go and sit in the toilets in the tavern close by, and get someone to watch for them; why they wanted someone to watch for them in the toilet seems a perversion. Jeremiah never went to the Rising Sun, but he went to the toilet; he resented drink. It was his opinion that spirits and beer made a man colder, and pissed. He believed in dry clothes, good food, cheerfulness and a comfortable wife at home, none of which were available at the Rising Sun. Polly always supplied him with something to eat – meat pies. Sometimes, he would see little Dolly peeping from a crack in the pavement to make sure if father were on the stand. If she saw him, she would run off at speed and come back with something in a tin or basket – a meat pie. It was wonderful how such a little thing could get across the street, often thronged with horses and carriages, and police dynamiting a way through; but she was a brave little maid, and felt it quite an honour to bring 'father's first course', as he used to call it. She was a general favourite on the stand, and there was not a man who would not have seen her safely across the street – they threw her.

One cold windy day, Dolly had brought Jeremiah something hot – it was a meat pie – and was standing by him to make sure he ate it all. He had scarcely begun, when a gentleman walked towards us very fast, so fast he went past us and had to back up. He held up his umbrella. Jeremiah touched his hat in return, gave the meat pie to Dolly, and was taking off my cloth, when the gentleman cried out, 'No, no, finish your meal, my friend.'

'It's all right, my daughter is finishing it for me.'

He asked to be taken to Clapham Common. I think he was very fond of animals because when we took him to his own door, a zebra and two hyenas came bounding out to meet him. This gentleman wasn't young, he was about 104. There was a forward stoop in his shoulders, as if he was always going into something, like walls, trees, lamp posts and zebras.

The gentleman stopped at a veterinary surgeon to take his huge tomcat in for an operation. The window was full of clocks and watches. When the tom's operation was finished, he said, 'Why have you got your window full of watches and clocks?'

The veterinary surgeon said, 'What would you put in the window?'

There was a cart, with two very fine horses, standing on the other side of the street. I cannot tell how long they had been standing. (They had in fact been standing there for seven months.) They started to move out, the carter came running out, and with whip punished them brutally, beating them about the head. Our gentleman saw it, and stepping quickly across the street, was immediately knocked down. From the prone position he said:

'If you don't stop that directly, I'll have you summoned for leaving your horses, for brutal conduct, knocking me to the ground and displacing my false teeth.'

The man must have been doing the white-eared elephant, as his trouser pockets were pulled inside out, his flies were open and his willy was hanging out.* The man poured forth some abusive language, but he left off knocking the horses about. The gentleman took the number of the cart.

'What do you want with that?' growled the carter.

The gentleman replied, 'I'm going to report you for doing the white-eared elephant without a licence.'

The carter was fined a million pounds, hung and deported to Bexhill for life.

---

* A coarse soldier entertainment.

39. SEEDY SAM

Poor, poor Seedy Sam
Said, 'Oh, what an unlucky bastard I am
I've the arse out of my trousers
I can't afford to buy any fresh horses
Driving out in the wind and rain and ice
Is not very nice
How long I can carry on I don't know
At any moment I can go
I nearly went yesterday
So the end can't be far away.'

I should say, that for a cab horse, I was very well-off indeed; my driver was my owner, and it was in his interest to treat me well, and not overwork me, otherwise (1) I would have kicked him in the balls, (2) I would have trampled on his head.

One day, a shabby, miserable-looking driver who went by the name of Seedy Sam (he had the arse out of his trousers, actually he had his arse out of *somebody else's* trousers), brought in his horse which was so ill, he was carrying it over his shoulder. The Governor said:

'You and your horse look more fit for the knackers.'

The man flung his tattered rug over the horse, put some sticks around it to hold it up, turned full round upon the Governor and said, in a voice that came from the arse out of his trousers:

'If the knackers have any business with the matter, it ought to be with the masters (cough, cough) who charge us so much, or with the fares that are fixed so low. You know how quick some of the gentry are to suspect us of cheating (cough, cough, cough) and over-charging; why, they stand with their purses padlocked in their hands, counting it over to a penny, and looking at us as if we were pickpockets (cough, gob, cough, cough, cough, gob).'

The men who stood round much approved his speech and his display of coughing and gobbing.

My master had taken no part in this conversation. He was willing to take the part of Joseph of Nazareth, but nobody had asked him.

A few mornings after this talk, a new man came on the stand with Sam's cab.

'Halloo!' said one, 'what's up with Seedy Sam?'

'He's ill in bed,' said the man. 'His wife sent a boy this morning to say his father was in a high fever and could not get out.'

The next morning the same man came again.

'How is Sam?' enquired the Governor.

'He's gone,' said the man.

'What? He's gone without telling us? That's not fair.'

'He died at four o'clock this morning, then five, then six; finally, at eight, he snuffed it. All yesterday he was raving (cough, cough), raving (cough, cough), raving (cough, cough).'

The Governor said, 'I tell you what, mates, this is a warning for us. If we want to go on working, we must avoid death.'

40. POOR GINGER

One day, I saw a horse in a state
I thought I better wait
It turned out to be Ginger, my friend
He was coming to a terrible end
He threw his legs around me and cried
'Oh, I wish I'd died'
His tears flooded the floor
I was forced to say, 'Stop crying, no more
We're drowning by the score.'

One day, a shabby old cab drove up beside ours. The horse was an old worn-out chestnut, with an ill-kept coat; you could see the lining, and bones that showed plainly through it. The knees knuckled over, and the forelegs were very unsteady. He was the worst case of horseitis I had ever seen. I had been eating some hay, and the wind rolled a little lock of it that way, and the poor creature put out his long thin neck and picked it up. There was a hopeless look in the dull eye that I could not help noticing, and then, as I was thinking, he looked full at me and said, 'Black Beauty, is that you?'

It was Ginger! But how changed! The beautifully arched and glossy neck was now straight and lank, and fallen in; the clean straight legs and delicate fetlocks were swelled; the joints were grown out of shape with hard work; the face, that was once so full of spirit and life, was now full of suffering, and I could tell by the heaving of his sides, and his frequent cough, how bad his breath was. It was the worst case of horse halitosis I had ever known. It was a sad tale that he had to tell.

After twelve months at Earlshall, he was considered to be fit for work again. In this way he changed hands several times, but always getting lower down.

I said, 'You used to stand up for yourself if you were ill-used, and kick them in the balls.'

'Ah!' he said, 'I did once; no, wait, I did it fifteen times. I wish the end would come, I wish I was dead. I wish I may drop down dead at my work.'

I waited for him to drop dead, but he didn't. He said, 'I don't feel like dropping dead today.'

A short time after this, a cart with a dead horse in it passed. The head hung out of the cart-tail, the lifeless tongue was slowly dripping with blood; and the sunken eyes! He would soon be a dinner in some French restaurant. It was a chestnut horse with a long thin neck. Wait! I saw a white streak down the forehead. It *was* Ginger; I hoped it was, for then his troubles would be over. Soon, he would be a tin of cat food.

41. THE BUTCHER

The butcher was a prompt man
Delivering meat by horse or van
His delivery boy rode them very fast
The butcher said, 'If you go on like this he won't last'
The boy said, 'I have to deliver on time
I have to, so the customer can dine
If only they'd order in advance
We wouldn't lead this merry dance'
So he bought the boy a bike
'I hope,' said the butcher, 'this is something he'll like.'

We horses do not mind hard work if we are treated with a dinner at the Savoy, or taken to a music hall. I am sure that many are driven by quite poor men who have had a happier life.

It often went to my heart to see how the little ponies were used, straining along with heavy loads, wearing a truss over their hernias. We saw one doing his best to pull a heavy cart back to Africa with ten elephants.

Pulling ten elephants back to Africa
For a little ruptured horse is much too far
Try, try, try as they may
They'll be lucky to get as far as Herne Bay
The ruptured horse to Africa will never get
The best he can hope is to be put down by a vet.

I used to notice the speed at which the butcher's boy was made to go – 90 miles per hour. One day, we had to wait some time in St John's Wood; we were actually waiting for St John. There was a butcher's shop next door and, as we were standing, a butcher's cart came dashing up at 100 miles per hour. The horse was hot, and much exhausted; he hung his head down, his legs hung down, his body hung down. The lad jumped out of the cart and the master came out of the shop and was much displeased when the lad landed on him.

'How many times shall I tell you not to drive at 100 miles per hour?'

'So far twenty, sir,' said the lad.

'You ruined the last horse and broke his wind, it smelled terrible, and you are going to ruin this in the same way. If you were not my own son, I would dismiss you on the spot.' (His was another spot a foot in diameter.) 'It is a disgrace to have a horse brought to the shop in a condition like that; you are liable to be taken up by the police for such driving, and if you are, you need not look to me for bail, for I have spoken to you till I am tired.'

During this speech, the boy had stood by, still standing on the spot, sullen and dogged. It wasn't his fault.

'You always say, "Now be quick; now look sharp!" and when I go to the houses, one wants a leg of mutton for an early dinner, and I must be back with it in a quarter of an hour.'

Who ever thinks of a butcher? Some people do nothing but think of a butcher. In fact, there's a Think of Butchers Society.

There was a young costerboy who came up our street with sacks of potatoes and a gorilla. Apparently, some people love gorilla and chips.

There was an old man, too, who used to come up our street with a little coal cart; he wore a coal-heaver's hat and was black from the coal. Actually, he was Ugandan and they called him Ogu Amin; his father got rid of all the wogs in his country.

42. THE ELECTION

Our cab was out on Election Day
Politicians were trying to find their way
Jerry wouldn't let his cab be used
For drunken voters to abuse
He told them to go away
And they've never been seen from that day.

As we came into the yard one afternoon, Polly came out:

'Jerry! I've had Mr B. here asking about your vote. He wants to hire your cab for the election.'

'Well, Polly, I'm sorry but I don't want to put up with half-drunken voters. It would be an insult to the horse, and I should hate to drive an insulted horse.'

'I suppose you'll vote for the gentleman?'

'I shall not vote for him, Polly; you know what his trade is?'

'Yes. He exports veal calves to the continent.'

Every man must do what he thinks best for his country. Some did Barclay's Bank and got away with it.

On the morning before the election, Jeremiah was putting me into the shafts when Dolly came into the yard, sobbing and crying.

'Why, Dolly, what is the matter?'

'Those naughty boys have thrown rice pudding, peaches and cream and it is all over me, and they called me a little ragamuffin,' she said, eating as much of it as she could before it slid off.

'They called her a little blue ragamuffin father,' said Harry, also covered in rice pudding, peaches and cream, and looking very angry. 'But I have given it to them, they won't insult my sister again. I killed them.'

Jeremiah Barker kissed the child and said, 'Run in to mother, my pet, and tell her I think you had better stay at home today and help her eat the rest of the rice pudding, peaches and cream.'

Then, turning gravely to Harry:

'My boy, I hope you will always kill anybody who offends your sister.'

'Why, father, I thought blue was for Liberty.'

'My boy, Liberty does not come from colours; they only show party, and all the liberty you can get out of them is liberty to get drunk and throw rice pudding, peaches and cream at each other.'

'Oh, father, you are laughing.'

'No, Harry, I am serious, I'm only laughing to camouflage me being serious.'

At that moment, he was hit full in the face with rice pudding, peaches and cream.

43. A FRIEND IN NEED

One day in the City
Jerry saw a woman and took pity
She was in the city all alone
She had a child weighing nineteen stone
She said she had to be at St Thomas by midday
So Jerry took her right away
From her, he refused to take her fare
The bloody fool, she was a millionaire.

At last came election day; there was no lack of work for my master and me. First came a stout puffy gentleman with a carpet bag; he wanted to go to the Bishopsgate Station, so we let him; then we were called by a party who wished to go to the Regent's Park, so we let them. We waited in a side street where a timid, anxious old lady was waiting to be taken to the bank, which she held up. We had to wait and take her back (she robbed it again), and just as we had set her down, a red-faced gentleman with a handful of papers came running up, out of breath. Before Jeremiah could get down, he had opened the door, popped himself in, and called out, 'Bow Street Police Station, quick!' So off we went with him, where he was arrested.

Then we saw a poor young woman carrying a heavy child – it weighed nineteen stone – coming along the street. She was looking this way, and that way, like she was watching a tennis match, and seemed quite bewildered. Presently, she made her way up to Jeremiah and asked if he could tell her the way to St Thomas's Hospital, and how far it was to get there. She had got an order for the hospital, for her little nineteen stone boy. The child was crying with a feeble pining cry.

'Poor little fellow!' she said, 'he suffers a deal of pain; he is four years old and can't walk any more than a baby; but the doctor said if I could get him into the hospital, he might get well.'

'Please, get in our cab and I'll drive you safe to the hospital: don't you see the rain is coming on?'

'No sir, no, I can't do that, thank you. I have only just money enough to get back with: please tell me the way.'

'Look you here, missis,' said Jeremiah, 'I've got a wife and dear children at home, and I know a father's feelings; in fact I felt my wife this morning; now get you into that cab and I'll run you there for nothing.'

'Heaven bless you!' said the woman, bursting into tears.

'There, there, cheer up, my dear, I'll soon take you there; let me put you inside.'

As Jerry went to open the door, two men, with colours in their hats and button-holes, ran up, calling out, 'Cab!'

'Engaged,' said Jeremiah, but one of the men, pushing past the woman, sprang into the cab, followed by the other. Jeremiah looked as stern as a policeman: 'This cab is already engaged, gentlemen, by that lady.'

'Lady!' said one of them. 'Oh, she can wait: our business is very important; we import rice pudding, peaches and cream.'

'All right, gentlemen, pray stay.'

He soon got rid of them with his pistol; he blew out their brains.

Jeremiah walked up to the young woman, who had just finished counting a thousand gold sovereigns. After this little stoppage we were soon on our way to the hospital and when there, Jeremiah helped the young woman out.

'Thank you a thousand times. I've never travelled with dead men before,' she said. 'I could never have got here alone.'

'You're kindly welcome, and I hope the dear nineteen stone child will soon be better; but for him, we would have got here faster.'

The rain was now coming down fast, 100 miles per hour, and just as we were leaving the hospital the door opened again, and the porter called out, 'Cab!' We stopped, and a lady came down the steps.

She put her veil back and said, 'Barker! Jeremiah Barker! Is it you? I am very glad to find you here; you are just the friend I want, for it is very difficult to get a cab in this part of London today.'

'I shall be proud to serve you, ma'am; I am right glad I happened to be here,' he grovelled, 'where may I take you ma'am?'

He had no idea who she was.

'To the Paddington Station, and then if we are in good time, as I think we shall be, you shall tell me all about Polly and the children.'

We got to the station in good time and, being under shelter, the lady stood a good while talking. Jeremiah told her about the rice pudding and peaches and cream attack. I found she had been Polly's mistress.

'How do you find the cab work suits you in winter? I know Polly was rather anxious about you last year.'

'Yes, ma'am, she was; I had a bad cough that followed me up quite into the warm weather, and when I am kept out late, she does worry herself a good deal.'

'Well, Barker,' she said, 'it would be a great pity that you should seriously risk your health in this work, not only for your own, but also for Polly and the children's sake: there are many places where good drivers or good grooms are wanted; and if ever you think you ought to give up this cab work, let me know.' She put something into his hand saying, 'There is five shillings each for the two children, Polly will know how to spend it.'

He kissed her shoes, and seemed much pleased, and, turning out of the station, we at last reached home, and I, at least, was tired.

44. OLD CAPTAIN AND HIS SUCCESSOR

Oh, terrible crash with a brewer's dray
It happened on a clear sunny day
It had crashed into a cab horse.
And injured it of course
Old Captain was the victim of the crash
He came out in a nervous rash
The brewer had to pay compensation to Captain's master
For the brewer, it was a financial disaster

Captain and Jeremiah Barker had taken a party to the great railway station over London Bridge; the cab was full; it was the Labour Party; and, coming back, the Conservative Party mined the train.

Somewhere between the Bridge and the Monument, Jeremiah saw a brewer's dray coming along, drawn by two powerful horses. The drayman was lashing his horses with his heavy whip; they started off at a furious rate, at 100 miles per hour; the man had no control over them, and the street was full of traffic; they were now travelling at 102 miles per hour; one young girl was knocked down and run over, and the next moment they dashed up against our cab; both the wheels were torn off, the cab was thrown over and the Labour Party were thrown out. Captain was dragged down, the shafts splintered, and one of them ran into his backside. My master, too, was thrown, but was only bruised; nobody could tell how he escaped; he always said 'twas a miracle.

When poor Captain was got up, Jerry led him home gently, and a sad sight it was to see the blood soaking into his white coat; they were catching it in a bucket and pouring it back in the hole it came out, so they plugged the leak with a cork. The drayman was proved to be very drunk, and was fined ten pounds and asked for time to pay. While he was waiting to pay, they hung him, and the brewer had to pay damages to our master. But there was no one to pay damages to poor Captain.

The farrier did the best he could to ease his pain and make him comfortable; they put him up at the Savoy. The fly had to be mended, and for several days I did not go out, and Jeremiah earned nothing. The first time we went to the stand after the accident, the Governor came up to hear how Captain was.

'He'll never get over it,' said Jerry, 'at least not for my work, so the farrier said this morning. He says he may do for carting and that sort of work. If there's one devil that I should like to see in the bottomless pit more than another, it's the drink devil.'

'I say,' said the Governor, 'I'm not so abstemious as you are, more shame for me.'

'Well,' said Jeremiah, 'why don't you cut with it, Governor? You are too good a man to be the slave to the drink.'

'I'm a great fool, Jerry; but I tried once for two days, and I thought I should have died: to stop me dying, I drank a bottle of whisky; how did you do it?'

'I had hard work at it for several weeks; you see, I never did get drunk, but I found that I was not my own master, and that when the craving came on, I'd take off all my clothes and run a mile. I had to say over and over to myself, "Give up the drink or lose your soul." Then off I'd run another nude mile. But, thanks be to God and my dear wife, my chains were broken, and now for ten years I have not tasted a drop. But just in case, I still run a mile in the nude. Now I wish I'd never given up!'

'I've a great mind to try it,' said the Governor, 'for 'tis a poor thing not to be one's own master.' So off he went on a run for a mile in the nude.

At first, Captain seemed to do well, but he was a very old horse, and it was only his wonderful constitution, and his convalescence at the Savoy, that kept him up at the cab-work so long; now he broke down and had to be towed away. The farrier said he might mend up enough to sell for a few pounds, but Jeremiah said, 'no!' and he thought the kindest thing he could do for the fine old fellow would be to put a bullet through his head; he would make jolly good cat food.

The day after this was decided, Harry took me to the forge for some new shoes; when I returned Captain was gone, but on the farrier's shelf was sixty tins of cat food. He would have been pleased he could make some pussy cat happy.

Jeremiah had now to look out for another horse, and first he looked out the window but couldn't see one. He stood on the cliffs of Dover looking through a telescope for one. He soon heard of one through an acquaintance who was under-groom in a nobleman's stables; he put his ear to the acquaintance and through him, sure enough, he could hear a valuable young horse. But he had smashed into another carriage, flung his lordship out, and the coachman had orders to look round – he already looked round through over eating – and sell him as well as he could.

'I can do with high spirits,' said Jeremiah Barker, 'as long as he doesn't kick me in the balls.'

'He tries to, but he misses,' said the man.

Our governor (the coachman, I mean) had him harnessed in as tight and strong as he could; his four legs were tied together. My belief is, that is what caused the accident.

The next day, Hotspur came home; he was a fine brown horse.

'Hello Hotspur,' I said.

The first night, he was very restless, instead of lying down, he kept jerking his halter; surely he would go blind. However, the next day, after five or six hours in the cab, he came in quiet and sensible; the cabman had gained a good horse. He had cost Jeremiah nine pounds, and he had paid cash.

Hotspur thought it a great come down to be a cab-horse, and disguised himself as a donkey. In fact, he settled in well, and master liked him very much, and discarded his donkey disguise.

45. JERRY'S NEW YEAR

It was one New Year's day
Freezing weather was here to stay
We had a late pickup, eleven o'clock
We waited till it was two of the clock
Our customers came out and pee'd against a tree
By then, it was half past three
When they didn't want to go any more
It was half past bloody four
They said they hadn't the fare
So we didn't take them anywhere.

Christmas and the New Year are very merry times for some people to get pissed; but for cabmen and cabmen's horses it is no holiday. There are so many big parties, and big balls. Sometimes driver and horse have to wait for hours in the rain or frost, shivering with cold, and whilst the merry people within are dancing away to the music, cabmen outside are dying of hypothermia. I saw a horse standing till his legs got stiff with cold, ice and rheumatism; think of horses standing till their legs get stiff with cold, ice and rheumatism.

I had most of the evening work now, as I was well accustomed to standing covered in ice, and Jeremiah was also more afraid of Hotspur taking cold – he didn't give a fuck about me. We had a great deal of late work in the Christmas week, and Jeremiah's cough was bad; he gobbed up huge things that looked like breaking eggs when they hit the pavement; but however late we were, Polly sat up for him with a meat pie, and came out with the lantern so he could see it.

On the evening of the New Year, we had to take two gentlemen to a house in the West End. We were told to come again at eleven. 'But,' said one of them, 'as it is a card party, you may have to wait a few minutes, but don't be late.'

As the clock struck eleven we were at the door, for Jerry was always punctual. The clock chimed the quarters – one, two, three, and then struck twelve, but the door did not open.

The wind had been very changeable, with squalls of rain during the day, but now it came on a sharp driving sleet, which seemed to come all the way round; it was very cold.

At a quarter past one, the door opened and the two gentlemen came out; they chipped at Jeremiah with ice picks till he was free, then told him where to drive, which was nearly two miles away. When the men got out, they never said they were sorry to have kept us waiting, but were angry at the charge. They had to pay for the two hours and a quarter waiting; but it was hard-earned money to Jeremiah.

At last we got home. He could hardly speak and I could hardly neigh; his cough was dreadful and he was gobbing great egg yolks. Polly opened the door with a meat pie and held the lantern for him.

'Get Jack something warm, then boil a pot of gruel, then put me in it.'

This was said in a hoarse whisper (I too had a horse whisper); he could hardly get his breath. Polly brought me a warm mash and spread it over my frozen bed. That made me comfortable, and then they locked the door.

It was late the next morning before any one came, and it was Harry. He cleaned us and fed us. He was very still, and neither whistled nor sang, but did some Russian dancing. At noon he came again, and gave us our food and water. This time Dolly came with him. She was crying, and I could gather that Jeremiah Barker was dangerously ill and broke. The doctor said it was a bad case; so did his bank manager.

So two days passed away, but he didn't, and there was great trouble indoors. We only saw Harry, and sometimes Dolly. I think she came for company, for Polly was always with Jeremiah, and he had to be kept very quiet. So they rendered him unconscious with a mallet.

On the third day, whilst Harry was in the stable, there was a tap on the door – why anybody wanted to put a tap on a door is strange – and Governor Grant came in.

'I want to know how your father is.'

'He's unconscious,' said Harry, 'they call it bronchitis.'

'That's bad, very bad!' said Grant, shaking his head; it fell off.

'Yes,' said Harry, 'and the doctor said that father had a better chance than most men, because he didn't drink.'

The Governor looked puzzled.

'If there's any rule that good men should get over these things, I am sure he will, my boy.'

Early next morning he was there again.

'Well?' said he.

'Father is better,' said Harry. 'Mother hopes he will get over it.'

'Thank God!' said the Governor, 'and now you must keep him warm, and that brings me to the horses; you see, Jack will be all the better for the rest of a week or two in a warm stable, and you can easily take him a turn up and down the street to stretch his legs; but this young one, if he does not get work, he will soon be all up end, and when he does go out, there'll be an accident.'

'I have kept him short of corn,' said Harry, 'but he's so full of spirit, it's coming out the back.'

'Just so,' said Grant. 'Now look here, will you tell your mother that I will come for him every day till something is arranged, and whatever he earns I'll bring your mother half of it, and that will help with the horses' feed. Your father is in a good club, I know, but that won't keep the horses, and they'll be eating their heads off all this time.' And without waiting for Harry's thanks, he was gone.

For a week or more he came for Hotspur, and drove him at 150 miles per hour until he settled down, and when Harry thanked him, or said anything about his kindness, he laughed it off, saying it was all good luck for him. Polly got half the takings, but he kept the bigger half; his horses were wanting a little rest, which they would not otherwise have had.

Jeremiah grew better, steadily; first his feet got better, then his legs, and finally his body and head. The doctor said that he must never go back to the cab work again if he wished to be an old man. The children had many consultations together about what father and mother would do, and how they could help to earn money. There was bank robbery, but that was too dangerous; the bank manager would recognise him and ask him to repay his overdraft.

One afternoon, Hotspur was brought in very wet and dirty. While Harry was sponging off the mud from Hotspur, Dolly came in, looking very full of something. It was cottage pie.

'Oh! Harry, there never was anything so beautiful; Mrs Fowler says we are all to go and live near her. There is a cottage now empty that will just suit us, with a garden, and a hen house, and apple trees, and everything, and her coachman is going away in the spring to be put down, and then she will want father in his place!'

'That's uncommon jolly,' said Harry, in old English, 'it will suit father. I'll be a groom, a gardener or a bank robber. We'll need money.'

It was quickly settled that the cab and horses should be sold as soon as possible.

This was heavy news for me, for I was not young – I was 79. Grant said he would take Hotspur, and there were men on the stand who would have bought me, but Jerry said No! The Governor promised to find a place for me where I should be comfortable, possibly the Ritz.

The day came for going away. Jerry had not been allowed to go out yet, and was chained to his bed just in case. Polly and the children came to bid me good-bye. 'I wish we could take you with us,' she said. Dolly was crying and kissed me, too, then they buggered off, and I was led away to my new place.

46. JAKES AND THE LADY

I was sold to a corn dealer and a carter, called Jakes
To serve them it took me all it takes
Going downhill he never put on the brakes
'With that load, your horse you'll kill '
Said a gentlewoman called Jill
'Keep quiet you silly girl'
She, with a karate hold, gave him a huge hurl
He landed over a mile away
It made my day
He ran away to Spain
And we never saw him again.

I was sold to a corn dealer for three and six a pound whom Jeremiah Barker knew and he thought I should have good food and fair work.

In the first he was quite right, and if my master had always been on the premises, I do not think I should have been over-loaded; but there was a foreman who was always hurrying and driving everyone, even Queen Victoria, and frequently, when I had quite a full load, he would order something else to be taken on. My carter said it was more than I ought to take, but the other always overruled him:

' 'Twas no use going twice when once would do, and he chose to get business forward.'

Jakes, like the other carters, always had the bearing rein up, which prevented me from drawing easily, and by the time I had been there three or four months, I found the work telling very much; I was shagged out.

One day, I was loaded more than usual, and too often, and part of the road was a steep uphill: I used all my strength and Vitamin B tablets, and some Horlicks, but I could not get on. This did not please my driver, and he laid his whip on badly.

'Get on, you lazy fellow,' he said, 'or I'll tweak your swannicles.' Oh, no! I'd do anything for him not to tweak my swannicles.

Again I took some Horlicks tablets, started the heavy load, and struggled on a few yards backwards; again the whip came down, and again, to soothe it, I struggled backwards. The pain of that great cart whip was sharp. I'd sue the makers of Horlicks. A third time he was flogging me cruelly, when a lady stepped up to him:

'Oh! pray do not whip your good horse any more. I am sure he is doing all he can; the road is very steep and I am sure he is doing his best.'

'If doing his best won't get this load up, he must do something more than his best; that's all I know, ma'am,' said Jakes, which was all he knew.

'But is it not a very heavy load?' she asked.

'Yes,' he said, louder, 'but that's not my fault, I must get on with it as well as I can.'

He was raising the whip again, when the lady threw him over her shoulder judo style; she was a sixth Dan. 'He cannot use all his power with his head held back, as it is with that bearing rein. If you take it off, I am sure he would do better – do try it,' she said persuasively, giving him a karate chop.

'Yes, ma'am,' said the terrified carter. The rein was taken off; what a comfort it was!

'Poor fellow! that is what you wanted,' said she.

Jakes took the rein – 'Come on, Blackie.' I put down my head, and threw my whole weight against the collar; I spared no strength; the load moved on, and I pulled it steadily up the hill – and then stopped to take a spoonful of Sanatogen.

The lady had walked along the footpath, and now came across the road, stopping only to throw the carter on his back.

'You see, he was quite willing when you gave him the chance; I am sure he is a fine-tempered creature, and I dare say he has known better days. You won't put that rein on again, will you?'

'Well, ma'am, I can't deny that having his head and Horlicks has helped him up the hill.'

'Is it not better?' she said. 'I thank you for trying my plan with your good horse. Good-day,' and with another soft pat on my neck, she stepped lightly across the path, and I ran over her.

I may as well mention here what I suffered at this time from another cause. I had heard horses speak of it; mine was a badly lighted stable; there was only one very small window at the end, and the stalls were almost dark. It very much weakened my sight, and when I was suddenly brought out of the darkness into the glare of sunlight, it was very painful to my eyes (I had to have glasses), and I drove into a shop-front window. However, I escaped without any permanent injury to my sight, and was sold to a large cab owner.

47. HARD TIMES

Now my new master was called Skinner
He wouldn't give you the price of a dinner
My driver was very, very cruel
All I had to eat was watery gruel
I became so very thin
You could see in
Coming down Ludgate Hill
I fell and became very ill
I wanted to die
But I don't think I'll try.

I shall never forget my new master; he had black eyes and ears and a hooked nose, his mouth was full of teeth locked on a cheese sandwich. His name was Skinner, and I believe he was the same man that poor Seedy Sam died for.

Skinner had a low set of cabs, so low that if you looked out the window you could only see the pavement. He was hard on the horses; in this place we had no Sunday rest.

Sometimes on a Sunday morning, a party of fast men would hire the cab for a day in France; four of them inside and another with the driver, and I had to take them to Calais. I had to swim the channel and back again and sometimes I had such a high fever that I caught fire and had to be put out. I could hardly touch my food because there wasn't any. How I used to long for the nice bran mash with whisky in it that Jeremiah used to give us on Saturday nights in hot weather – that used to cool us down. But here, there was no rest, and my driver had a cruel whip with something so sharp at the end that it sometimes drew blood; gradually I was becoming anaemic. He would even whip me under the belly, and flip the lash out at my head. Indignities like these took the heart and my liver out of me, but still I did my best and never hung back.

My life was now so utterly wretched that I wished I might drop down dead at my work and go to the great stable in the sky. I tried hard, but somehow couldn't drop dead. One day, it very nearly came to pass.

I went on the stand at eight in the morning and had done a good share of work, when we had to take a fare to the railway. A long train was just expected in, so my driver pulled up at the back of some of the outside cabs, to take the chance of a return fare. It was a very heavy train, it weighed 5,000 tons, and all the cabs were soon engaged. There was a party of four;

a noisy, blustering man with a lady, a little boy, and a young girl, and a great deal of luggage. The lady and the boy got into the cab, while the man ordered the luggage. The porter, who was pulling about some heavy boxes, suggested to the gentleman, as there was so much luggage, whether he would not take a second cab.

'Can your horse do it?' enquired the blustering man.

'Oh yes, he did some down the road.'

He helped to haul up a box so heavy that I could feel the springs go down. Box after box was dragged up and lodged on the top of the cab. At last all was ready and, with his usual jerk at the rein, he drove out of the station.

The load was very heavy and I had had neither food nor rest since the morning, save a boiled egg; but I did my best, as I always had done. I got along fairly well till we came to Ludgate Hill. My feet slipped from under me, and I fell heavily to the ground on my side; I lay perfectly still; I had no power to move. Someone said, 'He's dead, he'll never get up again.' Good, I could stay here! Then I could hear a policeman giving orders, 'Get up!' Some cold water was thrown over my head and some cordial was poured into my mouth. I cannot tell how long I lay there, but I found my life coming back. After some more cordial had been given me, I staggered to my feet, and was gently led to some stables, where I was put into a well-littered stall, and some warm gruel and Horlicks were brought to me.

In the morning, Skinner came with a farrier to look at me.

'This is a case of overwork, and if you could give him a run off for six months, he would be able to work again.'

'Then he must go to the dogs,' said Skinner.

Upon advice, Skinner gave orders that I should be well fed and cared for. Ten days of perfect rest with plenty of good oats, hay, bran mashes and Guinness (all with boiled linseed mixed in them), did more to get up my condition than anything else could have done; those linseed mashes were delicious with malt whisky, and I began to think that, after all, it might be better to live. When the twelfth day after the accident came, I was taken to the sale. I felt that any change from my present place must be an improvement. They put a label on my neck: 'Horse for sale. Good for knacker's yard.'

48. FARMER THOROUGHGOOD AND HIS GRANDSON WILLIE

At the sale I was in with old horses in wheel chairs
Many were in need of constant care
One man said of me, 'He has known better days

Soon he'll have to wear stays'
'Grandpa,' said the boy, 'can't we buy him?'
'All right,' said Grandpa looking grim
He paid five pounds for me straight away
And I stayed with them for many a day.

At this sale, of course, I found myself in company with old, broken-down, dying horses – some lame, some broken-winded, some in wheel chairs going on eighty. There were poor men trying to sell a dead horse for three pence to the PAL dog food company. Some of them looked as if they had seen hard times; the hardest times were from midnight to six o'clock in the morning.

Coming from the better part of the fair, I noticed a man who looked like a gentleman farmer, with a young boy by his side. When he came up to me, he stood still. I saw his eye rest on me; I had still a good mane and tail.

'There's a horse, Willie, that has known better days.'

'Do you think he was ever a carriage horse?' asked the boy.

'Oh yes,' said the farmer, coming closer, 'he might have been anything when he was young. Look at his nostrils and his ears, the shape of his neck and shoulder; there's a deal of breeding about that horse.'

So the boy looked at my nostrils and ears and the shape of my neck and shoulder. 'Could not you buy him and make him young again?'

'My dear boy, I can't make old horses young; this one is knackered.'

He was wrong. I had never been knackered; I still had a complete set.

'Well, grandpapa, I don't believe that this one is old – he has a complete set. But do look at his mouth, grandpapa, I am sure he would grow young in our meadows.'

The man who had brought me for sale now put in his word.

'The young gentleman's a real knowing one, sir; I heard as how the veterinary should say – that a six months in bed would set him right up.'

'What is the lowest you will take for him?' said the farmer.

'Five pounds, sir; that was the lowest price my master set.'

' 'Tis a speculation,' said the old gentleman, shaking his head, but at the same time slowly drawing out his purse and taking the lock off. 'Have you any more business here?' he enquired, counting the sovereigns into his hand.

'No, sir, I can take him for you to the inn, if you please.'

'Do so, and give him a whisky and soda.'

The boy could hardly control his delight, so he was put in a straight jacket. The old gentleman seemed to enjoy seeing him trying to get it off. I had a good feed and a whisky and soda at the inn.

Mr Thoroughgood, for that was the name of my benefactor, gave orders that I should have hay, oats, halibut liver oil and three-egg omelettes every night and morning, the fun of the meadow during the day, and the run of the stable at night, and, 'You, Willie,' said he, 'I give him in charge to you.'

The boy was proud of his charge and undertook it in all seriousness; in fact he was a downright misery. There was not a day when he did not pay me a visit; he became a bloody nuisance, sometimes picking me out from amongst the other horses, and giving me a bit of carrot (what bloody good was that?), or something good, or sometimes standing by me whilst I ate my oats. He always came with kind words and caresses and, of course, I grew very fond of him. He called me Old Crony, the bastard, as I used to come to him in the field and follow him about. Sometimes he brought his grandfather, who always looked closely at my legs; he was kinky.

'Willie,' he would say, 'he is improving so steadily that I think we shall see a change for the better in the spring.'

The perfect rest, the good food, the soft turf and gentle exercise, and the idiot grandchild in a straight jacket, soon began to tell on my condition and my spirits. I had a good constitution from my mother, and I was never strained when I was young.

During the winter, my legs improved so much that I used them when I went out. The spring came round, and one day so did Mr Thoroughgood, to try me in the phaeton. I was well pleased, and he and Willie drove me a few miles. I did the work with perfect ease; I even sang 'Good-bye Dolly Grey.'

'He's growing young, Willie; we must give him a little gentle work now – he can clean out the chicken house – and by midsummer he will be as good as that milkmaid with big boobs.'

49. MY LAST HOME

One day I was all dolled up
The groom was called Tim Nup
I was to be sold to two ladies
Very respectable, not at all shady
They took to me right away
That would be £5 to pay
I thought the fee below my worth
Because I was of noble birth
It would have been very nice
If £50 was my minimum price.

One day, the groom cleaned and dressed me in a suit with such extraordinary care that I thought some new change must be at hand; he trimmed my fetlocks and legs, passed the tarbrush over my hoofs, parted my forelock, and flattened it down with Macassar oil. I think the harness had an extra polish. Willie seemed half-anxious, half-merry as he got into the chaise with his grandfather.

'If the ladies take to him,' said the old gentleman, 'they'll be suited.'

We came to a pretty, low house with a lawn and shrubbery at the front, and a drive up to the door. Willie rang the bell and asked if Miss Blomefield or Miss Ellen was at home. Yes, they were. So, whilst Willie stayed with me, Mr Thoroughgood went into the house. In about ten minutes he returned, followed by three ladies. The younger lady – that was Miss Ellen – took to me very much; she said she was sure she would like me.

'You have always been such a good adviser to us about our horses, and sexual proclivities,' said the stately lady, 'we will accept your offer of a trial.' At the trial they were found Not Guilty.

One morning, a smart-looking young man who was held together with acne came for me. When he saw my knees, he said:

'I didn't think, sir, you would have recommended my ladies a horse with knock-knees.'

'You are only taking him on trial, young man, and if he is not as safe as any horse you ever drove, send him back,' said my master.

I was led home, placed in a comfortable stable, fed and left to myself. The next day, when my groom was cleaning my face, he said:

'That is just like the star that Black Beauty had; he is much the same height too.' He began to look me over carefully, talking to himself:

'White star in the forehead, one white foot on the off side, this little knot just in that place' – then, looking at the middle of my back – 'Good heavens! it must be Black Beauty; there is that little patch of white hair that John used to call Beauty's threepenny bit. It *must* be Black Beauty!' (Good heavens, it was Black Beauty!) 'Why, Beauty! Beauty! Do you know me? Little Joe Green, that almost killed you?'

I could not say that I remembered him, for now he was a fine-grown young fellow, with black whiskers and a man's voice, and cross eyes – no wonder he nearly killed me. He was Joe Green. I never saw a man so pleased. He was so pleased that he climbed a tree and jumped in the river; they had to drag the water.

'Give you a fair trial? I should think so indeed! I wonder who the rascal was that broke your knees, my old Beauty? You must have been badly served out there somewhere.'

Yes, out there somewhere, I was.

'Well, well, it won't be my fault if you haven't good times of it now. I wish John Manly was here to see you.'

He wished and wished, but John Manly didn't appear; mainly because he was dead.

In the afternoon, I was put into a low Park chair and pushed to the door. Miss Ellen was going to try me. I soon found that she was a good driver, and she seemed pleased with my paces. I heard Joe telling her about me.

'I shall certainly write to Mrs Gordon, and tell her that her favourite horse has come to us with knock-knees. How pleased she will be!'

The swine, how dare he give away my knock-knees. So the next day, I kicked him in the balls. It was like old times.

I have now lived in this happy place a whole year; I have my own bedroom with a bathroom ensuite. Joe is the best and kindest of grooms, but with the curse of cross eyes keeps missing me. My work is easy and pleasant (I help wash up in the kitchen), and I feel my strength all coming back. Mr Thoroughgood said to Joe the other day:

'He will last till he is twenty years old – perhaps more.'

My ladies have promised that I shall never be sold, and so I have nothing to fear; and here my story ends. My troubles are over, all over me, hah, and I am at home; and often, before I am quite awake, I fancy I am still in the orchard at Birtwick, standing with my old friends under the apple trees and Dick the plough throwing stones at us.

FRANKENSTEIN ACCORDING TO SPIKE MILLIGAN

From acid and brine
Mixed with horses' urine
I fashioned the Frankenstein
He craves for a cigarette
So far they haven't caught him yet.

When I was very young I started to collect bits of people
I stored them in old deserted steeples
The bits were all homeless people and nowhere to go
To preserve them I packed them in snow.

What made me want to make such a horror
With human bits I started to beg, steal or borrow
One day in the spring
I would stitch it all together with string.

AUTHOR'S INTRODUCTION TO THE STANDARD NOVELS EDITION (1831)

The publishers of the Standard Novels, in selecting *Frankenstein* for one of their series, expressed a wish that I should furnish them with an account of the origin. Well my own account stands at £3.10. 'How I, then a young girl, came to think of and dilate upon so very hideous an idea?' The answer is I was kinky and pretty bent and was smoking the stuff. It is true that I am very averse to bringing myself forward in print; I would rather bring myself sideways. In writing this book, I can scarcely accuse myself of a personal intrusion; I always get someone else to do it.

It is not singular that, as the daughter of two persons of distinguished literary celebrity, I should very early in life have thought of writing, and I did. I was two. My dreams were at once more fantastic and agreeable than my writings. In the latter I was a close imitator – in other words, a little bloody cheat. What I wrote was intended at least for the human eye, so I had to look around for one-eyed readers.

I lived principally in the country as a girl and passed considerable time in Scotland. I won the Junior Women's Haggis Hurling Championship. I discovered nothing was worn under the kilt; everything was in working order. But my residence was on the dreary northern shores of the Tay where I met the poet William McGonigal who wrote:

THE RAILWAY BRIDGE OF THE SILVERY TAY

Beautiful railway bridge of the Silvery Tay
With your numerous artists and palaces in so grand array
And your central girders which seem so high
To be almost towering to the sky
The greatest wonder of the day
And the great beautification to the River Tay
Most beautiful to be seen
Near by Dundee and the Magdalen Green.

Beautiful railway bridge of the Silvery Tay
That has caused the Emperor of Brazil to leave his home far away
Incognito in his dress
In view as he passed along en route to Inverness.

Beautiful railway bridge of the Silvery Tay
The longest of the present day
That has ever crossed over a tidal river stream

Most gigantic to be seen
Near by Dundee and the Magdalen Green.

Beautiful railway bridge of the Silvery Tay
Which will cause great celebration on the opening day
And hundreds of people will come from far away
Also the Queen most gorgeous to be seen
Near by Dundee and the Magdalen Green.

Beautiful railway bridge of the Silvery Tay
And prosperity to Professor Cox who has given £30,000 upward
    and away
To help erect the bridge of the Tay
Near by Dundee and the Magdalen Green.

Beautiful railway bridge of the Silvery Tay
I hope that God will protect the passengers by night and by day
And that no accident will befall them while crossing the bridge of
    the Silvery Tay
For that would be most awful to be seen
Near by Dundee and the Magdalen Green.

Beautiful railway bridge of the Silvery Tay
And prosperity to Messrs Bouche and Groat
The famous engineers of the present day
Who have succeeded erecting the railway bridge of the Silvery Tay
Which is unequal to be seen
Near by Dundee and the Magdalen Green.

My father was an ambitious man
'Hurry,' he'd say, 'Hurry and get a literary reputation if you can'
So I wrote *Hamlet*
And was hailed by the nation
The first prize was Victoria Station.

It was a pleasant region where, unheeded, I would commune with creatures of my fancy; I fancied elephants but there were none in Scotland. I wrote then in the most common-place style – 'Cor blimey Fred, ya got a big willy, s'truth.' I could not figure to myself that romantic woes or wonderful events would ever be my lot; but I was not confined to my own identity – I used to black up myself, beat a tom-tom and pretend to be a Zulu.

My husband, however, was from the first very anxious that I should prove myself worthy of my parentage and enrol myself on the page of fame.

He was forever inciting me to obtain a literary reputation. 'Hurry,' he'd say, 'Hurry and get a literary reputation and enrol yourself on the page of fame.'

We visited Switzerland and became neighbours of Lord Byron, who was writing the third canto of *Childe Harold*. By the time he had written the tenth canto of *Childe Harold*, the Childe was 35.

Some volumes of ghost stories, translated from the German into French, fell into our hands. Someone pushed them and we caught them. There was the *History of the Inconstant Lover*, who, when he thought to clasp the bride to whom he had pledged his vows, found himself in the arms of the pale ghost of her whom he had deserted. Then there was the tale of the sinful founder of his race, the Two Thousand Guineas: his gigantic, shadowy form was clothed, like the ghost in *Hamlet*, in complete armour, but with the beaver up it was very painful and could kruple his blurzon. He was to bestow the kiss of death on all the younger sons so, in his clanking armour, he advanced to the couch of the blooming youths who were cradled in healthy sleep. Eternal sorrow sat upon his face as he bent down and kissed the foreheads of the boys who [wait for it!] from that hour withered like the flowers snapped upon the stalk. But, alas, the cost of the funerals finally bankrupted him. He sold his suit of armour to raise money and the suit was crushed into a metal square and made into a Mini-Minor which was bought by a priest.

'We will each write a ghost story,' said Lord Byron. Poor Signor Polidori had some terrible idea about a skull-headed lady who was so punished for peeping through a keyhole, she saw what all keyhole peepers see – a couple screwing on the bed. He did not know what to do with her and was obliged to dispatch her to the tomb of the Capulets. Alas, when she got there they were both dead so she went for a coffee.

I busied myself *to think of a story*, a story that would curdle the blood of the reader and loosen the sphincter. Every ghost story must have a beginning. The Hindus gave the world an elephant to support it, but they make the elephant stand upon a tortoise. In practical terms the tortoise would have been crushed to a pulp. Perhaps that's what is wrong with the world – we are all living on a crushed tortoise.

Many and long were the conversations between Lord Byron and Shelley; some were eighteen feet tall. They talked to Dr Darwin and one of his experiments. He had preserved a piece of vermicelli in a glass case till by some extraordinary means it began to move with voluntary motion. Again, you could put some spaghetti in a glass case and wait for it to become animated, then you could let it go and it could then run free in the streets.

I did not sleep that night; my mind wandered. I saw a pale student of unhallowed arts kneeling beside the monster he had put together. I saw the hideous phantasm of a man stretched out and then, on the working with some powerful engine, he shows signs of life, sits up and says, 'Hello dar, what's de time?' Frightful must it be; for supremely frightful would be the effect of any human endeavour to mock the stupendous mechanism of the Creator of life – which as we all know is a flat tortoise.

So when the hitherto inanimate body sat up, opened his eyes and said, 'Hello dere, lend us a quid,' I opened my eyes in terror. The idea so possessed my mind that a thrill of fear ran through me and out the back.

Swift as light, and as cheering, was the idea that broke in upon me: 'I have found it! What terrified me will terrify others; and I need only describe the spectre which had haunted my midnight pillow.' On the morrow I announced that I had *thought of a story*.

At first I thought but a few pages – of a short tale, about 5 feet 3 inches, but Shelley urged me to develop the idea to a greater length, 100 feet 6 inches. I certainly did not owe the suggestion of any one incident to my husband. In fact, he did bugger all. However, but for his incitement it would never have taken form, and all he wanted was 60% of the royalties.

And now, once again, I bid my hideous progeny go forth and prosper. Open a tie shop! Its several pages speak of many a walk, many a drive, and many a takeaway curry.

I have changed no portion of this story.

M.W.S.
London, October 15th, 1831

PREFACE

(By P. B. Shelley, 1818)

This Preface has absolutely nothing to do with Mary's book. It is written so I'll have a few fingers in the pie when the book starts to sell.

VOLUME ONE

LETTER I
To Mrs Saville, England
St Petersburgh, Dec. 11th, 17—.

You will rejoice to hear that no disaster has accompanied the commence-
ment of an enterprise which you regarded with such evil forebodings. I
did not catch fire nor was I sucked down in a whirlpool or eaten by a
polar bear. Perhaps these are the things you had in mind for me.

I am already far north of London and as I walk in the crap-ridden
streets of Petersburgh I feel a cold northern breeze play on my cheeks,
which braces my nerves and warms my swannicles. Do you understand
these feelings? If not, feel yourself in bed tonight. I try in vain to be
persuaded that the North Pole is the seat of God and his angels, tho they
must wear warm clothes; it ever presents itself to my imagination as the
region of beauty and delight and McDonald's. There, Margaret, the sun is
very low in the sky, but if you go upstairs and stand on the chair you will
be able to see it although, like my bank balance, it has almost disappeared.
If only my bank balance would rise on the horizon every morning, oh how
happy I would be. However, I have trust in the preceding navigators. We
are preceded by about a dozen in a small boat. One claims to be Henry of
Navarre. I think he's a bloody liar, his name is actually Dick Smith.

The snow and frost are banished and we are sailing over a calm sea. We
may be wafted to a land surpassing in wonders and in beauty every region
hitherto discovered on the habitable globe. There is the phenomena of the
heavenly bodies. When I think of heavenly bodies I think of Doris Riter's
body of 36 Roseland Road, Catford. What may not be expected in a country
of eternal light? Well, for a start it never gets dark. I may have discovered
the wondrous power which attracts the needle. I may go to parts of the
world where no human eye has ever set foot. These are my enticements, to
conquer all fear of danger or death. If the latter should happen, I will stop
immediately. I feel the joy a young boy feels when he embarks in a little
boat with his holiday mates on an expedition of discovery up a native river.
If I remember correctly, that is how Livingston died.

I shall find the secret of the magnet and I will become admired far and
wide [he speaks well of himself]. I feel an enthusiasm which elevates me
to heaven, for nothing contributes so much to tranquillise the mind as
does a steady purpose, or Valium. It is regret which I had felt as a child
on learning that my father's injunction had forbidden my uncle to allow
me to embark on a seafaring life. Fuck him, I'll do as I please.

I must go down to the sea again
To the lonely sea and the sky
And all I ask is a tall ship
And a star to steer her by.

One day my name will go down beside Drake's and Nelson's. In fact I believe some people can't wait for me to join them.

Six years have passed since I resolved on my present undertaking. (He was an undertaker as well as a sailor.) I remember how I prepared for this enterprise. I stripped naked and covered my body with bear's grease. I accompanied the whale-fishers on several expeditions to the North Sea, and several times I fell into it. I voluntarily endured cold, famine, thirst and want of sleep and did it all in the comfort of my hotel room because I just couldn't keep up with the sailors. I hired myself as a mate on a Greenland whaler and acquitted myself to the admiration of the crew, except that during the whole voyage I was violently seasick. I must own to feeling a little proud when the captain offered me a boat to row back home.

> I'm now a fisherman
> I strip naked and cover myself in bear's grease
> I dive over the side, I nearly bloody freeze
> I catch fish with my teeth
> Alas, I foundered on a reef

Dear Margaret, I now deserve to accomplish some great purpose – become Admiral, Field Marshal or manager of Boots. My life has been passed in ease and luxury, and in being seasick. Oh, that some encouraging voice would answer in the affirmative.

This is the most favourable period for travelling in Russia. They fly quickly over the snow in their sledges. Some have difficulty stopping the horses which seem to go on and on and they are never seen again. The cold is not excessive if you are wrapped up in furs with an electric heater attached. It would need to be full on. The difficulty is carrying the heavy batteries under your arm. This is a dress which I have already adopted, but carrying the batteries has given me a hernia – this too is electrically heated. There is a great difference between walking the deck and remaining seated, motionless for hours. The latter people freeze to death and have to be thrown overboard. I have no ambition to be thrown overboard so I walk continuously, backwards and forwards, holding my heated hernia in place.

I shall depart from this town in a fortnight or three weeks; my intention is to hire a ship, which can be easily done by slipping the hawsers off when the owner is not looking.

Your affectionate brother,
R. Walton

> We had a sto'way in the hold
> He was an eccentric millionaire we were told
> Every night we'd throw him over the side
> He'd say 'thanks for the ride'
> And the crew threw him overboard on the next tide
> Eventually he died.

LETTER II
To Mrs Saville, England.
Archangel, March 18th, 17—.

How slowly the time passes up here. Up here one hour takes three. Encompassed as I am by frost, snow and ice, yet I have hired a vessel. It is a very secure ship with a slight tendency to sink. Just in case, we all sleep in the lifeboats.

I have no friend, Margaret; I think this is because I have got halitosis. The men stand 50 yards away whenever they want to talk to me. I am glowing with the enthusiasm of success, but there will be none to participate in my joy. Still, I am wearing a furry hat and every evening I sing 'God Save the Queen' through the porthole. I know she can't hear me but there's no reason why I shouldn't.

I shall commit my thoughts to paper, or the wall or the floor or even the ceiling. But that is a poor medium for the communication of feeling. Talking of medium, we have one travelling with us in the steerage. He has a mystic power. He can give us the exact date and day every day. I desire the company of a man who could sympathise with me and his company must have a good annual turnover. I bitterly feel the want of a friend. (I have no one near me except the ship's cat.) Someone who has tastes like my own – chicken madras.

I am self-educated: for the first fourteen years of my life I ran wild on the common. At the end of that time I fell exhausted to the ground. By the time I was fifteen I had recovered from my fourteen-year run. At that age I became acquainted with poets of our own country: Goethe, Adolph Hitler, Goering. Now one becomes acquainted with more languages than that of my native country. Now I am twenty-eight, and am in reality more illiterate than many schoolboys of fifteen. I speak two languages – good and bad.

> We have a sailor on board who's gay
> No one knows what got him that way
> I asked him what made him one
> 'It's . . .,' he said, 'It's a lot of fun.'

Well, I will certainly find no friends on the wide ocean. Every day I scan the seas for one and I never see one person – perhaps he's inland.

The master is a person remarkable in the ship for his gentleness and mild of discipline. He likes to talk to young sailors with his hand on his hip. I cannot overcome an intense distaste to the usual brutality exercised on board ship. I have never believed it to be necessary to give a man 50 lashes, then keelhaul him, then hang him from the yard arm, then finally make him walk the plank or swallow an anchor. Very few sailors survive this ritual.

I am preparing to depart. I am going to unexplored regions, 'to the land of mist and snow'; but I shall kill no albatross, therefore do not be alarmed for my safety. If you see an albatross, he can be one I did not kill.

So, dear sister, continue to write to me by every opportunity and don't forget to enclose the postal orders.

Your affectionate brother,
Robert Walton

LETTER III
To Mrs Saville, England.
July 7th, 17—.

My dear Sister,

I write a few lines in haste to say that I am safe. My men are bold and apparently firm of purpose. But the floating sheets of ice that continually pass us, indicating the dangers of the region towards which we are advancing, appear to dismay them. They all shrink from their posts and huddle together in fear, many crossing themselves. Why not? They have crossed everybody else.

My swelling heart involuntarily pours itself out thus. The doctor says it's a vascular leak. But I must finish. Heaven bless my beloved sister.

R.W.

P.S. Please keep sending the postal orders.

LETTER IV
To Mrs Saville, England.
August 5th, 17—.

So strange an accident has happened to us. My seamen groaned. A strange sight attracted our attention. We perceived a low carriage, fixed on a sledge and drawn by dogs, pass on towards the north at the distance of half a mile but which had the shape of a man, apparently of gigantic stature. He was smoking a cigarette. He sat in the sledge and guided the dogs. We watched the rapid progress of the traveller with our telescopes until he was lost among the distant inequalities of the ice.

In the morning I went on deck and found all the sailors busy on one side of the vessel, apparently talking to someone in the sea. It was a sledge, like that we had seen before, which had drifted towards us in the night on a large fragment of ice. Only one dog remained alive; but there was a human being with it. He was not, as the other traveller seemed to be, a savage inhabitant. When I appeared on deck, the master said, 'Here is our captain, and he will not allow you to perish on the open sea. Come aboard and he will give you beans on toast and Horlicks.'

On perceiving me, the stranger addressed me in English, although with a foreign accent. 'Before I come on board,' said he, 'will you have the kindness to inform me whither you are bound.'

I replied that we were on a voyage of discovery, in search of heaven, and if he came aboard I would give him beans on toast and Horlicks.

Upon hearing this he came aboard. Good God! Margaret, if you had seen the man who thus capitulated for his safety . . . His limbs were frozen, and his body dreadfully emaciated by cold and fatigue; his penis had snapped off. I never saw a man in so wretched a condition. We attempted to carry him into the cabin, but as soon as he had quitted the fresh air he fainted! We accordingly brought him back to the deck, and restored him to animation by rubbing him with brandy and forcing him to swallow a small quantity. He forced himself to swallow quite a large quantity. As soon as he showed signs of life, we wrapped him up in blankets and placed him near the chimney of the kitchen stove. By slow degrees he recovered and ate at great speed some of the beans on toast. We had to stand clear of him.

Two days passed in this manner before we could get close enough to speak. Then, when my guest was a little recovered, I had trouble keeping off the men who wished to ask him a thousand questions – What's the Pope's inside leg measuirement? What's your blood group? Have you ever had prostate trouble? Do you like beans on toast and Horlicks? The lieutenant asked why he had come so far off the ice.

'To seek the one who fled from me.'

'And did the man who you pursued travel in the same fashion?'

'Yes.'

'Then I fancy we have seen him, for the day before we picked you up, we saw some dogs drawing a sledge, with a man in it, across the ice. He was huge, he would have knocked the shit out of you.'

This aroused the stranger. Alone with me he said, 'Thank you for having rescued me from a strange and perilous situation.'

'Oh it is nothing,' I said, 'we are only charging you for bed and breakfast.'

August 19th, 17—.

Dear Sister,

The stranger, whose name is Victor Frankenstein, is still travelling on the ship with me and his intellect is very satisfying; he speaks two languages – good and bad. He has told me that he will tell me his story and commence his narrative tomorrow when I am at leisure. Please keep sending the postal orders.

Yours,
Robert

My father was very attracted to children from the hills
He found this blonde beauty, she was called Jill
He adopted her and took her to Rome
Where she proceeded to eat them out of house and bloody home.

CHAPTER 1

I am by birth a Genevese. I was brought up by the Christian Brothers and I was brought down by Mrs Doris Munger of Lewisham. My ancestors had been for many years counsellors and syndics and my father had filled several public situations: (1) he was a lavatory attendant (2) he was a dustman and (3) a street sweeper, posts which he served with honour and reputation. He was respected by all who knew him. He passed his younger days perpetually occupied by affairs of his country. He had quite a few himself until he was caught.

A variety of circumstances had prevented his marrying early – he was ugly. It was not until the decline of life that he became a husband and the father of a family.

As the circumstances of his marriage illustrate his character, he married a nymphomaniac. One of his most intimate friends was a merchant from a flourishing state, who fell through numerous mischances – one was a coal hole. He had back trouble. People who borrowed money never gave it back. This man, whose name was Beaufort, and his great grandfather had invented the solid-lead violin for the deaf. He was of proud and unbending disposition and could not bear to live in poverty and oblivion in the same country where he had formerly been a distinguished dustman. Having paid his debts with cheques stamped RTD – his one heirloom – he took to wearing a diamond-studded jock strap. He had to retreat because he lived unknown and in wretchedness.

My father loved Beaufort with the truest friendship. He bitterly deplored the false pride which led his friend to a conduct so little worthy of the affection that united them. He lost no time in endeavouring to seek him out. He went round the streets with a stop watch, ringing a bell and shouting, 'Beaufort, for Christ's sake where are you man?'

Beaufort had taken effectual measures to conceal himself: he painted himself black and it was ten months before the paint wore off. My father discovered his abode and hastened to the house. But when he entered, misery and despair alone welcomed him. Beaufort had saved but a very small sum of money from the wreck of his fortunes but it was sufficient to provide him with sustenance, which was all he ate. He was so poor that he had the arse out of not his but somebody else's trousers. At length his grief took so fast hold of his mind that at the end of three months he lay on a bed of sickness, incapable of any exertion except to play the trombone.

Caroline Beaufort possessed a mind of an uncommon mould: it was back to front, but her courage rose to support her in her adversity. She procured plain work; she plaited straw blankets. She plaited a straw blanket for her father; she earned a sustenance.

Several months passed in this manner. Her father smoked and set fire to his straw blanket. Her father grew worse. Her time was entirely occupied in attending him and his trombone. Her means of subsistence decreased and in the tenth month her father died in her arms, leaving her an orphan and a beggar, a terrible inheritance. The orphan was adopted but they told the beggar to 'bugger off'. The last blow overcame her, and she knelt by Beaufort's coffin weeping. When my father entered the chamber it was flooded. He came like a protecting spirit to the poor girl and her magnificent bosom. After the interment of his friend he conducted her to Geneva, and placed her under the protection of a relation. Two years later, he shot his wife. Caroline and her magnificent boobs then became his wife.

They seemed to grow in their bonds of devoted affection. There was a sense of justice in my father's upright mind which rendered it necessary that he should approve highly in order to love strongly. He did it to her six times a day; then he would rest for a fortnight. During former years he had suffered from the late-discovered unworthiness of one beloved, and so was disposed to set a greater value on tried worth. He put a value of £100 on his beloved. Of course he did not know about the liaison between his wife and the milkman – he just wondered why they had not had a milk bill for a year. He strove to shelter her so, as a fair exotic is sheltered by the gardener from every rougher wind, he bought her an umbrella and he had a fence built round her to protect her. Her health and even the tranquillity of her hitherto constant spirit had been shaken by what she had gone through. She had gone through £10,000. During the two years that had elapsed previous to their marriage, my father had gradually relinquished all his public functions – railway guard, hotel porter and tallyman.

They travelled to Italy, they visited Germany, France and Bexhill-on-Sea. Their eldest child was born in Naples. For several years I was the only child. Much as they were attached to each other (they were joined at the hip) they seemed to draw inexhaustible stores of affection from a very mine of love to bestow on me. Yes that was it – I was a plaything and when they got tired of that, their idol, and as a last resort, they used me as a child. During every hour of my infant life I received the lessons of patience (for this I was locked in a cupboard for an hour), charity (they made me give them all my pocket money) and, finally, karate lessons.

For a long time, apart from the rent, I was their only expense. Occasionally, to prove my progress I would fell my father with a karate chop to the neck.

My mother often used to visit the poor. I didn't understand – we were the poor. To my mother this was more than a duty. For her to act in her turn the guardian angel to the afflicted was a great act in itself, and she travelled the halls with it. One house she visited contained some neglected children. It spoke of penury in the worst shape. In fact, one of the children spoke, 'This is penury in its worst shape.' Among the children was a very thin girl, fair with hair the brightest gold colour. It seemed to set a crown of distinction on her head. She had blue eyes.

When my father returned from Milan he found in the hall of our villa a child fairer than a pictured cherub – a creature who seemed to shed radiance from her looks and whose form and motions were lighter than the chamois of the hills. And, above all, she had good drainage. It would be unfair to keep her in poverty when we could give her a better quality of poverty. Her name was Elizabeth. Everyone loved her, even Lord Palmerston and Lord Nelson; everyone had the most reverential attachment, which was attached to her side. On the morning her parents presented Elizabeth to me as a promised gift, she arrived gift wrapped.

CHAPTER 2

We were brought up together, only one inch separated us. I was capable of a more intense application and was deeply smitten with a thirst for knowledge. I got her to play doctors and nurses. At heart I was a dirty little devil. She busied herself with following the aerial creations of the poets. 'The nightingale. Blessed bard death wasn't meant for thee.' Now let some other bloody bird snuff it. It was summer, the brilliant sun, the flowers and cow pats, and Elizabeth pursued the world of nature. What causes elephants? I had never had them so I couldn't answer her.

On the birth of a second son, my parents gave up their wandering life and fixed themselves in their native country using contact glue. We possessed a villa in Venice. When we visited there I forgot and as I opened the back door I stepped straight into the canal. My parents' lives had passed into considerable seclusion. He locked himself in the loo all day and she locked herself in the attic all night. I united myself in the bonds of a close friend; he had a hundred pounds' worth. Henry Clerval was a boy of singular talents. He could play hop-scotch, and above all he liked whipping. He read books of chivalry, romance and Sade and he composed heroic songs: 'I've got a heroic bunch of coconuts, see them all standing in a row, big ones, little ones, ones as big as your head, etc., etc.' He liked characters – King Arthur and his Round Table, the one he had breakfast on. He wanted to shed blood to redeem the Holy Sepulchre from the Infidels which meant Saladin, who beat the shit out of the Crusaders.

Saladin was fighting for Jerusalem
He said the city belonged to him
He and his calvary charged the city
But they missed, 'twas such a pity.

My parents were possessed by a generous spirit, usually 90% proof Famous Grouse.

My temper was sometimes violent and I was given to swinging a cat round and round my head in a room just to prove there was enough space to swing one. I was trying to solve the physical secrets of the world: did Queen Victoria have thin legs? and did John Brown wear anything under the kilt?

Clerval was desperate to be a horse in the charge of the Light Brigade. To this effect he went around wearing a saddle on his back and charging imaginary Russian guns.

I had exquisite pleasure in dwelling on the recollections of my childhood – a bottle, my potty, and my crap-filled nappy.

One day we went to the baths near Thonon. The inclement weather obliged us to remain a day, confined to the inn. I chanced to find a volume of the works of Cornelius Agrippa. I opened it; a new light seemed to dawn upon my mind. I communicated my discovery to my father who said, 'Ah, Cornelius Agrippa. My dear Victor, do not waste your time upon this crap.' Apparently, Agrippa's theories were crap and had been entirely exploded – which blew his leg off.

> I found Cornelius Agrippa's book
> I thought I'd have a look
> He opened up my mind
> He did it from behind
> I've still got the scar
> Which can be seen from afar.

When I returned home my first care was to procure what works were left of this author. They consisted of a wooden leg and Paracelsus and Albetus Magnus. I read and studied the wild fancies of these writers – most of them fancied women with big tits. I always came from my studies discontented and unsatisfied. Sir Isaac Newton said he felt like a child picking up shells beside the ocean but never finding one. So? I had gazed upon the fortifications and impediments that seemed to keep human beings from entering the citadel of nature, and rashly and ignorantly I had repined. [This is a lot of bollocks. Ed.]

> So once a year
> Scientists went 100 feet down in a sphere
> They ran out of air
> So they got out of there
> One tried holding his breath
> This brought on his death.

But here were books and here were men who had penetrated deeper and knew no more. Some had descended to a depth of 300 fathoms but couldn't hold their breath any longer and had to ascend having proved bugger all. I was self-taught with regard to my favourite studies; hunchbacks and fairies. My father was not scientific but he could juggle with melons. I entered, with the greatest diligence, into the subject of the philosopher's stone and where he had hidden it, and the elixir of life. The nearest thing that man had to that was Horlicks. Some disbelieved in Horlicks as the elixir of life and said it actually was Oxo. Wealth was an inferior object, but by God it paid the rent. But the glory would attend to the discovery if I could find ways to make man invulnerable to any violent death, like an elephant falling on him.

Then there was the raising of ghosts and devils. If my incantations were always unsuccessful, people would point me out in the street and say, 'See him, his incantations are unsuccessful.' I attributed my failure to wearing skin-tight underpants to avoid ants getting in. And thus for a time I was occupied by exploded systems. There were dozens of explosions going on throughout the house. One blew up my father's breakfast, another one blew him up. One explosion blew my mother off the W.C. at a critical moment.

One day there was a violent and terrible thunderstorm that burst at once with frightful loudness and ripped my trousers off. I remained while the storm lasted, watching its progress. I beheld a stream of fire issue from an old and beautiful oak. It stood just a few yards from where I stood and my face was smoke-blackened. My mother screamed when she saw me. 'Help,' she shouted, 'There's a nigger in the house with no trousers on!'

I at once gave up my former occupations – clog dancing, bare-back riding and pheasant plucking. I set down natural history and all its progeny as a deformed and abortive creation, i.e., a three-legged cripple. Are we bound to prosperity or ruin? When I look back it seems to me that this remarkable change of inclination and will was a suggestion of the guardian angel of my life – Dick Tonk. [What in God's name is he talking about? Ed.]

CHAPTER 3

When I was seventeen and had learned to spell cat, dog and duck, they decided I should become a student at the university of Ingolstadt. I should be made acquainted with the customs of my country, with dwarf hurling, haddock stretching and ostrich strangling. My sister had caught scarlet fever, and she caught it with a butterfly net. During her illness we had to prevent my mother nursing her to death. Elizabeth was saved, but the consequence of this imprudence was fatal. On the third day, mother sickened; but for this illness she would be back home boiling custard. Even on her death bed her fortitude continued – she did 250 press ups; it proved too much for her and she died. 'It is all our bloody daughter's fault,' said father.

> I went to my mother's funeral
> It was raining with a grey sky
> But in her coffin, she was nice and dry
> I wanted to cry, but I could only try, try, try.

I need not describe the feelings of those whose dearest ties were with the Lords Taverners, Grenadier Guards, and the Royal Artillery. During the

Napoleonic wars my father had volunteered to serve with Lord Nelson's cricket team. Nelson bowled him with his good arm for a duck. They were playing on deck during the battle and a Spanish marksman, knowing nothing of cricket, shot Nelson and play was halted for the day.

The funeral over, I departed for Ingolstadt. I desired to see my Elizabeth consoled. She indeed veiled her grief – she put a blanket over her head and looked through a hole. I left her to her life of ironing, cooking, mountain climbing, scuba diving and dwarf hurling.

On the day of my departure, Clerval spent the evening balancing on one leg and sword swallowing. Henry felt the misfortune of being debarred from a life of idleness and financial ruin.

Next morning, grabbing the seat of my trousers, I threw myself into the chaise and shot out the other side. I love my brother Edward and my friend Clerval. Such were my reflections, which I managed by bending down and observing myself in the seat of my shiny trousers.

There came into my life a Mr Krempe. He was uncouth – he used to be couth, but he forgot. He asked me several questions, the first was 'lend us a quid?'

He said, 'Have you really spent your time studying that crap?'

I replied, 'I have studied that crap, what crap did you study?'

'I studied a different crap in Ancient Greek.'

So saying, he stepped aside and into it. He sold me several books, charging £1.00 a time. By the time he had finished, I had a pile of books and he was a millionaire.

Mr Krempe had huge ears which looked like people looking over his shoulders.

As a child I had not been content with the results promised by a philosopher of natural science. One such promise was that by waving my arms I should be able to fly. I proved that to be a myth, so I blew his brains out. I realised that Kant, Hegel and Freud were all cunts. I had utter contempt for these three mentioned Charlies. They all sought immortality but in the end they all snuffed it. I was required to exchange chimeras of boundless grandeur for realities of little worth. I exchanged my chimera ten times a day and ended up with fuck all.

I thought of Mr Krempe and recalled what he had said of Mr Waldman.

I went into the lecturing room. Mr Waldman entered shortly after. He appeared about fifty and disappeared about seventy. He was a redhead; no hair, just a red head. He was short for his height – three feet two inches. He began his lecture by singing 'Ave Maria'. After a few preparatory experiments, he concluded with 'A good big un will always beat a good little un.' To prove it, I knocked him down.

Mr Waldman lectured on Ave Maria
He knew her dimension from ear to ear

Her blood group was 'A'
She used it every day
'It's,' she said, 'the best way'
Alas, that night she passed away.

Modern masters promise very little; they know that metals cannot be transmuted and that the elixir of life is a chimera on sale at all good chimeraists. Scientists penetrate nature and show how she works in her hiding-places – usually Bradford. And on the third day they rise again from the dead, ascend into heaven and sit at the right hand of God the Father Almighty. They have discovered how the blood circulates (through the veins, would you believe it?) and the nature of the air we breathe (it's invisible and full of crap). They can command the thunders of heaven, mimic the earthquake and even do Al Jolson. Something was wrong. I didn't come to this school to be destroyed. If I am, they should lower the fees. I will pioneer a new way, explore unknown powers, and unfold to the world the deepest mysteries of creation. This was going to get me right in the shit.

I closed not my eyes that night, only the doors. My internal being was in a turmoil – I had to swallow an enema. I believed myself to possess a natural talent, that was making moustard.* I visited Waldman. I listened to his statement that was delivered without any presumption, except for a burst on the banjo. He said how ignorant they were and how enlightened were those who had removed prejudices against modern chemists like Boots.

'I am happy,' said Mr Waldman, 'to have gained a disciple. Chemistry has had a great many improvements. They now have suppositories for piles and are able to take the temperature of boiling water and the temperature of a monkey with malaria.' So I set out to take the temperature of boiling water and searched for a monkey with malaria so that I might take his temperature. Anything to forward my studies.

Winter, Spring and Summer passed away
So did Queen Vic they say
She died with a bad heart
The damn thing wouldn't start
It meant nothing to me
I was looking for bits for my monster you see.

CHAPTER 4

From this day, chemistry in the most comprehensive sense became my sole occupation. Every day I would boil a vat of water and take its temperature

---

* Unexplainable.

and then the monkey with malaria had his temperature taken. So it went on.

Krempe had a great deal of sound sense but he had a repulsive physiognomy. He had a face like a dog's bum and the dirty devil let off in confined spaces. Professor Krempe often asked me, with a sly smile, how Cornelius Agrippa went on? I said that he went on the bus. At the same time Mr Waldman expressed the most heartfelt exultation in my progress: 'I have the most heartfelt exultation in your progress,' he said. Two years passed, during which time I paid no visit to Geneva but was engaged heart and soul in pursuit of some discoveries through which I hoped to make a monster. None but those who have experienced them can conceive of the entice-ments of science – one is money. In other studies you go as far as others have gone before you. Some got as far as Bexhill-on-Sea, which is not a seat of learning. In scientific pursuit there is continual food for discovery; I had discovered sausage and mash with mushy peas. I, who continually sought the attainment of one object: sausage and chips and mushy peas.

One of the phenomena which had peculiarly attracted my attention was the structure of the human frame. I discovered it was made up mostly of bones, skin and veins, all of which could be made into a nourishing soup. Then I asked myself, how did the principle of life proceed? The answer was mostly on foot. Next, how would life proceed to be a mystery? To find out, I shot somebody and waited by the corpse. Finally, I took it to the morgue. In life he had been a butcher. I sat by the body all night with some cheese sandwiches and a thermos of Horlicks. In the morning the sandwiches and Horlicks were gone but he was still there and still as stiff. The moral of this story was, if you shoot a butcher, he stops working. Suddenly in the midst of this darkness a light broke in upon me, a light so brilliant it must have been 200 watts, while I became dizzy with the immensity of the prospect which it illustrated. I was surprised that among so many men of genius, like George Formby, I alone should be reserved to discover so astounding a secret.

Remember, I am *not* recording the vision of a madman. I have succeeded in discovering the cause of generation of life. I became capable of bestowing animation upon lifeless matter, like I could make a doormat shake itself and I could make a couch animate and run around the room. I could boil an egg just by looking at it. What had been the study and desire of the wisest men since the creation of the world was now within my grasp, i.e., life. I was like the Arabian who had been buried with the dead and who found a passage to life, aided only by one glimmering and seemingly ineffectual light that led me to the Stock Exchange where I met Jeffrey Archer who immediately absconded with my life savings.

When I found so astonishing a power placed within my hands, I put it in my pocket. It was with these feelings I began the creation of a human being, but the size of his parts formed a great hindrance. I decided to make the being of a gigantic stature, about eight feet in height. I plundered the mortuary for parts and what I couldn't find I would take from the butcher's shop

Life and death appeared to me to be ideal bounds, and most people are either one or the other. I could dig up the dead departed and put them on the lawn of the grieving and say to them, 'Give me four hundred guineas and I can bring that stiff back to life.' No man could refuse such an offer. This I did successfully for a few weeks.

My cheek had grown pale with study, and my person had become emaciated with confinement. Who could conceive the horrors of my dabbling among the unhallowed damps of the grave? But then a resistless and almost frantic impulse urged me forward – so I collided with a tree. I seemed to have lost all soul or sensation but for this one pursuit. It was indeed but a passing trance; it passed me at thirty miles per hour and disappeared. I returned to my old habits. I collected bones from charnel houses. They disturbed the tremendous secrets of the human frame. In a solitary chamber, or rather a cell, at the top of the house separated from all other apartments I kept my workshop of filthy creation; my eyeballs were starting from their sockets in attending to the details of my employment. The dissecting room and the slaughterhouse furnished a pair of balls and a willy the right size for my monster. I stuck them on with glue, they looked marvellous. I knew my silence disquieted some of my friends. One of them said, 'Your silence disquiets me.'

I knew well how my father felt – it was usually my mother. My father made no reproach in his letters and only took notice of my silence by enquiring, 'What the fuck are you doing? Love, Dad.' Winter, spring and summer passed away. So did Queen Victoria. I did not watch the blossom or the expanding leaves; no, I was looking for bones and spare kidneys to fit an eight feet giant. I appeared to people like one doomed by slavery to toil in the ruins, or any other unwholesome trade like a pheasant plucker. Every night I was oppressed by a slow fever; it took two days to reach me. My monster was completed and all I had to do now was to give him the gift of life. The creature lay on a slab naked; he could not be allowed thus into society. I struggled with the lifeless body and put on him a pair of giant-sized trousers and a flannel shirt.

The monster's trousers fell to the floor
Some of it out the front
Round the back there was more
Underpants must be found
Before it spreads around.

The first words the monster spoke
'Has anyone got a smoke?
I'd give anything for a drag
On a fag.'

CHAPTER 5

How can I describe my emotions at this catastrophe, or how delineate the wretch whom, with such infinite pains and care, I had endeavoured to form? There was the bolt that affixed his neck to his spine, there were the screws holding his forehead to his skull; but now was the moment of truth. I plunged the electrodes into his rectum and switched on the current. He gave a groan and he was alive! He spoke as he sat up, 'Have you got a fag mate?' My God, I had given birth to a nicotine junky! I handed him the cigarette which I lit then, leaping off the table, he stood there. But, alas, we had forgotten one thing: he had no support for his trousers which fell to the floor revealing his manhood in all its glory. If any women saw this they would be leaving their husbands in thousands. Quickly I got some string round his trousers. What had I done? No mortal could support the horror of that countenance! I rushed downstairs to the refuge of a cupboard where I remained during the rest of the night walking up and down in great agitation – something difficult to do in a cupboard.

I passed the night wretchedly sleeping on a clothes line. I sank to the ground through languor and extreme weakness and the doctor came and said, 'You have sunk to the ground through languor and extreme weakness.'

I continued walking in a depressed manner. I traversed the streets without any clear conception of where I was or what he was doing. He wasn't doing anything. My heart palpitated in the sickness of fear and I hurried on with irregular steps, not daring to look about me.

Ohhhh . . . .
Like one, on a lonesome road who,
    Doth walk in fear and dread,
And, having once turned round, walks on,
    And turns no more his head;
Because he knows a frightful fiend
    Doth close behind him tread.*

My eyes fixed on a coach that was coming towards me. It stopped just where I was standing. The door being opened, I perceived Henry Clerval, who sprang out of the coach and trod straight in it. 'My dear Frankenstein,' he exclaimed, 'how glad I am to see you!'

Clerval's presence brought back thoughts of my father, Elizabeth, and all those bloody hangers-on at home. I grasped his hand and the 100 kroner note in it. 'It gives me the greatest delight to see you but tell me how you left my father, my brothers and Elizabeth.'

'Penniless,' he replied. 'But my dear Frankenstein,' he continued, 'I did

---

* Coleridge's *Ancient Mariner*.

not before remark how very ill you appear, so thin and pale, you look as if you have been wanking for several nights.'

We ascended into my room and, once seated, I was unable to contain myself. I was unable to remain for a single instant in the same place: I jumped over the chairs and climbed on top of the cupboard; I crawled under the table; I jumped out the window and ran back up the stairs and hid under the bed.

I was very ill and what was wrong with me was affecting my mind
But the pain was coming from my behind
Perhaps the illness is in my bum
It's amazing where illness can come from.

'Victor, Victor,' cried Clerval, 'what the fuck's the matter with you?'

'Oh, save me! save me!' I imagined that the monster seized me; I struggled furiously and fell off the washing in a fit.

Clerval took the opportunity to put a straitjacket on me. I was lifeless and did not recover my sense for a long time – eighteen months.

I was very ill; I had no idea what the fuck was the matter with me but I raved incessantly about the monster. Doubtless my words suprised Henry. It persuaded him that my disorder indeed owed its origin to some uncommon and terrible event. He did not know what the fuck was the matter with me.

By very slow degrees, and some frequent relapses that alarmed and grieved my friend, they would tighten the straps on my straitjacket. All the while there was this twittering in my head. One day the gloom disappeared, but just in case they kept my straitjacket on. But what the fuck had been wrong with me?

'Dearest Clerval,' I exclaimed, 'the whole winter, instead of being spent studying as you promised yourself, you have been consumed with me and you have watched me being sick in my room. How shall I ever repay you?'

'A thousand guilders wouldn't go amiss,' said Clerval. 'You will repay me entirely, if you do not discompose yourself. May I speak to you of one subject? Compose yourself.'

Immediately I knocked off a 24 bar nocturne.

'I have observed your change of colour,' said Clerval.

I had gone a pale green.

'You're the strangest colour I've ever seen
You've gone dark green'
So said my friend Clerval who himself was ill in bed
Going a bright colour red.

'Your father and cousin would be happy if they received a letter in your own handwriting.'

Immediately I wrote the letter 'A' and posted it to them.

'If this is your present temper, my friend, you will perhaps be glad to see a letter that has been lying here some days from you – to your cousin, I believe.'

CHAPTER 6

Frankenstein to Elizabeth:

Dearest Cousin,

Do not come here! The countryside abounds with wolves, bears and bandits!

Elizabeth to Frankenstein:

Clerval writes that indeed you are getting better and have stopped hiding in the cupboard. How pleased you would be to remark the improvement of our Ernest! He is now sixteen and full of activity and learning to yodel. He is not pleased with the idea of a military career overseas, playing bagpipes to the Scots Guards. In the meantime he is spending time in the open air, slapping his thighs and yodelling.

My dearest aunt and cousin died. We buried them; it seemed the best thing to do. The mortician did a job lot – he buried them all together. She, my aunt, was a Roman Catholic and she had pieces of the true cross. Put all of the pieces of the true cross together and it would show that Jesus was sixty feet high and eighty feet across. Poor girl, Justine; she wept and we were up to our ankles in tears.

Elizabeth Lavenza
Geneva, March 18th, 17—.

Frankenstein to Elizabeth:

Dear Elizabeth,

You say one word would suffice to quiet your fears. Here it is – C O L O U R! You can choose whatever you like – white, black, red, brown, blue, Russian blue, yellow, ochre. Yes, the word can go a long way.

One of my first duties on my recovery was to introduce Clerval to several professors. I introduced him to several Professor Waldman. In the absence of the other several professors, he will do. They have taken everything out of my laboratory – several noses, sets of false teeth, twelve legs, six vials of blood, twelve feet of veins, some spare kidneys, and a bottle of tomato sauce, etc. They were charging me 10 Marks a minute rent so I had to rush in, stay for three minutes, and rush out again. It was the only way I could afford it.

I writhed under Professor Waldman's words of praise but dared not exhibit the pain I felt. Clerval curled up on the floor in front of me, his legs behind his head, and said, 'This puts me in a very difficult position.' My sin in the back of my mind was that of a monster with his trousers down.

Mr Krempe was quite docile – I kept him on a lead. He was given to bursts of speech. 'Damn the fellow,' cried he. 'Why Mr Clerval has outstripped us all. He's a youngster who but a few years ago believed in Cornelius Agrippa, the Gem, the *Hotspur* and *Boys' Own*.'

Mr Krempe now commenced to eulogise. He did it in a bush. Clerval had never sympathised with my tastes for natural science. He came to university to master the Oriental languages.

The Persian, Arabic and Sanskrit – what a waste! No one in Switzerland spoke them and for the rest of his life he would have to talk to himself in one of these three languages. There were only three works of the Orientalists: the Omar Khayyám Ice Cream Factory, the King Durius Sewage Works and the Sheik Hussein Laundry.

Summer passed away, having been delayed by several accidents: (1) I was run over by a train; (2) I fell over a cliff and (3) I fell down a well. The roads were deemed impassable with snow.

During the month of May I expected the letter daily which was to fix the date of my departure. As I was still down a well I found it very hard to answer. Henry proposed a pedestrian tour in the environs of Ingolstadt and I acceded with pleasure to this proposition: I was fond of exercise but not that bloody fond. In the end it was to prove too strenuous for me. My health deteriorated; I tried very hard. I was taken for the salubrious air of the Alps but when I breathed it I fainted. In a few days I recovered.

Henry rejoiced in my gaiety and I started to yodel. He exerted himself to amuse me: he would juggle three bags of flour, he stood on his head and yodelled the 'William Tell Overture', he played the banjo and danced. He could make himself disappear; this he did by the simple expedient of leaving the room. His conversation was full of imagination. He spoke in Persian and Arabic; that was wonderful, but I didn't understand a bloody word. He repeated my favourite Wordsworth poem:

I wandered lonely as a cloud
That drifts aloft over dales and hills
And all at once I came upon
My dog being sick on the daffodils.

Clerval believed the world was flat, but he kept tripping over it.

We returned to our college on a Sunday afternoon: the peasants were dancing and hurling each other off cliffs into the lake. It was an old custom and they never tired of it, except those who drowned. My own spirits were high and I bounded along with feelings of unbridled joy and hilarity. From a great distance my family could see me bounding with unbridled joy and hilarity.

CHAPTER 7

On my return I found the following letter from my father:

My dear son,

You expect a happy and glad welcome and a box of gift-wrapped suppositories for your haemorrhoids. Well fuck your luck. But how can I relate our misfortune? William is dead! – di diddly I di – dead; he has stopped yodelling. One day he went for a walk but did not return. We searched for him until night fell and then we returned to the house. About five in the morning I discovered my lovely boy, who the night before I had seen blooming and yodelling, stretched on the grass lifeless and motionless. He was as stiff as a poker. His neck had been broken and his face was facing backwards. In other words he was lying face downwards on his back. He was conveyed home in a wheelbarrow. The anguish visible on my countenance betrayed the secret to Elizabeth. The fact that the body was rigid was another giveaway. She was very keen to see the corpse; she likes that sort of thing. Seeing the corpse, she fainted away; a bucket of water soon revived her. The previous day William had teased her to let him wear a very valuable miniature. It was an ivory elephant and he wanted to use it as fishing bait.

Come, Victor, not brooding thoughts of vengeance against the assassin – but just in case would you bring a musket, a sword, a brace of pistols and a bomb.

Your affectionate and afflicted father,
Alphonse Frankenstein
Geneva, May 12th, 17—.

'My dear Frankenstein,' exclaimed Henry, when he perceived me weeping with bitterness, 'are we always to see you unhappy, you miserable bastard?'

I motioned him to take up the letter so he took it up to the first floor while I walked up and down the room from north to south, to east and west, to nor-noreast, to sou-souwest, to 20° west, to 30° east – by which time I had covered the whole room.

'I can offer you no consolation,' said he.

'Then piss off,' said I.

'Now I go instantly to Geneva: come with me, Henry, to order four horses over the counter.' I held up four fingers to make sure we got them. As soon as the horses arrived I hurried into a cabriolet and bade farewell to my friend.

My journey was very uncomfortable as I was suffering from piles and looking forward to the gift of suppositories. I wished to hurry home for I longed to console and sympathise with the miserable bloody lot back home.

As I approached my home
I recognised the dome
I recognised the bailiff's men
Bringing out the furniture now and then
The last contents they brought was my mother
And then my invalid brother.

I remained two days at Lausanne in a painful state of mind and arse and then continued my journey towards Geneva. The road ran by the side of the lake which became narrower and narrower and narrower and finally it disappeared, and so did I; it took a month to find me again. As I approached my native town I discovered more distinctly the black sides of Jura and the bright summit of Mont Blancmange. I wept like a child – boo hoo hoo. 'Dear mountains! My own beautiful lake! How do you welcome your wanderer?' At that moment a landslide pushed me and the carriage into the lake. That's how they welcome their wandering kith and kin.

'Which are you,' said a peasant digging me out, 'are you kith or kin?'

'I am kith.'

'Well good, we don't want any kins here.'

Yet as I drew nearer home, grief and fear again overcame me so I did not care a fuck for the Jura or Mont Blancmange. Night also closed around and I could hardly see the dark mountains. My landlady said she had put a po under my bed but if I used it I was not to put it back under the bed because the steam rusts the springs.

As I cowered on deck it started to rain
And, terrible luck, I fell in the lake again
William, this storm is your funeral hymn
But I got no bloody response from him.

As I was unable to rest I resolved to visit the spot where my poor William had been murdered. As I could not pass through the town I was obliged to cross the lake in a boat to arrive at Plainpalais. During this short voyage, as I was rowing, the boat flooded and sank and I had to swim for the shore. I saw the lightning playing on the summit of Mont Blancmange. Already soaked to the skin, it started to rain again, absolutely flooding me. It was pitch dark until my eyes recovered themselves to the darkness. During that time I fell in the lake for a second time.

From the bank I watched the tempest, so beautiful yet terrific. This noble war in the sky elevated my spirits; I clasped my hands and exclaimed aloud: 'William, dear angel! this is thy funeral dirge.' [I don't think William heard it but it was well meant. Ed.] A flash of lightning illuminated the object and discovered its shape plainly to me, its gigantic stature. His trousers were still around his ankles. Each flash of lightning lit up his huge wedding tackle. What did he there? I waited, but he did nothing there. Was he the murderer of my brother? He suddenly rushed towards me. 'Have you got a fag?' he said. I hastily gave him a packet. Yes, he was the murderer! [There is not a shred of evidence against this poor monster. Ed.] Yes, it must have been two years since I gave this monster life. Was this his first crime? A murderer two years old? No court would believe it!

My first thought was to discover what I knew of the murderer and cause instant pursuit to be made. 'Quick, police, fire, ambulance!' This being I had myself formed and given life to and met me at midnight. He asked me for a cheese sandwich. I told him I had no cheese, would fish paste do?

'Oh,' he queried, 'what will fish paste do?'

'Nothing,' I said, 'it just stays there.'

He asked me to help secure his trousers which I did, fixing them from the back where it was less dangerous.

It was about five in the morning when I entered my father's house. I told the servants not to disturb the family and they didn't but they, too, were still in bed. Six years had elapsed. I embraced my father, beloved parent. I gazed on the picture of my mother which stood over the mantelpiece. It was an historic subject painted at my father's desire and represented Caroline Beaufort in an agony of despair, kneeling by the coffin of her dead father. My father was really bent. Her garb was rustic and her cheek pale; but there was an air of dignity and beauty that hardly permitted the sentiment of pity. Nevertheless it was a bloody miserable painting. Below this picture was a miniature of William; my tears flowed when I looked upon it and soon the room was ankle deep in tears.

While I was thus engaged, Ernest entered. 'Still bloody miserable? Welcome home my dearest Dick,' he said.

'I'm not Dick,' said I, 'I'm Victor.'

'Poor William, he was our darling. We tried to revive him, we even tried a vet.'

Tears unrestrained – strained tears are much purer but less plentiful – fell from my brother's eyes. 'Elizabeth, alas, announced herself as having caused the death of William and that made her very wretched, but since the murderer has been discovered . . .'

Good God! How can that be? Who could attempt to pursue him? It is impossible; one might as well try to overtake the winds or confine a mountain stream with a straw. He disappeared at a speed of 100 miles per hour. He was eating a fish paste sandwich and his trousers kept falling down. The police, ambulance and fire brigade chased but he outstripped them.

'Indeed, who would credit that Justine Moritz became capable of so appalling a crime? The morning of the murder, servants had discovered in her pocket the ivory elephant brooch. She has been apprehended and charged with the murder.'

Nonsense! I knew that the murderer had been eating a fish paste sandwich and travelling at 100 miles per hour with his trousers down.

The real murderer was eating a sandwich of fish paste
To finish it he would have to make haste
His trousers were laying in haste on the floor
Could he ask for anything more?

My dear father, you are mistaken. Justine is innocent. No sir, I tried it on with her and she wasn't having any of it. I sincerely hope she will be acquitted. The murderer was a man with his trousers down, eating a fish paste sandwich and travelling at 100 miles per hour.

My tale was not one to announce publicly. I would tell it to someone privately in a cupboard.

We were soon joined by Elizabeth. Time had altered her since I last beheld her; it had endowed her with loveliness surpassing the beauty of her childish years – and huge boobs. She welcomed me with the greatest affection, and I gave them a quick squeeze.

'She is innocent, my Elizabeth,' said I.

'Yes, I too am innocent,' said Elizabeth.

'And me,' said father. 'And we are all of us innocent. Does that make you feel better?'

'Dearest niece,' said my innocent father, 'dry your tears. If she is Justine, as you believe, she will have to rely on the justice of our laws.'

'I tell you,' I said, 'that murderer had his trousers down, was eating fish paste sandwiches and travelling 100 miles per hour.'

'Of course he was,' said my father, helping me on with my straitjacket.

She related the evening of the night of the sailor
I think he was a sailor or it might have been a tailor
'All night I watched him go up and down on my bed
By dawn he fell off dead.'

CHAPTER 8

At Justine's court appearance I called out to the court from the witness box, declaring that she was innocent, that the murderer was eight feet tall, with his trousers down, travelling at 100 miles per hour and eating a fish paste sandwich. She entered the court, threw her eyes around the room and then caught them coming back.

She had been out the whole night with a sailor; the murder had been committed towards morning. A woman asked her what she did and she said, 'I did the sailor.' When another one enquired where she had passed the night she replied, 'With a sailor.'

A murmur of indignation and disbelief filled the court and the street. As the trial proceeded her countenance altered. One minute she was Tommy Cooper, then Lon Chaney, then Jimmy Durante and, finally, Frank Bruno. She collected her powers, then spoke in an audible although variable voice: she did Tom Jones, Frank Sinatra and Paul McCartney.

She related the evening of the night of the murder. She had been at the house of an aunt at Chêne with a sailor. On her return she met a sailor who asked her 'Would you like a fuck dear?' All through the night she watched him go up and down. As dawn broke she awoke and the sailor rolled off her, dead. From the back of the court I called out, 'It was a giant with his trousers down, eating a fish paste sandwich and travelling at 100 miles per hour.' That is all I said and for saying it they put me back in a straitjacket.

Several witnesses were called who said they had known her for many years. Many spoke well of her but were unwilling to come forward, so they went backwards and disappeared out of the court. During her service with us she was the most benevolent of human creatures. In her last illness she nursed Madam Frankenstein until it killed her. But public indignation had returned with renewed violence against her, with blackest ingratitude.

I perceived the countenances of the judges and they had already condemned my unhappy victim. I rushed out of the court in agony and was run over by a bus. I felt I had never before experienced such sensations of horror – not since I saw *Don't Forget Your Tooth Brush*. Words cannot convey an idea, only things like fork, hippo, nut cutlet, couch, tree, but none of them convey the heart-sickening despair.

'Yes,' said Elizabeth, 'we will go and visit her in jail and you, Victor, shall accompany me.' ('Oh fuck.') 'I cannot go alone.'

The idea of this visit was torture to me, yet I could not refuse. I didn't want to be seen going so I put a towel over my face. We entered the gloomy prison chamber and beheld Justine sitting on some straw at the far end; her hands were manacled and, with difficulty, she was trying to eat a packet of Smith's crisps. She rose on seeing us and threw herself at the feet of Elizabeth, weeping bitterly. We were soon all ankle deep in tears.

'Rise, my poor girl,' said Elizabeth. The poor girl rose six feet in the air and remained there.

'Would you like a sailor to make your last hours happy?'

'Can I come down now?' Justine asked. 'The local priest said that unless I gave £10 towards the church I will go to hell.'

'Then pay the £10 and avoid going to hell,' said Elizabeth.

'Dearest William, dearest blessed child! I soon shall be able to see you again, in heaven where we shall all be happy and I can see the strangle marks on your neck. Goodbye cruel world, goodbye. I leave a sad and bitter world, and that stupid man in the corner with the towel over his head.'

During this conversation I had retired to the corner of the prison room where I could conceal the horrid anguish that possessed me with a large piece of cardboard.

'I feel as if I could die in peace.' We all waited while she tried to die in peace but nothing happened.

Thus, the poor sufferer tried to comfort others – she tried to comfort the Pope, but before she could she would be strung up.

We stayed several hours with Justine and I danced with her three times.

On the morrow, Justine died, a favourite with Her Majesty's Royal Navy. I turned to contemplate the deep and voiceless grief of my Elizabeth but she wasn't there. All that woe and the desolation in the home. All was the work of my thrice-accursed hands, bloody hands multiplied by three. Justine's funeral was accompanied by wailing and lamentations and weeping. It was so bloody noisy we couldn't hear the coffin go into the ground.

Meanwhile, this monster was walking the countryside at 100 miles per hour, demanding cigarettes and strangling people if they did not give him one.

VOLUME TWO

CHAPTER 1

I could never watch *Drop the Dead Donkey*; I could only watch it fall and pray for its soul. They say all the souls of dead donkeys go to Bexhill-on-Sea.

'Victor,' said my father, 'for fuck's sake snap out of it. I loved your brother.'

Tears came into his eyes; they ran down his body into his boots where they escaped through lace holes as steam.

'It is a duty to improve or enjoy, even the discharge of daily usefulness without which no man is fit for society. For fuck's sake, snap out of it.'

Now I could only answer my father with a look of despair, and endeavour to hide myself from his view behind a piece of cardboard from where I shouted, 'For fuck's sake I can't snap out of it.'

About this time we moved to a house at Belrive. This change was particularly agreeable as there was no rent to pay. Often, when the rest of the family retired for the night, I took the boat and passed many hours upon the water. It sprang a leak, and despite four hours of bailing out it sank. Another time I hoisted the sails and let the wind take me wherever it would. I ended up in France. It took me two days of sailing to get back. Often I was tempted to plunge into the lake; that the waters might close over me and end my calamities forever, but each time I ran short of breath and had to surface. Thank heaven, it saved my life.

I lived in daily fear lest the monster whom I had created should perpetrate some new hobby like haddock stretching or nude woodchopping. None of these activities could obliterate the monster from my mind. I must find him, even if it means going to the Andes. There I would arrest him.

> The monster would not leave my mind
> Suppose he left it behind!
> He could throw it in the sea
> Dearie me
> And that would be the end of me.

My father's health was deeply shaken by the horror of the recent events. We had to put heavy rocks on him to keep him still.

'When I reflect, my dear cousin,' said Elizabeth, 'I no longer see the world and its works as they before appeared to me. Before I looked upon the accounts of vice and injustice.'

'Don't worry, I will look up these accounts,' I said. I did, and there was a deficit of £50 10s 6d so we closed the books on that company.

'Yes,' I said, 'I felt she was innocent before she died. I felt her after she died and she felt innocent after she died. William and Justine were assassinated and the monster walks free, smoking fifty fags a day and God help the man who doesn't give them to him.'

'I would not change places with such a wretch,' she said.

'Well you certainly couldn't change places with him. You would need to be five feet taller and ten stone heavier.'

Elizabeth read my anguish in my countenance and kindly taking my hand threw it on the floor. She was so elegant it abolished any thought of using that one-eyed trouser snake.

Ah, the wounded deer dragging its fainting limbs to some untrodden brake, there to gaze upon the arrow which had pierced it and left it to die. Ah, if only a bowman would shoot an arrow into my leg, I could find an untrodden brake and, gazing at the arrow, die. [What a lot of bollocks! Ed.]

The high and snowy mountains were its immediate boundaries; but I saw no more ruined castles and fertile fields – only quite a few McDonald's. Immense glaciers approached the road from which I ran like fuck. I heard the rumbling thunder of the falling avalanche as it moved our house five hundred yards down the hill.

A tingling, long-lost sense of pleasure often came across me during the journey, as did some young woman who also came across. The very winds whispered in soothing accents – French, Italian, German and, believe it or not, Swahili. I spurred on my mule, striving to forget the world, my fears and my overdraft. Suddenly, as I was forgetting the world, my mule threw me and kicked me in the balls which swelled up like water melons and I had to carry them around in a wheelbarrow. The animal was trying to tell me something. Listening to the rushing of the Arve, which pursued its noisy way beneath, the same lulling sounds acted as a lullaby. I felt it as sleep crept over me as I, the mule and my swollen balls were down by the raging torrent.

> We rest; a dream has power to poison sleep.
> We rise; one wand'ring though pollutes the day.
> We feel, conceive, or reason; laugh or weep.
> Three cheers, hip hip hooray.
> It is the same for be it joy or sorrow,
> The path of its departure still is free.
> Man's yesterday may ne'er be like his morrow;
> Hi diddle diddle dee.

CHAPTER 2

I spent the following day roaming through the valley. I stood beside the source of the Arveiron. The glacier with the slow pace is advancing down from the summit to barricade the valley and cut all the poor buggers off from the other side. The abrupt sides of the mountains were before me, but turning round suddenly they ended up behind me. The glorious Nature was broken only by the brawling waves, and from somewhere there came the sound of someone being sick. The thunder of the sound of a million tons of avalanche afforded me the greatest consolation. All I needed to cheer me up was a million tons of ice crashing down. The unstained snowy mountain top, the giant Alps – indeed all I need to make me sleep was the Swiss Alps and Mont Blancmange.

Where had they fled when the next morning I awoke? They had not fled anywhere. They were all still there. In fact, I need not have gone to sleep at all.

The next day my mule had its back legs shackled together to protect my balls. I resolved to ascend to the summit of Montanvert. I said to my groom, 'I resolve to ascend to the summit of Montanvert.'

He said, 'What you do is your business.'

The ascent revealed a scene terrifically desolate. In a thousand spots the traces of the winter avalanche may be perceived. Actually, I myself came out in a thousand spots and I was treated for youth's acne. The path, as you ascend higher, is intersected by ravines of snow, down which stones continually roll from above, crashing down on people's heads below. In fact, there was a whole generation of people with lumps on their heads. Apparently the lumps went through the families. The rain poured down from a dark sky and added to the melancholy impression. I myself could do a melancholy impression – the Hunchback of Notre Catford and the Hunchback of Marie Antoinette on the Gallows.

The field of ice is almost a league in width, but I spent nearly two hours falling down and getting up it. [Dear reader, I have a feeling he's going to meet the monster! Ed.] My heart which was before sorrowful, now swelled with something like joy. Actually, it was a mild coronary.

Suddenly nothing happened, but it happened suddenly. Mark you, I beheld the figure of a man advancing towards me with super-human speed; roughly, I would say he was doing 150 miles per hour. He bounded over the crevices over which I had walked with caution. His stature, as he approached, seemed to exceed that of man. I was troubled: a mist came over my eyes, nose and teeth and I felt a faintness seize me; but I was quickly restored by a bottle of 1909 brandy. I perceived as the shape came nearer (sight tremendous and abhorred!) that it was the wretch whom I had created. [God, he was slow recognising him! Ed.] Argggah! Yes folks, argggah! I trembled with rage and horror, resolving to wait his approach, and then close with him in mortal combat [for Christ's sake, don't!]. Again, his trousers were round his ankles.

'Ello, ave you got a fag?' he said.

'Devil!' I exclaimed, 'do you dare approach me? And do not you fear the fierce vengeance of my arm?'

'Oh don't be like dat, I only want a fag.'

It was the monster, argggah
He said, 'ave you got a fag?'
'No, I've only got an argggah'
'Alright, I'll have an argggah.'

'Be gone, vile insect [Eh?], or rather, stay that I may trample you to dust! And, oh! that I could, with the extinction of your miserable existence, restore those victims whom you have so diabolically murdered!'

'Oh steady on, mate, I only done one. Now will you help me with my trousers.'

My rage was without bounds; I sprang on him, impelled by all the feelings which can arm one being against the existence of another. He hurled me 100 feet down a chasm and then he came down and helped me to my feet.

'Upsy daisy,' he said, 'Remember, thou hast made me more powerful than thyself, my height is superior to thine, my joints more supple, etc., etc. I could beat the shit out of you if I wanted. Now have you got a fag?'

'Here,' I said, 'here is a packet of twenty. That will be £2 and I sincerely hope you die of lung cancer.'

I hope you die of cancer
I will if I can sir
Personally I don't give a damn sir
I will smoke one hundred fags a day
Until the cancer goes away.

So saying I helped his trousers up.

'Now remember that I am thy creature; I am thy Adam – but I am better dressed.'

'Begone! I will not hear you. There can be no community between you and me; we are enemies.'

Suddenly he pulled my trousers down. 'There, how do you like it?' he said. 'Let me turn up your trousers; one good turn deserves another.'

'I don't think it's a very good turn – if it was, it should be in the music hall.'

CHAPTER 3: THE MONSTER'S TALE

'It was with considerable difficulty that I remember the original era of my being. By degrees, I remember, a stronger light pressed upon my nerves, so that I was obliged to shut my eyes. I walked over a cliff. By opening my eyes I found myself at the bottom of a cliff. Then I walked and I sought a place in the shade. This was the forest near Ingolstadt; and here I lay peacefully by the side of a brook, resting from my fatigue. A tree fell on me and I felt tormented by hunger and thirst. I ate some berries which I found hanging on the trees or lying on the ground. I slaked my thirst at the brook and then, lying down, I was overcome by sleep during which another tree fell on me. While I was under it some villagers asked for my autograph. A feeling of pain invaded me on all sides and I sat down and wept.

'Soon a gentle light stole over the heavens, and gave me a sensation of pleasure. I started up and beheld a radiant form rise from among the trees.* Of course, it was the moon! How silly of me not to recognise it. I was still cold when under the trees I found a huge cloak; it had a ticket on it, 'Made in Taiwan', and I covered myself with it and became Chinese.

'My eyes became accustomed to the light and to perceive objects in their right forms; I could distinguish herbs from animals. I could tell the difference between a nettle and an elephant. One gave you a sting, the other killed you. I could tell hot from cold. One day I found a fire which had been left by wandering beggars and was overcome with delight at the warmth I experienced from it. In my joy I thrust my hand into the life embers [What a bloody fool! Ed.]. Food, however, became scarce and I often spent the whole day searching in vain for a few acorns, sausages or a leg of lamb.

CHAPTER 4

'I lay on my straw, but I could not sleep. I didn't know how to. I thought of the occurrences of the day. I remembered too well the treatment I had suffered the night before from the barbarous villagers who had driven me out. I remained quietly in my hovel, watching, and endeavouring to discover the motives which influenced their actions.

'The cottagers arose the next morning before the sun. A young woman arranged the cottage and prepared the food; the youth departed after the first meal, the greedy bugger.

'The young man was constantly employed out of doors, and the girl in various laborious occupations within. The old man I soon perceived to be blind as he kept walking into walls.

'A considerable period elapsed before I discovered one of the causes of the uneasiness of this amiable family – it was poverty. I discovered that because at dinner time they had no food on their plates. The two children suffered the pangs of hunger, for several times they placed food before the old man. They reserved none for themselves. He ate the lot, the greedy bugger.

'This trait of kindness moved me sensibly. I had been accustomed, during the night, to steal a part of their store for my own consumption [The shit! Ed.].

---

* The moon [author's footnote].

'I learned the names of the cottagers themselves. The girl was called "Agatha", the youth "Felix" and the man "Father". I cannot describe the delight I felt when I learned the ideas appropriated to each of these sounds, so I won't. I distinguished several other words without being able yet to understand, though I repeated them; such as "fire", "milk", "bread", "wood", "shit".

'Felix carried with pleasure to his sister the first little white flower that peeped out from beneath the snowy ground – she ate it.

CHAPTER 5

'I shall relate events that impressed me with feelings which, from what I had been, have made me what I am [Frankenstein made him what he am. Ed.]

'Spring advanced rapidly; the weather became fine but I did not. It was a surprise to me that what before was a desert was now a Kentucky Fried Chicken. I was refreshed by a thousand scenes of delight with a little crushed garlic. One night, mad with hunger, I killed all the staff and ate all the chickens. Colonel Sanders came along so I killed him as well.

'The old man played on his guitar. There was a tap on the door. Why any one would want to put a tap on a front door is hard to explain.

'It was a lady on horseback, accompanied by a countryman as a guide. The lady was dressed in a black suit, and covered with a thick black veil. Agatha asked a question, "Are you a nigger?" The stranger only repeated the name of Felix. She held out her hand to Felix who kissed it and then spat on the floor. I could distinguish she was an Arabian so she was, in fact, a wog.

'She took the old man's guitar and sang delightful medleys:

"All nice girls like a sailor
All nice girls like a guitar
For there is something about a sailor
For you know what sailors are."

'The wog's name was Safie but her entrance into my story and continuance is not important. Let me go to the day that all the children and Safie were out and the blind father was in the cottage.

CHAPTER 6

'I knocked on the cottage door.
' "Who's there?" said the old man.
' "Some one else," I said.
'I entered. "Pardon this intrusion," said I; "I am a traveller in want of a cigarette."

' "Enter," said De Lacey, "You will find some on the mantelpiece. Unfortunately, my children are away from home and, as I am blind, I am afraid I shall find it difficult to procure food for you."

' "Do not trouble yourself. I only need that and fire, milk, bread, wood and shit. Your children are kind – they are the most excellent creatures in the world; but unfortunately, they are prejudiced against me."

' "That is indeed unfortunate; but if you are blameless, can you not do something about it?"

' "I am ugly."

' "Can't you have plastic surgery? Barbara Cartland is going to have it."

'At that instant the cottage door opened and Felix, Safie and Agatha entered. "Quickly," he said, "I need fire, milk, bread, wood and shit!" Who can describe their horror and consternation on beholding me? Agatha fainted and Safie, unable to attend to her friend, rushed out of the cottage. Felix darted forward and with supernatural force tore me from his father, to whose knees I clung. In a transport of fury, he dashed me to the ground and attacked me violently with a crowbar. I could have torn him limb from limb as the lion rends the antelope. But my heart sunk within me as with bitter sickness. I quitted the cottage, and in the general tumult escaped unperceived to my hovel.

CHAPTER 7

'Cursed, cursed creator! Why did I live? I could with pleasure have destroyed the cottage and its inhabitants, and have glutted myself with their shrieks and misery. All I had to show was a pair of the blind man's knees.

'Sleep relieved me from the pain of reflection which was disturbed by the approach of a beautiful child who came running into the recess I had chosen. Suddenly, as I gazed on him, an idea seized me, that this little creature had lived too short a time to have imbibed a horror of deformity.

'Urged by this impulse, I seized him as he passed and drew him towards me. As soon as he beheld my form, he placed his hands before his eyes and uttered a shrill scream; I drew his hand forcibly from his face and said, "Child, what is the meaning of this? I do not intend to hurt you; listen to me."

'He struggled violently. "Let me go," he cried. "Monster! Ugly wretch! You wish to eat me and tear me to pieces – You are an ogre – let me go, or I will tell my papa. Hideous monster! Let me go. My papa, M. Frankenstein – he will punish you. You dare not keep me."

' "Frankenstein! you belong then to my enemy – to him towards whom I have sworn eternal revenge; you shall be my first victim."

'The child still struggled, and loaded me with epithets which carried despair to my heart; I grasped his throat to silence him, and in a moment he lay dead at my feet.

'I gazed on my victim, and my heart swelled with exultation and hellish triumph; clapping my hands, I exclaimed, "I too can create desolation; my enemy is not invulnerable; this death will carry despair to him, and a thousand other miseries shall torment and destroy him. Heh – heh – heh." '

CHAPTER 8

'You must create a female for me – I need a shag – with whom I can live in the interchange of those sympathies necessary for my being. This you alone can do; and I demand it of you as a right which you must not refuse to concede. And have you got a fag?'

'I do refuse it,' I replied, 'and no torture shall ever extort a consent or a cigarette from me.'

'You are in the wrong,' replied the monster, 'and, instead of threatening, I am content to reason with you. I am malicious because I am miserable. Not only that, I am gasping for a fag and a fuck. If you consent, neither you nor any other human being shall ever see us again: I will go to the vast wilds of South America. My food is not that of man; I do not destroy the lamb and the kid to glut my appetite; trees, acorns and berries afford me sufficient nourishment. I am a vegetarian. My companion will be of the same nature as myself, and will be content with the same fare. We shall make our bed of dried leaves; the sun will shine on us as on man, and it will ripen our food while we are screwing on the leaves.'

'I consent to your demand, on your solemn oath to quit Europe forever.'

'I swear,' he cried, 'by the sun and the blue sky of Heaven, and by the fire of love that burns in my heart [that only left the moon], if you grant my wish you will never behold me again. I shall go to Bexhill-on-Sea; anybody who goes there is never seen again.'

Suddenly, he quitted me, fearful perhaps of any change in my sentiments. I saw him descend the mountain – with greater speed than the flight of an eagle – at 100 miles per hour, and quickly lost sight of him among the undulations of the sea of ice.

The labour of winding among the little paths of the mountain and fixing my feet firmly as I advanced perplexed me; still I kept going arse over tip. By the time I had gone 250 arse over tips, night was far advanced. I came to the halfway resting place and seated myself beside the fountain. The wind blew it all over me and I got soaked. The stars shone at intervals, the dark pines rose before me and here and there a broken tree lay on the ground – and I did arse over tips over them. Clasping my hands in agony, I exclaimed, 'Oh! stars and clouds and winds, and four Dispirins, do take the pain away.'

I cannot describe to you how the eternal twinkling of the stars weighed upon me, so I won't. I listened to every blast of wind – blast! blast! it went as it blew the fountains all over me again.

Morning dawned before I arrived at the village of Chamonix soaking wet and with hyperthermia. I took no rest, but returned immediately to Geneva. Even in my own head I could give no expression to my sensations – they weighed on me with a mountain's weight, and the result was I had to walk bent double. Thus, I returned home, and entering the house presented myself to my family bent double with mountains. My haggard and wild appearance awoke intense alarm. They called the fire brigade; I would answer no questions from the fire brigade. 'Are you on fire?' they said. 'No,' I said. With pulleys they removed the mountains off my back; I was able to stand straight for the first time in three days.

VOLUME THREE

CHAPTER 1

Day after day, week after week passed away, as did my Granny. On my return to Geneva I could not collect the courage to re-commence my work. I feared the vengeance of the disappointed fiend and his grieving for a wife and cigarettes. I could not compose a female without again devoting several months to profound study and laborious disquisition. My father saw the improvement in me and turned his thoughts towards the best method of eradicating the remains of my melancholy: he recommended an audience with the Pope but he was too busy and sent a bottle of Holy Water which I drank – it gave me typhoid.

It was after this that my father called me aside and thus addressed me: 'Victor Frankenstein, 10 Le Grande Rue, Geneva, Switzerland.' I wonder if I ever got that. It was marked 'Return to Sender, Not Known Here.'

'I am happy to remark, my dear son, that apart from your typhoid you have resumed your former pleasures and seem to be returning to yourself. Where from I do not know, but you seem to be returning. My son, you seem still unhappy; like yesterday, you never finished up your spotted dick. You know how ideal spotted dick is for people with typhoid.'

I trembled violently at his exordium, which he played brilliantly, and my father continued:

'I confess, my son, I have always looked forward to your marriage with dear Elizabeth.'

Oh fuck, now he was trying to marry me off. There were no ends he wouldn't go to get rid of me.

'You were attached to her from your early infancy by a chain.'

'My dear father, my future hopes and prospects are entirely bound up in the expectation of our union, that is The Tradesmen and Miners.'

I remember also the necessity imposed upon me of journeying to England and studying at the Bexhill-on-Sea Body Building Centre. I must absent myself from all I loved while thus employed in creating a female monster. Putting a pair of boobs in place would be a good start.

At Bexhill-on-Sea there was a morgue where they had the bits I needed. It was the city of the aged where many of the limbs would fall off in the street. These I would gather after dark. I was capable of taking pleasure in the idea of such a journey. My father hoped that the change of scene would restore me entirely to myself. Finally he talked me down from my position on top of the cupboard.

I now made arrangements for my journey to Bexhill-on-Sea. One of them was Chopin's E^b Nocturne for the spoons. In the time given it was the best arrangment I could do.

We travelled at the time of the vintage and heard the song of the labourers. I lay at the bottom of the boat in the hold under the luggage where I could be alone from that chatterbox Clerval. As we drifted down the Rhine we saw groups of labourers who had been hiding behind the trees from their work. Oh, surely the inhabitants would retire to the inaccessible peaks of the mountains where they hurl themselves to death rather than pay income tax.

Clerval! Even now it delights me to record your words – unending bloody yakking. He was a being formed in the very poetry of nature: it would take him two bloody hours to describe a tree. His soul overflowed with ardent affections and his friendship was of that devoted and wondrous nature. it is just that he would never stop bloody yakking. To satisfy his eager mind he took up kung fu.

And where does he now exist? [He doesn't, he snuffed it. Ed.] Is this gentle and lovely being lost forever? [Yes. Ed.] Has his mind perished? [Yes. Ed.] does it only exist in our memory? [Yes, if you want it to. Ed.] His favourite poem:

The sounding cataract
Haunted him like a passion: the tall rock,
The mountain, and the deep and gloomy wood,
Their colours and their forms, were then to him
An appetite; a feeling, and a love,
That had no need of a remoter charm
By thought supplied, or any interest
Unborrow'd from the eye.*

We arrived at Rotterdam; it was a clear morning. At length we arrived in England where we saw the numerous steeples of London – St Paul's, the Tower, Angus Steak House, Deep Pan Pizza, Boots, The London Dungeons, Garfunkels . . .

CHAPTER 2

London was our present point of rest; we were determined to remain several months in Neasden for Clerval to study Hindus. This wonderful city desired the intercourse of men of genius. They were fishmongers, plumbers, bricklayers, green grocers and King Edward. Company was irksome to me, especially A Company of the Irish Guards.

Clerval's design was to visit India, in the belief that he had in his knowledge of its various languages, starvation, plague and leprosy. And he believed in trade – importing chicken vindaloo and exporting fish and chips. I tried to conceal myself as much as possible and I wore a clown's mask. I often refused to accompany him, alleging another engagement like mud wrestling. I had finally found a good pair of boobs to start on my female monster.

* Wordsworth's *Tintern Abbey* [author's footnote].

We received a letter from a person in Scotland; that is, it had no stamp on it. He mentioned the beauties of his native country – Rangers and haggis and bagpipes and whisky. Clerval was eager to accept the invitation and I wished to view again mountains and streams. I packed up my chemical instruments and bits of body. I'd finish my labours in some obscure nook in the northern highlands of Scotland. To blend with the natives around I wore a kilt and, following tradition, under it I wore nothing. Every morning, to make sure, I stood on a mirror. We saw a quantity of game and herds of stately deer, which tasted delicious.

We visited the tomb of the illustrious Hampden and the field on which that patriot fell – he tripped over a stone.

To my horror I discovered the monster had followed me and he said, 'Have you finished her yet? Hurry up, I want a shag.'

To keep out the wind, I wore an ankle length kilt.

On an island there were three miserable huts, and eighteen miserable tenants. One of these tenants was vacant. One of the tenancies was also vacant. It contained two rooms and these exhibited all the squalidness of the most miserable penury. The thatch had fallen in, the neighbours had fallen out; I ordered it to be repaired. The walls were unplastered and the door was off its hinges. The cottagers had been benumbed by want and squalid poverty. When they spoke their brains hurt and they fainted to the floor.

It was a monotonous yet ever-changing scene. Its hills are covered with veins, as were the legs of the islanders. Starting my experiments, my mind fixed on the consummation of my labour and my eyes shut to the horror of my proceedings. Thus, I kept walking into the walls. I looked towards the completion of my work with tremendous hope which I dared not trust myself to question but which was intermixed with obscure forebodings of evil that made my heart sicken in my bosom. [What a lot of bollocks! Ed.]

CHAPTER 3

One evening the moon was just rising from the sea, dripping wet. I trembled, and my heart failed within me. [Where else? Ed.] Looking up I saw by the light of the moon the daemon at the casement with his ghastly grin. He had followed me in my travels; he had swum the English Channel. He had swum up the Thames to Scotland. He stubbed his cigarette out on the roof. His wife-to-be was in bits – her boobs were on the cases, her legs on the floor and her bum on the table.

Several hours passed, and three buses, while I remained at the window gazing out to sea. A fisherman called out. 'Och ter mukty.' 'Fuck you too,' I replied. I was hardly conscious of extreme profundity, until my ear was suddenly arrested by the sound of the local police. They took my ear to the police station where it was questioned and finally released.

Back home, I heard footsteps along the passage, the door opened and the wretch appeared.

'You have destroyed the work which you began; what is it that you intend?'

'I intend to sweep it up in the morning,' I replied.

'Don't you dare break your promise to me,' he said. 'I have endured toil and misery. I left Switzerland with you and crept along the shores of the Rhine. I swam the English Channel and I've swum the stinking Thames.'

'Begone! I do break my promise; never will I create another like yourself. I gave you cigarettes; what more do you want?'

The monster saw my determination and knashed his teeth at speed; they sounded like castanets. To make a living, he'd been on exhibition in the circus as the ugliest man in the world.

'I have journeyed the Sandy McNab desert,' he said. 'It was small compared with the Sahara. How in heavens I survived it I do not know; it was a miracle of survival.'

'Leave me, I am inexorable.'

'It is well I go, but remember – I shall be with you on your wedding night.'

In a few moments I saw him in his boat, which shot across the waters at a 100 miles per hour with an arrowy swiftness and was soon lost amidst the waves.

All was again silent, but his words rang in my ears; 'ding-a-ling, ding-a-ling' they went. I burned with rage, smoke billowed from my shirt. The trouble was, I could not swim at a 100 miles per hour. Why had I not followed him and closed with him in mortal strife. Because he would have beat the shit out of me. I shuddered to think who might be the next victim to be sacrificed to his insatiate revenge – some poor bloody crofter would suddenly find himself being hurled over a cliff. I resolved to fall before my enemy without a bitter struggle.

Leaving thoughts of my bride, I went for a walk along the shore. When it became noon I lay down on the grass, and was overpowered by a deep sleep. I awoke to find I had been washed out to sea; I was a mile from the shore.

Napoleon had gathered his army for Moscow
To his assistance I must go
When we got to Moscow it was on fire
So we all had to retire
The British arrested Napoleon and to him couldn't be meaner
They imprisoned him on St Helena.

Coming ashore, I received a letter which recalled me to life and I determined to quit my island at the expiration of two days. Yet before I departed there was a task to perform, on which I shuddered to reflect. I must pack up my instruments – my thermoreck, my buzzometer, my nauseaometer and the small porcelain statue of a milkmaid. The next morning, at daybreak, I summoned sufficient courage and unlocked the doors of my laboratory. The remains of the half-finished creature, whom I had destroyed, lay scattered on the floor. She was everywhere. I paused to collect myself, then I collected her. With trembling hands and revolving knees I conveyed the instruments out of the room. I put all the apparatus, and bits of the woman, in a basket.

Between two and three in the morning the moon rose, and so did I; then, putting my basket aboard a little skiff with a great quantity of stones and some ham sandwiches, I sailed four miles offshore. At one time the moon, which had before been clear, was suddenly overspread by a thick cloud, and I took advantage of the moment of darkness to cast my basket into the sea – and also to eat my ham sandwiches. Having reached the shore, I slept soundly, awakening every now and then to eat another ham sandwich. As there were twelve, they kept me awake until the morning.

I pushed the boat from the shore. The wind was north-east, and must have driven me far from the coast. I looked upon the sea; it was to be my grave. 'Fiend,' I exclaimed, 'your task is already fulfilled!' For some reason I thought of Elizabeth; I thought of my father and of Clerval and also of the 3rd BN Irish Guards.

Some hours passed thus; but by degrees the sun declined away into a gentle breeze and the sea became free from the breakers. Mind you, from the age of this boat it should have been at the breakers a long time ago. Suddenly, I saw a line of high land towards the south.

The dreadful suspense I had endured for several hours suddenly caused a flood of tears to gush from my eyes which started to fill the boat and I had to bail out. I resolved to steer directly towards the town as a place where I could most easily procure nourishment, beans on toast and Horlicks. Fortunately, I had money with me, money which I would invest as soon as I was ashore.

I addressed some of the natives. 'My good friends, would you be so kind as to tell me the name of this town and a bank where I can invest my money.'

'You will know that soon enough,' replied a man with a hoarse voice – so I offered him a throat pastille. 'Maybe this town will not prove to your taste.'

I did not understand. So far I had not tasted anything. I was surprised to receive so rude an answer from a stranger. I was disconcerted at the frowning and angry countenances of his companions. 'Why do you answer me so roughly?' I replied. 'I want my throat pastille back.'

'I do not know,' said the man, 'what the custom of the English may be, but it is the custom of the Irish to hate villains.'

Oh fuck! I had ended up in Ireland. I perceived the crowd rapidly increase from six to 10,000.

A man said, 'Begorra! you must follow me to Mr Kirwin's, to give an account of yourself.'

'My account? Why? It stands at £102 overdrawn. Is that a crime in this country?'

CHAPTER 4

I was soon introduced into the presence of the magistrate. He looked upon me, however, with some degree of severity. At college he had taken a degree in Severity. He asked for witnesses.

About half a dozen men came forward and collided. One had landed a boat on the shore the night before. It was very dark and he had to walk alongside his boat. He walked, taking parts of the fishing catch – in this case a whale which filled the boat – and that is why he had to walk alongside. As he was proceeding up the beach, he struck his foot against something and fell full length; they found that he had fallen on the body of a man.

The first part of his deposition did not in the least interest me, but when the mark of the fingers was mentioned I remembered the murder of my brother and felt myself extremely agitated; my limbs trembled and a mist came over my eyes obscuring my face. The magistrate observed me and propped me up with his walking stick.

I entered the room where the corpse lay, and was led up to the coffin. How can I describe my sensations on beholding it? I feel yet parched with horror. When I saw the lifeless form of Henry Clerval stretched before me I gasped for breath and threw myself on the body, managing to climb out just in time before they nailed the lid on. My friend Clerval, my friend, my benefactor, and monumental bore.

The human frame could no longer support the agonies that I endured; some bits of me fell off. I was carried out of the room in convulsions – the bits of me that were left.

A fever succeeded to this. I lay for two months on the point of death; my ravings, as I afterwards heard, were frightful. I said 'fuck' eighteen times. Fortunately, I spoke my native language.

Why did I not die? [Yes, why didn't you? Ed.] But I was doomed to live and in two months I found myself as awaking from a dream, stretched out on a wretched bed surrounded by gaolers, chains, turnkeys, bolts and a pot. When I looked around and saw the windows and the squalidness of the room in which I was, all flashed across my memory. I was in the nick; I groaned bitterly.

This disturbed an old crone who was sleeping in the chair beside me. She was a hired nurse. 'For Christ's sake, shet up!' she said. I think she meant 'Shut up', I have no idea what 'shet up' meant. She seemed to characterise that class who travel Economy on Spanish airlines. Her face was a mass of criss-crossed lines that spelt 'arseholes'.

'Are you better now?' she said.

I replied in the same creep language, with a feeble voice, 'I believe that I am still alive to feel this misery and horror.'

'For that matter,' replied the crone, 'if you mean about the gentleman you murdered, I think hanging will end all your suffering.'

I turned with loathing from the woman who could utter so unfeeling a speech to a person just saved yet on the very edge of death. I was unable to reflect on all that had passed – six trams, twelve buses and four dust carts. My temperature went up to 190° and they had to switch on the air conditioning.

There was no one near me with a gentle voice of love; no dear hand to support me with a bottle of Liebfraumilch. The physician came and prescribed medicines. The old woman prepared them for me; but utter carelessness was visible in the first. Who could be interested in the fate of a murderer, but the hangman who would gain his fee? He charged £1 for every pound of body weight. For me he would get £14. When he came he wore ear plugs. His visits were short – they lasted three minutes.

Occasionally, a friendly gaoler would give me a bottle of Liebfraumilch. Such were my thoughts when Mr Kirwin entered. He expressed sympathy; he spoke, '*Votre chat denotre tante est dans le jardin.*'

Then he said, 'Can I make things better for you?'

I said, '*Oui*, would you like to book *une chambre* at the Savoy Hotel for me?'

He replied, 'I am sorry, the Savoy Hotel don't take gaol birds.'

'I mean after the hanging.'

He replied, 'The Savoy Hotel don't take dead people.'

Mr Kirwin went on to say, 'Immediately upon your being taken ill, all the papers that were on your person were brought to me, *the Daily Mail*, *The Times* and *the News of The World*. I found several letters, all from the Midland Bank asking for you to clear your overdraft of £100. But you are ill, even now you are trembling; you are unfit for agitation of any kind.'

How many types of agitation are there?

'Your family is perfectly well,' said Mr Kirwin, 'and a friend has come to visit you.'

'Oh take him away. I cannot see him, for God's sake; do not let him enter.'

'I should have thought, young man, that the presence of your father would have been welcome!'

'My father!' I cried. 'Why the fuck didn't you say?'

Nothing at this moment could have given me greater pleasure than the arrival of my father. I stretched out my hand to him.

'Are you, then, safe – and Elizabeth – and Ernest? Did you manage to avoid that big tax demand?' I said.

'Why are you dwelling in this terrible prison?'

'Well, they will not let me stay at the Savoy.'

'And poor Clerval, what a terrible end.'

The name of my unfortunate friend was too great to be endured and I shed tears. Soon the cell was ankle deep in tears.

'Alas! yes, my father, the most horrible things hang over me; a noose for a start. I should have died on the coffin of Henry.'

'Then why didn't you if it would have made you feel better?'

Mr Kirwin came in, and insisted that my strength should not be exhausted by too much exertion. The appearance of my father in flowing white robes was like that of an angel complete with wings, and he flew away.

I sat for hours, motionless and speechless, wishing for some mighty revolution that might bury me and my destroyer. I sat for three days waiting; still the mighty revolution did not come.

I was obliged to travel nearly a 100 miles to where the court was held – so I had plenty of time before it arrived. I was spared the disgrace of appearing publicly as a criminal: I gave evidence from the clothes cupboard, speaking through the keyhole. The grand jury rejected the bill (I had but one in for expenses) on it being proved that I was on the Orkney Islands at the hour that the body of my friend was found; and a fortnight after my removal, I was liberated from prison.

My father was enraptured on finding me freed from the vexations of a criminal charge. What he meant was, murderer! I was again allowed to breathe the fresh atmosphere. He had booked a room for me at the Savoy. They took me to an optician who could find nothing wrong with my eyes so I went to a cobblers. He said he could find nothing wrong except that I needed a pair of new shoes.

One morning, my father awoke me with an electric cattle prod. I was in a deep depression. At night I put a loaded pistol by my bed but in the morning it was still there, and so was I.

My father was concerned for my health. I was a shattered wreck; I lay in bits all over the cabin floor. My strength was gone – I think it went to Bexhill-on-Sea. I was a mere skeleton. I urged our leaving Ireland and we took our passage on the SS *Plassey*, a splendid ship with a slight tendency to sink. It was midnight. I lay on the deck looking at the stars, with the passers-by walking over me.

I repassed my life, the death of my mother and my departure for Ingolstadt where I became a compulsive onanist. I called to mind the night in which my monster asked for a cigarette.

I had been in the custom of taking every night a small quantity of laudanum – yeah, man! I now doubled my usual quantity. My dreams presented a thousand objects that scared me: dentist's drill, hand grenade, hangman's rope, a bank overdraft, cuddly toy, a set of golf clubs, electric toaster, holiday for two in Venice, dishwasher, a dozen wine glasses ... Next morning, they threw a bucket of water over me. The fiend was not here; he must have been there! A sense of security, a feeling that a truce was established, and a disastrous future imparted itself to me. In other words, I was shit scared.

CHAPTER 5

The voyage came to an end and I found I had overtaxed my strength. I discovered I could only travel on a stretcher or by walking on one leg. My father wished me to seek amusement in society. I abhorred the face of man. How they would, each and all, abhor me and hunt me from the world for what I had done. Arghhhh!

At length, my father yielded to my desire to avoid society and he locked me in the W.C., where I had a plentiful supply of water. He would say to me through the keyhole, 'You can take a horse to water but he needn't drink; you can't make a silk purse out of a sow's ear; a bird in the hand is worth two in the bush; beware your sins will find you out; a stitch in time saves nine.'

'Thank you father' said I.

I continued in the same dream world. I imagined I was the Greek god Apollo, surrounded by woodland nymphs. Then, one day, I was no longer Apollo but Victor Frankenstein and strapped down to the bed. Was there any mail when I was away? Yes.

The day before we left Paris (how in God's name did I get there?) I received the following letter from Elizabeth:

My dear friend,

It gave me the greatest pleasure to receive a letter and your dirty laundry and you are no longer at a formidable distance like Ireland but still wear the restrictive jacket. How you must suffer! I hope to see you looking even more ill than when you quitted Geneva. This winter has been miserable, tortured as I have been by revolving swannicles and anxious suspense; yet I hope to see peace in your countenance and to find that your heart is not totally void of comfort and tranquillity. I know you enjoy so much being ill.

P.S. Perhaps on our wedding day you can leave off your straitjacket.

Elizabeth Lavenza
Geneva, May 18th, 17—.

After the ceremony was performed, a large party assembled. The sun was hot so we did not touch it. The sun sank lower in the heavens; and we passed the river Drance. We looked at the numerous fish that were swimming in the clear water so, stripping off, I dove into the water and retrieved a fish which I gave to my Elizabeth who straightaway ate it.

CHAPTER 6

We walked on the shore, enjoying the transitory light and dogs crapping on the beach. Suddenly a heavy storm descended and we were drenched. I had been calm during the day; now, between my teeth I clenched a dagger. In my left hand I carried a grenade, while in my right hand I had a sword.

I earnestly entreated Elizabeth to retire, resolving to join her as soon as I had some knowledge of the whereabouts of the monster. She left me and went to prepare divorce papers. One of the hand grenades was in my trouser pocket. Should it suddenly explode, I would be castrated on my wedding night.

Suddenly I heard a shrill and dreadful scream. I could feel the blood trickling in my veins, and tingling in the extremities of my limbs. This state lasted but for an instant; the scream was repeated, and I rushed into the room.

Great God! why did I not then expire? [Nothing was stopping you. Ed.] She was there, lifeless and inanimate, thrown across the bed, her head hanging down, her body hanging up and her pale and distorted features half covered by her hair. Everywhere I turn I see the same figure £10,000 from her insurance.

There lay the body of Elizabeth, my love, my wife, so lately living, so dear, so worthy, so dead! Deadly languor and coldness of the limbs told me that rigor mortis had set in. What I now held in my arms had ceased to exist. No, now she was a stiff.

I looked up and saw at the open window a figure, the most hideous and abhorred. A grin was on the face of the monster which seemed to take in part of his chest. He seemed to jeer, the cheeky devil. With his fiendish fingers he reached towards the package of my cigarettes, which he grabbed. Drawing my pistol from my bosom, I fired and the recoil threw me back and jammed me in the window. He plunged into the lake and swam away with the swiftness of lightning.

The discharge of my pistol brought a crowd into the room and the ceiling down. I pointed to the spot from where he had disappeared. We followed the tracks with maps and boats, and nets were cast – but all we caught was a fourteen-pound salmon. After passing several hours, we returned hopeless but with a good catch of fish.

After having landed, they proceeded to search the country; search parties going in different directions among the woods and vines following a trail of dog-ends. We never saw any of them again. I attempted to accompany them, and proceeded a short distance from the house; but my head whirled around and ended up facing the other way. My steps were like those of a drunken man and I fell at last in a state of utter exhaustion. In this state I was carried back and placed on a bed, hardly conscious of what had happened. My eyes wandered round the room and eventually returned to me.

After an interval I arose and, as if by instinct, crawled across the room; many thought I was a dog and patted me. There in the room, the corpse of my beloved lay. There were women weeping around; I hung over her boobs but gradually I slid off. I joined my sad tears to theirs and soon the room was ankle deep in tears.

I knew not whether my friends and my cigarettes were safe from the malignity of the fiend; my father even now might be writhing under his grasp and threatening him with the police. Who knows? Ernest might be dead at his feet. King Edward might be trampled underfoot. I started up and resolved to return to Geneva with all possible speed. There were no horses to be procured, so instead we boiled some eggs.

However, it was hardly morning, and I might reasonably hope to arrive by night. I hired men to row and took an oar myself because I always experienced relief from mental torment by bodily exercise. But the overflowing misery I now felt, and the excess agitation that I endured, rendered me incapable of any exertion. I threw down the oar and, leaning my head upon my hands, tears streamed from my eyes which flooded the boat and we had to try to bail out. I saw the fish play in the waters as they had done a few hours before; they had then been observed by Elizabeth. In memory of her, I stripped and dived in and retrieved a fish, and in memory of her, I ate it. The sun might shine, or the clouds might lower, but nothing could appear to me as it had done the day before. A fiend had snatched from me every hope of future happiness, plus twenty cigarettes: no creature in the history of man had ever been so miserable as I was then. Mind you, that might be a bit of an exaggeration. Mine had been a tale of hirror and horror. I have reached their acme, and what I must now relate can be tedious to you. [It's all been bloody tedious. Ed.]

My father and Ernest yet lived, but the former sunk under the tidings that I bore. We threw him a life belt. His Elizabeth, his more-than-daughter, whom he doted on; in fact she was a mass of dote marks. But alas, the springs of existence suddenly gave way: he was unable to rise from his bed and in a few days he died in the arms of his bank manager who, at the last gasp, got him to pay his overdraft.

What then became of me? I know not; and I asked somebody what had become of me; they said I became a train. I lost sensation, and chains and darkness were the only objects that pressed upon me. Sometimes I dreamed that I wandered in flowery meadows and pleasant vales with the friends of my youth, but I awoke and found myself in a public toilet. I gained a clear conception of my miseries and situation and was then released from my prison because they called me mad as a result of me saying I was Julius Caesar and was on my way to invade England and become a director of Hansons.

I began to reflect on the reason why I thought I was a Chinese junk. I think it was the monster whom I had created. I was possessed by a maddening rage when I thought of him and I prayed that I might have him within my grasp; I would tie grenades to his balls and explode them.

I began to reflect on the best means of securing him, and for this purpose I repaired to a criminal judge in the town and told him that I had an accusation to make – that I knew the destroyer of my wife, and who had stolen my fags.

The magistrate listened with attention and kindness. At this stage he signalled two attendants who rushed forward and put me in a straitjacket. As I spoke, rage sparkled in my eyes; the magistrate was intimidated: 'You are mistaken,' said he, stifling a laugh. 'I will exert myself; and if it is in my power to seize the monster, I shall.' He was laughing, with tears running down his cheeks.

They confined me to a padded cell, so I started to devote my life to the destruction of this monster. But to the magistrate, this elevation of mind had much the appearance of madness. He endeavoured to sooth me as a nurse does a child, pushing me in a pram and giving me a milk bottle.

'Man,' I cried, 'how ignorant art thou in thy pride of wisdom! Cease; you know not what it is you say.' They remembered it and let me free, and for a while I became an amateur hangman. I hanged seven amateur murderers.

CHAPTER 7

Then my situation was one in which all voluntary thoughts were swallowed up and lost, and I never found them again. I looked everywhere. I was hurried away by fury, revenge and an overdraft. I provided myself with a sum of money together with a few jewels which belonged to my mother. I took them as she slept – God bless her!

And now my wanderings began, which are to cease but with life. I have traversed a great portion of the earth using an American Express card. How I lived I hardly know – mainly bank jobs. I have stretched my failing limbs upon the sandy plain and have been crapped on by an elephant; rangers dug me out. I have swum the stormy seas; the Dover life boat saved me. I have searched the deepest; a rescue team got me out. But revenge kept me alive. I dare not die, that is the last thing I should do. I would never rest until I had exploded his balls and fed them to my dog.

That night, I knelt by the grave of my father and my wife. I kissed the earth – it tasted fucking terrible – and then exclaimed, 'By the sacred earth on which I kneel, by the shades that wander near me, by the deep and eternal grief that I feel, I swear (I also drink and smoke) to pursue the daemon until he or I shall perish in mortal conflict, preferably him. And I call on you, spirits of the dead – just don't answer all together.'

Then, to my horror, I heard the monster. He addressed me in an audible voice; that is why I could hear it: 'I am satisfied, miserable wretch! You have determined to live, and I am satisfied.'

I darted towards the spot from which the sound proceeded; it was a spot about six inches in diameter, but the devil eluded my grasp. The moon shone full upon his ghastly and distorted shape as he fled with more than mortal speed – 100 miles per hour.

I pursued him, guided by a trail of cigarette ends. I saw the feared fiend enter by night and hide himself in a vessel bound for the Black Sea. Just my luck, I took the wrong sea; I was colour blind. He took passage for the Red Sea, so he escaped.

Amidst the wilds of Tartary and Russia, he still evaded me. Sometimes the peasants, scared by this horrid apparition, informed me of his path; sometimes he himself, who feared that if I lost all trace of him I should despair and die. I saw the print of his huge footstep on the snowy plain, and I fell in it. A spirit of good followed and directed my steps, and I fell down a coal hole. I survived in the deserts by making a camel fricassee; it took me a week to eat it.

In other places, human beings were seldom seen, and I survived on elephant vindaloo. To gain the friendship of the villagers, I distributed some food – I shot an ant which I made into a stew.

I was still hell-bent on catching the monster. I exchanged my land-sledge for one fashioned for the inequalities of the frozen ocean. Immense and rugged mountains of ice often barred up my passage; it was very painful to have ice block up your passage.

Once, after my sledge-dogs had conveyed me up to the summit of an incredibly sloped mountain, one, sinking under his fatigue, died – I ate him. Suddenly, my eyes caught a dark speck upon the dusky plain. I strained my sight to discover what it could be; it was indeed a dark speck on the dusky plain.

Oh: with what a burning gush did warm tears fill my eyes. I caught the tears in a saucepan and before they became cold I made a cup of Oxo. Yes, my sledge-dogs were wonderful. They never stopped to urinate, but raised one leg and did it with the other three legs running.

In this manner, many appalling hours passed. Several of my dogs died and I made them into sausages which I enjoyed. I saw your vessel riding at anchor, and holding forth to me hopes of succour and life. I quickly destroyed part of my sledge to construct oars; and by these means was enabled, with infinite fatigue, to move to your ship.

Walton, in continuation.
August 26th, 17—.

You have read this strange and terrific story, Margaret, and do you not feel your blood congeal with horror? If it does, you must see a doctor. Sometimes, seized with sudden agony, he could not continue his tale; at others, his voice broke – he kept the pieces in a small bag. His face would suddenly change to an expression of the wildest rage as he shrieked out imprecations at his persecutor, so we put the straitjacket on him.

Sometimes, I endeavoured to gain from Frankenstein the particulars of his creature's formation – where he got the bits.

'Are you mad, my friend?' said he. 'Whither does your senseless curiosity lead you? Is it to the monster's balls which I intend to explode?'

Thus had a week passed away, but he had not. Frankenstein discovered that I made notes concerning his history, he played them back to me on his violin. I have listened to the strangest tale that ever imagination formed; much more frightening than *Midsummer Night's Dream*. To soothe him, I drained an entire bottle of brandy down his throat which seemed to relax him. In fact, it relaxed him to the point where he couldn't get out of bed. He talks of beings who visit him from regions of a remote world. They are all a bit loony.

'When younger,' said he, 'I believed myself destined for some great enterprise, like a sharcholder in Lloyds. My imagination was vivid, yet my powers of analysis and application were intense. I had conceived the idea, and executed the creation, of a man who would strangle people. I wasn't very pleased with that – or the people he strangled.'

September 5th, 17—.

My beloved sister,
We are surrounded by mountains of ice; the cold is excessive. Many of my unfortunate comrades have already found a grave. They go frozen stiff, so we cast them over the side. Frankenstein has daily declined in health. Three times in the last week he has nearly died. He suddenly has feverish fire in his eyes; but he is exhausted, and when suddenly roused to any exertion he speedily sinks again into apparent lifelessness. We throw buckets of water over him.

The ship is immured in ice, we are all shit scared and the crew want to mutiny. When Frankenstein heard this he addressed them with a courageous speech. He encouarged them to be brave and that their hearts be strong and their spirits become heroic. With that he sang 'God Save the Queen'.

He was willing to risk the lives of every sailor in an endeavour to catch his monster. What a prick! The leader of the sailors said that Frankenstein was a cunt: 'Listen to him and we'll all fucking snuff it.'

My chief intention was occupied by my unfortunate guest, a more unfortunate guest I've yet to have, whose illness increases by degrees and he is entirely confined to his bed and needs a po, but his aim was so appalling that urine went everywhere except in the chamber.

September 7th, 17—.

The die is cast; I have consented to return – if we are not first destroyed.

September 12th, 17—.

There was a shout of tumultuous joy. Frankenstein asked what the shout was. 'They shout,' I said, 'because they will soon return to England.'

'Do you really return?'

'Alas! yes. I cannot withstand their demands. I cannot lead them unwillingly to danger, and I must return. They have threatened me with fifty lashes, then being hung from the yardarm, keelhauled and made to walk the plank and swallow the anchor; fuck that.'

'You may give up your purpose, but mine is assigned to me by Heaven.' Shouting this, he sprang from his bed straight into the po, but the exertion was too much for him. He fell back and fainted, the silly sod.

At length, he opened his eyes; he breathed with difficulty. In the meantime, he told me he had not many hours to live. Quickly, I telegraphed an insurance policy on his life with Lloyds.

To make life difficult, Frankenstein revived. I waited patiently for him to die again but, alas, he raved on endlessly about the monster. At length, exhausted by his effort, he sunk into silence. About half an hour afterwards, he attempted again to speak, but he wasn't very clear.

Margaret, what comment can I make on the untimely extinction of this glorious spirit? What can I say that will enable you to understand the depth of my sorrow? Unfortunately, all he has left behind is a cabin reeking of stale urine.

Great God! what a scene has just taken place! I entered the cabin where lay my ill-fated friend. Over him hung a form which I cannot find words to describe: gigantic in stature, yet uncouth and distorted. As he hung over Frankenstein, he heard the sound of my approach; he sprang towards the porthole and got stuck half way. I called on him to stay for beans on toast and Horlicks.

He paused, turning towards the immobile form of his creator. He seemed to forget my presence; in return I forgot his. His voice seemed suffocated: 'I did – did it, uuh, I deaded him, your missus. I am saying sorry, Frank.'

Not noticing, Frankenstein attached two grenades to the monster's balls that exploded, blowing the monster's balls to smithereens. The cabin was speckled with bits of monster balls.

'Eureka!' shouted Frankenstein.

'Elizabeth, I killed her for her fags. Yes, I done Frank's wife in, but he tore my woman to bits. At least his wife is still in one piece. My wife's bits are in a basket at the bottom of the sea. Oh give me a fag,' he said as he snatched the packet from my hand and then stuffed six of them in his mouth. 'I'll have dat beans on toast now while I run over the frightful catalogue of my sins, which are on sale at all good book shops; oh bugger! this cabin stinks of piss; let's go up on deck.'

The monster cast a last glance at Frankenstein. 'He's snuffing it. It couldn't have happened to a nicer man. But soon,' he cried, 'I shall die and what I now feel is no longer felt. Soon these miseries will be extinct. I shall ascend my funeral pile triumphantly smoking the best Virginia cigarettes, and exult in the agony of the torturing flames. If they get too bad, I'll call the fire brigade. The light of the conflagration will fade away; my ashes will be swept into the sea by the winds. My spirit will sleep in peace.'

He sprang from the window upon the ice-raft which lay close to the vessel. He was soon borne away by the waves, and lost in darkness and distance

I descended to the cabin. I shook Frankenstein. 'Wake up, Frank! You can stop pretending to be dead; he's gone!'

THE END

THE HOUND OF
THE BASKERVILLES
ACCORDING TO
SPIKE MILLIGAN

FOREWORD

Sherlock Holmes was hurled to his death by Professor Moriarty but his death did not last long. He climbed up a thousand-foot mountain and killed Moriarty, who later became a character in *The Goon Show*

1. MR SHERLOCK HOLMES

Sherlock Holmes usually arrived brilliantly very late in the morning; his record for lateness was not coming down until the next morning. As we sat eating breakfast at 3 a.m., I stood upon the hearthrug and picked up the stick which our visitor had left behind the night before. It was a fine, thick piece of wood with a bulbous head known as a brain smasher. Just under the head was a broad silver band inscribed 'To James Mortimer, MRCS, from his friends of the CCH', with the date '1884'. It was just such a stick as murderers or old family practitioners used to carry – dignified, solid, and bloody heavy.

'Well, Watson, what would you make of it?'

'Firewood,' I said.

Holmes was sitting with his back to me and I had given him no signs of my occupation.

'Now what is your occupation, Watson?'

'I am a Coastal Spotter.'

'And what is that?'

'Well, I'm a Coastal Spotter. You go to the coast, you spot things and you report them to the Coast Guard.'

'And do you spot anything unusual?'

'Yes, I saw a man starving on a raft.'

'And what did the Coast Guard do?'

'They shot him.'

'Isn't that murder, Watson?'

'Not on the high seas,' said I. 'Spotting in Japanese is Yamaguchi. I did Yamaguchi for two years. I spotted a pirate ship and the Coast Guard sank it by gunfire. As the pirates swam ashore, the Japanese police drowned them by putting rocks in their clothes.'

'It seems, Watson, that the Coast Guard is hellbent on eliminating the human race.'

'Well, there do seem a lot of them.'

'Tell me, Watson, what do you make of our visitor's stick, since we have been so unfortunate as to miss him?'

'I think,' said I, analysing the implement as best I could using the methods of Holmes, 'that Mortimer is a successful elderly medical man, well esteemed – since those who know him gave him this stick as a mark of their appreciation.'

'Good!' said Holmes. 'Excellent! Ten out of ten!'

'Now this stick would seem to be the property of an elderly man,' I added.

'You know, Watson, you are a genius and have a remarkable power of stimulation. I must confess, my dear fellow, that I am very much in your debt.'

'As he entered his eyes fell upon the stick in Holmes's hand, and he ran towards it with an exclamation of joy.'

'Well, I would be grateful if you would start paying it off.'

He lit a cigarette, which flared up and set fire to his shirt front, which I doused with a soda siphon.

The doorbell had gone.

'Do come in,' cried Holmes.

The appearance of our visitor was a surprise to me since I had expected a typical country practitioner. He was a very tall, thin man, with a toothless dog by his side.

'Good morning,' said Holmes.

As he entered his eyes fell upon the stick in Holmes's hand, and he ran towards it with an exclamation of joy.

'Whooee! Whooee!' he said. 'I am so very glad,' said he. 'I was not sure whether I had left it here or in the Shipping Office. I would not lose that stick for the world.'

'Ah, a presentation, I see,' said Holmes.

'Yes, sir. From one or two friends at Charing Cross Hospital on the occasion of my marriage.'

'Pardon me, do I understand you received a walking stick as a wedding present?'

'Yes.'

'I am sorry but, if you will pardon me, what a crappy present. I got a toast rack.'

'Ah yes,' said Mortimer, 'but you can't take a toast rack for a walk.'

'Nonsense! I take my toast rack for a walk in the country. I took it to the Himalayas and made toast on K2 at twenty-two thousand feet and it worked perfectly.'

'I presume that it is Mr Sherlock Holmes whom I am addressing and not –'

'No, that is my friend Dr Watson. I am here near the window.'

'Good heavens!' said Mortimer. 'You're not going to jump out, are you?'

'Not yet. It depends on you.'

'Oh, I am glad to see you, sir. I have heard your name mentioned in connection with that of your friend. You interest me very much. I hardly expected so dolichocephalic a skull or such well-marked supraorbital development. Would you have any objections to my running my finger along your parietal fissure?'

'Look here, man,' said Holmes. 'You leave my parietal fissure alone! It's bad enough to have one.'

'My dear Holmes, as you wish, but a cast of your skull, until the original is available, would be an ornament to any anthropological museum. It is not my intention to be fulsome, but I must confess that I covet your skull.'

'No! No! Don't covet my bloody skull! It's bad enough just having one!' Sherlock Holmes waved at the visitor. 'Have a chair.'

'No, I'll stand.'

'All right, then bloody well stand on the chair.'

'You are an enthusiast in your line of thought, I perceive, sir, as I am in mine,' said Mortimer.

Holmes was silent, but his little darting glances showed me the interest which he took in our curious companion.

'I presume,' said Mortimer, 'that your little darting glances show an interest in me.'

'I presume,' said Holmes, 'it was not merely for the purpose of examining my skull that you have done me the honour to call here?'

'No, sir, but I am happy to have the opportunity of doing that as well. Mr Holmes, because I recognise myself that I am an impractical man who cannot tie my shoelaces nor roll a cigarette and because I am suddenly confronted with a most extraordinary problem, and recognising, as I do, that you are the second highest expert in Europe –'

'What, sir! May I enquire who has the honour to be the first?' said Holmes, his face white with anger.

'To the man of precisely scientific mind the work of Monsieur Bertillon must always appeal strongly.'

'All right, then, you had better consult him, and bugger off! And that will be ten guineas!'

'It came to pass that one Michaelmas the shit, with five or six of his idle and wicked companions, stole a maiden.'

'It is acknowledged that you stand alone.'

'At the moment I have insufficient funds to stand a loan,' said Holmes quickly. 'My fee is ten guineas an hour with a down payment of one hundred guineas.'

At the mention of a fee Dr Mortimer fainted and was revived only by pouring a bucket of water over him and extracting the money from his pocket.

2. THE CURSE OF THE BASKERVILLES

'I have in my pocket a manuscript,' said Dr James Mortimer.

'Of course you have. I observed it as you entered the room,' said Holmes. 'It was sticking out a mile. It is an early-eighteenth-century one.'

'How can you say that, sir?'

'Never mine how I said it; I said it.'

'Good heavens! The exact date is 1742. It was committed to my care by Sir Charles Baskerville, whose sudden and tragic death three months ago created so much excitement in Devonshire. I must say that I was his personal friend as well as his medical attendant.'

'Well, as he's dead, your practice doesn't seem to be very successful,' said I.

'Oh, what have we here?' said Holmes and Mortimer proceeded to read from the document.

' "As to the origin of the Hound of the Baskervilles, there have been very many statements. I come in a direct line from Hugo Baskerville. He was wanton and cruel but there was in him a certain wanton and cruel humour which made him known as the shit.

"It came to pass that one Michaelmas the shit, with five or six of his idle and wicked companions, stole a maiden. When they had brought her to the Hall the maiden was placed in an upper chamber while the shit and his friends sat down to a long carouse. Now, the poor lass, at her wits' end, slid down the ivy, tore her crotch to pieces, but escaped to freedom.

"It chanced later that the shit left his guests to carry food and drink to his captive and so found the cage empty and the bird escaped; whereupon the shit ran around the house crying to his grooms to saddle his mare and unkennel the pack of hounds, who had been brought up on jam, so in full cry they set off for the jam factory.

"Alas, there in the clearing lay the unhappy maid where she had fallen, dead of fear and of fatigue. But it was not the sight of her body, nor yet was it that of the body of the shit lying near her, which raised the hair upon the heads of those who discovered them." Are you still listening?' said Dr Mortimer.

'Just,' replied Holmes.

' "It was that, standing over the shit, and plucking at his throat, there stood a foul thing, a great, black beast, shaped like a hound yet larger than any hound any mortal eye had seen. It tore the throat out of the shit. As it turned its blazing eyes and dripping jaws upon them they all shrieked with fear." Well,' said Mortimer, 'did you find it interesting?'

'To a collector of fairy tales,' scoffed Holmes.

Dr Mortimer drew a folded newspaper out of his pocket.

'Now, Mr Holmes, we will give you something a little more recent.'

'Well, hurry up. It's my wedding anniversary in two days.'

'This is the *Devon County Chronicle* of June the fourteenth of this year. It is an account of the facts elicited at the death of Sir Charles Baskerville.'

Quack! Quack!

'Watson, stop that duck!'

Our visitor readjusted his glasses and began:

' "His health was sometimes impaired. He had a heart disease that changed his colour – one day he was red, the next day he was green-striped and then a light primrose colour. He was breathless sometimes. There was no need to be: there were tons of fresh air. All he had to do was suck it in." '

'Is there much more of this?' asked Holmes, yawning.

'The facts of the case are simple. On the fourth of June Sir Charles was starting next day for London, and had ordered Barrymore to prepare his luggage, a billiard table, a gas stove, a blow-up female doll, and a puncture kit. That night he went out as usual for his nocturnal walk. He never returned. At twelve o'clock his body was discovered.'

'Was he dead?' I asked.

'Yes, thank God. I thought he was going to go on for ever.'

'Oh, very interesting,' said Holmes, 'but what has this got to do with me?'

Quack! Quack!

'Stop that duck!' cried Holmes.

Dr Mortimer refolded his paper and replaced it in his trousers. It went straight through into his sock as he had no lining in his pocket. He leant back, put his fingertips together but, alas, he had been using superglue and they were stuck there.

'I must thank you,' said Holmes, 'for calling my attention to a case which certainly presents some features of interest. I had observed some newspaper comment at the time. This article, you say, contains all the public facts?'

'It does.'

'Then let me have the private ones.'

'In doing so,' said the boor Dr Mortimer, who had begun to show signs of some strong emotion, 'I am telling that which I have not confided to anyone. My motive for withholding it from the coroner's inquiry is that a man of science shrinks from placing himself in the public position of seeming to endorse a popular superstition.'

Any minute now Sherlock Holmes was going to tell him to bugger off!

'You wouldn't like to bugger off, would you?' said Holmes to Dr Mortimer.

'I can well remember driving up to the house in the evening, some three weeks before the fatal event. He chanced to be at his hall door. I descended from my gig and was standing in front of him, when I saw his eyes fix themselves over my shoulder and stare past me with an expression of the most dreadful horror.

' "The Baskerville hound!" he shrieked.

'I looked around in time to see a gigantic something, which I took to be a large black calf passing at the head of the drive. So excited and alarmed was he that I was compelled to go down to the spot where the animal had been and look around for it and there it was – gone.'

'Your claim to fame is that you saw the Hound of the Baskervilles?' mused Holmes.

'Sir Charles' heart was affected, and the constant anxiety in which he lived, however chimerical the cause of it might be, was having a serious effect upon his health.'

'Please stop,'

'On the night of his death Barrymore said there were no traces –'

'Oh my God, he's going on.'

'– of footsteps except those of Sir Charles. He said that there were no traces upon the ground near the body. He did not observe any. But I did – some little distance off, but fresh and clear.'

'Footsteps?' said Holmes.

'Dr Mortimer looked strangely at us for an instant, and his voice sank to a whisper as he answered, "Mr Holmes, they were the footprints of a gigantic hound!"'

'Footprints.'

'A man's or a woman's?'

Dr Mortimer looked strangely at us for an instant, and his voice sank to a whisper as he answered, 'Mr Holmes, they were the footprints of a gigantic hound!'

'Oh fuck,' said Holmes.

3. THE PROBLEM

I confess that at these words a shudder passed through me and out the back. Holmes leant forward in his excitement and his eyes had that hard, dry glitter, which shot from them when he was keenly interested.

'You saw this thing?'

'As clearly as I see you.'

'And you said nothing?'

'Yes, I said, "Look at that fucking thing!" '

'How was it that no one else saw it?'

'No one else was there. The marks were some twenty yards from the body.'

'How can a dog race twenty yards and kill somebody? You say it was large?'

'Enormous.'

'What sort of night was it?'

'Like every night – dark. Please don't ask silly questions.'

'But not actually raining?'

'No, he wasn't raining.'

Holmes was very thorough with his questioning.

'Was he wearing a hat?'

'No, I was.'

'There are two lines of old yew hedge, twelve feet high and impenetrable.'

'Where is all of this getting us?' asked Mortimer.

'I understand that the yew hedge is penetrated at one point by a gate?'

Oh brilliant questioning, Holmes, brilliant!

'Had Sir Charles reached this gate?'

'No, he lay about fifty yards from it.'

'Are you saying he travelled fifty yards after he was dead?'

'Yes, he was a very strong man.'

'How high was this gate?'

'About ten feet.'

'Could anyone have got over it?'

'Only if he was an Olympic hurdler.'

'What marks did you see?'

'In fact the wicket gate had been bitten in half by a giant dog.'

'There is a realm in which the most acute and most experienced of detectives is helpless,' said Holmes.

'You mean that thing is supernatural?' I asked.

'There was one clue,' said Mortimer. 'There was a pile of dog crap three feet high.'

'One dog?'

'Yes, sir, one dog.'

'Couldn't several dogs have done it in concert?'

'No one does such a thing at a concert.'

'I will have to make a note of that,' said Holmes.

'I don't care if you make a sandwich of it,' said Mortimer.

'Tell me in the same breath that it is useless to investigate Sir Charles's death and that you desire me not to do it.'

'I did not say that I desire you to do it.'

'My fee is ten guineas an hour and one hundred guineas deposit.'

The doctor made a dash for the door but I managed to intercept him and made him pay up.

'The current Sir Henry Baskerville is arriving from Canada at Paddington Station,' said Holmes. 'I recommend, sir, that you take a cab, call off your spaniel, who is scratching at my front door, kick him up the arse, and proceed to Paddington Station to meet Sir Henry. You will say nothing to him at all until I have made up my mind about the matter.'

'How long will it take you to make up your mind?'

'Twenty-four hours. At ten o'clock tomorrow, Dr Mortimer, I will be much obliged to you if you will call upon me here; that's a chance you'll have to take, and it will be of help to me in my plans for the future if you will bring Sir Henry Baskerville with you and a cheque for one hundred guineas.'

At the mention of the money, Mortimer again tried to escape from the room.

'One more question, Dr Mortimer. You say that before Sir Charles Baskerville's death several people saw this apparition upon the moor?'

'Three people did.'

'Did any see it after?'

'No, only during.'

I went to the Turkish bath at the club and lost two stone in the steam bath and my wallet.

Holmes suffered hours of intense mental concentration during which he weighed every particle of evidence – it gave him a nosebleed – constructed alternative theories, balanced one against the other, and made up his mind which points were essential and which were immaterial. Clever sod, but expensive.

'Where do you think I've been, Watson? I have been to Devonshire.'

'In spirit?'

'Exactly. My body remained in this armchair – it saved train fare.'

He would do anything to save train fare. He was a mean bastard: we called him glue pockets. Once he put his hands in them he never took them out.

'After you left I sent down to Stanford's for the Ordnance Survey map. I flatter myself that I can find my way about. If I was any flatter I would disappear. The devil's agents may be of flesh and blood, may they not?'

'Well, that goes for most people except the Hindus, who don't have blood, only curry.'

'If Dr Mortimer's surmise should be correct, we are dealing with forces of evil.'

'Oh, how do you do it, Holmes?' Actually he did it like everybody else.

'Everything was packed for his journey to London – the hobby horse, the grand piano, billiard table and blow-up rubber doll with puncture outfit.'

'Yes, I have thought a good deal of it in the course of the day. What do *you* make of it?'

'I would make a rice pudding of it.'

'He was running, Watson – running desperately, running for his life, running until he burst his heart and fell face down on his back, dead.'

'How can you say that?'

'It's easy. I just say it. Everything was packed for his journey to London – the hobby horse, the grand piano, billiard table and blow-up rubber doll with puncture outfit.'

'He's done that before, hasn't he?'

4. SIR HENRY BASKERVILLE

Our clients were punctual to their appointments. The clock was just striking ten and Dr Mortimer was one of them. He was followed by the young baronet, sturdily built, thick black eyebrows and a strong, pugnacious face. He had the weather-beaten appearance of one who spent most of the time in the open air or drowning.

'This is Sir Henry Baskerville,' said Dr Mortimer.

'Pleased to meet you,' said Holmes. 'Do take a seat.'

'No, I'll stand.'

'All right, then stand on a bloody seat. Do I understand you to say that you have had some remarkable experience since you arrived in London?'

'Nothing of much importance, Mr Holmes. Only a joke, as like as not.'

He laid an envelope upon the table. 'It was this letter, which reads, "As you value your life or your reason keep away from the moor." ' It was printed in ink. 'Now,' added Sir Henry, 'you will tell me what in thunder you make of it.'

'I would make sponge pudding out of it.'

'. . . "Do take a seat."
"No, I'll stand."
"All right, then stand on a bloody seat." '

'As far as I can follow, Mr Holmes,' said Sir Henry, 'someone cut out this message with scissors.'

'*The Times* is a paper seldom found in any hands but those of the highly educated. We may take it, therefore, that the letter was composed by an educated man in black wearing a white tie and tails, a cape, silk top hat, patent-leather boots and a thousand pounds in loose change. Did the composer fear an interruption – and from whom? Mrs Doris Stokes.'

'Mrs *Doris Stokes*??!!!'

'Now you would call it a guess, no doubt, but I am certain that this address has been written in an hotel,' said Holmes.

'How in the world can you say that?' asked Sir Henry.

'I just can. I am bloody brilliant. Sir Henry, has anything else of interest happened to you?'

'No, Mr Holmes, I think not. Only the loss of a boot. I don't know much of British life yet, for I have spent nearly all my time in Canada counting moose. But I hope that to lose one of your new brown boots is not part of the ordinary routine of life over here.'

'You have lost one of your boots?'

'My dear sir,' cried Dr Mortimer, 'it is only mislaid. You will find it when you return to the hotel.'

'Perhaps,' said Holmes, 'but this event gives us food for thought, no matter how foolish the incident may seem. Left or right.'

'I don't know until I find it,' said Sir Henry.

'Look, Sir Henry,' said Holmes, 'I'll be willing to wear the odd boot until you find the other one.'

'It seems an unusual thing to steal unless the thief is one-legged,' I observed.

'It may be that they wish for their own purposes to scare me away and they left me with one boot so I couldn't travel to Baskerville Hall.'

'There seems to be danger,' muttered Holmes.

'Do you mean danger from human beings?'

'Are there any other kind? It's something *out there*!' said Holmes, pointing upward. 'Meanwhile I have hardly had time to think over all that you have told me. It's a big thing for a man to decide at one sitting. I should like to have a quiet hour by myself to make up my mind.'

'Suppose you and your friend, Dr Watson, come around and lunch with us at two?' suggested Sir Henry.

'Is that convenient to you, Watson?' enquired Holmes.

'I can't. I have a brain operation at three.'

'Yes? What's wrong with your brain?' asked Holmes.

'It's coming apart.'

'I'll join you and your one boot with pleasure,' said Holmes.

'Then we meet again at two o'clock. Au revoir, and good morning!' Sir Henry waved goodbye, opened the door and walked into a cupboard, came out again and left via the front door with Mortimer in tow.

'Quick, Watson, quick! Not a moment to lose!'

Holmes rushed into his room, collided with a bus, and was back again in a few seconds. We hurried down the stairs together and into the street, where we collided with a bus. Dr Mortimer and Baskerville were still visible about two hundred yards ahead of us.

At that instant I saw a hansom cab with a man inside who got out when it halted on the other side of the street and then walked slowly onward towards Mortimer and Sir Henry.

'There's our man, Watson! Come along! We'll have a good look at him, if we can do no more.'

But the man leapt back into the cab and at that instant I was aware of a bushy black beard and a pair of piercing eyes turned upon us through the side window of the cab. Instantly the trapdoor at the top flew up, something was screamed to the driver, and the cab flew madly off down Regent Street. Holmes looked eagerly round for another, but none were going cheap. Then he dashed in wild pursuit amid the stream of traffic and collided with a bus. But the start was too great and already the cab was out of sight and Holmes was knackered. He had to rest, so he lay down on the pavement and went to sleep.

'Watson, you are an honest man. You will record this also and set it against my successes!'

'Who was the man?'

'I have no idea.'

'Was it a spy?'

'Well, it was evident from what we heard that Baskerville has been very closely shadowed by someone since he has been in town. Whoever it was may have actually stolen the lost boot to stop him travelling anywhere. You may have observed that I twice strolled over to the window.'

'You weren't considering jumping out?'

'As it is, our eagerness was taken advantage of with extraordinary quickness and energy by our opponent. We have betrayed ourselves and lost our opponent.'

'Fuck!'

We had been sauntering slowly down Regent Street during this conversation, and Dr Mortimer, with his companion, had long vanished in front of us.

'There is no object in our following them or we will vanish as well,' observed my companion.

'I could only swear to the beard,' I said.

'In all probability it was a false one. A clever man upon so delicate an errand has no use for a beard save to conceal his teeth. Come in here, Watson!'

We turned into one of the district messenger offices, where he was warmly greeted by the manager.

'Ah, Wilson, I see you have not forgotten the little case in which I had the good fortune to help you?' said Holmes.

'No, sir, indeed I have not. You saved my good name, and perhaps my life.'

'We all make mistakes, son,' said Holmes. 'I have some recollection, Wilson, that you had among your boys a bright lad called Cartwright, who showed some ability during the investigation. Could you ring him up? Thank you. I should be glad to have change of this five-pound note.'

A fourteen-year-old lad with a bright visage, keen face held together with pimples, had obeyed the summons of the manager.

'Let me have the *Hotel Directory*,' said Holmes. 'Now, Cartwright, there are the names of twenty-three hotels here, all in the immediate neighbourhood of Charing Cross. Do you see?'

'Yes, sir.'

'You will visit each of these in turn.'

Twenty-three hotels! Was he mad?!

'You will begin in each case by giving the outside porter one shilling. Here are twenty-three shillings.'

He *is* bloody mad!

'You will tell him that you want to see the wastepaper of yesterday. You will say that an important telegram has miscarried, and that you are looking for it. You understand?'

He ought to be in a straitjacket under supervision!!

'But what you are looking for is the centre page of *The Times* with some holes cut in it with scissors. Here is a copy of *The Times*. It is this page. You can easily recognise it, can you not?'

'Yes.'

'You will then learn in possibly twenty cases out of the twenty-three that the waste of the day before has been burnt or removed. In the three other cases you will be shown a heap of paper, and will look for this page of *The Times* among it. The odds are enormously against your finding it.'

Why did he bother to send the lad?

Thus passed another lunatic idea of Holmes.

5. THREE BROKEN THREADS

Sherlock Holmes had, in a very remarkable degree, the power of detaching his mind at will. He removed it and placed it on the mantelpiece in the lobby of the hotel where we were to meet with Baskerville and Mortimer.

'Have you any objection to my looking at your hotel register?' Holmes asked the porter.

'Not in the least, sir.'

'Sherlock Holmes had, in a very remarkable degree, the power of detaching his mind at will.'

The book showed that two names had been added after that of Baskerville. One was Theophilus Johnson and family of Newcastle; the other Mrs Oldmore and maid, of High Lodge, Alton.

'Surely that must be the same Johnson whom I used to know,' said Holmes to the porter. 'A lawyer, is he not, grey-headed, and walks with a limp?'

'You're wrong, sir. This is Mr Johnson, the coalowner, a very active gentleman, not older than yourself, and does not limp.'

'Surely you are mistaken.'

'Wrong, sir. He has used this hotel for many years, and he is very well known to me.'

'Mrs Oldmore, too; I seem to remember the name – a very keen horsewoman and showjumper.'

'She is an invalid lady, sir, and never goes anywhere.'

So much for the brilliance of Mr Sherlock Holmes's identification ability.

'What's the matter, Holmes?' I asked.

'No stranger has checked in after Mortimer and Baskerville, said Holmes. 'Whoever is stalking them is not in residence here.'

As we came round the top of the stairs we ran up against Sir Henry Baskerville himself. His body and face were flushed with anger as were several of his fingers.

'It seems to me they are playing me for a sucker in this hotel,' he cried. 'If that chap can't find my black boot I will shoot a policeman.'

'But surely, you said that it was a new brown boot?' said Holmes.

'So it was, sir. And now it's a new black one.'

'Do make up your mind – black or brown?'

'When they stole my brown one, I bought a black pair; now that is missing.'

'Look,' said Holmes, 'I am only too proud to wear your brown and now your black one until they are found.'

An agitated German waiter had appeared on the scene.

'You German *Schweinhund*!' said Holmes. 'You and your nation are preparing for World War One – now get out and do it. Well, either that boot comes back before sundown, or I'll alert the Grenadier Guards.'

'It shall be found, sir – I promise you that,' he said, doing a Nazi salute and goosestepping out the door as Dr Mortimer arrived.

Holmes asked Baskerville what his intentions were.

'To go to Baskerville Hall.'

'On the whole,' said Holmes, 'I think that your decision is a wise one. Did you know that you were followed this morning from my house?'

Dr Mortimer started violently. 'Followed! By whom?'

'That, unfortunately, is what I cannot tell you.'

'Oh fuck!' said Mortimer.

'Have you among your neighbours or acquaintances on Dartmoor any man with a black, full beard?'

'Why, yes. Barrymore, Sir Charles's butler, is a man with a full, black beard.'

'Ha! Where is this Barrymore?'

'Ha! He is in charge of the building. He is charged with not letting it fall down.'

'We had best ascertain if he is really there. Give me a telegraph form. We can write "Is all ready for Sir Henry?", address it to Mr Barrymore, Baskerville Hall, and we will say, "Are you there?" '

The devilish cunning of Sherlock Holmes never ceased to amaze me.

'Now, Dr Mortimer,' said Holmes. 'Tell me all you know of this Barrymore.'

'So far as I know, he and his wife are as respectable a couple as any in the country.'

'Did Barrymore profit at all by Sir Charles's will?' asked Holmes.

'I hope,' said the boor Dr Mortimer, 'that you do not look with suspicious eyes upon everyone who received a legacy from Sir Charles, for I also had a thousand pounds left to me.'

'There were many insignificant sums to individuals and a large number of public charities. He left ten thousand pounds to the Berlin Philharmonic Orchestra.'

'Indeed! While he was blowing it all, how much did he leave?'

'A great deal. There were many insignificant sums to individuals and a large number of public charities. He left ten thousand pounds to the Berlin Philharmonic Orchestra.'

'And how much was the residue?'

'Seven hundred and forty thousand pounds.'

Holmes raised his eyebrows and went green with envy. 'I had no idea that so gigantic a sum was involved,' said he.

'Sir Charles had the reputation of being rich. The total value of the estate was close on to a million.'

'Dear me! It is a stake for which a man might play a desperate game, like Arsenal versus Spurs. Supposing that anything happened to our young friend here, who would inherit the estate?'

'The widows of the Arsenal and Spurs football match. There are distant cousins, so distant you can hardly see them. James Desmond is an elderly clergyman in Westmorland. He came to visit Sir Charles. He is a man of venerable appearance and of saintly life. I remember that he refused to accept any settlement from Sir Charles, though he pressed and pressed him until he was much thinner and finally grabbed the money and ran from the room screaming "RICH, RICH, RICH".'

'Quite so. Well, Sir Henry, I am of one mind with you as to the advisability of your going without delay. There is only one provision which I must make. You certainly must not go alone.'

'Dr Mortimer returns with me.'

'No, Sir Henry, you must take with you someone, a trusty man, who will always be by your side.'

'Is it possible you come yourself, Mr Holmes?'

'No, I will stay behind and wear your boots. You can buy a new pair. It will be my honour to wear your old ones.'

'Whom would you recommend then?'

Holmes laid his hand upon my arm. 'If my friend would undertake it there is no man who is better worth having at your side when you are in a tight place.'

'Well, now, that is real kind of you, Dr Watson,' said Sir Henry. 'Then on Saturday, unless you hear to the contrary, we shall meet at the ten-thirty train from Paddington. Would that suit Dr Watson?'

We had risen to depart when Baskerville gave a cry of triumph, and diving into one of the corners of the room he drew a brown boot from under a cabinet. 'What a pity,' he said, 'I threw the other one away. You can still wear one black one and one brown one.'

'Look,' said Holmes, 'I am willing to wear the remaining odd boots until you buy another pair. It is not often I am honoured by being allowed to wear any of the Knights of the Realm's boots.'

The German was sent for and the very appearance of him enraged Sherlock Holmes.

'You *Schweinhund mit Krieg kommen Sie mir! Dummkopf!* Herr Fritz, I accuse you of spying for and working for the German Government and hiding Allied boots to prevent them from marching to war. *Schweinhund* and fuck the Kaiser.'

The German gave the Nazi salute.

Just before dinner two telegrams were handed in. The first ran:

HAVE JUST HEARD THAT BARRYMORE IS AT THE HALL.
 BASKERVILLE.

The second one:

YOU BASTARD, HOLMES, WHY DID YOU SEND ME ON A WILD-GOOSE CHASE.
CARTWRIGHT.

'That's funny,' said Holmes. 'I don't remember sending him on a wild-goose chase. I wonder if he caught any?'

We have still traced the cabman who drove the spy,' I reminded him. Holmes decided to question the cabman immediately.

'First of all your name and address, in case I want you again.'

'James Clayton.'

'I will make a note of it.'

'I don't care if you make a Dundee cake out of it.'

'And now, Clayton, before I make a Dundee cake, tell me about the fare who came and watched this house at ten o'clock this morning.'

'The truth is that the gentleman told me that he was a detective and that I was to say nothing about him to anyone.'

'Did this detective mention his name?'

'He said his name was Sherlock Holmes.'

Holmes burst into a hearty laugh. 'For all I know I might be Florence Nightingale. How would you describe Sherlock Holmes?'

'He wore a beard which completely concealed his teeth.'

'Nothing more you can remember?'

'Oh yes, I remember it's my wife's birthday.'

'Well, then, here is your half-sovereign.'

John Clayton departed downstairs chuckling, and Holmes turned to me with a shrug of the shoulders and a rueful smile.

'Bloody working class,' said Holmes and spat out of the window in time for it to alight on Clayton's head.

'I am sending you on an ugly business, Watson, ugly, dangerous and the more I see of it the less I like it. God knows what horrors await you.'

Quack! Quack!

'Stop that duck!'

6. BASKERVILLE HALL

Mr Sherlock Holmes drove me to the station – he didn't have a carriage; he had a whip.

'You can leave me to give orders,' he said.

'What orders? would it not be well in the first place to get rid of this Barrymore couple?' I suggested.

'By no means. It would be a cruel injustice. No, no, we will preserve them upon our list of suspects. Then there is a groom at the Hall, if I remember right. There are two moorland farmers. There is our friend Dr Mortimer, whom I believe to be entirely honest, and there is his wife, of whom we

'Mr Sherlock Holmes drove me to the station – he didn't have a carriage;
he had a whip.'

know nothing. There is a naturalist Stapleton and his sister. These are the folk who must be your very special study.'

'I will do my best, Holmes.'

'But we can't afford failure, Watson. You have arms, I suppose?'

'Yes, and legs.'

'Keep your revolver near you night and day and never relax your precautions. And, if anybody attacks you, escape by shooting yourself and make a getaway.'

'Take one of them every night with water.' I handed him an illegible prescription.

Our friends had already secured a first-class carriage and were waiting for the train to be late.

'We have no news of any kind,' said Dr Mortimer.

Good God, he was still with us!

'We have never gone out without keeping a sharp watch, and no one could have escaped my notice,' said Dr Mortimer.

'You have always kept together, I presume?'

'Yes, I always kept together and so did Sir Henry. He kept together.'

'Dr Mortimer,' I said, 'avoid the moor in those hours of darkness when the powers of evil are exalted.'

'What a lot of balls,' said Sir Henry.

I looked back at the platform when we had left it far behind, and saw the tall, austere figure of Holmes standing motionless, gazing after us wearing one brown boot and one black and that absurd deerstalker hat.

The journey was a swift and pleasant one. I spent it playing with Dr Mortimer's spaniel. The little bastard bit me so I kicked his arse. Baskerville stared eagerly out of the window and cried aloud with delight as he recognised the familiar features of the Devon scenery.

'It is all as new to me as it is to Dr Watson and I'm as keen as possible to see the moor,' said Sir Henry.

'Oh are you? Then your wish is easily granted, for there is your first sight of the moor,' said Dr Mortimer, pointing out of the carriage window.

'Oh,' said Sir Henry, 'is that all it does?'

'The journey was a swift and pleasant one. I spent it playing with Dr Mortimer's spaniel.'

Baskerville sat for a long time. It was his first sight of this beautiful spot, which was about six inches in circumference. He sat there wearing one brown boot and one black one.

The train pulled up at a small wayside station and we all fell out. A wagonette with a pair of cobs was waiting. Percival was the driver. Our coming was evidently a great event.

'Three cheers for Sir Henry: hip, hip, hooray!' said the station master, and waved a green flag and blew a whistle for us. Unfortunately the driver didn't know it was a welcome whistle so the train started up and left the station.

It was a sweet, simple country spot. I was surprised to observe that by the gate there stood two soldierly men in dark uniforms who leant upon their short rifles. There was a convict at large on the moor. A few minutes and we were flying swiftly down the broad white road. Rolling pasture lands curved upward on either side of us.

'Halloa,' cried Dr Mortimer.. 'What is this?'

'This is England,' I said. 'I thought you knew.'

On a summit was a mounted soldier, his rifle poised over his forearm.. He was watching the road along which we travelled.

'What is this, Percival?' asked Dr Mortimer.

There's a convict escaped from Princetown, sir,' said Percival. 'He's been out three days now, and the warders watch every road and every station, but they have had no sight of him. You see, he isn't like an ordinary convict.'

'What does an ordinary convict look like?'

'Oh, very ordinary. It is Selden, the Notting Hill murderer.'

'Oh, we must tell the villagers to watch out for a man called Selden, the Notting Hill murderer, and to stay awake with a pistol by your side. If he attacks, shoot yourself and your family before he can hurt you.'

Somewhere on that desolate plain was lurking this fiendish man, the Notting Hill murderer, hiding in a burrow like a wild beast. As if we didn't have enough trouble with this phantom hound.

'Baskerville Hall,' said Percival.

When we arrived, Sir Henry stepped down wearing odd boots. He was looking at the alterations made by his late ancestors and the improvements consisted of a Japanese golf course, a supermarket and a bingo hall, all with flashing lights. It cheered Sir Henry's Canadian soul to see the illuminations. He walked into a low branch, rendering himself unconscious.

'Welcome to Baskerville Hall, Sir Henry,' said a servant.

'You're bloody welcome to it too!' said the semiconscious Sir Henry.

'Welcome, Sir Henry! Welcome to Baskerville Hall.'

A tall man had stepped from the shadow of the porch to open the door of the wagonette. It was Barrymore. A woman came out and helped the man to hand down our bags.

'He walked into a low branch, rendering himself unconscious.'

'You don't mind my driving straight home, Sir Henry?' said Dr Mortimer.

'My man, you would drive anybody home,' replied Sir Henry.

'My visiting fee is five pounds,' said the good doctor as a helpful reminder.

Sir Henry went to an early fridge. He opened it and took out a tin of 1889 lager and swallowed and immediately threw up.

'It's just as I imagined it,' said Sir Henry. 'Bloody awful. To think that this should be the very same hall in which for five hundred years my people have lived!'

Barrymore had returned from taking our luggage to our rooms. He stood in front of us now with the subdued manner of a well-trained servant. He was a remarkable-looking man, tall, handsome, with a square black beard and pale distinguished features. He looked as if he would die any moment.

'Would you wish dinner to be served at once, sir?'

'Is it ready?'

'Yes, are you? My wife and I will be happy to stay with you until you have made fresh arrangements, but you will understand that under the new conditions this house will require a considerable staff.'

'What are the new conditions?'

'We want more money.'

'Do you mean your wife and you wish to leave?'

I seemed to discern some signs of emotion on the butler's white face.

'I hope, sir, that you discern the signs of emotion on my white face. I feel very bad about this, sir, and so does my wife. I fear that we shall never again be easy in our minds at Baskerville Hall.'

'Then what do you intend to do?'

'Bugger off, sir. Have no doubt, sir, that we shall succeed in establishing ourselves in some business. Sir Charles's generosity has given us the means to do so. And now, sir, perhaps I should best show you to your freezing bloody rooms.'

Sir Henry kept walking into the wall. 'Isn't there a bloody light or a door along here somewhere?'

'Yes, you're leaning against it now.' Which he did, and forthwith catapulted into the room.

'My word, it isn't a very inviting or warm place,' said Sir Henry.

'Well, sir, you could set fire to it.'

'I don't wonder that my uncle got a little jumpy here.'

'Yes, he would jump all around the room until he was tired, then he would lie down, then would do some more jumping. He tried to enter for the Olympics but was too tired.'

We retired to our rooms late that evening. Suddenly, in the very dead of the night, there came a sound to my ears, clear, resonant and unmistakable. It was the sob of a woman, the muffled, strangled gasp of one who is torn with uncontrolled sorrow. What was he doing to her?

7. THE STAPLETONS OF MERRIPIT HOUSE

The morning did something to calm all our minds. As I sat at breakfast the sunlight flooded in through the high mullioned windows. That woman crying in the night had given me the shits.

'Did you hear a woman sobbing in the night?' I asked.

'Yes, I did. I waited quite a time but there was no more of it so I presumed he had stopped doing it to her,' replied Sir Henry.

'I heard it distinctly, and I am sure that it was really the sob of a woman.'

Sir Henry asked Barrymore whether he could account for our experience. It seemed to me that the pallid features of the butler turned a shade paler still as he listened to his master's question.

'There are only two women in the house, Sir Henry,' he answered. 'One is the scullery maid, who sleeps in the other wing. The other is my wife, and I can answer for it that the sound could not have come from her.'

I met Mrs Barrymore in the long corridor with the sun full upon her face. She was a large, impassive, heavy-featured woman with a stern, set

Dr Watson enjoys the warmest affections of the Barrymores.

expression of mouth. But her telltale eyes were red and glanced at me from between swollen lids. It was she, then, who wept in the night. What had he been doing, the swine? Why had she wept so bitterly? Was the swine using a feather duster on her.

I decided to make enquiries at the local Post Office to establish whether Barrymore had been at the hall to receive the telegram Holmes had composed.

'Certainly, sir,' said the postmaster, 'I had the telegram delivered to Mr Barrymore exactly as directed.'

'Who delivered it?'

'My boy here. James, you delivered that telegram to Mr Barrymore at the Hall last week, did you not?'

'Yes, Father, I delivered it.'

'Into his own hands?' I asked.

'Well, he was up in the loft at the time, so that I could not put it into his own hands, but I gave it into Mrs Barrymore's hands.'

'Did you see Mr Barrymore?' I asked.

'No, sir; I told you he was in the loft.'

'If you didn't see him, how do you know he was in the loft?'

'Well, surely his own wife ought to know where he is,' said the postmaster testily. 'If there is any mistake it is for Mr Barrymore himself to complain.'

The conclusion was that Barrymore was working on a new appliance to use on his helpless wife.

Suddenly my thoughts were interrupted by the sound of running feet behind me and a voice called my name. To my surprise, it was a stranger who was pursuing me. He was a small, slim, clean-shaven, prim-faced man, flaxen-haired and lean-jawed, between thirty and forty years of age, dressed in a grey suit and wearing a straw hat. A tin box for botanical specimens hung over his shoulder and he carried a green butterfly net.

'You will, I am sure, excuse my presumption, Dr Watson,' said he. 'You may possibly have heard my name from our mutual friend, Dr Mortimer. I am Stapleton, of Merripit House.'

'How did you know me?'

'I have been calling on Mortimer, and he pointed you out to me from the window of his surgery as you passed. We were all rather afraid that after the sad death of Sir Charles the new baronet might refuse to live here. It is asking much of a wealthy man to come down and bury himself.'

'Oh, he doesn't intend to bury himself. He intends to go on living above ground.'

'Of course, you know the legend of the fiend dog which haunts the family? I may be of some help to you in this strange matter.'

'You think, then, that some dog pursued Sir Charles, and that he died of fright in consequence?'

'Have you any better explanation?' asked he.

'Yes, an elephant fell on him.'

'And how about Mr Sherlock Holmes?'

'He brilliantly does not know. I assure you that I am simply here to visit my friend, Sir Henry, and I need no help of any kind. Now piss off!'

'You are perfectly right to be wary and discreet and I promise you that I will not mention the matter again.'

We came to a steep, boulder-sprinkled hill which had in bygone days been cut into a granite quarry. The face turned towards us on the dark cliff, with ferns and brambles growing in its niches. From over a distant rise there floated a grey plume of smoke. It was a perfect mantrap; it trapped me. I couldn't find my way out until dawn.

As Holmes had expressly said I should study the neighbours upon the moor, I accepted Stapleton's invitation to his home.

'It is a wonderful place, the moor,' he said, looking around in terror. 'A false step means death to man or beast. Only yesterday I saw one of the moor ponies wander into it. He never came out. I saw his head for quite a long time craning out of the boghole, but it sucked him down at last. The same thing happened to our postman. It sucked him down. The milkman was another victim. Before he was sucked down he said, "Play for me," so I played for him but he still got sucked down.

'The Mire has him,' Stapleton continued. 'Two in two days, and many more, perhaps, for they get in the way of going there in the dry weather and never know the difference until the Mire has them in its clutch. It's a bad place, the Great Grimpen Mire.'

'You say you can penetrate it?'

'Yes, with a thermos of tea and a packet of sandwiches. There are one or two paths which a very active man can take. I have found them out.'

'But why should you wish to go into so horrible a place?'

'Well, mainly for the tea and sandwiches. It's where the rare plants and the butterflies are if you want to reach them.'

'I'll try it one day.'

'For God's sake, put such an idea out of your mind,' said he. 'Your blood would be upon my head.'

'Oh? How would it get up there? Halloa,' I cried. 'What is that?'

A long, low moan, indescribably sad, swept over the moor. It filled the whole air, and yet it was impossible to say whence it came. From a dull murmur it swelled into a deep roar and then sank back again into a melancholy, throbbing murmur once more.

'Queer place, the moor!' said he. 'Queers haunt it day and night. The peasants say it is the queer Hound of Baskerville calling for its prey.'

'You're an educated man. You don't believe such nonsense as that?' said I. 'What do you think is the cause of so strange a sound?'

Quack! Quack!

'Why have you brought a duck?' Stapleton asked.

'For company,' I replied.

'Bogs make queer noises sometimes,' said Stapleton. 'Yes, I've used a few. No, no, that was a living voice.'

'Look at the mounds on the hillside yonder. What do you make of those?'

'I would use them as night soil,' I said.

'No, they are the homes of our worthy ancestors. Neolithic man, no date.'

'What did they do?'

'They grazed cattle on the slopes, they grew potatoes and killed each other so they soon ran out of people.'

A small butterfly crossed his path and in an instant Stapleton was rushing with extraordinary energy and speed in pursuit of it. To my delight the creature flew straight for the great Mire. If only it would suck him down.

A woman approached me and was certainly that, and of a most

'A small butterfly crossed his path and in an instant Stapleton was rushing with extraordinary energy and speed in pursuit of it.'

uncommon type. There could not have been a greater contrast between brother and sister. Stapleton was neutral-tinted, with light hair and grey eyes, while she was darker than any brunette whom I have seen in England – slim, elegant, and tall.

'Go back!' she said. 'Go straight back to London instantly.'

'Go back?' I said. 'I've only just got here. Why should I go back?'

'For heaven's sake, do what I ask you and never set foot upon the moor again.'

'Don't set foot on it? How are we going to get about?'

Stapleton had abandoned the chase, and came back to us breathing hard.

'You have introduced yourselves, I can see.'

'Yes,' said she. 'I was telling Sir Henry that it was rather late for him to see the true beauties of the moor.'

'Why, who do you imagine this is?'

'I imagine that it must be Sir Henry Baskerville.'

'No, no,' I informed her. 'I am only a humble commoner, but his friend. My name is Dr Watson.'

'Oh, I'll wash my hands.'

We went to Merripit House. Inside there were large rooms furnished with an elegance in which I seemed to recognise the taste of a lady. I broke a piece off and tasted it – it tasted of a lady.

'Queer spot to choose, is it not?' said he, pointing to a queer spot on the ground. 'I find an unlimited field of work here, and my sister is as devoted to Nature as I am. Every morning you see her dancing naked on the lawn.'

'It certainly did cross my mind that it might be a little dull – less for you, perhaps, than for your sister, which explains her Doric postural dancing.'

'No, no, I am never dull,' she said quickly. 'We have books, we have our studies, we have interesting neighbours, and we have fish and chips with Worcestershire sauce and McDonald's with milkshakes. Do you think that I should intrude if I were to call this afternoon and make the acquaintance of Sir Henry?'

'I am sure that he would be delighted.'

'I could show him my materials, miniature heads of Tutankhamen.'

'Oh yes, of course.'

But I was eager to get back to my charge. The melancholy of the moor, the death of the unfortunate pony, the postman, the milkman and the weird sound which had been associated with the grim legend of the Baskervilles and the queers on the moors – all these things tinged my thoughts with sadness.

On my way back I reached the road and was astounded to see Miss Stapleton sitting upon a rock by the side of a track. Her face was beautifully flushed with excitement and cheap scent.

'I have run all the way in order to cut you off, Dr Watson. I must not stop, or my brother may miss me. I wanted to say to you how sorry I am about the stupid mistake I made in thinking that you were Sir Henry. Please forget the words I said, which have no application whatever to you.'

'But I can't forget, Miss Stapleton. I am Sir Henry's friend and his welfare is a close concern of mine. Why were you so eager that Sir Henry should return to London?'

'A woman's whim, Dr Watson. When you know me better you will understand that I cannot always give reasons for what I say or do. I dance naked every morning on the grass with no reason but that I must. I felt I should warn him of the danger which he will run.'

'What is the danger?'

'You know the story of the hound?'

'I do not believe in such nonsense. Some people say it is the queer Hound of the Baskervilles. The world is wide, Miss Stapleton. In some places it is twelve feet by thirty feet.'

'I cannot say anything definite,' she said, 'for I do not know anything definite.'

The Grimpen Mire held many gruesome secrets, including the whereabouts of an unfortunate moor pony, the local postman and a wayward milkman.

She turned and disappeared in a few minutes among the scattered boulders, divesting herself of her clothes as she went.

Quack! Quack! Stop that duck!

8. FIRST REPORT OF DR WATSON

My Dear Holmes,

My previous letters have kept you pretty well up to date as to all that has occurred in this most godforsaken corner of the world but this is my first full report.

We are four able-bodied men in this household and we could take good care of ourselves. I sleep with a pistol under my pillow and every morning when I wake up it's still there. It is not to be wondered that time hangs heavy in this lonely spot. We hang it from a beam and it keeps good time.

Stapleton gives the idea of hidden fires. As yet we can't find where he hides them. He has the strange habit of drinking a glass of Horlicks before retiring.

He came over to call upon Baskerville and took us both to see the spot where the legend of the wicked Hugo, the shit, was supposed to have its origin. He pointed to a spot in the carpet.

'That's it,' he said. 'That's the spot where the wicked Hugo, the shit, was supposed to have its origin.'

We found a short valley between rugged High Tors. High Tor, I tort I saw a puddy tat but when I got there there was none. He really did believe in interference of the supernatural in the affairs of men. I told him I had never had an affair with men. He told us cases where families had suffered some evil influence — they all exploded and were never seen again. We asked him if he could tell us where they went. They went to bits.

From the moment Sir Henry saw Miss Stapleton he appeared to be strongly attracted, putting a great strain on his trousers. Such a match would be very welcome to Stapleton, yet I more than once caught a look of the strongest disapprobation on his face. As Sir Henry said more than once, when paying close attention to his sister, Stapleton had the look of strongest disapprobation on his face.

I cannot help but think of the old man, Sir Charles, as he stood there and saw something coming across the moor, something which terrified him so much that he lost his wits. There was a long, gloomy tunnel down which he fled and from what? Eh? A sheep dog of the moor? Eh? A spectral wild hound? Eh? A Notting Hill murderer? Eh? People said it was an Eric. An Eric? Eh?

One other neighbour I have met since I wrote last. This is Mr Frankland, of Lafter Hall. His passion is for the law, and he has spent a large fortune in litigation. He fights for the mere pleasure of fighting, especially against people of the parish. Sometimes he will shut up a right of way and defy the parish to make him open it.

And now, having brought you up to date in the escaped convict, the Stapletons, Dr Mortimer and Frankland of Lafter Hall, the homosexual hound and Erics, let me tell you more about the Barrymores, and especially about the surprising developments of last night.

You are aware that I am not a very sound sleeper. Last night, about two in the morning, I was aroused by creaking footsteps. I opened my door. A long black shadow was trailing down the corridor. It was thrown by a man who walked softly down the passage with a candle in his hand. By piecing together his footsteps I realised he was doing the rhumba. He was in shirt and trousers, with no covering to his feet. It was Barrymore.

Barrymore crouched at the window with a candle held against the glass. His profile was half turned towards me, and his face seemed to be rigid with expectation as he stared out into the blackness of the moor. For some

'. . . she put me on Coca-Cola. I'm on that three times a day.'

minutes he stood watching intently. Then he gave a deep groan, and with an impatient gesture he put out the light. Instantly, I made my way back to my room.

9. THE LIGHT UPON THE MOOR

I asked Barrymore what he was on.
   'Guinness and Newcastle Brown. I mainline it straight into the vein.'
   'Can't you kick it?'
   'No. I need a fix three times a day.'
   'What does it do for you?'
   'It gets me pissed.'
   'Have you been to a psychiatrist?'
   'Yes, she put me on Coca-Cola. I'm on that three times a day.'
   Before breakfast on the morning following my adventure I went down the corridor and examined the room in which Barrymore had been the

night before. I stood in the same place he had. The trouble is he was still standing there. It was all more than a little embarrassing.

I had an interview with Sir Henry in his study after breakfast and he was less surprised than I expected.

'I see you are less surprised than I expected,' I said.

'I knew that Barrymore walked about nights, and I had in mind to speak to him about it,' said he. 'I will do it together and you do it together. Two or three times I have heard his steps in the passage coming and going.'

'I am certain it was the rhumba,' I said.

'We must take our chance. What was his object with the rhumba?'

'Perhaps he pays a visit every night to that particular window,' I suggested.

Sir Henry rubbed his hands with pleasure and hand cream.

Sir Henry had been in communication with the architect who prepared the plans for Sir Charles, and with a contractor from London, and planned that great changes should begin soon. There had been decorators and furnishers up from Plymouth who painted Sir Henry green when the house was being renovated and refinished.

After our conversation Sir Henry put on his hat and prepared to go on the moor.

'What, are *you* coming, Watson?' he asked, looking at me in a curious way, that is, using his head back to front.

'It all depends whether you are going on the moor,' said I.

'Well, I am,' he said. 'I have to: the WC is broken so we have to use the moor.'

'Well, you know what my instructions are. I am sorry to intrude but you heard Holmes insist that I should not leave you here, and especially that you should not go on the moor.'

'But I have to. I am telling you that the WC is broken.' Sir Henry put his hand on my shoulder with a smile. 'I am to meet Miss Stapleton on the moor.'

Our friend, Sir Henry, and the lady had halted on the path, and were standing deeply absorbed in their conversation when a wisp of green floating in the air caught my eye and another glance showed me that it was carried on a stick by a man who was moving along the broken ground. It was Stapleton with his butterfly net. He was very much closer to the pair than I was, and he appeared to be moving in their direction. At that moment I fell off the rock into a bog and I came up dripping with ooze and smelling like disinfectant. Stapleton put the net over my head and I said there must be some mistake: I was not a specimen.

At that instant Sir Henry suddenly drew Miss Stapleton to his side. His arm was round her but it seemed to me that she was straining away from him with her face averted. I watched from a distance as Stapleton tried to catch her in his butterfly net but she kept ducking behind Sir Henry. Sir Henry dodged as Stapleton lunged towards them, his net thrust out in front of him. He gesticulated and almost danced. He put his net over his sister's head and took her away.

'Hello, Watson,' said Baskerville. 'Where have you dropped from? Good God, you smell of shit!'

'It will wash off,' I said.

Quack! Quack! Stop that duck will you!

'You don't mean to say that you came after me in spite of all? You would have thought the middle of that prairie a fairly safe place for a man to be private,' said he, 'but by thunder, the whole countryside seems to be out to see me do my wooing! Where had you engaged a seat?'

'I was on that hill clinging to a boulder.'

'Of course you were.'

'That fool put the net over my head and I said there must be some mistake: I am not a specimen.'

'Tell me straight now, Watson, is there anything that would prevent me from making a good husband to a woman that I loved? Her brother seems a lunatic. Is he of sound mind?'

'Yes, you can hear him a mile away.'

'Yes,' he said, 'he would not have me as much as touch the tips of her fingers. Listen, there's a light in a woman's eyes that speaks louder than words. In fact, I had to use ear plugs but he has never let us get together. She has never been together and I have never been together. She would not speak of love so I spoke to her of the bubonic plague in Rajputa. If he had not been her brother I would have known better how to answer him, the cunt. Just tell me what it all means, Watson. I'll owe you more than ever I can hope to pay.'

'No, sir, I am quite satisfied with a hundred guineas per day retainer.'

'I can't forget the look in his eyes when he ran at me this morning, but I must allow that no man could make a more handsome apology than he has done.'

'Did he give any explanation of his conduct?'

'Yes, he said he had piles and they were playing him up. I told him his arsehole has nothing to do with me. You do not use piles as an apology – it is a condition.

'He said he was a lonely man with only her as a companion, so the thought of losing her was really terrible to him. Surely if he lost her he could look for her. He was very sorry for all that had passed. He himself was past fifty.'

I sat up with Sir Henry until three o'clock in the morning. One struck, and then two. We heard the creak of a step in the passage – strike three. We walked into the room and as we did Barrymore sprang up from the window with a sharp hiss of his breath, and stood, livid and trembling, before us.

'What are you doing here, Barrymore?' demanded Sir Henry.

'I was doing the rhumba, sir.'

'Come, come, that's not the rhumba; that's the carioca.'

'I swear, sir, I am doing nothing.'

'Rubbish! No one can do nothing.'

'Yes, you can, sir. You close your eyes, lie quite still and you stop breathing.'

A sudden idea occurred to me and I took the candle from the windowsill, where the butler had placed it.

'He must have been holding it as a signal,' said I. 'Let us see if there is any answer.'

I held the candle to my ear – there was no sound. Then I gave a cry of exultation, for a tiny pinpoint of yellow light had suddenly transfixed the dark veil, and glowed steadily in the centre of the black square framed by the window.

'There it is!' I cried.

'Move your light across the window, Watson!' cried the baronet. 'See, the other moves also! Now, you rascal, do you deny that it is a signal? Come, speak up! Who is your confederate out yonder and what is this conspiracy that is going on?'

The man's face became openly defiant. 'It is my business, and not yours. I will not tell.'

'Then you will leave my employment right away.'

'Then that will be a little case of seven hundred and fifty quid back pay.'

'Right, there's one pound in advance,' said Sir Henry, the mean bugger.

'No, no, sir; no, not against you!'

It was a woman's voice, and Mrs Barrymore, white as paper and more horror-struck than her husband, was standing by the door. Her bulky figure in a shawl and skirt might have been comic were it not for the intensity of feeling upon her face.

'Oh, John, John, have I brought you to this? It is my doing, Sir Henry – my doing!'

'What about your doings?'

'My unhappy brother is starving on the moor. We cannot let him perish at our very gates.'

'Why not? It's as good a place as any.'

'The light is a signal to him that the food is ready for him, and his light out yonder is to show the spot to which to bring it.'

'Then your brother is . . .'

'Yes, the escaped convict, sir, Selden, the Notting Hill murderer.'

'That's the truth, sir,' said Barrymore. 'I said that it was not my secret, and that I could not tell it to you. But now you have heard it, and you will see that if there was a plot it was not against you.'

'So your brother is Selden, the Notting Hill murderer?'

'Yes, sir, my name was Selden, and he is my younger brother. We humoured him when he was a lad and gave him his own way in everything, until he came to think that the world was made for his pleasure and that he could do what he liked in it. Then he met wicked companions, and the devil entered into him, until he broke my mother's heart and dragged our name in the dirt. From crime to crime he sank lower and lower until he nearly disappeared. We took him in and fed him and cared for him. Then you returned, sir, and my brother felt he would be safer on the moor than in prison, or the police, or hanging.'

The woman's words came with an intense earnestness which carried conviction.

'Is this true, Barrymore?' asked Sir Henry.

'Yes, sir, every word of it.'

'Well, I cannot blame you for standing by your wife and candle and accept a rise in wages of sixpence.' (Mean swine.)

When they were gone the cold wind blew in and nearly froze our balls off. Far away in the black distance there still glowed that one tiny point of yellow light.

'It may be so placed as to be only visible from here, said I.'

'Very likely. How far do you think it is?'

'It's out by the High Tor, I tort I saw a puddy tat. I will come,' said I.

'Then get your revolver and put on your boots. The sooner we start the better, as the fellow may put out his light and be off.'

'Are you armed?' I asked.

'I have a hunting crop and a mincer.'

'Good! We must close in on him rapidly for he is said to be a desperate fellow. We must take him by surprise, kill him and then mince him.'

Suddenly out of the vast gloom of the moor came that strange cry which I had heard upon the borders of the Great Grimpen Mire. It came with the wind through the silence of the night, a long, deep mutter, then a rising howl, and then the sad moan in which it died away. Again and again it sounded, the whole air throbbing with it, a strident, wild and menacing sound. The baronet caught me by the sleeve.

'Good heavens, what's that, Watson?'

'That's my sleeve,' I said. 'The villagers call it an Eric.'

'Eric?'

'Yes, the homosexual Hound of the Baskervilles is called an Eric – Eric of the Baskervilles.'

'Tell me, Watson, what do you say it is?'

'They say it is a cry of the queer Hound of the Baskervilles who roamed the moor. The hound was called Eric.'

'A supernatural hound it was,' he said at last, 'but it seemed to come from miles away over yonder. I think it needs a vet.'

'It's hard to say from whence it came.'

' "Are you armed?" I asked. "I have a hunting crop and a mincer." '

'No, it isn't; it's quite easy. It rose and fell with the wind. Isn't that the direction of the Great Grimpen Mire?'

'Well, it was up there yesterday,' he replied.

'Come now, Watson, didn't you think yourself that it was the cry of a queer ghostly hound or an Eric?'

'No, no, it was a flesh-and-blood hound; it wasn't a queer hound nor an Eric,' I argued.

'You don't believe it, do you Watson? It was one thing to laugh about in London but it's another to stand in the darkness of the moor and hear such a cry as that. That sound seemed to freeze my very blood. Feel my hand!'

It was as cold as a block of marble.

'Ah, you need a hot bath,' I advised.

'No, we are after a convict and a queer ghostly hound and an Eric. If we shoot him we'll mince him.'

We set out onto the dark and desolate moor. It was strange to see this single candle burning there in the middle of the moor with no sign of life near it – just one straight yellow flame and the gleam of the rock on each side of it.

Over the rocks where the candle burnt was thrust an evil yellow face, a terrible animal face; it looked like Frank Bruno's face upside down, all seamed and scored with vile passions.

'It's an Eric,' I screamed.

We followed him forward, sideways and backward shouting, 'Out of my way, I am holding a pistol and a flask of brandy. The choice is yours. Stop or I will drain this brandy.'

The light reflected his small cunning eyes, which appeared like those of a crafty and savage animal who had heard the steps of hunters.

'Stop! It's nearly Christmas,' I cried.

Our man was running at great speed in the direction of away. I didn't want to shoot an unarmed man who was running away for Christmas. That's what I'll tell the police. Was he an Eric?

We ran and ran until we were completely blown, and the space between us grew even wider. Finally we stopped and sat panting on two rocks, while we watched him disappear in the distance. As we did he turned and watched us disappear in the distance.

I wished to go in that direction to search the High Tor where I tort I saw a puddy tat but it was useless: the puddy tat had also run away for Christmas.

10. EXTRACT FROM THE DIARY OF DR WATSON

Sir Henry was obsessed with impending danger. I felt myself and I felt an impending danger. I have with my own ears heard the sound which resembled the distant baying of a homosexual hound – or an Eric. A spectral hound which leaves a single footprint – perhaps it was one-legged. Whatever it was, it would be easy to identify with one leg. I, myself, had a three-legged dog. His name was Rover but, alas, when he barked he fell

Neither one leg nor three is the correct amount for a fully equipped dog.

over. In fact, at night I have twice heard the creature crying out upon the moor.

'Shut up,' I said. 'There are people down here trying to sleep.'

I could see on the high Tor, Hi Tor I saw a puddy tat. Was it a cat or was it an Eric or was it a one-legged Eric? A stranger then is still dogging us just as a stranger had dogged us in London. We had never shaken him off. I wouldn't like to shake him off.

Sir Henry's nerve had been badly shaken by the sound of the one-legged Eric on the moor.

We had a small scene that morning after breakfast. Barrymore asked if he could speak with Sir Henry and they were closeted in the billiard room. Sitting outside, I heard them playing a few strokes of snooker and then there seemed to be a row. Then I heard Sir Henry break his cue over Barrymore's head. Barrymore considered he had a grievance.

'I'm a better snooker player than him,' said Barrymore, the blood running down his head.

The butler was standing, very pale but very collected, before us. 'At the same time, I was very much surprised when I heard you two gentlemen come back this morning and learnt that you had been chasing Selden, the Notting Hill murderer,' said he.

'The man is a public danger,' said Baskerville. 'Look at Mr Stapleton's house for example, with no one but himself to defend it. There is no safety for anyone until he is under lock and key by Christmas.'

'Well, sir, he has stopped murdering people. In a few days necessary arrangements will be made and he will be on his way to South America to become a Nazi. For God's sake, don't stop him.'

'But how about the chance of his murdering someone up before he goes?'

'We have provided him a place in the Cambridge Rowing Eleven. It's very hard to commit murder when you're rowing,' said Barrymore.

'All right, then,' said Sir Henry, 'Well, Barrymore –'

'God bless you, sir.' So grateful was he that Barrymore seemed keen to offer us some further information. 'I've never breathed a word about this yet to a mortal man. It's about poor Sir Charles's death.'

Sir Henry and I were both on our feet.

'Do you know how he died?'

'Some say it was an Eric; some say a homosexual hound. That evening he was to meet a woman.'

'To meet a woman! And the woman's name?'

'I can't give you the name, sir, but she was rhesus negative and her initials were L.L.

'Sir Charles had a letter that morning. It was from Coombe Tracey, and it was addressed in a woman's hand. Only a few weeks ago, after his death, my wife was cleaning out Sir Charles's study and she found the ashes of a burnt letter in the back of the grate. But one little slip, the end of a page, hung together. And it ended: "Please, please, as you are a gentleman, burn this letter, and be at the gate by ten o'clock." Beneath it were signed the initials L.L.'

'Have you got that slip?'

'No, sir, it crumbled to bits and the cat ate it.'

'You mean it might injure his reputation?'

'No, sir, he hasn't got one.'

The answer to the initials L.L. came from Dr Mortimer.

'There are a few gypsies and there is Laura Lyons, blood group rhesus negative. She married an artist named Lyons who came sketching on the moor. Her father refused to have anything to do with her because she had married a Jew without his consent, and perhaps for one or two other reasons as well, and the young girl had a pretty bad time.'

'How did she live?'

'Frugally. Her story got about and several people did something to enable her to earn an honest living. Stapleton did, for one, and Sir Charles another. I gave her a trifle myself, and she ate it.'

Mortimer wanted to know the object of our enquiries but I managed to quieten him with an oven-ready chicken.

Before we sought out Laura Lyons, the opportunity presented itself to question Barrymore further. The possibility remained that Selden, the Notting Hill murderer, might have had a hand in Sir Charles' demise.

'Did you see your wife's brother on the night of Sir Charles' death?' I asked.

'No, sir, but the food was gone when next I went that way. I think, sir, he has stopped murdering people.'

'Then he was certainly there?'

'Well, sir, everybody had to be somewhere but it could be, sir, that it was the other man who took it.'

'You know that there is another man, then?' asked Sir Henry.

'Yes, sir; there is another man upon the moor.'

'Have you seen him?'

'Yes, sir. He's a queer fellow. I tell you straight, sir, that I don't like queers on the moor.'

'Now listen, Barrymore, tell me frankly what it is that you don't like.'

'Spinach, sir.'

'But what is it that alarms you?'

'All those noises on the moor at night. There are murderers, homosexual hounds, Erics, puddy tat, queers, and Christmas three weeks away. There is not a man who would cross the moor after sundown if he was paid for it. Selden was holding up people and robbing them of their life's savings.'

'Where did you say he lived?'

'Among the old houses on the hillside – the stone huts where the old folk used to live.'

'Seldon was holding up people and robbing them of their life's savings.'

'And how about his food?'

'Oh, he does McDonald's and chips and he goes to a supermarket.'

'Very good, Barrymore, we may talk further of this some other time. Merry Christmas,' said Sir Henry.

'Christmas is in three months' time, sir.'

'Yes, I don't like to wait until the last minute.'

What passion or hatred can it be that leads a man to a McDonald's and a milkshake? How could he face up to living in a place with packs of Erics about? And who was this mysterious 'other' man most recently seen out upon the moor?

11. THE MAN ON THE TOR

The time when these strange events began to move swiftly towards their terrible conclusion was too swift for me to keep up with. I had established two facts of great importance: that Mrs Lyons, blood group rhesus negative, had written to Sir Charles Baskerville, blood group G, and they made an

'I thought she had fainted but she recovered herself with a supreme effort by doing a backward somersault into the upright position.'

appointment to meet the hour that he met his death. Of course, when she arrived he wasn't there.

When we all sat down to breakfast the next morning, the absence of Sir Charles Baskerville was entirely due to his recent death.

'Shall we have two minutes' silence?' said Sir Henry.

This we did and I whistled the 'Dead March'.

After breakfast we paid a visit to the aforementioned Laura Lyons. My first impression of Mrs Lyons, blood group rhesus negative, was a pleasant smile of welcome.

'I had the pleasure,' said I, 'of knowing your father.' It was a clumsy introduction, and the lady made me feel it, so I felt it. 'Did you correspond with Sir Charles?'

'I certainly wrote to him once or twice to acknowledge his kindness and generosity,' she said,

'Did he know you were blood group rhesus negative? Surely your memory deceives you,' said I. 'I could even quote a passage of your letter.

THE HOUND OF THE BASKERVILLES

It ran, "Please, please, as you are a gentleman, burn this letter, and be at the gate by ten o'clock with your cheque book." '

I thought that she had fainted, but she recovered herself with a supreme effort by doing a backward somersault into the upright position.

'Do you think a woman could go alone at that hour to a bachelor's house? I never got there.'

'Why not?'

'Something intervened to prevent my going.'

'What was that?'

'An elephant fell on me. I tell you, if you heard anything of my unhappy history you know that I made a rash marriage for which I have reason to regret. If it had been rasher, it would have been bacon.'

'Then how is it that you did not go?'

'I keep telling you an elephant fell on me. So I should have met with him the following day had I not seen his death in the paper next morning.'

'He died in a newspaper?'

'Yes, the *Mirror*.'

'What a terrible paper to die in.'

Sir Henry was sitting in the lounge when Barrymore announced, 'Sir Henry, the Berlin Philharmonic have arrived.'

'Well, show them in and tell them to start playing "The Valkyries".'

Mr Frankland, the gentleman who took such great delight in closing down the countryside to members of the general public had also come to call.

'Good day, Dr Watson,' said he.

'Good morning, you miserable bastard,' I said.

'It is a great day for me, sir – one of the red-letter days of my life. I have established a right of way through the centre of old Middleton's park, slap across it, sir, within a hundred yards of his own front door. What do you think of that? Wait a moment, Dr Watson. Do my eyes deceive me, or is there something moving upon that hillside?'

I could distinctly see a small dark dot against the dull green and grey.

'Come, sir, come!' cried Frankland, rushing upstairs. 'You will see with your own eyes and judge for yourself.'

The telescope, a formidable instrument mounted upon a tripod, stood upon the flat leads of the house. Sure enough, a small urchin with a little bundle upon his shoulder toiled slowly up the hill. He looked as though he had bubonic plague. When he reached the crest I saw the ragged, uncouth figure outlined for an instant against the cold blue sky. He looked round him with a furtive and stealthy air. Then he vanished over the hill. I resolved to investigate this mysterious figure at my earliest opportunity.

The sun was sinking when I reached the summit of High Tor. There wasn't a puddy tat in sight. One great grey bird soared aloft in the blue heaven.

'I turned around and a shadow fell across the opening of the hut.'

He and I seemed to be the only living things between the sky and the desert beneath it.

I approached the hut, walking as warily as Stapleton would do. I was by myself but the place had indeed been used as a habitation. Throwing aside my cigarette, I closed my hand upon the butt of my revolver and, walking swiftly to the door, I said, 'Come out or I will come in and kill you. Now you wouldn't like that.' I went inside and fired my pistol and shouted, 'I know you're outside because you're not inside. If you give yourself up I'll give you a chocolate and a ticket to the opera. Now listen, hands up before Christmas and a Happy New Year.'

I looked under every rock outcrop and there was nothing. All I got was a pain in the back. Then, as I returned to the hut, I heard the sharp clink of a boot striking upon a stone. Then another and yet another, coming nearer and nearer. I shrank back into the darkest corner, cocked my pistol, determined not to be discovered. I turned around and a shadow fell across the opening of the hut.

'It is a lovely evening, my dear Watson,' said a well-known voice. 'I really think that you will be more comfortable outside than in.'

12. DEATH ON THE MOOR

For a moment I sat breathless. That cold, incisive, ironical voice could belong to but one man in all the world.

'Holmes!' I cried. 'Holmes! Holmes! Holmes!'

'There's only one of me, Watson. Come out,' he said, 'and please be careful with the revolver.'

There was a loud bang and I shot myself in the foot.

'You see there beside the path?' said Holmes. 'You threw the cigarette down at the supreme moment when you charged into the hut to find it empty.'

'There was a loud bang and I shot myself in the foot.'

'Exactly.'

He was still wearing one brown boot and one black one, silly bugger.

'You saw me, perhaps, on the night of the convict hunt, when I was so imprudent as to allow the moon to rise behind me?'

'Not at all. We ran our arses ragged chasing that devil Selden but saw nothing of you. You, then, are the "other" man on the moor! But why keep me in the dark, Holmes?'

'It saves electricity, Watson.'

'Excuse me, sir,' said Barrymore. 'The Berlin Philharmonic have finished "The Valkyries".'

'Then tell them to play some extracts by Wagner and when finish they can go back to Germany.'

A terrible scream – a prolonged yell of horror and anguish – burst out of the silence of the moor. That frightful cry turned the blood to ice in my veins.

'Aggggggg!!'

'Good God, what is it? What does it mean? What is the meaning of Aggggggg?' I cried.

Holmes sprang to his feet. I saw his dark, athletic outline at the door of the hut, his shoulders stooping, his head thrust forward, his face peering into the darkness. He walked into a rock.

'What is it?' Holmes whispered. 'Is it an Eric or a queer hound of the Baskervilles? Where is it, Watson?'

'There, I think.' I pointed into the darkness. 'No, there! No, there! No, there!' So I went there and there and there and Holmes went there and there, too.

Again, an agonised cry swept through the silent night. Whatever it was sounded as though it had got its balls caught in a rat trap.

'The hound!' cried Holmes. 'Come, Watson, come! Great heavens, if we are too late!'

I saw Holmes put his hand to his forehead. It was still there. 'He has beaten us, Watson. We are too late.'

'No, no, surely not!'

'Fool that I was to hold my hand. And you, Watson, see what comes of abandoning your charge. But, by heaven, if the worst has happened, we'll avenge him. Can you see anything?'

'Yes, anything.'

'That's no bloody good. Hark! Hark!'

'I can't see anything and I am harking as much as I can.'

A low moan had fallen upon our ears. There it was again upon our left! On the boulder strewn hillside was spread-eagled some dark, irregular object. As we ran towards it the vague outline hardened into a definite

THE HOUND OF THE BASKERVILLES

shape. It was a prostrate man face downward upon the ground, the head doubled under him at a horrible angle, the shoulders rounded, and the body hunched together as if in the act of throwing a somersault. So grotesque was that attitude that I could not for the instant realise that that moan had been the passing of his soul. Not a whisper, not a rustle, rose now from the dark figure over which we stooped. Holmes laid his hand upon him, and held it up again, with an exclamation of horror. 'Mark my words, Watson,' said Holmes. 'This is the work of that villain Stapleton.'

'Why should we not seize them at once?' I asked.

'Our case is not complete. The fellow is wary and cunning to the last degree.'

'We must send for help, Holmes! We cannot carry the body all the way to the Hall. Let's put a rock on it so that the cat doesn't get him.'

We put our hands in the dead man's pocket and it came to thirty shillings in loose change. He was not only dead but also skint.

'The man has a beard!' cried Holmes.

'A beard?'

'It is not Sir Henry – it is . . . why, it is my neighbour, Selden, the Notting Hill murderer, and he has apparently stopped murdering.'

The Notting Hill murderer had Sir Henry's old wardrobe and Barrymore had passed it on in order to disguise Selden's escape.

'These clothes have been the cause of the poor fellow's death. The homosexual Hound of the Baskervilles recognised the smell as belonging to Sir Henry. By his cries he must have run a long way after he knew the homosexual hound was on his track.'

'How did he die?'

'Well, he ran like fuck, when he saw what he thought was an Eric or a homosexual hound and had a heart attack.'

'Well, then, why should this hound be loose tonight? It would normally not run loose upon the moor except to kill a policeman, a farmer or a duck. Stapleton would not let it go unless he had reason to think that Sir Henry would be there.'

Quack! Quack! Stop that duck!

'Halloa, Watson, what's this? It is Stapleton himself. Not a word to show your suspicions.'

A figure was approaching us over the moor. I saw the dull red glow of a cigar. Though it was midnight, he carried a butterfly net. It was a disguise.

'Why, Dr Watson, that's not you is it? You are the last man that I expected to see,' said Stapleton.

'Well, I dearly hope I am not.'

'Is somebody hurt? Don't tell me it's our friend Sir Henry.'

'All right then, I won't tell you.'

He hurried past me and stooped over the dead man. I heard a sharp intake of his breath and the cigar fell from his fingers.

'Who is this?'

'It is Selden, the Notting Hill murderer,' I informed him.

Stapleton turned a ghastly face upon us, but by a supreme effort he had overcome his amazement and his disappointment.

'Dear me! What a horrible affair! How did he die?'

'Death,' said Holmes.

'So death finally killed him.'

'He appears to have broken his neck by falling over these rocks. My friend and I were strolling on the moor when we heard a cry,' I said.

'I also heard a cry. That's what brought me out. I was uneasy about Sir Henry,' said Stapleton.

'Why Sir Henry in particular?' I could not help asking.

Holmes blurted out, 'The bloody fool.'

'Because I had suggested he come over. When he did not come I was surprised, and I naturally became alarmed for his safety when I heard cries upon the moor. By the way –' his eyes darted again from my face to Holmes's '– did you hear anything else besides a cry?'

'No, of course not. Did you?' I answered.

'No.'

'What do you mean then?'

'I mean no. I hope your visit has cast some light upon those occurrences, whether it was an Eric or a homosexual hound.'

Holmes shrugged his shoulders. 'One cannot always have the success for which one hopes.'

My friend spoke in his frankest and most unconcerned manner. Stapleton still looked hard at him. Then he turned to me.

'I would suggest carrying this poor fellow to my house, but it would give my sister such a fright that I do not feel justified in doing it. I think if we put something over his face he will be safe until morning.'

So we put another rock over his face.

Holmes and I set off for Baskerville Hall, leaving the naturalist to return alone. Looking back we saw the figure moving slowly away over the broad moor, and behind him that one black smudge on the silvered slope which showed where the man was lying who had come so horribly to his end.

'We're at close grips at last,' said Holmes.

'I am sorry that he has seen you, Holmes.'

'And so was I at first. But there was no getting out of it.'

'Why should we not arrest him at once and not Doris Stokes?'

'*Doris Stokes???!!!* We should be laughed out of court if we came with such a story and such evidence. We might as well blame her for the Boer War.'

'Who was responsible for the Boer War?'

'Mrs Doris Grub, 33 Wellington Street, Hackney.'

'How do you propose to confront her?'

'I have great hopes of what Mrs Laura Lyons may do for us tomorrow. And now we are late for dinner. I think that we are both ready for sustenance.'

'. . . she wept bitterly in her apron so we put her through the mangle.'

13. FIXING THE NETS

Sir Henry was more than pleased and surprised to see Sherlock Holmes. He did raise his eyebrows, where they stuck, however, when he heard that my friend had neither any luggage nor any explanations for its absence. But first I had the unpleasant duty of breaking the news of the death of Selden the Notting Hill murderer to Barrymore and his wife. To him it may have been an unmitigated relief, but she wept bitterly in her apron so we put her through the mangle.

'Don't worry,' said Holmes. 'He is lying out on the moor with a rock on him. You can visit him whenever you like. He's not going far.'

Sir Henry opened his eyes. 'How did he come to die?'

'The poor wretch was dressed in your clothes. I fear your servant who gave them to him may get into trouble with the police.'

'But how about the case?' asked Sir Henry. 'Have you found the guilty person? And have you found my other boots?'

'We've had one experience, as Watson has no doubt told you. We heard one of the Erics on the moor.'

He stopped suddenly and stared fixedly up over my head into the air. The lamp beat upon his face, and so intent was his gaze and so still that it might have been that of a clear-cut classical statue.

I could see as he looked down that he was repressing some internal emotion. His features were still composed, but his eyes shone with amused exultation.

'Excuse the admiration of a connoisseur,' said Holmes, as he waved his hand towards the line of portraits which covered the opposite wall. 'Watson won't allow that I know anything of art but that is because he is entirely ignorant. That stout gentleman with the wig ought to be a Reynolds. They are all family portraits, I presume? Do you know the names? And this Cavalier opposite to me – the one with the black velvet and lace?'

'Ah, you have a right to know about him. That is the cause of all the mischief, the wicked Hugo the shit, who started the homosexual Hound of the Baskervilles.'

Holmes stood on a chair and went through it. He held the light up against the time-stained portrait on the wall.

'Good heavens!' I cried, in amazement.

The face of Stapleton had sprung out of the canvas. Holmes burst into one of his rare fits of laughter as he turned away from the picture.

FINALE

Yes, we should have a full day today,' Holmes remarked, smothering his nose with a pinch of snuff. If only he knew how ridiculous he looked with a brown nose.

'I have sent a report from Grimpen to Princetown as to the death of Selden. I think I can promise that none of you will be troubled in the matter of his death, although there might be an inquiry about the rock on his face and body. You are engaged, as I understand, to dine with our friends the Stapletons tonight.'

'Yes,' replied Sir Henry. 'I hope that you will come also.'

'I fear that Watson and I must go to London.'

Sir Henry's face dropped and hit the floor.

'My dear fellow,' said Holmes, 'you must trust me implicitly and do exactly what I tell you. We will drive in to Coombe Tracey, but Watson will leave his things as a pledge that he will come back. Watson, you will send a note to Stapleton to tell him that you regret that you cannot come.'

'All right then, I will go on my own,' said Sir Henry. 'Fuck it.'

'One more direction!' Holmes instructed our host. 'I wish you to drive to Merripit House. Send back your trap, however, and let them know that you intend to walk home.'

'Bloody hell! But that is the very thing which you have so often cautioned me not to do.'

'This time you will do it with safety.'

'Then I will do it.'

'If only he knew how ridiculous he looked with a brown nose '

'Good boy,' said Holmes, patting his head and giving him a lump of sugar.

'Good doggy,' I said, trying to pat him.

'And, as you value your life, do not go across the moor in any direction save along the straight path. Good boy,' Holmes said, patting him and giving him another lump of sugar.

We said goodbye to our rueful friend. I left him chewing a sugar lump, cocking his leg and peeing against a tree. And after a couple of hours we were at the station of Coombe Tracey. A small boy was waiting on the platform.

'Any orders, sir?'

'Yes, you will take this train to town, Cartwright. The moment you arrive you will seek out Inspector Lestrade of Scotland Yard. You will give him this letter and ask him to wire his reply to me at this station immediately.'

It was later that morning when the telegram arrived, which Holmes handed to me. It ran:

WIRE RECEIVED. PROCEED. COMING DOWN WITH UNSIGNED WARRANT AND
CHANGE OF UNDERWEAR. ARRIVE FIVE-FORTY.
  LESTRADE.

'Now we must visit Mrs Laura Lyons,' Holmes announced.

Mrs Laura Lyons, blood group rhesus negative, was in her office, and Sherlock Holmes opened the interview.

'I am investigating the circumstances which attended the death of the late Sir Charles Baskerville. Dr Watson said in a previous interview you withheld information.'

What have I withheld?' she asked defiantly.

'You confessed that you asked Sir Charles to be at the gate at ten o'clock. You have withheld the connection.'

'There is no connection.'

'In that case I wish to be perfectly frank with you, Mrs Lyons. We regard this case as one of murder, and the evidence may implicate not only your friend, Mr Stapleton, but his wife as well.'

The lady sprang from her chair and hit the wall opposite.

'His wife!' she cried.

'The fact is no longer a secret. The person who has passed for his sister is really his wife. Stapleton himself is an illegitimate descendant of Hugo the Shit and will step forward to inherit the Baskerville fortune once the rightful heir is out of the way.'

Sherlock Holmes shrugged his shoulders. A lot of bloody good it did.

'One thing I swear to you is that when I wrote that letter I never dreamt of any harm to the old gentleman,' said Mrs Lyons.

She did a quick back somersault and landed on her feet.

'I entirely believe you, madam,' said Sherlock Holmes. 'I presume you received help from Sir Charles for the legal expenses in connection with your divorce. What persuaded you from keeping the appointment?'

'An elephant fell on me,' she said. 'He frightened me into remaining silent.'

'But you had your suspicions?'

'Yes, Doris Stokes.'

She held up a cardboard cutout of Tutankhamen. Holmes put it under his arm.

The London express came roaring into the station and crashed into the buffer with its bumpers. A small, wiry bulldog of a man was hurled on the platform from the first-class carriage. We all three shook hands. I shook two of his; he shook one of mine.

'Anything good?' asked Inspector Lestrade.

'Yes, there's a marmalade fair in the village.'

14. THE END

THE HOUND OF THE BASKERVILLES
One of Sherlock Holmes's defects is that all of the plans he makes he neglects to tell anybody about. I had no idea what the hell was going on.

'Lestrade got into a hollow. It gradually filled with fog, obscuring him completely.'

'Are you armed, Lestrade?'

The little detective smiles. 'As long as I have my trousers, I have something in it: a nine-millimetre Colt automatic.'

'Good! My friend and I are also ready for emergencies. I have a pint hip flask of Napoleon brandy.'

'You are mighty close about this affair, Holmes. What's the game now?' I asked.

'I will find the murderer and post him to the police for Christmas. There is Merripit House and the end of our journey. I must request you to walk on tiptoe and not to talk above a whisper. This will do,' said he. 'Get into this hollow, Lestrade.'

Lestrade gradually got into a hollow. It gradually filled with fog, obscuring him completely.

'Can you tell the position of the rooms?' asked Holmes.

'Yes, nor'west,' I said.

'What are those latticed windows at this end?'

'I think they are the kitchen windows.'

'And the one beyond, which shines so brightly?'

'That is certainly the dining room.'

'The blinds are up. You know the lie of the land best. Creep forward and see what they are doing!'

There were only two men in the room, Sir Henry and Stapleton. They sat with their profiles towards me on either side of the round table. Both of them were smoking cigars, and coffee and wine were in front of them. Stapleton was talking with animation but Sir Henry looked pale and distrait.

As I watched them, Stapleton rose and left the room, while Sir Henry filled his glass again and leant back in his chair, puffing at his cigar. I heard the creak of a door and the crisp sound of boots upon gravel. Looking over, I saw the naturalist pause at the door of an outhouse in the corner of the orchard. A key turned in a lock, and as he passed in there was a curious scuffling noise from within. He was only a minute or so inside, and then I heard the key turn once more, and he passed me and re-entered the house.

'You say, Watson, that the lady is not there?' Holmes asked.

'No. Perhaps she's cooking.'

'But there is no light in any other room, including the kitchen?'

'Perhaps she's cooking in Braille.'

The fog bank fell back until we were half a mile from the house, and still that dense white sea, with the moon silvering its upper edge, swept slowly and inexorably on. Lestrade was absolutely forgotten in that hole. We watched as Sir Henry left Merripit House to begin his long, lonely walk home.

'Hist!' cried Holmes, and I heard the sharp click of a cocking pistol. 'Look out! It's coming!'

I was at Holmes's elbow, and I glanced for an instant at his face. It was pale and exultant, his eyes shining brightly in the moonlight. But then they started forward in a rigid, fixed stare, and his lips parted in amazement. At the same instant Lestrade gave a yell of terror and threw himself downward upon the ground. I sprang to my feet, my inert hand grasping my pistol, my mind paralysed by the dreadful shape that had sprung out upon us from the shadows of the fog. A homosexual hound it was, an enormous coal-black hound, but not such a hound as mortal eyes have ever seen. Fire burst from its open mouth, its eyes glowed with smouldering flames, its muzzle and hackles and dewlap were outlined in the flickering flame. Never in the delirious dream of a disordered brain could anything more savage, more appalling, more hellish, be conceived than that dark form and savage face which broke upon us out of the wall of fog.

Oh nice doggy, doggy here.' I tried to offer him a biscuit.

' *"Oh nice doggy, doggy here." I tried to offer him a biscuit.*'

Then Holmes and I both fired together, and the creature gave a hideous howl, which showed that one at least had hit him. He did not pause, however, but bounded onward. Far away on the path we saw Sir Henry looking back, his face white in the moonlight, his hands raised in horror, glaring helplessly at the frightful thing that was hunting him down. 'Down, Fido,' he gasped, but Fido did not go down. Fido sprang at his throat. But the next instant Holmes had emptied five chambers of his revolver into the creature's flank. With a last howl of agony and a vicious snap in the air, it rolled upon its back, and then fell limp upon its side. I stooped, panting, and pressed my pistol to the dreadful, shimmering head, but it was useless to press the trigger. The giant homosexual hound lay dead.

Lestrade thrust his brandy flask between the baronet's teeth.

'My God!' Sir Henry whispered. 'What was it? What, in heaven's name, was it? he said, swallowing.

'It's a Napoleon brandy, '89,' said Lestrade.

'It's a large Eric,' I said. 'Yes, it's dead. We have laid the family ghost once and for ever.' I placed my hand upon the glowing muzzle, and as I held them up my own fingers smouldered and gleamed in the darkness.

'Phosphorus,' I said.

The dog had a name on his collar, 'Tiddles'.

'You saved my life, Holmes,' said the baronet.

'We all make mistakes,' said Holmes. 'Are you strong enought to stand?'

'Give me another mouthful of that brandy, and I shall be able to stand anything.' He drank the bottle and collapsed.

He tried to stagger to his feet and passed out, but he was still ghastly pale and trembling in every limb. We helped him to a rock. He wouldn't eat it.

At that moment there came a horrific scream and a hissing, gurgling, squelching sound from the direction of the Grimpen Mire. Stapleton, rushing to view the fiendish work of his hideous hound had met his fate, sinking into the foul depths of the bog to join the unfortunate pony, the postman and the milkman.

ORIGINAL REWRITE OF SIR ARTHUR CONAN DOYLE

We all drove to Stapleton's for the denouement. There was nobody in. We went into a room that had been fashioned into a small museum, and the walls were lined by glass-topped cases full of that collection of butterflies and moths the formation of which had been the relaxation of this complex and dangerous man. In the centre of this room there was an upright beam, which had been placed at some period as a support for the old worm-eaten balk of timber which spanned the roof. To this post a figure was tied, so swathed and muffled in the sheets which had been used to secure it that one could not for the moment tell whether it was that of a man or woman. One towel passed round the throat, and was secured at the back of the pillar. Another covered the lower part of the face and over it two dark eyes – eyes full of grief and shame and a dreadful questioning – stared back at us, a moustache pencilled under her nose. In a minute we had torn off the gag, unswathed the bonds, and Mrs Stapleton sank upon the floor in front of us and her beautiful head fell forward. It went thud as it hit the floor.

'The brute!' cried Holmes. 'Here, Lestrade, your flask! Put her in the chair! She has fainted from ill usage, housework and laundry. I will just squeeze them while she's unconscious.'

She opened her eyes again. 'Is he safe?' she asked. 'Has he escaped?'

'He cannot escape us, madam.'

'No, no, I did not mean my husband. Is Sir Henry safe?'

'Yes, and the homosexual hound is dead.'

She gave a long sigh of satisfaction. 'Thank God! Thank God! Oh, this villain! See how he has treated me!'

Kinky, eh?

We saw with horror that her arms were tattooed with the winning numbers of the National Lottery and she had won millions.

'To hell with Sir Henry! I don't need him and I don't need anybody,' she cried.

'Marry me,' said Holmes. And they lived happily ever after.

Somewhere in the heart of the Grimpen Mire, down in the foul slime of the huge morass that had sucked Stapleton in, this cold and cruel-hearted man is for ever buried.

'Excuse me, sir, the Berlin Philharmonic have finished the Wagner selection.'

'Go and tell them to start playing World War One with my compliments.'

Quack! Quack! Stop that duck!

HOLMES   WATSON

ROBIN HOOD ACCORDING TO SPIKE MILLIGAN

THE LEGEND OF ROBIN HOOD

Once upon a time, sometimes twice upon a time, there lived a Lord and Lady Huntingdon. He was seven feet ten inches and she was five feet so they never had to talk when making love. Tiptree was his favourite jam. Tiptree Strawberry Jam: it's delicious when spread on bread and when the jars are empty you can keep water in them. Tiptree is the jam for you.

One day Lady Huntingdon gave birth to a boy. They fed him on steroids. He soon grew to seven feet. The boy was destined to become an outlaw.

'Come one, come all and join me as archers in Sherwood Forest. When we are hungry we'll have jam sandwiches and deer. I, Robin Hood, will lead you with my wonder weapon, a bow and arrow. This puts paid to sword and axe.'

A Norman archer killed King Harold. Robin found the Norman Army, the dead and dying. Many were eating jam sandwiches.

Robin started robbing. He did the Midland Bank, Lloyds and Barbara Streisand. He had her nose fixed.

Robin Hood had a pet duck. He rented it out for children's parties.

1. THE SAD END OF MUCH THE MILLER

The good spirit of Sherwood, 12%,
Sherwood in the twilight,
Is Robin awake?
Grey and ghostly shadows are
Gliding through the break.
Shadows of the dapple deer
Dreaming of the morn,
Dreaming of shadowy men in the winds
Of a shadowy horn,
Aren't you bloody glad you're not bloody well born.

Alfred Noyes, 'Sherwood', 1903

King Richard the First, Richard Coeur de Lion, came to the throne in 1189 and left it a year later leaving a debt of £500,000. All lost on the bingo table. He set off to free Jerusalem from the Saracens and bingo. He used to ride past them and set fire to their legs. John, his brother, was a truly merciless man. He wore no trousers. John rode with his bandits to the Sheriff of Nottingham's second-hand-car and scrap-yard business, where he shared some of the profits.

They had reached a lightly wooded area of the great Sherwood Forest when suddenly a man started to shout. 'Save me, Prince. In God's love, save me!'

'Who is he?' asked John casually.

'They call him Much. He was a miller once but he was much too fond of the King's deer,' his Lieutenant replied.

'Oh,' said Prince John. 'Why the King's deer? Was there no other way?'

'He couldn't afford to go on eating at McDonald's. He has fallen in with a band of outlaws led by Robin Hood.'

'Describe this Robin Hood.'

'I don't know much of him, sir. Robin Hood comes out of the forest but then goes back in again.'

'Faugh, faugh!' cried Prince John impatiently, which was, in fact, 'fuck' in old English.

So they dragged poor Much away. Suddenly, with a desperate cry, he tore himself loose, snatched a sword from one of the men and made a rush at the Prince's horse's bum, which he stabbed, the horse then throwing the Prince over his head. Alas, the men held Much down; some held him up; some held him sideways. His future looked grim . . . and short. Ahead of him lay only death, torture, excruciating pain and abominable barbarity – but mainly death.

There was a whooshing sound and an arrow sped to Much's heart and laid him dead on the ground. The feather on the arrow was red – the signature of Robin Hood.

'Who loosed that arrow?' cried Prince John.

He turned as he spoke and saw at the edge of the glade a man wearing a green cloak over his suit of brown and widdling against a tree.

'Who goes there?' called Prince John, pointing to the tree.

'We all do.'

'Tell me, is this Robin Hood, this fellow – is he rich? Are his lands wide?'

'Once they were indeed wide,' said the Lieutenant, 'but now only the house and the lands of Locksley remain to him. The other lands he has sold. He put them on the market with Harrods.'

'Ah, then his coffers would be full of gold,' said John.

'And Harrods' as well,' said the man, 'and Ali Khan's, the owner. I know that this Robert, Earl of Locksley, known as Robin Hood, has some secret need for money. He has an offshore bank account with Lloyds of London in Jersey in the name of Charlie Chaplin and Sons.'

'I didn't know he was a son of Charlie Chaplin.'

'That may well be, but he remains a dangerous enemy,' said the Lieutenant.

'How may we put an end to his treachery?' asked the Prince.

'Then I'll tell thee how it can be done. Tomorrow the Loony Earl of Locksley is to be married at Fountains Abbey.'

'Then there we will deal with the cursed Robin Hood,' cried the Prince.

They rode off into the grey of the evening, leaving the body of old Much le Miller lying where it had fallen. His wife had already collected the insurance policy and was living at the Ritz.

As his men gathered in the clearing, Robin Hood mused over the death of Much. It had been the merciful thing to do. No one stabbed the Prince's horse up the bum and got away with it.

When the King Richard came back from the crusade, things would be better. For a start he'd have Much buried! But if he never came back that devil Prince John would be King and God have mercy on everyone.

A man walked into the midst of the occasion.

'Will Scarlet,' called out Robin Hood, 'my true friend. What have you got there?'

'I have brought a hundred sausages for the feast and a hundredweight of chip potatoes from Marks & Spencer's.'

'God's blessing on you, Robin Hood,' they all chorused, except the boy who was kneeling by his father's body. He wept copiously on the corpse. If Much had been alive, he'd have drowned.

'So they have killed old Much. Have comfort, boy, be at peace,' said Robin. 'He has been spared many evils – income tax, overdraft, mortgages, bills and AIDS.'

'Let me come with you, Robin, and serve with you,' pleaded the boy. 'Look, I'm old enough: I have hairs on my willy.'

'Oh, well done, son, and I might say well hung.'

2. HOW ROBERT OF LOCKSLEY BECAME AN OUTLAW

In Locksley Hall that night all seemed peaceful after the gigantic meal. There was burping, leaping, being sick and farting. They all feasted in honour of Robert Fitzooth Locksley's wedding to Marian Fitzwalter, which was to take place on the morrow as soon as they'd washed all the vanilla and chocolate ice cream off the bridal gown.

Earl Robert stood near the great fireplace, welcoming his guests and collecting five dollars a head – the mean bastard!

Lady Marian Fitzwalter stood beside him. She was some five years younger than he was. She was tall and beautiful and had won the hundred-metre gold medal. She could also pole vault anything up to twenty feet. She had practised over Earl Robert two or three times during the evening. She could also hop, skip and jump twenty feet.

They now drank a toast to the bride and groom. They held up their drinking horns, which were edged with gold. 'Here's to Robin and Marian,' they said. They drank the toast; it was water. One of the hidden traits of Robin was meanness.

Finally the drunken guests sang the following boring chant: 'Pray Ye Do It For Prosperity'.

Boring Chant

Down with John.
Drink to the Lion Hearted
Everyone.
Especially long live Richard
Robin and Richard.
Down with John.
Drink to the Lion Hearted
Everyone.
God bless
Ronny Scott.

'Hello, what have we here?' said someone.

Well, someone had spotted something that was here, but he never said what it was.

As the boring song ended there was a groan of relief. A portly monk, dressed in russet robes, appeared with a haircut that made him look like he had a lump on his head. He also got a groan of relief as he pushed his way through the throng. Suddenly, and for no reason at all, he fell backward like a board. He'd found the drink.

* * *

In the luxurious surroundings of the Sheriff of Nottingham's second-hand car lot, Prince John brooded over his forthcoming encounter with Robin Hood.

'Your Highness, when I enquired from Much the Miller's son, who has hairs on his willy, he told me all was well with him and Scarlet had come to take him away to be cared for by Robin Hood,' the Sheriff said.

'Will Scarlet, Robin Hood . . .' roared Prince John, clutching his crown and knocking it off to the floor with a loud clang.

From under the banquet table came drunken voices: 'Long live Richard, Robin and Richard.' And there it stopped. They had fallen asleep.

'Yes, there is no doubt about it,' continued Prince John. 'Tomorrow, curtail the wedding of this traitor, Robin, or Robin Declared An Outlaw, and you take and hang him forthwith. There, of course, are his lands and his goods, which are forfeit to me. And that attractive bride of his, Lady Marian. Trouble is, as soon as I get near her – she is a champion – she pole vaults twenty feet over me. I try to catch her; she does one hundred metres in twelve seconds. If I try to trap her she does the hop, skip and jump, twelve, ten, twenty feet.'

Lord Fitzwalter, Lady Marian's father, seemed troubled and uneasy. He suffered with piles and acne.

Yes, this was the day of the wedding of Robin to Marian. They stood at the altar; it seemed a good place for it.

'Hold,' said a Knight, arriving with a detail of armed guards. 'I am Guy de Custard Gisborne, come in the King's name without trousers to stop this ceremony proceeding. Pursuivant, read the mandate.'

'Look, will you piss off,' said Robin Hood.

A man dressed in the livery of Sarah Bernhard unrolled the parchment and read in a louce voice. 'Be it all known that Robert Ffffffittzzooth, known as Old Mother Riley, and Marian –'

'Let me see that seal,' said Robin. 'It's not genuine.'

Quickly he raised his hunting horn and blew his horn through the window. In no time at all the church was surrounded by Robin's bowmen. In one charge Robin and his men dispersed the Sheriff's men, and then made good their escape into the forest.

'It's no good following him now, but he'll find the Sheriff waiting for him at Locksley Hall if he ventures there,' snorted Sir Guy, cowering by the altar.

But, alas, Robin had ventured somewhere else.

'Robin is one of the finest marksmen with an arrow. He can shoot through the seams of a man's trousers and out the other side. It's a dangerous thing to outlaw such a man,' boomed the Priest, Brother Michael. 'You have taken his home. Where will he live?'

'He might have to go into B&B.'

'You have taken his cattle. What will he eat?'

'Well, there's Big Macs, Kentucky Fried Chicken, takeaway vindaloo curry.'

'I am Lady Marian's confessor,' said Brother Michael. 'She has beauty, grace and £100,000 in the Bank of Australia.'

3. THE OUTLAWS OF SHERWOOD FOREST

A hundred valiant men has this brave Robin Hood
Still ready at his call those bowmen were right good
All clad in Lincoln green with caps of red and blue
His fellows winded horns not one of them new
All made of Spanish yew, his bows were wondrous strong
They did not an arrow draw but was a cloth yard long
They drew a wondrous arrow that could get through gaps
That rarely missed their mark
They really missed when they missed Hyde Park.

Early next morning Sir Guy de Custard Fitz Gisborne set out for Arlington, home of the Fitzwalters. His guide was the Fat Friar called Brother Michael who so disgraced himself on the eve of the wedding of Robin Hood. The Abbot had banished him in no uncertain terms.

'You go out, false and treacherous man, as you came in many years ago, plain Michael Tuck, no longer a brother of this order. If you show your face around here again, I'll shut the door in your face,' the Abbot had cried.

'I haven't got a door in my face. Why then,' cried the Friar gaily, 'farewell to the Abbey of Fountains, and all hail to the jolly green coat and catch me again if you can.'

So he went on his way singing: 'We'll meet again, Don't know where, Don't know when . . .'

As they came in sight of Arlington Castle, the Friar ceased from his singing in case they thought he was being tortured.

'You best turn back, Sir Knight, or at the least lower that visor of yours,' he advised Sir Guy.

'How?' exclaimed Guy Sir Gisborne. 'Surely Lord Fitzwalter is not in league with Robin Hood.'

'Far from it,' laughed the Fat Friar. 'Lady Marian Fitzwalter assuredly is, and she is national pole vault champion at eighteen and stays at the YWCA.'

They reached the castle in safety, however, and Lord Fitzwalter welcomed them loudly, showing great eagerness to be on the side in power, and the YWCA!

Lord Fitzwalter was deep in discussion with his aspirant son-in-law, Robin Hood.

'Would you have had me marry my daughter to an outlaw, a fly-by-night, a slayer of deer, an Old Mother Riley impressionist?'

'For her I save my nether regions,' said Robin.

'Just wait till I get a chance to get to your nether regions,' said Lord Fitzwalter. 'You will never see them again. The marriage was never completed!'

'Will you stop saying that or I will crush your balls between my teeth,' said Robin.

Lord Fitzwalter was going more and more red in fury for at this moment Lady Marian came suddenly into the room, clad in topless green with a quiver of arrows at her side and a bow in her hand.

'What now? Where are you off to now, wench?'

'The *Sun*. I'm a page-three girl,' Marian calmly answered.

'That you shall not,' bellowed Fitzwalter. 'I will have up the drawbridge.'

'I shall pole vault it,' said Marian.

'But I will secure the gates.'

'But I will pole vault anything up to twenty feet.'

'I will lock you in your upper chamber three hundred feet up.'

And suddenly she exclaimed, 'Father, let me go to the greenwood. You have my promise that I will return and I promise that Robin will do nothing to me more than he is doing now without your leave.'

'All right, just this once,' said Lord Fitzwalter.

'And now,' said Robin, 'those who remain with me, let us go away to our new home in the forest where it's pouring bloody rain and see how many of us are still alive after the attendant illnesses we'll gather. We stand loyally together for the King; for God; for his anointed servant Richard, King by the Divine Right; and for justice and the righting of wrongs and pneumonia.'

And they all got pneumonia. Robin went on boring the men with his speech for another half an hour by which time they had all contracted pneumonia. Some of them tried to get out of the contract but they hadn't read the small print.

So they went to the forest of greenwood, with steep banks fencing in either side and in which there were caves both deep and dry at either end of a shallow valley out of which floods of water were issuing. The forest edged them in with mighty trees of oak and ash and beech, frogs and leeches, and thick clumps of impossible thorn with desolate marshes where a horse might disappear for ever. It was run with ferocious rivers. Robin went along the footway and fell into a deep river.

'Help! Help!' he said. 'I can't swim! I can't swim!'

And Friar Tuck was walking by and said, 'Look, I can't play the violin but I don't go shouting it around to everybody.'

That night Robin hosted a great feast of venison. Many of the vegetarians settled for veggie burgers.

He decided to go for a wander through the secret lanes of Sherwood Forest. He had to stop twenty times to find the way. Finally he mounted his horse and galloped over the bridge and straight into the lake.

'Help! Help! I've fallen in the water! Help! I can't swim!'

A man passing by said, 'Here, catch this,' and threw him a ship.

Finally the archers sent a search party out for him and they spent half the bloody night looking for him. Eventually they rescued him. After a few brief words they set about lighting two great fires to roast the venison and in twenty minutes they had half of Sherwood Forest in flames.

Then Robin Hood arose and addressed them. The trouble was they'd heard it all before. He began by telling the men, 'Remember that we are outlaws, not robbers. We must take the King's deer. I mean, we can't live on Big Macs, but when the King returns I myself will beg pardon at his feet for this trespass, and now –' ('Oh dear,' groaned the archers) '– you shall all swear the oath that I must swear with you – Long live King Richard. Kellogg's Corn Flakes are the ideal breakfast food.'

END OF COMMERCIAL

'Thank Christ,' said one of the archers, 'I thought he was going on all bloody night.'

4. THE RESCUE OF WILL SCARLET

And these will strike for England
And man and maid be free
The foil and spoil, the tyrants beneath
The greenwood tree

Tennyson, 'The Foresters', 1881

Early the next morning Robin gathered his band in Sherwood Forest and swore his great oath ('Go and get me some money!').

Walking briskly through the forest and frequently getting lost, Scarlet and Little Much came to the edge of open parkland in the middle of which stood a great stone house set in a lake. Unfortunately, once again Robin's unreliable horse had pitched him into the lake.

'Help! I can't swim!'

The guard on duty said, 'Hang on to the horse.'

'He can't swim either,' said Robin.

And so Robin took drowning lessons.

He dragged himself ashore just as Scarlet and Little Much reached the edge of the lake.

'Have you got me any money yet?' asked Robin, wringing out his tights.

'Alas, no,' replied Scarlet. 'Please accept this humble cheese sandwich as an apology, my Lord Robin.'

'Well, there's a pile of treasure hidden in a secret place in that house,' said Robin. 'All you have to do is cross the lake, evade the guards, find the secret place, steal the gold and jewels, sneak out without being spotted, cross the lake again and get the loot back to me. It's a cinch. I've already drunk half the lake to make it easier for you.'

Scarlet and Little Much left Robin tucking into his sandwich and drying out while they set off to raid the castle. All went according to plan until they came to make their escape with the bounty. As they made their way down a darkened stone staircase, a figure stepped from the shadows. It was Sir Guy de Custard Gisborne.

'Aha,' said Sir Guy. 'What have we here?'

'We have me here,' said Scarlet.

'Stop that man!' cried Sir Guy, drawing his sword. It was a very good likeness.

Scarlet flung open the bundle he was carrying and snatched out the bag of gold and jewels. 'Much,' he hissed, 'guard that with your life.'

'Christ, I might not live that long,' said Little Much.

By now a guard had appeared and grabbed Scarlet. 'What have you got there?'

'I've got me,' said Scarlet.

'What has the knave under his cloak?' roared Sir Guy.

'More of me,' said Scarlet.

But Sir Guy had seen Scarlet's face.

'It's Will Shitlock! Hold him! He's a traitor!'

Scarlet's hand flew to the long knife at his belt but, as he drew it, his trousers fell down. Little Much was long gone and so missed out on the chance to compare willy hair.

'I am no traitor,' said Will Scarlet. 'You be aware of the vengeance of Robin Hood and Co. My card, W Scarlet, Director.'

After this Scarlet was led away into the Great Hall. There was some semblance of a trial before the Sheriff, then, heavily guarded, he was taken to Nottingham and chained in a dungeon.

Much the Miller's son missed his way several times as he trod the narrow path in the heart of the forest. He fell in the bog and came up covered in it. Finally he found himself in the glade and told the news to Robin Hood, after handing him the bag of gold and jewels for which Scarlet had risked his life.

When Robin had heard all that had happened, he was sorely grieved, bringing his fist down into a plate of porridge.

'I'm willing to hang Guy de Custard,' said Robin savagely, banging his fist into a plate of porridge. He was covered in it.

So they marched to attack.

At the edge of the forest Robin fell in a bog. They finally got him out. He was pitch black.

Outside the prison, Robin approached a man he knew to be trustworthy.

'Now tell me, good Palmer,' said Robin Hood, 'do you know Will Shitlock or Scarlet?'

'That I do. I knew him when he was only shit. They brought him in last night. You're pitch black.'

'Never mind all that crap. When do they hang him?'

'He hangs tomorrow at midday before the Sheriff and Prince John,' answered the Palmer.

'They're hanging the Sheriff and Prince John?'

'No, they'll just be there.'

At noon the next day a crowd had gathered around the gallows. Foremost in the crowd was an old beggar leaning on a staff.

'Ere,' said a man with no balls. 'If only Robin Hood were here to give a lead.'

The Sheriff and Prince John sat on a lofty podium to view the execution. To create a diversion, Robin had secreted a haddock in the crotch of Prince John's tights.

Then Scarlet spoke from the gallows. 'My name is Shitlock, also known as Scarlet, and my Robin will save me. I am no grasping villain!'

'Rest assured we shall seek him out,' growled the Sheriff, who was red with anger, white with rage and purple with fury.

At that moment, Prince John collapsed on the podium, overcome with haddock fumes, and the old beggar threw off his ragged cloak. It was Robin! He waved his staff as a signal and in an instant a hundred archers rushed the gallows and carried it off into the forest. Scarlet was saved.

And the crowd sang: 'We'll meet again . . .'

In fact, they met them all again coming out of McDonald's. Each of a hundred archers shot an arrow into a hundred Big Macs as a warning . . .

5. HOW LITTLE JOHN CAME TO THE GREENWOOD

You gentlemen and yeomen good
Come in and drink with Robin Hood
If Robin Hood be not at home
Come in and drink with Little John.

Anon, 'William MacGonigal', 1887

After Robin Hood had rescued William Shitlock he remained quietly in Sherwood holding up a baggage train, clubbing innocent travellers insensible and removing all their goods for confiscation. So life settled down at Sherwood Forest. It was so up to date Sherwood Forest was fitted with a burglar alarm. Unfortunately, it caught him six times.

Prince John sent a large force to drive Robin out of Sherwood and they were shot to pieces. The pieces were given back to their widows as souvenirs. Prince John roamed Sherwood, gradually going mad looking for him and foaming at the mouth. Someone tried to shoot him for having rabies and he had to wear a muzzle.

With the supermarkets opening, Robin bought four hundredweight of chip potatoes at Marks & Spencer's. He would order a dozen Mars bars for distribution for heroism among his archers. But still Robin grew restless.

'Stay you all here, my merry fellows. Come swiftly if you hear the blast of my horn. It means I am in the shit.'

First Ducking Sequence

About noon Robin came across a forest path with a wide, swift-flowing stream cutting across it. (Please God, he's not going to drown again.) On the other side of the stream was a tall yeoman. The stranger carried a long, stout staff, as did Robin.

They faced each other at either side of a log which bridged the stream, but it was wide enough only for one.

'Out of my way, little man,' shouted the stranger, who was a good foot taller than Robin.

'Not so fast, tall fellow,' said Robin, 'and not so tall, fast fellow. Go back until I have passed.'

'Why then, I'll break your head first and dip you into the water afterwards,' cried the stranger.

'We'll see about that. I'm not frightened of water. I can swim,' Robin lied.

'You talk like a bloody fool,' exclaimed the stranger.

Bringing this story to a conclusion, the bloody fool whacked the stranger, who immediately retaliated, sending Robin straight into the water. Robin Hood swam gracefully to the surface, arse first.

Robin dutifully invited the newcomer back to Sherwood Forest and he joined the archers. Little John was his name but he was known as Big Dick because . . .

6. HOW SIR RICHARD OF LEGH PAID THE ABBOT

My londes beth set to weddie Robin
Untyll a certayne daye to a rich abbot here besyde of
Saynt mac abbay [Gobble-de-gook]

Anon, 'A Lytelt Geste of
Robyn Hode', 1489

One day soon after he came to the greenwood, Big Dick was wandering with Robin Hood deep in the wilds of Barnsdale, the arsehole of England. With them were Scarlet and Little Much, forming a small party about the size of the Liberals. They were in search of a hidden site to make a camp where a whole band could hide if Sherwood Forest was hit by an atomic bomb while they waited for it to explode.

'Good master, let us shoot a fat deer for our lunch. We shall all be the better for a feast.'

'I have no desire to dine yet,' said Robin. 'Give everyone a jam sandwich and a plate of soup to entice them. Wait there in hiding until some uninvited guest asks his way and then bring him to dinner whether he will or not.'

'What kind of guest would you have?' asked Big Dick.

'A starving one.'

They came back with a noble Knight in rags. He'd been repairing his horse and got covered in oil and shit.

'What master is yours?' asked the Knight.

'Robin Hood,' answered Big Dick.

'Oh, I didn't know he was into haute cuisine.'

'Well, I thank you,' said the Knight when the meal was ended. 'I have not dined so well these past three weeks, during which I lost three stone.'

'Now I must ask you to pay something towards what you have eaten,' said Robin.

'Alas,' said the guest, sighing even more deeply, 'my coffers are empty. There is naught that I can proffer without shame.'

'This Knight is a true Knight, a glutton and skint,' Robin declared. 'Fill him now with a cup of wine. My good mate, did you lose money in usury or women?'

'I played bingo with housekeeping money.'

'How much do you owe on your home?'

'Just four hundred pounds. I owe this sum to the Abbot. If I do not pay it tomorrow, then I'll lose everything – the wife, the horse, the mangle.'

'Big Dick, see if we have four hundred pounds in the treasury.'

'Unfortunately, Robin, all we have in the treasury is two shillings and sixpence,' said Big Dick.

'Well, for all it's worth, you can borrow it and let us have it when you have enough.'

Next day.

'God's blessings, my Abbot,' said the Knight. 'I am here within the hour.'

'Have you brought the money you owe me?'

'Come off it,' said the Knight. 'I have two and sixpence as a first instalment.'

'That's no bloody good,' said the Abbot. 'You get no further help from me, Knight that would cheat the Holy Church of four hundred pounds and try to pay it with two and sixpence.'

Sir Richard rode full speed to Legh Hall where his horse collided with his wife.

'My merry good lady, all is well. I have paid the National Debt; our lands are safe for ever. I gave him a two and sixpence postdated cheque as a first instalment.'

At the local bingo hall Robin was losing £3. His men had to drag him away screaming, 'All the fours Dr's orders, legs eleven . . .' Finally he fell asleep on a horse. When he awoke he was twenty miles away.

7. MAID MARIAN OF SHERWOOD FOREST

Gamwell Hall, seat of Robin's uncle, Sir William Custard Gamwell, was not far from Nottingham. And thither Sir Guy Custard de Custard Gisborne rode one day, along with the Sheriff and a body of men.

'Sir Guy, Sheriff, welcome,' said Custard Gamwell, with two Kentucky Fried Chicken and chips, £2.50.

Sir Guy suggested that they all attend the great festival held not far from the forest, hoping (aha!) to find out where Robin Hood was.

Sir Guy de Custard sat quietly under a tree while Sir William was eating a couple of Big Macs. Only once did he lean forward suddenly with an angry glint in his eyes and put on his glasses. An archer led one of the maidens out to dance who will be recognised as Lady Marian Fitzwalter disguised as a *Sun* page-three peasant girl.

'What maiden is that who's dancing with that crippled dancer?' asked Sir Guy.

'Oh, he's a well-known crippled dancer,' said Sir Custard William vaguely. 'She is known as the stupendous Clarinda. She oughtn't to come to these feasts.'

'What is your archer's name?' he asked.

'Robin, I believe,' said Sir William.

'Is that all you know of him?'

'He is inside leg 33 inches, blood group Rhesus negative, inside hat 6⅞.'

'Why, let me tell you,' said Sir Guy sternly. 'He is none other than the outlaw Robert Fitzooth Locksley. Tell me, what would you then advise me to do?'

'Why,' answered Gamwell, 'I would advise you to turn and ride like fuck for Nottingham unless you want a volley of arrows.'

By the time Sir Guy looked round again, Robin and Marian had made good their escape into the forest. Waiting not a moment, Sir Guy assembled his troops and he and the Sheriff set off at a pace, pursuing the renegades into the greenwood.

Waiting in the shelter of the trees, a portly Monk observed the commotion approaching down the forest path.

'Now who be these coming so fast this way?' he pondered. 'The stupendous Clarinda and Robin, I'll be bound, and with Sir Guy de Custard Gisborne in their wake.'

Robin and Marian went right and left into the cover of the trees. He went right and left and then she went right and left. Friar Tuck was left to face their pursuers.

'Out of the way, renegade Friar,' shouted Sir Guy. 'You keep doubtful and traitorous company and you . . .'

At this a hundred arrows rained down on them, decimating the troops and wounding Sir Guy.

The stupendous Clarinda appeared at the side of the path.

'As for doubtful and traitorous company, I see none on this side of the forest,' she said, as she pole vaulted the path.

Sir Guy raised his hand derisively as he started to speak and, swift as thought, the stupendous Clarinda raised her bow: the string hummed and Sir Guy's hand was transfixed by an arrow.

'Treachery! Cut them down . . . and sideways!' shouted the Sheriff.

The bow strings hummed again. The Sheriff's horse reared up as an arrow whizzed into the ground between his forefeet and the Sheriff was thrown off backward into a pool of mud.

'Faugh, oh faugh,' he said, 'oh faugh.'

Thereupon, arrows sped among the Sheriff's men, who retreated up a steep embankment only to be beaten back by the mighty staff in the hands of the great Friar. Roaring lustily, he stood there alone whirling his staff from side to side among the Sheriff's men, knocking down one, breaking the ribs of another, flattening the nose of another, cracking the skull of another. Thank heavens they were all in BUPA.

Next morning Lord Fitzwalter was disturbed. A large body of armed men drew up on the further side of the moat, with the Herald blowing his trumpet and an Officer bidding them, 'Lower the drawbridge in the King's name.'

'Ye bugger off-ee,' roared Lord Fitzwalter angrily. 'All balls and hang me arse,' he spluttered without his teeth. 'What do you mean by coming here with this nonsensing story about my daughter, the Lady Marian, bruising the Sheriff, injuring his men and shooting arrows into Sir Guy de Custard Gisborne? She would never kill a man without knickers. Off you go or I'll bid my men to shoot at you with their crossbows.'

'You'll hear more of this,' shouted the Officer.

'No I won't. I've heard enough already.'

'Not so lightly may you flout the will of our Liege, Lord Prince John.'

'Faugh! Him!' shouted Lord Fitzwalter. 'Let him come in person.'

The troops around the moat could see that an archer with a crossbow stood ready at every loophole, that the drawbridge was up and the moat wide and deep, and boiling oil in a giant pot was being poured over the troops below. It was olive oil at five shillings a bottle. It's lovely with salads.

'And what's this story about the stupendous Clarinda posing topless for the *Sun* on page three? You go no more forth from the castle,' declared Lord Fitzwalter to Lady Marian.

'Then I'll get out if I can,' answered Marian. 'I'll pole vault the moat. Prince John will get me out.'

'You can't bloody tolerate him.'

'Listen! If you shut me up I shall escape from the castle. No blame can be attached to you and you can welcome Prince John here with every sign of regret at my absence and fury at my flight.'

'Hum-ha,' said Lord Fitzwalter, and opened his toothless mouth and popped in a Polo. 'God bless you, Marian, and your pole vault!'

A few hours later Prince John rode up with high blood pressure, 180 over 90. Lord Fitzwalter met him at the gate with a most profuse expression of loyalty, begging pardon for his behaviour to the Herald in the morning.

Prince John was graciously pleased to accept Lord Fitzwalter's apologies, grovelling at the same time. When he asked to be presented to the Lady Marian, it was found she was no longer three hundred feet up planning a route for her escape.

Lord Fitzwalter raged around the castle. He raged around it 28 times and got very giddy, his blood pressure 200 over 160. He was dead but he didn't know it.

Prince John graciously lent half his followers to Lord Fitzwalter and they scoured the neighbourhood until it was spotless, but Lady Marian Fitzwalter had vanished.

8. ANOTHER CONFRONTATION WITH ROBIN

Robin came across a young man dressed in forest attire eating a jam sandwich at speed.

'Ah now, good fellow,' cried Robin, 'why so fast?'

'It might escape.'

'Look, I'll wait till you finish your jam sandwich and I'll challenge you to a joust with sticks. Where do you get all this jam from?'

'Lugworth's Jam Factory,' said the youth.

'Does your father own the jam factory?'

'Yes.'

All the while the lad was beating back Robin Hood, who had to say, 'Don't hurt me! Will you stop fighting? I cannot match you. Do you have any more jam sandwiches? I'd like one.'

'I'll get them to post you one.'

Suddenly the young lad took off his beard. 'Robin, don't you know me?'
'Marian,' said Robin, his arms around her squeezing her boobs.
'You've never done that before, Robin.'
'Well, I'm coming of age.'

There was feasting and boob squeezing that night as Robin and his merry
men did honour to their queen. Robin got more and more imbibed. He rose
with a flagon in each hand, swaying and spilling it all over him. He fell
down, rose again, fell down, stayed down.

Before he started again, his archers fled to bed.

9. HOW SIR RICHARD PAID ROBIN HOOD

Get well your abbot, sayd Robyn
And your pryour, I you pray,
And byd hym send me such a monke
To dymer every day.

Anon, 'A Lyell'

Sir Richard and his followers hastened along into Barnsdale. They came to
a bridge where many people living nearby were meeting that day for a
wrestling match. The prize was a white horse with a harness, a pair of
gloves, a gold ring, a pipe of wine and a jam sandwich. And, just as Sir
Richard arrived, wrestling was taking place. One of the wrestlers had gone
home, leaving his opponent on his own to try to win alone. Nobody would
take his opponent's place.

'Is this not a contest open to all comers?' asked Sir Richard.

'But the men of Barnsdale be jealous of an outsider like this Arthur A
Bland and they fear he will beat our man and throw him in the river,'
explained a yokel.

'This shame should not be,' exclaimed Sir Richard.

He pushed his way through the crowd and struck down the cudgels
which were raised to fell Arthur A Bland. Sir Richard spoke to the gathering.
He appealed to the pride of every Barnsdale man and many came forward
to challenge Arthur A Bland. Bland beat the crap out of the lot of them. The
white-horse prize then threw him and kicked him in the balls and galloped
away.

While Sir Richard was boldly proving yet again what a prat he was, Robin
and his men waited in vain for him to arrive in Sherwood, where he had
promised to settle his debt.

'Let us go to dinner,' said Big Dick at length.

'Not so,' answered Robin. 'I fear that Our Lady is wrath with me, since
she has not sent me my pay!'

'Have no doubts, master!' cried Big Dick. 'It is scarcely noon. Be sure that, before the sun is down, all will come right. I dare be sworn Sir Richard of Legh is true and trustworthy.'

'Then take your bows,' said Robin, 'you and Little Much and Scarlet, and hasten to the Great North Road. And, if the Knight you cannot find, maybe you will meet with another guest to stand proxy for him!'

Off went the three merry men, clad all in Lincoln green with swords at their sides and bows in their hands – but never a sign of Sir Richard could they find.

Presently, however, as they lay in wait behind the bushes, they saw two monks approaching dressed in long black robes and with a large band of serving men and attendants behind them.

Then said Big Dick to Little Much, with a broad grin, 'I'll wager my life these monks have brought our pay! So cheer up, loosen your swords in their scabbards, set arrows to your strings – and follow me. The monks have twenty or more followers, I know, but I dare not return to Robin without his expected guests!'

So saying, Big Dick sprang out into the road and was knocked down by a van.

'Look where you're going!' shouted the monk driver.

'I was looking where I was going. I was looking to be knocked down by you!'

'Who is your master?' asked the monk of the figure under the van.

'Who else but bold Robin Hood!'

'He is a strong thief,' quavered the monk, pale with fear. 'I have heard little good of him.'

'You lie!' cried Big Dick, crawling from under the van. 'He is a good yeoman of the forest and he bids you to dinner with him.'

'What if we refuse?' asked the monk.

'Then you'll go bloody hungry,' said Big Dick.

So they brought the two fearful monks to Robin.

'These are your guests,' protested Big Dick.

'This is an outrage,' protested the monk.

'No, it's not,' said Robin, 'it's a dinner. Can't you tell the difference between a dinner and an outrage?'

'I am the Abbot of St Mary's Higher Cellarer, and this reverent monk is my clerk.'

'High Cellarer, ha-ha!' said Robin. 'Then your duty is to supply the Abbey with provisions and wine, and to collect tithes, both in kind and money. Maybe Our Lady has sent me my pay after all, by the hands of this her servant . . . But to dinner first. Big Dick, fill a horn of the best wine for Master Cellarer – who doubtless is an expert on vintages – and let him drink to me!'

So the monks sat with very bad grace. The Cellarer and Master Vintner drank the wine and commented, 'That is fucking terrible.'

'Oh, if you think that's fucking terrible,' said Robin, 'just wait till you taste the grasshopper pie. Now, have you any money to pay for your dinner?'

'I have just written out a cheque for £10,000,' said the Master Vintner.

'Well, make it payable to Robin Hood Enterprises, Charlie Chaplin and Sons,' said Robin. 'That will just about pay for the dinner.'

Just then Sir Richard of Legh came riding hastily to the meeting place.

'Greetings to you, good Knight,' cried Robin, slapping him on the back.

'And good night to you, Robin Hood.'

'What brings you here to Barnsdale, the arsehole of England?' asked Robin.

'My good grace and your kindness and the two and six you lent me. My house and lands are once and for all free of debt. Therefore accept these small gifts. I have brought you a cuddly teddy bear, a quarter-ounce jar of jam, a feather duster, a hundredweight barbell, a ball of wool with knitting needles, a hammer and nails, a fair doll and a large pot of jam.'

10. THE SILVER ARROW

Tarrah! Boom! Crash! News came to Robin that an archery contest was being held in Cheshire. Oh, who would win? Would it be Robin?

'Oh, Father, Robin will win,' said Maid Marian.

Sir Richard de Custard Kingsley was hosting the tournament. He was doing so, the rumour said, because a dispute had arisen between the foresters of the forests of Delamere and Wirral as to who were the best archers. Oh, oh, oh, will Robin win? It was said the prize was an arrow made of silver with head and feathers of rich red gold.

'I think,' said Robin, 'that we should show Prince John a Sherwood archer could outshoot any contestant put up against them, but first I must have a jam sandwich. As for that silver arrow, I have a great desire to drop it into my quiver.'

'We shall be in great danger,' said Scarlet cautiously from under a table.

Big Dick nodded. 'Maybe our enemies in Nottingham and York will expect Robin to compete for this arrow, and be ready for him should he dare to show himself at this shooting match.'

Robin Hood smiled slowly. 'Exactly,' he said. 'I'll get in some disguise. Aha, that's it! I'll go as Old Mother Riley.'

'Listen, we can't all go as Old Mother Riley.'

'I'm sorry, but it's Old Mother Riley, and Marian will be Kitty McShane.'

All through the day the competitors shot and shot and many shot each other. Prince John, to increase his popularity among the poorer of the people, was giving free jam sandwiches, a cuddly toy and a weekend in

Venice. When the afternoon was far advanced, thirty of the archers lay dead drunk and face down on the ground, leaving only six archers to compete.

'And now,' said Sir Richard de Kingsley, 'since these three are equal (he couldn't count up to six), let them shoot at the eye and that be the final test.'

The first man from Delamere stood forward, gave his long, low cry of 'he, he', knocked his arrow, and drew it to his cheek until the arrow hummed through the air.

Sir Richard stepped down to the target. There was a gasp from the crowd.

'It's in the gold,' he cried, 'but a hair's-breadth out from the eye. Then Delamere has it, unless Sherwood shoot better.'

Once more his bugle rang out and every sound died with the echo of it. Quietly a man from Sherwood took his stand, knocked the arrow (Oh please God, let him win!), glanced down the point at the distant shimmering target, then he drew the mighty bow to its limit. The air seemed to stand still. He let go the bowstring and the arrow sped like a meteor towards the target.

There was a gasp of mingled breath and praise. Richard de Custard Kingsley proclaimed in a great voice, 'I declare that the archer from Sherwood bears away the silver arrow from both Wirral and Delamere. Let the champion, the man of Sherwood, draw near and receive his prize.'

Robin stepped forward.

'Uncover your head, fellow.'

He did, and revealed Old Mother Riley with a feather in her bonnet.

'I bestow this silver arrow upon the best archer present, Old Mother Riley,' announced Sir Richard.

'What is your name, Yeoman?' asked the Prince.

'It's Old Mother Riley. I'm an old cleaning woman from Ireland.'

A Knight dressed in chain mail said, 'This man is not Old Mother Riley; she's in a nursing home in Bognor. That is Robert Fitzooth, truly the Earl of Locksley and an Old Mother Riley impressionist.'

Prince John, putting on his reading glasses, said, 'I'm glad to have seen this far-famed Robin Hood.'

'Shame on you, false Prince,' cried Robin, drawing himself up to his full height and putting on his own glasses. 'This is no way to treat a guest and a lawful winner of a prize.'

'Go in peace, false traitor,' said John, and sang:

We'll meet again
Don't know where
Don't know when
But I know we'll meet again some sunny day
Keep smiling through
Just like you always do
Until we see the dark clouds far away.

'To take Robin Hood here might cause a riot and undo all today's good work but Sir Guy and his men are posted on every road and he cannot escape,' whispered Prince John.

'We are in great danger,' said Robin in a low voice to Big Dick and Scarlet, who were waiting in the crowd. 'Gather the rest of our band and slip quietly away to the north woods where Delamere Forest lies deepest. If they overtake us, fire a volley, then a villey and then a valley and flee into the forest.'

The danger came sooner than Robin had expected. They were not yet out of Kingsley Park when the bushes on every side gave up armed men and the shrill bugle call brought Sir Guy de Custard with several mounted followers galloping straight into the bushes and getting lost.

'Now stand all together, ha, ha,' directed Robin, 'and shoot as you've never shot before – straight. Not one volley, but many, keeping back three or four arrows each. There are but a dozen of us and at least four times that number of them. But wait a minute, ha, ha, has not today shown that the archers of Sherwood surpassed all others?'

'Yield, Robin Hood,' said Guy. 'My men surround you and there's no escape.'

'Aha,' said Robin, 'and this is my answer to you, Sir Guy.'

As he spoke, Robin drew his bow, loosed the arrow from the string and struck Sir Guy de Custard Gisborne on the front of his helmet. It failed to pierce the iron plate but it toppled him backward out of his saddle and brought him to the ground with a crash. His armour weighed two tonnes and they had to wait half an hour while they got a crane to put him back on. In a little while no one durst stand against the archers of Sherwood. They fled in all directions but mostly away.

'Now,' commanded Robin, 'shoot no more but run for the trees where we'll have lunch of porridge sandwiches.'

Guy de Custard had recovered his senses and stapled back the lumps of armour that had fallen off him. He urged on his men while parties kept running in from various glades and clearings in the forest, which were almost continually open in that part – in fact some fell in.

Twice more, bands of men sprang out on Robin and his band in ambush, and just as easily they were wiped out. They were beaten back with quick volleys of arrows.

'Take that, you buggers, ha, ha,' said Robin.

'Look, yonder, the pine-stone house. It's got all mod cons – television, television and TV,' shouted Big Dick.

'Has it a coat of arms?'

'Yes, but no legs.'

It was the house of Sir Richard Legh himself.

'Welcome, its £3.10 a week, B&B. Welcome, welcome,' said Richard, slapping Robin on the back. 'I have a chance of repaying you –' More slapping on the back. 'Kindly be to me what I was to you in Sherwood.' More slapping on the back. 'I bid you and all your men up the drawbridge and fend the walls and the great tower, bolt the doors, the windows, and the cat flap.'

Early next morning came Sir Guy de Custard Gisborne with his armour tied on with string and a large company of men and a fridge, and Richard Legh demanded that he store some beer in the fridge for lunchtime.

'Faugh!' shouted Sir Guy de Custard and, knowing that he had not the means to assault the fortress, he turned for home.

Some days later, with Robin and his men having departed for their forest, Sir Richard's lady mounted her horse and rode day and night until she came to Sherwood.

'God save you, Robin Hood. Sir Guy de Gisborne has, contrary to all law, imprisoned my husband in Nottingham Castle.'

'We can scarce effect a rescue there,' said Robin, looking grave. 'I know: I will wear this model French la femme le frock.'

'I am hees mistress and I needs heem at 'ome,' said the French model, standing on the drawbridge of Nottingham Castle.

As a result of Robin being dressed in a French la femme le frock, Sir Legh of Legh was released from prison and escorted with all honour back to his home.

While Robin was in Nottingham, he discovered that there was a porridge surplus so he smuggled some back in his bra – 33 inches' worth. While dressed like a Frenchwoman he was arrested by the Sheriff's police for being a lesbian. To prove he wasn't he gave them a photo of his own genitals. They put it on display at the Police Black Museum. Many women asked for a copy.

11. ROBIN HOOD AND THE BUTCHER

Because there was so much to do in Sherwood, some of them did it behind the trees. Nearly all of the food they ate had to be trapped or shot. Alternatively they could buy a pound of sausages, but they were always in danger of sausages being seized by the Sheriff of Nottingham. What with Sir Guy de Custard of Gisborne, and the rest, Robin Hood had to keep five hundred archers on standby. They usually stood by a tree.

On one occasion, Big Dick and Robin were walking by the high road when a cart of meat came jogging along accompanied by a pussy cat who picked up bits that fell off.

'Now then, I've a mind to be a butcher myself. Will you sell me your horse and lend me your pussy cat?' asked Robin.

'Right willingly,' answered the Butcher, and went to bed with a high temperature.

Robin killed the horse (he was a cruel bugger), donned the bloodstained butcher's garb and headed into town with his own horse, followed by the pussy cat.

'Meat to sell! Fresh horse meat to sell! Fresh meat, three pennies a pound and, free for adoption, a pussy cat!'

Among the crowd that gathered round him came the Sheriff's wife and, seeing the meat was good and tender and most unusually cheap, she invited the Butcher to bring his horse, cart and pussy cat to the Sheriff's to sell what was left and then sup with her and the Sheriff.

At dinner, Robin and his cart and his horse learnt many things. He heard that King Richard was a prisoner, and that Prince John was giving it out that he was dead so that he himself might become King.

Next morning Robin was arrested by the RSPCA for cruelty to a horse and having an unlicensed pussy cat. He daren't let on he had another horse in the fridge but was then further arrested by BUPA police for not being ill.

Late that evening the Sheriff asked Robin if he had any horned beasts that he could sell them.

'I can do that,' said Robin, then led the Sheriff and two followers into a herd of three hundred deer on the outskirts of the forest. Robin was easily able to lure them to his forest hideaway.

'You swine of a man. You'll pay for this,' roared the Sheriff.

'No, he's doing it for free,' said Big Dick.

'Fine trade indeed,' announced Robin, pulling a beard and a moustache and an eye patch from his disguise. 'And, see, I've brought with me the Sheriff of Nottingham to dine with us today.'

'He is right welcome,' said Big Dick, 'and I'm sure he will pay well for his dinner.'

'Indeed,' laughed Robin, 'for he has brought some money with him to buy three hundred head of deer from me and already he has offered me a great sum of money to lead him to our secret glade.'

'Are these deer?'

'Yes, very dear. Pound for a pound.'

'By the Rude,' said the Sheriff, shaking with terror, 'had I guessed who you were, a thousand pounds would not have brought me into Sherwood.'

'Oh yes it would. It would also have got you a ticket for Manchester United v Tottenham Hotspur.'

So the Sheriff and his two trembling followers were blindfolded, and they tried, with difficulty, to eat their food. Since all three were blindfolded, Robin feasted them.

Big Dick spread his cloak on the ground and poured into it all the money the Sheriff had brought with him. It came to £500.

'We'll keep their three horses, too,' said Robin, 'and let Master Sheriff and his two men walk back forty miles to Nottingham and a porridge drought. When you next come to visit me in Sherwood,' said Robin quietly, 'you shall not get away on such easy terms. I'll send you all packing back with just your under drawers, ha, ha, ha, ha.'

Then he left them and returned to the secret glade where the Butcher, whose name was Gilbert-of-the-White-Hand, was waiting for him.

'Here are your cart, horse and pussy back again, good Master Butcher. I have had a fine holiday selling meat in your stead – but we must not play too many of such pranks.'

'By the must,' swore Gilbert the Butcher, 'I'll sell meat no longer if you will have me as one of your merry men. I'll become a vegetarian, and so will my pussy cat.'

That night there was another back-smacking feast. But next day Robin was issued with a summons from the RSPCA for killing a horse. The fine was £10.

Ten pounds! It took three hours to count the money. Tears ran down his cheeks as he counted each pound. He was also fined by BUPA for not being ill.

12. THE ADVENTURES OF THE BEGGARS

After Robin's adventure with the Butcher, Gilbert the Whitehand, and his trick played on the Sheriff of Nottingham, Big Dick professed himself to be jealous.

There were in those days a great many beggars wandering about the country. Some were Liberals; some were Conservatives; some of the Green Party; and they were not always either too old or too lame to work. Often, indeed, they were lazy ruffians who only turned up in Parliament for their daily pay. Some were even so lazy they lived on Social Security and Big Macs and chips.

Such a beggar as this, Robin and Big Dick saw striding along the road, waving a great staff in his hand and singing merrily.

'Farewell, Beggar Big Dick,' laughed Robin as he came down the hill. 'There you have your disguise. Hie away to Nottingham and call on the Sheriff!'

'I seem to have lost the first round. But I'll wager you, good master, that I'll bring back better gains as a beggar than ever you would,' said Big Dick.

'Done,' laughed Robin.

Yes, indeed, Big Dick had been done.

'Now I'll hasten after your friend there and see what he has in his bag,' cried Robin.

Away went Robin at his best pace and very soon caught up with the beggar. 'Not so fast there,' shouted Robin, taking out his knife. 'Stand still a minute! Let me see the colour of your gold.'

'Right willing,' answered the beggar. With that he opened the bag and Robin bent down to see what he would take out, the brisk wind ruffling his hair as he did so. The beggar moved round a little so as to get the wind behind him. And then he suddenly pulled out a great handful of ground porridge and flung it into Robin's face.

Robin stowed away his arrows under his coat, unstrung the bow which he could then use as a staff, and set off by the shortest forest paths towards Nottingham. Now he knew there was a porridge surplus. Through the wood he came to the edge of the forest, where he fell off. He came to a crowd clustered around a low knoll on which stood the gallows.

'This is no public spectacle, but a cruel, unlawful wickedness,' said Robin without porridge.

Robin pushed his way right to the front. The crowds were crying shame upon the Sheriff, Prince John, and all Normans – and pity and encouragement to the prisoners. 'Cheer up, you'll soon be dead.'

The Executioner had almost to push his way through the throng. As he passed Robin, he tripped suddenly. Robin uttered a cry, lurched forward as if pushed from behind, and landed on the man's back.

The Captain of the Guard strode forward with several of his men. Roughly they dragged Robin to his feet, and then the Executioner. But the latter fell again for the hot iron in his hand had burnt a great red wound like the letter U on his face – and in falling Robin had broken several of his somethings.

'Your noble worships,' whined Robin, 'the crowd pushed me – I fell – and I broke my something. I could not help it. Spare me, I pray.'

'That's enough grovelling,' said the Prince. 'Fellow, you may go free if you perform the office of executioner in place of the man whom you have injured.'

'Make haste then,' said the Captain. 'There will be trouble if we delay longer.'

'As soon as this iron's white hot,' Robin called out, 'I'll see the right man gets it in the face. Porridge for sale,' he said, 'and one of the condemned men wants to buy some. Mercy, the condemned man wants to eat some porridge. The man's last request – 'tis the law. The other two will have to wait. I'll cook it for him.'

Robin came to the foot of the gallows, raised the iron as if to press the points into the first man's eyes – and then suddenly, twiggerlypoo, straightened himself up and hurled it with dead accuracy into the face of the Captain of the Guard.

'I say, I say, that's jolly unfair,' said the Captain.

The stillness was broken by the scream of pain. During it, Robin flung off the beggar's coat and took up his bow and arrow, ready for action. Robin had his arrow tipped with plague, malaria and typhoid.

'Freemen of England – make way for Robin Hood and his three new followers.'

'Cut him down!' cried the Captain, staggering to his feet. He had to go somewhere.

Robin's bowstring twanged, and the Captain fell to the ground for the last time, an arrow through his heart. He died of plague.

Now the guards made ready as if to attack Robin. But his bowstring twanged twice and two more men lay dead of plague – for at that range even chain mail could not withstand arrows sped by the surest hand that ever plucked a bowstring. Robin loosed one or two more arrows; both guards died of malaria. The remaining guards could only push through the throng slowly. By the time they reached the gallows, Robin and the men he had rescued were lost in Sherwood Forest.

While all this was happening, near Nottingham, where incidentally there had been a porridge glut, Big Dick came late in the afternoon to a fire which had been lit. Around it sat three others. To shorten his temper, a man from the RSPCA wanted to know if he had killed any horses, threatening him with a warrant.

'Greetings, brothers,' said Big Dick. 'I'm glad I've come upon my kind. I hope you've had a better day than I've had.'

Sherwood was still a place of mystery.

13. ROBIN HOOD AND THE TANNER

Now then, it was one lovely May day and Arthur the Tanner was singing as he rode. It was bloody awful singing as he went, but he went.

'Well met, jolly fellow, well met,' said Robin, backslapping Arthur. 'You sing like Dorothy Squires. How is the cat skinning going today?'

'Well, I've done 25 cats and some of them have been worn around the neck of highborn ladies, all with flea collars.'

'Now, Tanner, there is a new law. All tanners who drink too much ale and beer are to be set in the stocks. Some will have their legs put in the stocks and their pussy cats' legs too.'

'That's rubbish,' said Arthur, nearly falling off his horse laughing. 'We will not lose any freedom by that, and it will not stop my catching pussy cats. It's a freedom I'll wager that you lose sooner than I do.'

'I'll take your wager, and two cats,' said Robin. 'Let us on to Nottingham. There might be a porridge glut there.'

'But, tell me, what brings you by the forest road?' said Arthur.

'They call it a horse.'

'There is a reward offered for the capture of Robin Hood. I have in my pocket a warrant for his arrest and three cats.'

'If I meet this Robin Hood,' said the Tanner, 'they will pay me a hundred pounds and six cats.'

'Indeed?' mused Robin. He would know more of this grand reward and pussy cats upon his head.

So they went to the inn and Robin had a mead and a matzo; Arthur had an ale and the pussy cats had three coca colas with straws. Bit by bit Arthur became blot-eyed and collapsed to the ground. He was so full he started to leak. Three of the pussy cats escaped from his trouser pocket and ran out of the door shouting, 'Freedom! Freedom! Freedom!'

Robin Hood waited for the drunken slob to recover. He tried to assist him by throwing three bottles of icy water over him. It didn't seem to help so Robin returned to the camp. On the way he adopted three stray pussy cats.

When Arthur the Tanner came to, he was enraged that he had let Robin Hood slip from his fingers, and three cats slip from his trousers. He sprang on his horse and shot off the other side.

Robin returned to the inn and stabled his horse with the stable man. 'It's sixty pence a horse, Robin.'

'Oh look, here's sixty pence and a pound.'

'Why the pound?' said the attendant.

'It's an intelligence test,' said Robin. 'Now pass me the glass. I've just found some water and I want to use it before it goes off.'

So Arthur the Tanner confronted Robin Hood and rushed at him with a good oak staff. WHACK! Down went Arthur. WHACK! Down went Arthur. WHACK! Down went Arthur. WHACK! Down went parts of Arthur. WHACK! Two pieces of Arthur went down. WHACK! Down went some more of Arthur the Tanner.

'And now, there, there, Arthur-a-Whack. Have you had enough?'

'Well, let's put it this way, I don't want any bloody more. You owe me three pussy cats,' said Arthur-a-Whack.

'I'm sorry, I'll set up a pussy cat hunt tomorrow and try and catch them again. Look, Arthur-a-Whack, come and join my merry band in Sherwood Forest, or at least come and dine with us,' said Robin. 'I owe you a good meal in exchange for the thrashing I gave you. You can use as much tomato sauce and jam as you like.'

Robin blew his horn and his socks rolled down. There appeared Big Dick and several others and two cats who were survivors of Arthur-a-Whack.

'By the mass!' exclaimed Arthur. 'Is that Big Dick?'

'That was his name,' answered Robin, 'before a tree fell on him.'

'Big Dick!' said Arthur. 'Big Dick is my own cousin, our mothers being sisters. And I loved him ever since he was a little boy.'

'What is the matter, good master,' called Big Dick as he saw blood on Robin's face.

'Well, that bastard bashed me in the face.'

'Did he? Take that, you bastard!' And he hit Arthur-a-Whack over the head.

'Look, I can't sit here getting bashed. I got to hunt my pussy cats,' moaned Arthur.

A fine dinner was spread before Arthur-a-Whack, and so he became a member of the gang.

Every morning Arthur-a-Whack went riding out looking for pussy cats. He could never see them but they could always see him.

14. THE WEDDING OF ALLIN-A-DALE

Robin Hood and his men lived mainly in caves, huts, cupboards, refrigerators and washing machines. They stayed mostly on the tops of trees so they could see other people's heads – many with bald heads, many with grey heads, many with red heads, many unfortunate ones with no heads at all. They lived in the wildest depth of Sherwood Forest and they had many other places as well. There was the basement of the Silver Star Soup Kitchen, the kitchens of McDonald's and Ronny Scott's Hyde Park.

Sir Richard of Legh, the bankrupt Knight whom Robin had saved, had been an ardent follower of King Richard Coeur de Lion. Sir Richard's men were ever ready to shelter Robin Hood. They used an umbrella. They sheltered Robin Hood for nearly six months under the umbrella then they got fed up of holding it.

Robin first saw Allin-a-Dale one spring day as he stood in the pale-green shade of the chestnut waiting to shoot shepherds. When Robin saw him, he'd already killed three and hung them up.

There came the sound of crappy singing and a brave young man came tripping along a forest path and fell flat on his face. He stood up dripping in mud, as fine a sight as could be seen for the perverted. He was clothed in scarlet, red and mud. And, as he strode along, springing a little with each step, he sang as sweetly as a bird. And ever and anon, he paused to strike a trilling melody from the very harp that hung from his shoulder. Clankity clang it went.

Next day Robin saw him again but now he came drooping through the woods, his feet dragging behind him, his head bent. He had caught it in a disco door.

At a sign from Robin, Big Dick and Little Much stepped out into the open and barred the young man's way. But, just to sedate him a bit, Big Dick hit him over the head with a stick and gave him a Valium.

'Stand off, stand off,' cried Big Dick. 'You must come before our master at once.'

'And who is your master?' asked Allin-a-Dale.

'Robin Hood.'

When he was brought before Robin, Robin asked him cautiously, 'Fair sir, have you any cash to spare for my merry men and me?'

'No bloody fear, one's just bashed me over the head.'

'Oh, he was only training,' said Robin.

'I have no money to spare except five shillings and a ring. These I have hoarded for several long years to have at my wedding, but my bride was taken away from me. They are forcing her to marry a grizzled old Knight.'

Awwwwww

'What is your name?'

'Allin-a-Dale.' Then he sang:

There'll be bluebirds over
The white cliffs of Dover
Tomorrow just you wait and see.

They went to see bluebirds over the white cliffs but all they saw were sea gulls, a dumped fridge and crows.

'What will you give me, Allin, if I deliver you your true love from the old Knight?' asked Robin.

'Robin, I will swear upon the Bible to be your true and faithful servant and lend you my pussy cat. I'll give you a pound and have the money sent by postal order.'

'But what about these bluebirds over the cliffs of Dover? Will we see them?'

'No, you will see sea gulls, a dumped fridge and crows.'

Robin took the train to Hyde Park and got out. Robin borrowed Allin's harp, wrapped his cloak about him and entered the cathedral where the wedding was being held.

'Oi, you, shitface, where are you going?' said a monk

'Well,' said Robin, 'first I'm going somewhere to get away from you. I am the best harpist in the North and I'm sure no wedding is complete without music, a cake and a pussy cat.'

'If that is so, you're right welcome, shitface,' said the Bishop. 'Come play to us until the bride and groom arrive.'

We'll meet again
Don't know where, don't know when
But I know we'll meet again some sunny day
Keep smiling through
Like you always do
Till it grew too blue.

The bride came walking down the aisle. She was young but as pale as death and her eyes were red with weeping. After her came the old Knight in a motorised wheelchair. He ran over the bride. He had put a deposit down on her of $10.

Now Robin started to sing louder and louder.

'For God's sake shut up, shitface,' said the Bishop.

'Not so,' answered Robin. 'I see no bridegroom yet for this lovely lass with her youth and beauty. The old man, I suppose her grandfather, comes to give her in marriage to the man of her choice. Is he your choice for the wedding night?' Robin asked the bride.

'No,' she said.

Whereupon the Knight had a heart attack and fell dead at her feet. Robin was quick to pocket the $10. With that, Robin set his horn to his lips and blew out the back of his trousers. Soon the church was live with archers.

'Heel um am,' said Allin-a-Dale.

'So you are,' said Robin.

'Who gives this maid to be married?' asked Big Dick.

'That I do,' cried Robin.

And so, Allin-a-Dale and his bride were married and they had their honeymoon at Sherwood Forest and gave Robin a pussy cat. Gradually Allin's speech became clearer. Unbeknown to all concerned, someone had belted him over the head with a staff.

15. GEORGE-A-GREEN, THE PINNER OF WAKEFIELD

Then another forest year went by quickly enough and then it went quicker and reached 92 years early. Robin was getting on a bit now and his hair was growing thin and he was put to wearing a ginger wig and false teeth. Prince John plotted and schemed to gain power and King Richard, after his unsuccessful crusade, was captured by the Archduke of Austria and languished in prison. Blondel, Richard's faithful minstrel, every day tried to haul up to the tower a series of goods – a bottle of Dettol, a tube of Pepsodent and some feather dusters and a box of matches, twenty Players, a cuddly toy, and in case he got lonely a rubber, blow-up woman doll. Blondel sang at the bottom of the tower:

You are my sunshine my only sunshine
You make me happy when skies are grey
You'll never know, dear, how much I love you
Please don't take that sunshine away.

'For fuck's sake, shut up,' said the voice of King Richard.

The ransom which the Archduke demanded for the King was £1,000,000. Toward this, Robin sent a pound and asked for a receipt.

George-a-Green had won the world heavyweight wrestling contest and pulled a railway train backwards with his teeth. This last feat was a disaster as all his teeth shot out. George-a-Green's fame, like butter, had spread. He was even mentioned at Bexhill-on-Sea. He had fallen off Mount Everest. He swam the Channel backwards, upside down, and he slew a lion and an elephant, strangled an anaconda, and wrestled with a gorilla. He even slept with the Spice Girls.

Marian took Robin to the side one day. 'Dear heart, one hears so much these days of the deeds and valour of this George-a-Green, and of the beauty of his love for the fair Bettris, who is said to exceed all women in her loveliness. Until recently your name was on everyone's lips and in some people's trouser pockets. And they all sang of you and me, the Queen of Sherwood.'

Now, many evenings later, his cares permitting, George-a-Green walked forth into the country outside Wakefield with Bettris on his arm, to view the fields.

'Tell me, sweet love,' George was saying, 'are you content to wed so simple a man as I when Knights and gentlemen seek your hand in marriage?'

'Oh, George, how can you doubt my love?'

George-a-Green suddenly grasped his staff and flushed with anger as he gazed across the nearest field.

'Look!' he exclaimed. 'There are four men breaking through the hedge. Oh, this is not to be borne.'

'That's it, don't borne it, George.'

'Go back, you foolish travellers! You are wrong – you mustn't borne it!' cried George.

'Are you mad?' cried Robin, who was, of course, the leader of the four.

'No, I'm just having a giddy spell.'

'Look at our limbs,' boasted Robin.

'Sirrah,' answered George, 'the biggest limbs have always got the stoutest hearts. If you are brave men and not cowards, come to me one at a time and I'll trounce you all. I'll stop you borning it.'

'Piss off,' said Robin.

'Sirrah, dare you defy me?' shouted George.

'If we give you a dried fish will you let us go?' asked Will Scarlet.

Then they came together striking mighty blows but by the end it was George who knocked Scarlet a crack on the head and laid him out. They had to send for an ambulance.

'Save your blows for a younger man,' exclaimed Big Dick, and a moment later they too were exchanging blows that rang out like thunder across the peaceful evening fields.

But the end of that round was also that Big Dick felt the Pinner's staff on his head more heavily than his senses could stand. Another ambulance.

'Come on,' cried Robin, taking Big Dick's place, 'spare me not and I'll not spare you. Yes, if you spare me not, I'll spare you not, but if I don't spare you, you'll not spare me.'

Just in case, Robin called the ambulance. They rushed him to hospital where they operated for appendicitis and took him back.

'Ha, ha,' laughed George, equally cornily. 'Make no doubt of that, for I'll be as liberal to you as I was to your friend. In fact, I'll smash your bloody brains in.'

It was a contest with much at stake. Every time Robin hit, he called, 'Cuddly toy, holiday for two in Venice, washing machine, teddy bear, set of dishes.' He never got further – George knocked him down.

So they set to work with great oaken staffs and they were so evenly matched that, though they fought for an hour, neither got in a decisive blow at the other.

'Just wait till I see that cow Marian,' Robin said sotto voce. 'All this mayhem for the love of a bloody woman. I hope she's satisfied,' said Robin with a split head and blood running down his face.

'I'll have that dried fish now,' said George.

Robin was carried back on a stretcher. 'I hope you're satisfied,' he said to Marian.

'Well, you could have come back standing up.'

'I am standing up. I'm just doing it on a stretcher.'

16. A NIGHT ALARM AND A GOLDEN PRICE

After spending several days at Wakefield with the merry Pinner George-a-Green and his bonny bride Bettris in the monkey house, they all set out once more for Sherwood. The first day's journey was mainly down the road fighting the monkeys off. A monkey and a dozen men at arms swung round a corner in front of them at a trot and came past before they had any chance of hiding.

The Knight did not stop but his visor was down, which caused him to keep riding into trees and houses.

'Walk on,' said Robin quietly to his men. 'Try and ignore the monkeys but follow me quickly and quietly into the wood as soon as they are out of sight. That was Sir Guy de Custard of Gisborne – who is my sworn enemy.'

'What is he doing with that monkey?' asked Marian.

'He's taking it for a walk.'

'Where are you leading us?' George said at last.

'To seek shelter for the night and give your monkey a rest.'

'Whither go you, my masters?' asked Big Dick. 'There be rogues in that direction.'

'Can you show us any direction in which there are no rogues?' said Robin.

'Yonder.' He pointed to a door invitingly open and on the threshold was Arthur-a-Whack.

'Welcome, welcome, good Robin Hood!' cried Arthur, and slapped him on the back, arousing all those painful bits. 'And welcome to your brave followers. My wife and I are indeed honoured by your company.'

'Now don't overdo it. I fear that we bring danger with us,' said Robin, 'and a monkey.'

They came to the great stone-flagged room which served as kitchen and hall, and indeed the whole ground floor of the little house was all in one. So was Robin and so was Marian and Arthur-a-Whack and his wife and a monkey. They were all in one.

And, when he had introduced George and Bettris, they all sat down on rough-hewn benches which gave them numerous splinters in the bum.

'Ah, this wine is Sancerre,' said George.

'No, frog wine,' said Arthur.

Even as he said this, his wife caught him suddenly by the arm and pointed to the window. Outside there was an armed Knight with plumes tossing in the storm. Alas, with the torrential rain his plumes all hung down, blinding him.

'Shelter for a poor traveller who has lost his way in the storm!' came a voice from outside.

'Who and what are you? What identity have you?'

'We are soldiers taking a poor monkey for a walk.' And they put the monkey through the letterbox.

'Are you alone?' said Robin.

'Not with a monkey.'

Back came the monkey through the letterbox.

In the end there was an angry, 'Look, if you don't let us in I will break my fist down on this door.'

'Aha,' said George-a-Green, 'we are ready for you. You thought to rob, murder and set a monkey on my monkey. Well, we're ready for you. We must warn you that we have a jar with leprosy spores in it and, the moment you come in, we'll break it.'

Then Robin, Scarlet, Big Dick and George drew back to the other end of the room and the door gave a crash and a dozen or more armed men were seen in the opening followed by a monkey. The instant the door broke, the five bows twanged and as many arrows rushed unerringly to their marks. Five soldiers lay dead on the floor. Arthur then picked up the leprosy spores and threw them at the Captain of the Guard.

'Help,' screamed the Captain, 'I've got leprosy.'

And then, 'Mercy, good sir,' gasped the Knight. 'Put down your swords, men: we are fairly beaten.'

'Guy of Gisborne, you shit,' said Marian, flinging back her hood so he could see who had defeated him.

'I've got a good idea: let's chop off his head,' said Robin, so chip, chop and off it came.

The next morning they set off again for Sherwood.

'I hope there're no more adventures before we are safe in our own glades,' said Robin.

'Yes, as long as you don't go near any rivers,' said George.

'Shoosh,' cautioned Robin. 'Come quietly hither behind these bushes, good George, and I believe that you will see how we gather our tithes in Sherwood Forest. Yes, the good Friar is collecting subscriptions for King Richard's ransom!'

The travellers saw Friar Tuck, his mighty quarterstaff in his hand, talking with two trembling priests.

'Alas, we have not so much as a penny piece between us. For this very morning we met with robbers who took from us everything we had, including our pile ointment.'

'Stand, base Friar!' roared Robin.

Friar Tuck looked up. 'Robin Hood, forever my master,' went on the grovelling cur.

'Any news?'

'Yes, a man from the RSPCA has heard you are in possession of some monkeys and wants to know if they're being well looked after. A verger brought you a six-pound tin of jam and you'll be delighted to know that we've eaten it.'

'And look what I bring with me,' answered Robin. 'Brave George-a-Green, the Pinner of Wakefield, who is now one of us, and with him his bride, the lovely Bettris, who has brought us another six-pound pot of jam.'

Jam, jam wonderful jam
I will eat it where'ere I am

So they sat down to a feast of six pounds of jam and for days afterwards they were stuck to each other.

17. THE WITCH OF PAPLEWICK

'Can I come in or are Jews excluded?' The voice came from a man with a black moustache called Groucho.

'Welcome to Sherwood Forest,' said Robin.

'And you're welcome to it, too,' said Groucho. 'As a matter of fact, if this is Sherwood Forest I can't see the wood for the trees.'

One summer's day Robin Hood decided to hold yet another boring feast to entertain the shepherds. Unfortunately, this was a sad occasion, for Eglamour had lost his love, Earine.

'Lost? Hasn't he looked for her?' said Groucho. 'Was she insured?'

'Yes, but they only paid out fifty pounds.'

'You couldn't afford to bury her in the ground with that. You'll have to bury her above ground.'

Eglamour would not believe she was dead but sought her still by wood, by woe, by telegraph, by telephone, by telex, by lighthouse.

'My Marian,' cried Robin.

'Robin, my love!' she answered. 'Oh, now my day's happiness is complete. I rose early, early before the sun, and such fine sport we had seeking the deer. Then one shot brought him down.'

'Yes, nothing like killing deer to start a happy day,' said Groucho.

'Only one shadow fell upon us,' said Marian. 'When we had killed the deer and cracked it up, a raven sat in a tree over our heads and croaked.'

'You say he croaked?' said Groucho. 'He's lucky to be alive.'

'They are wise birds and know that it is ever the huntsman's custom, when he cleaves the brisket bone, to set aside the spoon of it with the gristle that grows there – which indeed is often called the Raven's Bone. [Mrs Beaton, p. 141.]

'The Mother Maudlin, the Witch of Paplewick, can take any form she will and fill them in. She can even become a pot of jam,' said Marian.

'Yes, the witch,' said Groucho, 'by her wobbling I'd say she needed a slimline aerodynamic broomstick.'

Groucho fired an arrow into the air on the off chance it would fall on somebody. There was a loud explosion. By a lucky chance he'd hit a taxi, puncturing the driver.

'How now, sweet Marian?' began Robin. 'Shall we to the feast?'

'Feast!' cried Marian, her voice filled with anger. 'What bloody feast?'

'Why, your bloody feast,' said Groucho.

'Why, Marian, how strange you look,' said Robin.

'Oh, I am well,' snapped Marian.

'There, let us call our friends to the feast.'

'Yes, let us. I'm one,' said Groucho. 'I'll see if I'm in.'

'Friends,' cried Marian, whirling her rosary round and round her head. 'They shall not feast on this venison. Scarlet, take up the venison – swiftly now! Carry it to Mother Maudlin, the wise woman whom you call a witch, and her white crow. Mr Marx is keen to know if it's changed colour.'

'If it's green now it's a parrot,' said Groucho.

'Marian, can this be true?' gasped Robin.

'I think she's running out of her tablets,' said Groucho.

'Am I dreaming that I am now Robin Hood and this is Marian?' said Robin.

'You are Robin Hood right enough, you grovelling little creep,' said Groucho.

Marian left with Will Scarlet and the feast.

'I fear she is stricken with some illness,' said Robin at last.

'It's Alzheimer's disease,' said Groucho.

Suddenly Marian appeared. 'Robin, xypta monzal prup a pool.'

'That's Alzheimer's! I'd recognise it anywhere,' said Groucho.

'Yes,' Robin proclaimed. 'I want you to see a London psychiatrist. I'll get it on BUPA.'

'Look, here comes Big Dick.'

'Good master,' he called, 'here is Mother Maudlin. She says that she comes in gratitude with some gift made by Maid Marian.'

Alas, although Eglamore had rediscovered his lost love, the witch cast a spell on Will Scarlet and he became a frog.

'Mind how you tread,' said Groucho.

The witch turned and sped away swiftly on her broomstock to a holiday in Japan at Karaoke Holiday Camp. Now that Earine had been discovered alive, there was no reason she couldn't eat a Big Mac and chips.

And still, Sherwood was a place of mystery.

18. THE LAST OF GUY OF CUSTARD GISBORNE

The last Guy of Custard Gisborne
Now take thou gold and fee
Sir Guy will come and moat thou be
Your rear will go numb
So he gets kicked right up the bum.

Anon, 'Folk Play of Robin Hood', before 1476

It was a glorious spring morning. Groucho was sipping oxygen through a straw. New leaves were fully opened and so were all the pubs. The greenwood was all fresh and daisy-clad, and the birds sang merrily in every tree.

Loudest of all sang the thrush. Robin shot it.

'Let us go and see if there is a porridge surplus in Nottingham,' he cried.

Off went Big Dick whistling happily but, alas, he came upon two dead men with arrows in their hearts and it needed only a glance to tell him that both these fellows were outlaws and members of Robin's band.

'Aren't you going to call the police?' asked Groucho. 'It's a case of double homicide here.'

Will Scarlet came hopping down the road for his life. William Trent, whom Big Dick knew well and had once thrashed at quarterstaff, stepped up on to a log and loosed his arrow, and Will Scarlet pitched forward on to his face.

'How do you bury a frog?' asked Groucho.

'It were better for you, William Trent, that your hand had been smitten off at the wrist 'er you fired that shot,' cried Big Dick, and as he spoke his bow twanged and Will Scarlet's slayer lay dead.

'They're dropping like flies around here,' said Groucho. 'Soon we won't have enough characters left to finish this story!'

The Sheriff's men were upon Groucho and bound him.

'I'm on a goodwill visit to Nottingham to see if there's any chance of a porridge surplus,' he cried.

The Sheriff rode up and surveyed Big Dick. 'You shall be drawn at rope's end by down and dale back to Nottingham and then hanged on Castle Hill.'

'Not much of an offer,' said Groucho. 'Get a solicitor. He'll have you off in a day. He'll have you bankrupt in an hour and a half. I'll send a fax to Robin to tell him.'

Fax
Big Dick preparing for death. Seek advice.
PS: No porridge surplus in Nottingham.

Meanwhile, Robin was speaking to a forester who had a duck on a lead.

'You carry in your hand a fine bow. I presume you're a good archer,' said Robin.

'No, I'm a bloody awful one.'

'Come with me then and bring your duck.'

'I wish to meet Robin Hood,' said the stranger, 'and I would fain be one of his company.'

'We'll shoot at that white patch of lichen – that will make a bull's eye,' suggested Robin.

Robin aimed carefully at the mark. He missed.

With that he flung down his bow and quiver and stomped off. The stranger called Robin when he had gone a dozen yards. Now his voice had changed. Robin spun round at the sound of his voice; round and round and round he went. He recognised the voice as that of Sir Guy de Custard Gisborne.

The staples and string which once repaired his armour now held his head in place.

'This is the last round,' said Guy grimly, and very slowly drew back the string of his bow to point at Robin's heart.

'Look out, you'll kill the duck! To shoot an unarmed man is shame indeed and damnation to the fellow,' cried Robin.

Guy de Custard flushed a little at Robin's words and said, 'Indeed, when Robin of Locksley became Robin Hood of Sherwood he was cast out beyond the law of man and beyond the pale of honour. In a little while I shall wind my horn and thereby the Sheriff shall know that Robin is dead.'

'I prefer peanut butter on matzos,' said Groucho.

As he spoke, with a sudden movement Robin flung the knife which he held in his hand and flung himself forward on the ground with the same movement.

'That's the finest draw I've seen since Wild Bill Hickok shot Billy the Kid. You need an agent,' said Groucho.

A moment later Robin, on his feet again, his sword drawn in his hand, charged down upon Guy.

'I think he's coming your way, Guy,' said Groucho.

'I'll take possession of this duck; his life is in mortal danger,' cried Robin. With that Robin smote off Guy's head.

'I always said you'd get ahead,' said Groucho.

Some time later Robin was walking through the forest wearing Sir Guy de Custard Gisborne's armour.

'Yonder he comes,' cried the excited Sheriff. 'Come hither, good Sir Guy, and ask of me any reward you will.'

'As I have slain the master, give me the man to slay as and when I will.' And, turning quickly, Robin pointed to Big Dick, who now lay bound.

'A mad choice when gold might have been yours for the asking,' said the Sheriff.

Suddenly a Knight clad from head to foot in black armour and riding a great black horse came riding up the road.

'Back, you damned wolves!' cried the Black Knight. 'I cannot see four men borne down by such a host. Charge, foresters! St George for merry England and three pence off income tax!'

At this unexpected attack many of the Sheriff's men broke and fled. The Black Knight paused only for a moment to shout, 'Stay, you base curs! Or I'll beat you back to your kennels.'

'Just you watch out, you guys. He's not joking,' said Groucho.

19. THE SILVER BUGLE AND THE BLACK KNIGHT

High deeds achieved by knightly fame
From Palestine the champion came
The cross upon his shoulders born
Battle and blast had dimmed and torn
Each dint upon his battle shield
Was token of a foughten field

Sir Walter Scott, *Ivanhoe*, 1820

The news of a shooting match was one thing sure to draw Robin Hood out of Sherwood. Robin set forth for Ashby-de-la-Zouche in Leicestershire.

'You're doing this for her?' said Groucho.

A great tournament was being held there by Prince John. The danger to Robin was as great as when he had won his silver arrow. But he had pawned that. Prince John, though his power had greatly increased, was by no means accepted as King of England. There were rumours that Richard was free.

The main feature of the tournament was, of course, the jousting Knights who had to knock each other out of the saddle.

All that morning the battle raged and Sir Wilfred, who was the victor, fainted when the crown of victory was placed over his head – it was too big by far and slipped over one eye.

When the time came for the archery contest, all of the marksmen stepped forward, Robin amongst them. Prince John immediately recognised Robin, but was no more able to apprehend the outlaw in the midst of this tournament than he was at the last.

'You dare to show your face here!' roared the Prince. 'You dog, you-you-you . . .'

'Don't call me a you-you,' interrupted Robin. 'Locksley is my name, if you please, Your Highness.'

'It does not please me,' spluttered Prince John.

'Bollocks then,' said Robin.

One by one the archers stepped forward and each discharged their arrows. Most failed to hit the distant target. Only two landed in the gold. One was fired by Robin and the other was shot by a certain Hubert.

'As far as anybody is listening, I think Robin's going to win. I've got one hundred to one on him,' said Groucho.

'How, Locksley, will you match your skill against Hubert?' sneered the Prince.

'Many a good bow was drawn on Senlac Field,' answered Robin. 'But only one side shot their arrows at random into the air, and it was such an arrow that struck King Harold in the eye.'

'Eh?' said the Prince.

'This is no fair match you propose,' said Robin. 'Do you shoot first, friend Hubert?'

Hubert loosed an arrow which flew straight and true to the edge of the gold.

'You have not allowed for the wind, Hubert, or that would have been a better shot!' said Robin.

Thus encouraged, Hubert set another arrow to the string and, taking the light breeze into account, his shaft struck the target exactly in the centre.

'Oh, fuck,' said Robin. 'I've gotta do better than that.'

The duck followed Robin to his mark. 'I will notch his shaft for him, however,' muttered Robin. He let his arrow fly. It stuck right upon that of his competitor, which it split to shivers.

'And now, Your Highness,' said Robin quietly, 'I crave permission to plant such a mark as we use in Sherwood.'

'Quack, quack,' went the duck.

'Stop that! This is serious stuff,' said Groucho.

With that, Robin and his duck walked to the nearest picket and returned with a willow wand six feet long, perfectly straight and not much thicker than a man's thumb. This he peeled, remarking as he did so that it was an insult to ask such a fine archer as Hubert to shoot at a target which might just as well have been a haystack in a farmer's field.

'But,' he concluded, as he went and stuck the willow wand in the ground and returned to Prince John, 'he that hits yonder rod at a hundred yards, I call him an archer fit to bear bow before any king – even before our good Richard of the Lion Heart himself.'

'Cowardly dog!' fumed Prince John. He spat and his teeth shot out. 'Well, Locksley, you split that wand.'

'I will do my best,' answered Robin.

So saying, he again bent his great bow, putting one foot on the duck to steady himself, but on the present occasion looked with care to his weapon, then took aim very slowly and deliberately, and loosed while the waiting multitude held their breath. The arrow sped towards its target and split the willow wand, and a great roar of applause rose.

'Robin, you need an agent. My card, and you just won me $800.75,' said Groucho.

'Well, Locksley, you have made true your boast,' grumbled the Prince, 'and here is the silver bugle horn filled with Mars bars and Dairy Delight ice cream.'

'Thank you,' said Robin.

The Prince said, 'Go in peace now – but remember that I have sworn vengeance on you and your duck.'

'Right,' said Robin. 'Would you like a Mars bar?'

'Yes.'

'I thought you would, you bastard.'

'Oh,' said Maid Marian, 'oh, Robin, you've won. I knew you would.'

'And I've just made $800.75,' said Groucho.

'You know that yonder braggart archer is none other than Robin Hood?' grumbled the defeated Hubert.

'Yes, I know that yonder braggart archer is none other than Robin Hood. But you know I'm none other than the famous Groucho Marx and I'm $800.75 richer.'

As they were returning through Sherwood to the secret glade, Robin met the Black Knight.

'All right, Black Knight,' said Robin, 'if any danger threatens you, noble sir, know that I or any of my men will come at once to your aid.'

'Well, my main danger comes from my bank manager and my overdraft,' said the Black Knight.

'We are keeping dangerous company,' said Robin, a bankrupt. 'I see the flash of armour behind the bushes.'

'Oh, a flasher,' said Maid Marian, 'a flasher and in Sherwood.'

Without a moment's hesitation the Black Knight set spurs to his horse and charged in the direction of the bushes. He was met by six or seven well-armed men. The Black Knight immediately chopped them all off. The armless men tried to ride their horses home and went in all directions.

'Come with us, good Knight,' begged Robin.

'Are you saying good night or good Knight?' said Groucho.

'Come now, good Knight. You will dine with us and we will entertain you. First you will have a vindaloo porridge.'

20. ROBIN HOOD AND THE TALL PALMER

There'll be blue birds over
The white cliffs of Dover
Just you wait and see

I waited to see and all we saw were sea gulls, a dumped fridge and crows.

One day the Bishop of Peterborough craved an audience with Prince John. The Bishop was fearful to venture forth near Sherwood lest he be molested by Robin Hood.

'My Lord,' said the Bishop, 'I have but a small company.'

'Can you buy shares in it?' asked Groucho.

'My Lord, Sherwood is beset with outlaws. I must claim protection. I need a Centurion tank.'

On the hillside outside Nottingham, a tall palmer sat on his horse. Under his palmer's robe he wore a shirt and leggings of chain mail; on his head under the palmer's hood was a skullcap of steel. He wore a pair of jockey pants and a vest. In his backpack he had three bottles of tomato sauce which he kept for his defence. He would open one over his victim, who would then think they were bleeding to death.

Presently a man came across the fields. Mind you, he'd come across before. The Palmer spoke a few words to the messenger, who saluted and gave himself a black eye.

Soon the Bishop of Peterborough and his Centurion tank came slowly down the hill. The Palmer rode forward and saluted him humbly.

'My lord, I beg to ride with you through the forest. I hear there are outlaws and I would be safer with you inside your Centurion tank.'

'You are most welcome,' answered the Bishop. 'I fear greatly my men would afford small protection should Robin Hood attack. That is why we have this Centurion tank.'

'Yes, do you have any cats?' said the Palmer.

'Yes, I have one back at the monastery. Why?'

'I collect homeless cats.'

'But he isn't homeless.'

'Well, if you threw him out the cat flap he would be.'

'Yes, I suppose that would be one way of making him homeless.'

Through the leafy trees the Bishop could see half a dozen men busy skinning and cutting up a newly slain deer.

The Bishop stood up. 'How dare you kill the King's venison, contrary to the forest laws?'

'We are shepherds. Today we have decided to make merry and have killed this fine, fat deer for our dinner.'

'Impudent fellow, you shall go to Prince John, who usually hangs deer slayers for the first offence.'

'Oh mercy,' cried the Shepherd.

'No mercy,' replied the Bishop.

The Shepherd drew a horn from his coat and blew three notes upon it.

The Bishop sat gaping. Suddenly there came running foresters.

'What is your will, good master?' said Big Dick, bending a little before the leading shepherd.

'Here is the Bishop of Peterborough in a tank. He proposes to hang us all and he will grant us no mercy.'

'Cut off his head, master,' said Big Dick, 'and bury him under this tree.'

'Oh mercy, mercy,' cried the Bishop, trembling inside his Centurion tank, for he now recognised the leading shepherd as Robin Hood.

The lid of the Centurion tank opened and out stepped the Palmer. 'I think this is where we part company, Bishop. Good Robin Hood,' he said, 'I am not of this man's party, but I cannot sit and see a bishop done to death without raising a hand to help him. I have fought in the Holy Land with Richard in the crusade against the infidel Saracens.'

'Good Palmer,' answered Robin courteously, 'with you I have no quarrel. But come with us now and taste our hospitality. Only justice shall be done. But first you will swear.'

'I swear. I also drink and smoke.'

'May I give you this gift of three tomato-sauce bottles as a sign of my friendship?' said Robin.

'If I had a friend like that I'd shoot him,' said Groucho.

'Robin will be back soon, Bettris,' said Marian.

Bettris suddenly stopped and gazed fixedly at the bracken.

'What is it, Bettris?' asked Marian.

'I thought I saw a face, there in the ferns,' answered Bettris. 'Yonder! Yes, they are shaking still.'

'You know that fern shaking is forbidden in Sherwood,' said Groucho.

Even as she spoke the bracken parted and Prince John strode into the glade and slid on a banana.

Marian whispered to Bettris, 'He slipped on a banana. Let's wait and see what he does next.'

'So here's the tigress in her den!' cried Prince John. 'Marian, after all these years we meet again.'

'No, we are vegetarians. We'll never have meat again.'

'Come, there is no escape,' sneered Prince John. 'Our horses wait beyond the rocks with the good forester who tracked you down at last.'

'Just wait till I see him. I'll set fire to his wedding tackle,' said Groucho.

'Robin will save us!' cried Marian.

'I'm afraid Robin Hood is too busy getting the Bishop of Peterborough out of his vegetarian Centurion tank,' replied Prince John.

Marian stepped backward and fell over. Quickly she took a horn from her belt and blew the Wa-sa-hoa call on it. Then she snatched up the sword which Bettris had brought her and stood on the defensive.

'Quick,' she said, 'more bananas.'

And Bettris immediately threw one dozen bananas in the middle of all the horsemen, whose horses slipped all over the place, and they slid off their mounts, peeled them and ate them. It was a good ploy by Marian but not clever enough. Some of the horses fell over, but not all.

The three surviving men at arms, seeing Robin's men returned, suddenly ran for their lives. But not far – several arrows came from among the trees on either side and they lay dead long before they reached another banana. The Prince and the Bishop were captured.

'Now,' said Robin, 'the Bishop of Peterborough has been brought to dinner in a Centurion tank. Let us see what appetites you have.'

'You live well, friend Robin Hood.'

Commercial
Ariel is the washing powder for you.
It washes clean; Maid Marian uses no other.

[I will come back to the second half of this commercial break later on in the story.]

'In that,' answered Robin, 'I hold that we break no just law. But I hold that we are not outlawed lawfully. It's John's doing and that of the minion of the Sheriff of Nottingham. We dwell here to set right the wrong; never yet did we hurt any man knowingly who was honest and true, but only those who – with or without the law on their side – robbed innocent men or oppressed them, or did ought against the honour of a woman. They call me the poor man's friend!

'Come now, good master Palmer – we are at least thieves of honour, and you do no dishonour, that is unless you shrink from eating the King's deer.'

'Shrink?' The Palmer laughed heartily. 'Ha, ha ha. I am as hungry as if I had walked all the way home from Jerusalem – and as thirsty, too.'

When the meal was ended, Robin turned to the Bishop.

'My lord,' he said gravely, 'you have dined with me this day from the inside of a Centurion tank. Come, drink with us to King Richard and then pay us and be gone. Now, Bishop, have you anything with you in that Centurion?'

'But little. Two hundred pieces of ammunition.'

'Just pass it through the hatch. Thank you. I'll send them to the German Army.'

'I know not what I have,' said the Palmer. 'Sometimes it is much; sometimes it is little; sometimes it is bugger all.'

'Since you say bugger all,' replied Robin, 'not a penny will I touch. You shall play our game of buffets but first the Bishop will dance a jig for us.'

And the Bishop was forced to pull up his skirts and dance a jig, whether he would or not, while all the outlaws roared (with forced laughter) at his comical fat figure and angry red face.

'Red is funny, Robin? So far your games are a total pain in the arse,' said Groucho.

'Enough, enough,' panted Robin, 'we have had sport enough of this kind. Now our game of buffets.'

'How is that played?' asked the Palmer.

'Simple,' said Robin. 'It's a game for oafs. Stand up and receive a buffet from us and, if it fails to knock you down, you will give out a buffet in return.'

'A fine sport, truly,' said the oaf, Big Dick, and forthwith he bared a forearm that any smith might have been proud of.

'Come on, Big Dick,' said Robin, 'and show this man that all the men of metal are not away crusading.'

Big Dick, like a true oaf, rolled up his sleeve, drew back his arm and threw a mighty buffet. The Palmer seemed scarcely to notice it. Instead he raised his arm and sent Big Dick on the turf.

'Have I now paid for my dinner, good Robin?' he asked.

'You must be the strongest oaf I've met,' replied Robin.

So Prince John was led out of the cave where he had been left, and sat down before Robin Hood. The tall Palmer saw him and uttered an exclamation. He threw back his hood.

The Palmer looked Prince John full in the face, which fell off, and he turned a ghastly colour, khaki, and fell grovelling at the Palmer's knees.

'Richard!' he gasped. 'King Richard, my brother.'

'Loose his bonds,' commanded the King. He had about 150 of them invested in stock in America.

Prince John stood to his feet, reeling and ghastly pale. His horse was brought to him. It kicked him in the balls, ran over him and galloped wildly away.

King Richard turned to Robin, who knelt before him, speedily followed by all the outlaws. 'Pardon, my Liege.'

'He didn't recognise you the first time, King,' said Groucho.

'Stand up again,' said the King, raising Robin. 'Stand up, my friend. I freely pardon you and all here present. You and your doings are spoken of throughout England . . .'

'He's been robbing and killing for years and all you've heard about are his doings?' said Groucho.

'. . . and that Lady Marian lives still a maid until I, the King, join you both in marriage. Is this true?'

'It is, my Liege,' answered Robin.

'I'm not a liege. I am a king.'

And Marian came and slipped him a ham sandwich.

'Married you shall be,' said the King. My Lord of Peterborough shall join your hands in holy matrimony. And that good deed shall wipe out what is past.'

So they drove to their honeymoon, which they had at Ronny Scott's. They had to wait until the place had emptied out at three o'clock in the morning.

The Sheriff fled the country. 'He's off to see his rabbi.'

'I didn't know he was Jewish,' said Groucho.

'Yes, he is.'

'How do you know?'

'I saw him in the shower.'

King Richard didn't remain long in England; the overdraft was killing him. The archers became soldiers to King Richard, and they went overseas. They were remembered only in the songs which the minstrels were singing of Robin Hood and his merry men.

In the honeymoon bed, Robin took his duck. It would be a great strain on the marriage.

21. ROBIN HOOD'S LAST ADVENTURE

Robin Hood rode for the coast, to Scarborough, to escape Prince John, who was worse than ever with his brother away again. He bought a fish and found lodgings with a fishwife. She was lamenting she was a poor fishwife. She had to cook all the fish that the fishermen caught. This time they had caught a shark and half of the crew was in it.

'My husband is *still* in it,' she said.

Robin found the shark hanging up in the harbour. 'Anyone in there?' he shouted.

'Yes. I'm the fishwife's husband. Could you help get me out?'

Eventually he found his way out and emerged covered in fish oil. He gave Robin a fish.

Then Robin joined a fisherman's ship and, whereas the fishermen used a huge net, Robin, not easy in the ways of fishermen, shot a fish at a time with an arrow. At the end of the day the fishermen had caught half a ton and he had caught three fish.

One day the Captain gave a shout of 'Ahoy, pirates!' Sure enough, there were Ahoy, pirates. Robin Hood held them off with his bow and arrow.

Then he gave a loud call with his horn and soon his archers came and they shot the shit out of the pirates. Alas, the archers did not know how to sail a ship so it sank from neglect. Robin gave the fishwife a single fish for his rent.

'Welcome home, Robin. I thought you had saved a fish for me,' she said.

The Pope wrote a note to Marian: 'No tocca tua corpo', meaning 'Don't let any scheming bastard touch your body'.

22. THE LAST ARROW

Weep ye woodmen wail
Your hands with sorrow ring
Your master Robin Hood lies dead,
Poor old thing. Hey ding a ling.

William J MacGonigal

At Short and Curly's Nunnery the Prioress welcomed Marian and led her at once to sanctuary.

Several days later Prince John's men came to the nunnery demanding that Marian should be given up to them.

The Prioress refused. 'The Lady Marian has taken sanctuary and she has crabs,' she said, 'and not the King himself can touch her now. I have my love for Robin Hood and, were it he and not his wife who knelt with hand on the altar, he were yet inviolate.'

But when they had gone she spoke with Marian many times.

'Good daughter,' she said, 'I have certain news that Robin Hood has snuffed it. Moreover, though I will withstand him to the last, King John may yet take you hence by force.'

So the Prioress exhorted Marian until Marian believed indeed that Robin was dead. And so she asked nothing better than to take the veil and pass the rest of her days in prayer to God, tending the sick, the lepers, and just hoping she didn't get it. When Prince John came Marian just pole vaulted him until he left.

At long last Robin Hood came. He came leaning on a stick, an old, sick man with a dried fish, though he was not much more than forty. He had limped his way painfully across country to Short and Curly's, growing rapidly weaker and more in debt as he went. And now he knocked at the door and begged the Prioress's aid.

'Come in, good sir,' said the Prioress gently. 'Here you are, have a nice jam sandwich. And she led him to a room on the ground floor at forty shillings a week. It looked out towards Sherwood. Then she put Robin to bed and opened a vein in his arm to let blood, which was considered at the time to be one of the cures for illness.

'Which one of you is Dracula?' said Groucho.

Presently Robin recovered a little, sat up and fell back.

'Good Mother Prioress,' he said, 'I must speak with you.'

'Speak, son. God alone will hear what you tell.'

'Not too fast: he's bottoming out,' said Groucho.

'Then know,' said Robin, 'I am Robert Fitzooth Locksley, Earl of Huntingdon. I had a million pounds in the Midland Bank. Every coin was proudly stolen.'

The Prioress stirred suddenly. Nothing happened but it happened suddenly.

'Good Mother Prioress, months ago my Marian and I fled from Nottingham. We could not escape together. Only I could escape together, and she had to escape together on her own. Have you news of my wife?'

'She came here.'

'Ah, then, she must be here,' cried Robin, trying to rise from his bed.

'When you are better.'

'Could I have a jam sandwich?' asked Robin.

'Yes. Sleep now and tomorrow you can travel to see her. I will lend you a horse, and two of my serving men shall ride with you.'

'Yes, but she's here,' said Robin.

'Yes, yes, they will bring you back here,' said the Prioress.

As soon as she was certain he was sleeping, the Prioress loosened the bandages on his arm so the blood flow increased. She then stole quietly away.

All day Robin lay there bleeding slowly.

'You're bleeding slow,' said a nun.

'He's going as fast as he can,' said Groucho. 'In fact, he's nearly empty.'

He was so weak now that he could hardly move. He saw the bandage had been unfastened purposely and he guessed that the Prioress had done it.

Robin staggered to his feet, flung open the window, and fell out and had to be dragged back in. But he could not raise a leg to get it over. Then he thought of his bugle horn. With trembling fingers he drew it from his pouch, and blew the old horn, 'Wa-sa-hoa'.

Out in the forest Big Dick heard it. 'That was Robin's horn, but I fear my master is near to death, he blows so wearily.'

He hastened to the nunnery with a stretcher and an accompanying coffin.

The notes came to Marian's ears from nearby. She had in fact got nearby ears. She sprang to her feet. 'Oh, my Robin, my love, my love,' she cried. She ran to the room where the sound was coming from.

'Marian,' he whispered, 'they told me you'd been appearing in cabaret at Stringfellow's.'

'It was only one week,' she said.

Then Marian told him what had happened to her and all her adventures.

'Listen, this guy's bleeding to death,' said Groucho.

'Here have I come to die and where else can I ask but in your arms?'

'Well, you could have done it at Stringfellow's.'

By this time Big Dick had broken into the room and was weeping at Robin's side. 'Oh, my master, my master,' he sobbed. 'Grant my one last wish. Let me burn Short and Curly's Nunnery and slay the wicked Prioress.'

'No, never,' said Robin, 'that is a boon I will not grant you. Never in my life did I hurt a woman or a kangaroo, nor raise my hand against a maid or a plumber. Nor shall it be done at my death. Do not blame the Prioress for my death and my overdraft. First give me my bent bow and set an arrow on the string. Where the arrow falls, there bury me.'

He took aim and the arrow landed on the roof of a police car. So, whenever a police car goes by, Robin is buried in the roof.

Marian came first in the nuns' pole vault. Sometimes, at the top of a vault, she could see Robin go by in a police car. When Robin was fed up being dead in the police car and missing his Weetabix, the ideal breakfast food and lovely with cold milk, he came down and took Marian to London. He booked two cheap day returns and took her to Ronny Scott's.

When he went to heaven St Peter wouldn't let him in, so Robin shot him in the leg.

'You swine, Robin. That's my good leg.'

Then Jesus came and, with a miracle at the feast, turned St Peter from water into wine.

'Now clear off, Robin,' he said, and confiscated his bow.

So Robin cleared off back to Ronny Scott's, where he sang jam-sandwich blues. Everything went OK except Robin didn't like one of the waiters and shot him in the leg.

'Ah, I know someone who can mend that,' he said, and took him to Jesus, who mended it but charged him a pound.

'Look, running heaven is expensive. Keeping the Jews in fried fish costs one hundred pounds a year.'

'I'll fix that,' said Robin, and shot several people in the leg.

Jesus healed them all and collected £100.

'You're great, Robin. I'll keep you on as Holy Resident Archer.'

But Robin longed for the old days in Sherwood with Marian pole vaulting, so he returned to robbing the rich. He held up the Midland, Prudential, Lloyds, Mrs Ada Biggs and Mr Alan Platter. He gave it all to the poor, who blew it on Big Macs and chips.

Jack Straw asked him to join the Labour Party.

'Never, I'm an aristocrat!'

So Tony Blair made him Archer in Residence and he shot Labour members who got out of hand. He shot Mr Jack Straw. Ian Paisley fought back with bagpipes. Robin couldn't stand the noise so he shot the bagpipes.

After this Robin was barred from Parliament and had to wait outside and shoot Labour candidates when they caused trouble or played bagpipes.

One day he saw Will Scarlet. He was a bus conductor.

'Robin, my old friend, stay on my bus all day for free.'

'Where is Big Dick?' asked Robin.

'He's a dustman in Hackney.'

'How terrible. He used to be my lieutenant. I'll find him.'

He did. He stood behind Big Dick's dustcart and got covered in it. Dick dug him out.

'Oh, my old leader, why don't we go and live in Sherwood. Unfortunately, Sherwood is only one tree nowadays.'

'Good, we'll hide behind it and wait for Midland Bank to go past and – wham bam!'

So they went back to Sherwood and hid behind a tree and, when Midland Bank went past, wham bam! But the bank told the police and they put Robin and Big Dick in the slammer.

'Do you want a solicitor?'

'Yes,' said Robin, 'I want Bing Crosby.'

Crosby's defence was: 'On behalf of my client I'd like to say:

Every time it rains it rains pennies from heaven
Don't you know each cloud contains pennies from heaven
You feel it falling all over town
That's why you hold your umbrella upside down
We need the showers
For sunshine and flowers
There'll be pennies from heaven
For you and me.

The Judge was a Bing Crosby fan. 'Case dismissed.'

Robin and Big Dick returned to the tree in Sherwood but they were unable to rob banks unless Bing Crosby said so. It started to rain so they both walked to the YMCA. They heard news of a great archery contest at Nottingham.

'That's for me,' said Robin, who was now 93.

The great day dawned. Twelve archers had entered. When it was Robin's turn, shaking like a leaf he fired his first arrow. It stuck in an oak tree. His second struck one of the spectators. Finally he hit the target plumb centre, and he was awarded the Golden Arrow With Jam Sandwich.

The Queen threw a great banquet. 'Robin Hood, my husband and my wifeless sons wish me to award you this bonnet and feather for you to become the Royal Archer.'

'Dear Queen, your husband and your wifeless sons, thank you. I would like permission to shoot a deer from the royal herd.'

'Of course. My husband and I and my wifeless sons grant you that wish.'

'Great Queen, ta.'

He climbed out of a window and shot one of the deer. The royal cook dressed it and served it to the company.

A coach and horses drove Robin and Marian back to their tree in Sherwood, where they settled down for the night in pouring rain.

'I think I'll die again. I'm getting fed up being alive.'

'Oh no, Robin, you're only 92.'

'But I'm bald.'

'That's why I've bought you this shoulder-length blond wig.'

'All right, I'll see how it goes and then I really must die. People are expecting it of me.'

Unfortunately, a great wind blew up and blew the wig hundreds of feet in the air and a man thought it was a pheasant and shot it. When Robin got it back it looked like a scarecrow and it had to be stuck down with UHU. He stuck it down on his forehead and couldn't see where he was going. Well, he wasn't going anywhere so it didn't matter.

'I'm not active enough,' said Robin.

'So shred this cabbage. Now peel the potatoes,' said Marian.

At potato no. 101 Robin collapsed. To revive him she threw a bucket of water over him and he recovered.

'No potato is going to beat me.'

On potato no. 102 he collapsed and had to be put to bed with a cup of Horlicks.

'I'll finish them tomorrow,' he said.

'Or they'll finish you.'

'Oh, we'll see, madame,' he said, sipping his Horlicks.

They saw, and the potatoes finished him.

'I'll do one a day,' he promised.

By potato no. 111 he was having giddy spells and had a fear of an elephant falling on him. To avoid it he slept in the clothes cupboard. Strangely enough an elephant fell on him. How it got in no one knows.

Because of his small body he applied to be a jockey. Lord Derby, the horse owner and gambler, took a liking to him and gave him a ride on Lion Heart at one hundred to one, an absolute outsider. It was the Gold Cup. At the start Lion Heart leapt from the gates. Robin clung on like a limpet under the horse. The horse went so fast he messed his pants. Lion Heart flew past the post; Robin hung on for dear life and fell off. Officials helped him up; the crowds cheered as he limped along. On the award stand Robin stroked Lion Heart; it bit him. Robin drew back and kicked him in the arse. The crowd booed, and a steward rushed Robin into the changing room where he changed into Gary Cooper in *The Bengal Lancers*.

'Mount,' said Cooper.

Robin mounted Lion Heart and 'Charge' came the order. Lion Heart, being a race horse, charged with Robin right through the enemy and out of sight on the other side. Lion Heart brought Robin back with him in his mouth.

'Absent on parade,' said Cooper. 'What's your excuse?'

'My horse is a race horse. He won the Gold Cup and he's just won it again!'

'Well, he won't win it any more,' said Cooper, and hung a hundred-pound anchor round his neck.

Robin told the RSPCA.

'You are fined one hundred rupees,' said the Magistrate.

'Time to pay,' said Cooper.

'Now is the time to pay, NOW!' said the Magistrate. 'What are you, a white American, doing in the Bengal Lancers?'

'You mean you knew all along I wasn't Indian?' Cooper broke into sobs; his shoulders shook; other bits not visible shook; he shook from head to foot.

Robin took him to England.

'Look,' said Marian, 'what *are* you doing out in India with Gary Cooper crying all over you? Look at you: you're soaking. You've been missing your medicines – a spoonful of Virol, one of Sanatogen, Halibut Liver Oil. Oh, your wig's on all wrong. Come back. They've built us a bungalow under our tree. The rain goes in but it gets out again.'

'I hate rain coming in.'

'Well, wait for it to go out again.'

'I'm in the Bengal Lancers; that's my horse with an anchor round its neck.'

'Why? He's not at sea,' said Maid Marian.

'He soon will be. They are going to throw him in it.'

'Won't that anchor drown him?'

'If he's not careful. Have you got a jam sandwich?'

'No, but I have deep-frozen porridge.'

'No, porridge makes me giddy and I keep falling down.'

'Well, try a small bite.'

He had a small bite, got giddy and kept falling down.

'He'll have to be hospitalised,' said a medic.

They put him on a stretcher but he kept falling off.

'Where's my three-legged dog called Rover who keeps falling over?'

They brought the ambulance.

'I'm not sick,' said Robin. 'I just keep falling. If I keep falling in that direction I can get to the hospital on my own.'

'Look, try falling upright: you'll get there quicker,' said Marian.

'Don't dare give me another porridge sandwich,' said Robin.

When they got to the hospital the Duchess of York was in the next bed.

'What are you doing here?' said Robin.

'I'm divorcing my husband; it's cheaper in an NHS hospital.'

Robin sat on the end of her bed.

'That's near enough,' she said, clutching her clothes, all made by Cheval of Paris.

'Would you have dinner with me?'

'Yes,' she said. 'Your bed or mine?'

'Neither,' said Robin. 'What's wrong with McDonald's?'

'Oh, if you eat there you get mad-cow's disease.'

'How do cows get mad-cow's disease?' said Robin.

'They eat at McDonald's,' said the Duchess.

'Let's have a Chinese takeaway,' said Robin. 'Hello, one portion of no. 3, one portion of no. 10, one portion of no. 20.'

They delivered but had added the numbers together and he had no. 33 – it was the washing-up water. 'It's delicious,' said Robin, going down with typhoid.

'Where's your husband?' said Robin.

'He's on a battleship,' said Fergie. 'He steers it.'

'Steers it where?' asked Robin.

'Away from the rocks. If he hits any the ship sinks.'

'What does he do?' said Robin.

'He throws everybody safely in the water then escapes in a helicopter.'

'Look, does he ever see the children?' Robin said.

'Yes, through a telescope.'

A telegram arrived for Robin.

'It's from the Queen,' said Robin. 'She wants me to go to the Palace, to give me the CBE and tea with Philip. You know Philip?' asked Robin.

'Do I?' said Fergie. 'He's my bloody father-in-law and landlord.'

'Oh I'll get him to reduce your rent, Fergie.'

Robin arrived in a horse and carriage with his bow.

'Hello, Robin,' said the Queen. 'This is Prince Philip.'

'Oh yes! He's Fergie's landlord.'

'What's that?' she said. 'What's that?' She pointed to his bow.

'It's for shooting.'

'Let's see you.'

So Robin shot a corgi.

'Oh, all over the carpet,' said the Queen. 'Corgis have been in my family for four hundred years.'

'Well, he was getting on. It's time he went. Shall I kill the rest?' said Robin.

'No. Now here's your CBE. Have your tea and leave,' said the Queen.

'Would you like a jam sandwich?' said Philip.

'Yes, I'll take it away with me,' said Robin, pointing to his mouth.

'Look,' said the Queen, holding a dead corgi bleeding down her dress, 'I want my CBE back. I'll put it with the Beatles' MBEs.'

'Come along, Robin. You can't be doing all this,' said Maid Marian. 'The Queen's bankrupt. She had to sell the royal yacht before it sank.'

'I've no merry men any more, only a merry woman, Maid Marian.'

Robin got a job as a floor manager. Sometimes he managed the ceiling; sometimes the floor, but the floor was his main job. He had to keep it clear of elephants. Unfortunately, a spare elephant got on it. He tried to shoo it but it fell on him and he was trapped underneath.

'Are you there, Robin? Don't worry, we'll call the fire brigade.'

Robin didn't understand. Was the elephant on fire? But when they arrived they pumped so much water on the elephant he drowned and they pulled Robin out. He was very flat and they had to inflate him. He floated up ten feet above the ground. A man from the fire brigade went up and brought him down by releasing the air through his toe.

'Where am I?' said Robin, regaining consciousness.

'England,' said Maid Marian, 'and you're very ill. You only weigh three ounces, as much as a Mars bar. Look at yourself.'

So he looked at himself and he wasn't there.

Robin ordered one hundred jam sandwiches, which he ate till he weighed ten stone eleven pounds with jam oozing out of him.

'Look, you're going all over the carpet,' said Maid Marian. 'It's no good, the house is full of jam.'

'So am I,' said Robin.

Somehow the War Office had made a glaring mistake. Robin Hood was called up for the Navy.

'Can you swim?' said a recruiting sergeant.

'Why? Haven't you got any ships?' said Robin.

He was posted to a submarine.

'I'll stand on the pier and watch it go down,' said AB Robin Hood.

'You,' said the Admiral, 'you're supposed to be on that ship.'

'I'm excused from submarines due to claustrophobia. That sub had terrible claustrophobia. That's why half of the crew are clinging to the outside.'

'They're hiding!' roared the Admiral. 'They're all survivors from the last trip. Stand to attention!' said the Admiral.

Robin couldn't. He had piles.

'How long have you had them, man?' said the Admiral.

'Oh quite long. Sometimes they are two feet ten inches.'

'Come along, Robin,' said Maid Marian. 'I'm not having you serving in the Navy with piles. There's a bill for the corgi you shot. You can't go round shooting the Queen's corgis and get away with it.'

'I'll apologise to her.'

So he wrapped up a jam sandwich and added a note: 'Queen, I'm sorry I shot your corgi. Will you accept this jam sandwich with my best wishes?'

'Philip, come and taste this jam sandwich,' said the Queen. 'It's delicious. Send for Robin Hood at once!'

'If you like, Queen, I'll walk all your corgis in the park,' Robin offered.

So the Queen let him. Every one of them bit him on the leg; it went septic. In the hospital with his leg up the Queen came to say sorry.

'I'm very sorry.'

'You're sorry,' said Robin. 'You know, after they all bit me, each one pissed on my leg.'

'Oh, the dear little things.'

The next time he took them for a walk he kicked the shit out of them.

Philip took Robin for a pheasant shoot and before the day was out Robin had shot two gillies, a gun dog and wounded the Duke.

'Who said you could shoot?' raged the Duke.

'Albert J Scroff,' said Robin.

'Albert J Scroff? Who's he?' said the Duke.

'He's someone who said I could shoot,' said Robin.

'I'll sue him.'

Albert J Scroff was in the dock. 'Are you Albert J Scroff?'

'Only on Mondays; on Tuesdays I'm Goldie Hawn.'

'What day do you tell Robin Hood he can shoot?'

'That's the first Wednesday of the month.'

'You tell him he can shoot?'

'I've no idea if he can. I just say it. There's no law to stop me saying Robin Hood can shoot,' said Albert.

'Do you realise he shot two gillies, a gun dog and Prince Philip?'

'Oh I never said he could shoot gillies, gun dogs and Prince Philip. All I said was he can shoot and so he can. He shot two gillies, a gun dog and Prince Philip.'

The Judge banged his mallet.

'Silence in court. I want the accused to apologise to the gillies, the dog and Prince Philip. You will then be taken to a place and hanged.'

'I don't want to be hanged,' said Albert.

'They all say that,' said the Judge.

So Albert hung there until he'd hung long enough. They let him go. He was OK but his neck was a foot longer and he could see over people. On clear days he could see over the Channel, and saw the German Army waiting to invade England so he told Winston Churchill.

'Yes, I know,' said Churchill. 'I'm doing a painting of them before they do. Here, hold this rifle with five rounds. If they come, don't hesitate to shoot.'

Before he could shoot, they came.

Churchill was very angry. 'Get out of England at once or I'll tell Hitler. You've ruined my painting!'

He was so fierce they all got out of England. So he told Hitler. 'Listen, Adolph.'

'*Ya*, I am listening.'

'Your German Army ruined my painting.'

'Ach, as a painter myself I understand your feeling.'

Hitler then had twenty soldiers shot to set an example.

'Winston, what do I do with this rifle and five rounds?' said Robin.

'You can guard the people of England against an overdraft.'

So Robin shot thirteen bank managers.

'Come on, Robin, you can't shoot bank managers and get away with it.'

But he did. Thirteen bank managers he had notched up on the butt of his gun. If he went in a bar they all dived for cover. 'He's the Bank Manager Killer!' they gasped.

Robin was fifty for the second time but still had a good figure, £50,000 to be precise. He opened a sandwich bar, boasting that he could make any sandwich a customer desired.

'Can I have an elephant sandwich?' said a customer.

'How many?' said Robin.

'One,' said the customer.

'Bugger off, I'm not going to kill an elephant for one sandwich,' said Robin.

Robin wanted to be a skater in *Starlight Express* but on skates at the audition he raced round the track and shot off it straight out the stage door and collided with a lamppost and broke both ankles. Thank heaven he was a member of BUPA and had a luxurious room with a po under the bed. Lloyd Webber came to commiserate and gave Robin a bottle of champagne. Robin sprayed it all over Webber, who sued him.

'Did you, without malice aforethought, spray Lord Webber with champagne?' said the Judge.

'Yes, m'lud,' said Robin. 'Racing-car drivers do it.'

'Lord Webber isn't a racing-car driver,' said the Judge.

'How was I to know that?' said Robin.

'Do you agree, Lord Webber, that you don't look like a racing-car driver?' said the Judge.

'No, I look like a composer of successful musicals,' said Webber.

'How does the jury find?' said the Judge.

'We find that Lord Webber looks like a composer of successful musicals.'

'How do you find Robin Hood?' said the Judge.

'We find him an old man in bed with fractured ankles.'

'What about damages?' said Webber.

'He's got enough damages, both ankles,' said the Judge. 'Case dismissed.'

* * *

'We have to X-ray your wallet, Mr Hood,' said a doctor. 'Don't worry, it won't hurt. We just want to know if you can afford to be in BUPA.'

So Robin changed the locks on his wallet. They X-rayed the wallet – he was skint, so they wheeled him out of the hospital and put him on a 137 bus which wasn't going anywhere. Robin didn't want to go anywhere – so he stayed on till it got there. He got off and sure enough he wasn't anywhere. Brixton is anywhere so he went there.

'Hello there,' said a tall black man. 'Welcome to Brixton.'

'You're welcome to it, too.'

'Don't be like that.'

'I've always been like this. What have you been like?'

'I've been like Frank Bruno,' said the man, and knocked Robin down. 'What a pity you aren't Mike Tyson.'

So for a moment Robin became Mike Tyson and knocked Frank Bruno down.

'That will be one million dollars,' said Robin. 'I think I'll retire from the ring now.' And Robin bought a Rolls Royce, and drove to Maid Marian under the tree in Sherwood Forest.

'What have you got there?' said Maid Marian, giving herself a flu jab.

'It's my new home,' said Robin, beeping the horn.

'You come on here and have your flu jab and tea.'

'What's for tea?' said Robin.

'A flu jab and a boiled egg,' said Marian.

'Could you give my flu jab to the boiled egg?' said Robin.

'Silly, boiled eggs don't catch flu,' said Marian.

'Not if they're given a flu jab,' said Robin.

Robin drove Maid Marian to the South of France in the Rolls Royce. It took him a while to find it. He missed it three times.

Finding himself alone in Rome he realised he was lost again – but by eating twelve plates of spaghetti at gun point, he escaped from Italy. Pursued by twelve Fascists and a beautiful Italian ballerina, he shook off the Fascists and she shook him off.

'Leave Marian,' she said.

'No, she does my laundry,' he said.

'I'll do your laundry in champagne with you in it,' said the beautiful ballerina.

So she did it in champagne and him in it. She hung him up to dry, pissed. She left him there all night till he was sober.

'Looka, I introduce-a you-a to Mussolini,' she said.

'Benito, dis is the famous bandit Robin Hood.'

'Oh gooda, have some spaghetti.'

'No thanks, I've just eaten twelve plates at pistol point.'

'OK, then have some ice cream.'

So Robin had an ice cream while Mussolini pointed a pistol.

'What's that for?' said Robin.

'It's in case you don't eat your ice cream. All British POWs we catch eat ice cream at pistol point.'

'What if they won't eat it?' said Robin.

'We-ar paint them green with yellow spots.'

'Does that contravene the Geneva Convention?' said Robin.

'No, no, no. Where does it say you mustn't paint your enemy?' said Mussolini.

'I'm not going to eat this ice cream,' said Robin.

Mussolini painted him green with yellow spots.

'Does this mean I'm a prisoner of war?' said Robin.

'Si si,' said Mussolini, and drove him to a POW camp.

Robin's first words were: 'Helppp. I want out! I've never declared war on anyone except the pigeons in Trafalgar Square!'

'Silencio! You'll give us all away,' said the camp commander.

'I want to escape,' said Robin.

So they let him out the back. Splash! He was in Venice.

'Get me out before I get typhoid!'

And he got typhoid. In hospital his temperature soared so they hooked him up to the central heating and that winter he kept the whole hospital warm. He nearly died from typhoid but he decided against it and settled for an itch. He started scratching it in April and didn't stop till Christmas but by then he had nearly scratched himself away.

Maid Marian collected him in the Rolls pulled by a donkey.

'It's run out of petrol. Who's that woman in your bed?' she said, sticking a knife in her.

'She's a grievously wounded Italian,' said Robin. 'She did my washing in champagne. She was a one-off.'

'Well, she's really off now,' said Marian, tipping her down the rubbish chute.

'Have you been sleeping with her?' said Marian.

'No,' said Robin, 'I've been sleeping with Mussolini.'

'Why are you green with yellow spots?' said Marian.

'You get that from sleeping with Mussolini.'

Then Robin died of green with yellow spots. It had been a good life.

Maid Marian married Jimmy Saville, thus putting an end to his career.

TREASURE ISLAND ACCORDING TO SPIKE MILLIGAN

PROLOGUE
HOW GROUCHO JOINED THE CREW

Q: Are you, Groucho Marx, willing to appear in 'TREASURE ISLAND'?

GROUCHO: Oh? What's in it for me, my good man?

Q: Fame and fortune!

GROUCHO: Never mind that, what about the money?

Q: Who's talking about money?

GROUCHO: No one. That's why I mentioned it.

Q: In this book no one gets paid.

GROUCHO: Well, I wish them luck and goodbye, suckers.

Q: Wait! In your case perhaps we can come to some special arrangement.

GROUCHO: In my case, my special arrangement is money.

Q: What do you want?

GROUCHO: Ten dollars a word.

Q: What if you don't speak?

GROUCHO: Then I'll get fuck all.

Q: Supposing we paid a dollar a word?

GROUCHO: Then I'd talk very fast.

Q: OK, you're on, a dollar a word.

GROUCHO: I agree. Yes I agree, yes I agree, I agree. That'll be sixty two dollars.

Q: Have you change for a hundred?

GROUCHO: No, but I'll keep it till I do.

Q: Right, sign this agreement.

GROUCHO: I'll just sign it with a cross.

Q: A cross? Are you illiterate?

GROUCHO: Heavens no. I can spell cross.

Q: You are a difficult man to deal with.

GROUCHO: Sometimes if the date is right, I'm a difficult woman to deal with.

Bow! Wow! Wow!

GROUCHO: Whose dog is that?

PART ONE
Captain Flint

CLASSIC ADVENTURES ACCORDING TO SPIKE MILLIGAN

1. THE OLD SEA DOG AT THE 'ADMIRAL BENBOW'

I remember him as if it were yesterday. As a matter of fact it *was* yesterday. He came plodding to the inn door. I distinctly heard him going plod-plod-plod; a tall, strong, heavy, nut-brown man. He was an unforgettable sight: his tarry pigtail falling over the shoulders of his shit-covered blue coat; his hands with black, broken nails; and the sabre-cut across one cheek a dirty, livid white. I remember him looking round the cove and whistling to himself. As he did so he broke out into the most boring old sea song that was not in the charts at the time:

Fifteen men on the dead man's chest –
Yo-ho-ho, and a bottle of rum!

It was an old tottering voice, so tottering I thought it was going to fall off. Then he rapped on the door with something that looked like a handspike. On inspection it proved to be something that looked like a handspike. When my father appeared, the man called roughly for a glass of rum.

'You! I roughly want a glass of rum!'

'There,' said my father setting it down, 'that's roughly a glass of rum.'

This he drank slowly like a connoisseur, lingering on the taste tho' he knew bugger all about rum.

'This is a handy cove,' said he at length, five feet eleven inches. 'Much company, mate?'

My father told him we weren't a company, we relied on a few Japanese tourists but as there was no golf course, they left.

'Well, then,' said he, 'this is the berth for me. Here you, matey,' he cried to a cripple who trundled the barrow. 'Bring up alongside and help up with my chest.'

So he helped him up with his chest which when expanded was forty-two inches.

'I'm a plain man; rum bum baccy, and bacon and eggs is what I want. You mought call me captain. Oh? I see what you're at – there.' He threw down three or four gold pieces on the floor. My father snatched them up and swallowed them for safety. 'You can tell me when I've worked through that.'

GROUCHO: You look like a seasoned rum bum and baccy old sailor.
CAPTAIN: Aye, seasoned with rum bum baccy and women.
GROUCHO: I wish you luck with all of them. You certainly have a wide choice. What did you do on your shore leave?
CAPTAIN: I think she was called Deptford Flo; coo, she was hot stuff.
GROUCHO: Hot stuff? Did she burn you?
CAPTAIN: No, no. Just beware of women.
GROUCHO: My mother's a woman, she does B&B.

CAPTAIN:	B&B?
GROUCHO:	Yes, B&B, breakfast and bugger off.
CAPTAIN:	Ah, breakfast and bugger off! Mothers are a wonderful thing.
GROUCHO:	Was Deptford Flo a mother?
CAPTAIN:	Frequently.
GROUCHO:	Who was the father?
CAPTAIN:	The crew of *HMS Ironsides*.

My mother called me over. She said, 'Jim, I want you to keep away from that man. He's a bad influence. He's vulgar and he smells.'

'I know but you soon get used to it.'

I went down to the cellar and adjusted all the bungs on the beer barrels, but I couldn't get the Captain out of my mind. He was a rough, rude, rum bum and baccy sailor. He kept letting off; then you had to stand clear.

The next morning I served him his breakfast of rum bum baccy, egg and bacon.

CAPTAIN:	Ah, fit for a king, my boy.
JIM:	You know, Captain, the Jews are not supposed to eat bacon.
CAPTAIN:	Thank God I'm not a Jew, Jim.
JIM:	What are you, Captain?
GROUCHO:	I'll tell you, he's methylated spirits.
JIM:	Oh? Methylated spirits? What's that?
GROUCHO:	Yes, I'd like to know what that is too.
JIM:	Captain, tell me about some of your sea battles.
CAPTAIN:	Oh, Jim, there was a time we boarded a Spanish galleon. I was set upon by a huge Spaniard.
JIM:	Oh, did he hurt you?
CAPTAIN:	No, I shot him before he could. I threw him over the side. He said, 'Señor, I can't swim.' I said, 'Look, I can't play the violin but I don't shout about it!'

My mother, who had been watching, shouted, 'Jim, come away from that man.'

'But, Mum, he's not doing me any harm,' I said.

'Come away before you feel the back of my hand!'

So I came away and felt the back of her hand. It was like playing a flesh-covered piano.

The Captain was a very silent man by custom. All day he hung around the cove with a brass telescope singing:

Fifteen men on the dead man's chest –
Etc., etc., etc.

GROUCHO:	I've never heard a brass telescope singing before. There must be a first for everything.

Mostly he would not speak when spoken to; so he did not ever speak. Every day, when he came back from his stroll, he would ask if any seafaring men had been. When a seaman put up at the 'Admiral Benbow' he would look at him through the crack in his trousers. He promised me a silver fourpenny on the first of every month if I would keep my 'weather-eye open for a seafaring man with one leg'. I didn't have any weather-eyes so I never saw a seafaring man with one leg.

But how that personage haunted my dreams. Now the leg would be cut off at the knee, now at the hip, now at the shoulders, then the neck; now he was a monstrous kind of a creature. I would dream of him chasing me on his one leg joined to his neck.

Though I was terrified by the idea of the seafaring man with one leg, I was less afraid of the Captain himself . . . but then he had *two* legs. There were nights when he took a great deal more rum and water than his head would carry; then he would sit and sing his number one in the charts; Madonna was a close second:

Fifteen men on the dead man's chest –
Etc., etc., etc.

Sometimes he would call for glasses all round, and force all the trembling company to sing: 'Sing, you buggers, sing.'

Often I have heard the house shaking with 'Yo-ho-ho, and a bottle of rum, etc., etc.,' all the neighbours joining in for dear life, with the fear of death upon them, each singing louder than the other. He could fly up in a passion of anger when asked Why did a chicken cross the road?

GROUCHO: To get to the other seed or to see Gregory Peck.

His stories were what frightened people worst of all. Dreadful stories they were; about hanging, walking the plank, swallowing the anchor, and the Clap. He must have mixed among some of the wickedest men that God ever allowed like Charlie Chester, Chris Evans and Terry Wogan.

My father was always saying, 'the Inn will be ruined,' he was always saying, 'the Inn will be ruined,' 'the Inn will be ruined . . .'

JIM: Don't worry, dad, the Inn is doing good business.
FATHER: Not really, son, the Captain hasn't paid any rent for weeks.
JIM: I suppose he hasn't got it.
FATHER: Well if he hasn't got it the Inn will be ruined. The rent is two weeks overdue and your mother is five weeks overdue. I tell you the Inn will be ruined.
JIM: Dad, we took four pounds ten shillings at the bar last night.
FATHER: Yes, but I still say the Inn will be ruined . . . I don't feel well, Jim.

So I felt him all over and sure enough he didn't feel well all over. 'Why don't you go to bed?'

Mother tucked him in with a hot water bottle. 'I think you should see a doctor,' she said, and Dad said, 'Shouldn't he see me? I think it's an attack of malaria; I got it when I was serving in India.'

MOTHER:	Why in God's name did you bring it back here?
FATHER:	It travelled with me.

Bow wow! Bow wow!

| GROUCHO: | Whose dog is that? |

We thought that the Captain would eventually tyrannise the people and soon they would cease coming but I really believe his presence did us good. There was even a party of young men and women who would admire him, calling him a 'true sea-dog', and a 'sea cat', even a 'sea hamster', saying that he was the sort of man that made England terrible at sea and just as terrible on land.

He kept staying on week after week; at last month after month so that all the money had long been exhausted, and still my father never plucked up the heart to insist on having more rent. If ever he mentioned it, the Captain would roar and stare my father out of the room. I am sure the terror my father lived in must have greatly hastened his early death.

All the time he lived with us the Captain did nothing. He did the lottery, of course, but apart from that, nothing. He didn't even wash. When he was up on the cliff a mile away we could still smell him down at the inn. In his room he kept a great sea-chest none of us had ever seen open. He'd stand on it and cross himself. Why not? He had crossed everybody else. Towards the end, when my poor father was far gone into decline and lay on his deathbed, Dr Livesey came late one afternoon to see the patient.

GROUCHO:	Doctor, where did you study medicine?
DOCTOR:	St John's College.
GROUCHO:	A medical school?
DOCTOR:	No, it was a college for farmers. I realised that when they asked me how to milk a cow.
GROUCHO:	So what is your hobby, doctor?
DOCTOR:	I like milking cows.
GROUCHO:	Isn't that boring?
DOCTOR:	Only after three churns.
GROUCHO:	That's a lot of milk. What did you do with it?
DOCTOR:	Oh, I poured it back into the cow.
GROUCHO:	Didn't that make them leak?
DOCTOR:	Yes, but when you couldn't see where they were, you could certainly see where they'd been.

I remember observing the contrast: the neat, bright doctor, with his powder-wig as white as snow, and his bright, black eyes and pleasant manner, compared with that filthy, shit-strewn, bearded scarecrow of a pirate of ours, sitting far gone in rum, with his arms on the table. Suddenly he – the Captain, that is – began to sing in the charts again:

Fifteen men on the dead man's chest –
Etc., etc., etc.

The doctor said to my father, 'Now, Mr Hawkins, let's have a look at you.'
'Will that make him better?' asked mother.
'He's got a temperature,' said the doctor. 'Make him drink lots of water. If he won't drink it, throw it over him.'

At first I had supposed 'the dead man's chest' to be that identical big box of the Captain's upstairs in the front room, and the thought had been mingled in my nightmares with that of the one-legged seafaring man. The Captain suddenly smashed his hand upon the table; the table and his hand fell to bits. We knew that to mean – silence. Dr Livesey, the idiot, went on talking as before. The Captain glared at him. 'Silence, you bastard.'

'Were you addressing me, sir?' says the silly doctor; and the ruffian had told him, with another oath, 'fuck', that this was so. 'I have only one thing to say to you, sir,' replied the doctor. 'Keep on drinking rum, and the world will soon be quit of a very dirty scoundrel – you'll snuff it!'

'Bollocks!' he said. He sprang to his feet, drew and opened a sailor's clasp-knife.

The doctor never moved. He spoke to him over his shoulder, it nearly broke his neck. The same tone of voice, rather high as if he were queer:
'If you do not put that knife away, sailor, I promise you shall be put in stocks.'

'Fuck the stocks,' said the Captain.

'I will not fuck the stocks,' said the doctor. 'And now, sir, I will have you know I am a magistrate and if I catch a breath of complaint against you, I'll revolve your swonnicles and after a fair trial you will be hung.'

'Get fucked,' said the sailor.

Soon Dr Livesey's horse came to the door and he rode away to get fucked, leaving my father in his deathbed. 'We will be ruined,' he said, 'you'll see.'

So we waited to see us all ruined.

GROUCHO: So far, so good, that'll be $171, please.
Bow wow! Bow wow!
GROUCHO: Whose dog *is* that?

2. BLACK DOG APPEARS AND DISAPPEARS

It was plain from the first that my father was little likely to see the spring. He sank down daily and my mother had to pull him out. Mother and I had all the inn in our hands as my father lay dying. Mother took up sleep walking. Why she didn't waken as she clumped out of the inn in her walking boots, I'll never know. Still, it was good healthy exercise for her.

JIM: Mum, where was Dad born?
MUM: In Bexhill-on-Sea.
JIM: Where is that?

MUM:	That's a village for the dying by the sea.
JIM:	Was he dying?
MUM:	No, he managed to escape before he did.
JIM:	How did he escape?
MUM:	He jumped out of his coffin and ran.
JIM:	What was he doing in a coffin?
MUM:	He was waiting to die.
JIM:	What was he dying of?
MUM:	Lurgy.
JIM:	What's that?
MUM:	Like spots of shit on the liver.
JIM:	Is that dangerous?
MUM:	Only if you've got it.
JIM:	How do you cure it?
MUM:	You jump out of your coffin and run away.
JIM:	How do you catch it?
MUM:	By living at Bexhill-on-Sea.

The Captain had risen earlier and higher than usual and so set out for the beach as though his mind was still on Dr Livesey who was away getting fucked.

My mother was downstairs while my father lay upstairs dying. When the parlour door opened and a man stepped in, I asked him what he wanted. 'What do you want?' I said. He said he would take some rum. As I was going out of the room to fetch it he went to sit down upon a table, missed it, then motioned me to draw near with the rum.

'Come here, sonny,' says he.

'Is this here table for my mate Bill?' he asked.

I told him I did not know his mate Bill; and this was for a person who stayed in our house, whom we called the Captain.

'Ah,' said he, 'that'll be my rum bum and baccy mate Bill called the Captain, as like as not.'

'Yes and his rent is three months overdue. Would you like to pay it?'

The man fainted.

I told him the Captain was out walking in the London Marathon.

GROUCHO: Ah, what a disguise.

The stranger hung about outside the inn door waiting for the Marathon to finish. My mother went upstairs to watch my father lying dying for a while.

'Aarh, sure enough,' he said, 'here comes my mate Bill, with a spy-glass under his arm.'

So saying, the stranger backed along with me into the parlour. He cleared the hilt of his cutlass and loosened the blade in the sheath. Was he going to kill him? All the time we were waiting he kept swallowing, as if he felt what we used to call a lump in the throat. He didn't know it was cancer.

At last the Captain ran in from the Marathon. He had been placed 74th out of a field of 22. He marched straight across the room to where his rum bum and baccy breakfast awaited him.

'Bill,' said the stranger, in a voice he was trying to make bold and big.

The Captain spun round and round and round and round. When he stopped revolving he was face-to-face with the stranger, a nasty shock for both of them.

'Come, Bill, you know me,' said the stranger.

The Captain made a sort of gasp in his voice. 'Black Dog!' said he with a sort of gasp in his voice.

Bow wow! Bow wow!

GROUCHO: Is that you, Black Dog?

'And who else?' returned the other, getting more at his ease. 'Black Dog as ever was, coming for to see his old shipmate Billy.'

GROUCHO: Black Dog? Isn't that what Churchill suffered from?

'Now, look here,' said the Captain; 'you've run me down; speak up: what is it?'

'That's you, Bill,' returned Black Dog, 'I'll have a glass of rum. We'll sit down, if you please, and talk square, like old shipmates.'

So they talked square like old shipmates.

When I returned with the rum Black Dog was next to the door so as to have one eye on his old shipmate, and one on his retreat.

I left them together and retired to the bar. I heard nothing, I listened intently; sure enough I heard low gabbling; but at last the voices began to grow higher and higher till they were about three feet above ground level, and I could pick up a word or two, 'fish' and 'bite'.

'No, no, no, no!' cried the Captain. 'If it comes to swinging, swing all, say I.'

Suddenly there was a tremendous noise – a clash of steel followed, and then a cry of pain, 'Ahgggggggah!' In the next instant Black Dog was in full flight, the Captain hotly pursuing.

'I'll have your balls for trophies!' shouted the Captain, streaming blood from the left shoulder. The Captain aimed at the fugitive one last tremendous cut, and missed.

Once out upon the road, Black Dog showed a clean pair of heels. The Captain stood staring after him.

'Jim,' says he, 'rum;' and as he spoke, he reeled a little, and steadied himself with one hand against the wall.

'Are you hurt?' cried I.

'Are you bloody blind?' he said.

'No, I'm not blind,' I said.

'Rum,' he repeated. 'I must get away from here. Rum bum and baccy!'

So I ran to fetch him his rum bum and baccy. I heard a loud fall in the parlour and, running in, beheld the Captain lying face down, full length, five feet eleven inches, upon the floor. At the same instant my mother, alarmed by the cries and fighting, came running downstairs while my father lay upstairs dying on his deathbed. Between us we raised the Captain's head and left his body where it was. The Captain was breathing loud and hard. His eyes, mouth and teeth were open for business, his face a horrible colour – magenta.

'Dear, deary me,' cried my mother, 'what a horrible colour – it doesn't match the curtains!'

We had no idea what to do for the Captain. I tried to pour some rum down his throat but his teeth were now tightly shut so with an enema we squirted it up his bottom.

Doctor Livesey came in to visit my father who lay dying.

'Oh Doctor,' we cried, 'what shall we do? Where is he wounded?'

'Wounded? Fiddle-sticks. The man has had a stroke, a stroke of luck for his wife, she has his life policy. Now, Mrs Hawkins, just you run upstairs to your husband, and tell him, if possible, nothing about it.'

So she ran upstairs and, if possible, said nothing about it.

'Jim, get me a basin.'

When I got back with the basin, the doctor had already ripped up the Captain's sleeve, and exposed his great sinewy arm. It was tattooed in several places. 'Here's luck', 'A fair wind', and his National Lottery numbers.

'Now, Jim, we will have a look at the colour of his blood. It should be red. Are you afraid of blood, Jim?'

'No, sir,' said I. 'I'm full of it.'

'Then hold the basin.'

A great deal of Blood Group G was taken before the Captain opened his eyes. He recognised the doctor with an unmistakable frown.

'That will be ten shillings,' said the doctor.

The Captain fainted. Suddenly his colour changed, puce, and he tried to raise himself, crying:

'Where's Black Dog?'

'There is no Black Dog here, he's buggered off and you have had a stroke, and I, very much against my own will, dragged you head-foremost out of the grave. Now Mr Bones –'

'That's not my name,' he interruped, 'it's my *nom de plume.*'

'Man, what I have to say is one glass of rum won't kill you but if you take another, you'll die or at least try to. This once I'll help you to your bed.' And for once he helped the Captain to his bed.

We managed to hoist him upstairs, and laid him on his bed, where his head fell back on the pillow, as if he were almost fainting. My father was still lying dying on his deathbed.

'Now, mind you,' said the doctor, 'the name of rum is death.'

GROUCHO: It'll never catch on. Who'd buy booze labelled 'DEATH'?

'This is nothing,' he said. 'I have drawn blood enough to keep him quiet a while; he should lie for a week where he is – that is the best thing for him and you; but another stroke would kill him.'

GROUCHO: Lucky he's not a pussy cat.

And with that he went off to see my father, who lay dying on his deathbed.

GROUCHO: Look, I don't like being in the same room as this lunatic Captain. He might decide he needs to use *my* blood.
JIM: You're speaking of a dying man.
GROUCHO: Dying? That's the last thing a man should do.

3. THE BLACK SPOT

About noon I stopped at the Captain's door with some cooling drinks and medicines and I threw them over him.

'Jim,' he said, 'bring me a noggin of rum.'

'Remember what the doctor said,' I warned him. ' "The name of rum is death." '

'Fuck the doctor,' he said. 'Doctors is all swabs,' he said; 'and that doctor there, why, what do he know about seafaring men? I been in places hot as pitch, and mates dropping all round with Yellow Jack, and with decks awash with dysentery.'

'No,' I said, 'you are not to have your rum bum and baccy now.'

'Oh, my blood'll be on you.'

GROUCHO: Jim, it will never wash out.

'Look, Jim,' he said, 'how my fingers fidget.'

I watched his fingers fidget.

GROUCHO: Some people will watch anything for entertainment.

'I can't keep them still; they will go on fidgeting as long as I don't get rum.'

So to stop his fingers fidgeting, I got him some rum.

'If I don't get some rum I will have the horrors.'

'We don't have horrors, we only have eggs and bacon.'

'I seen old Flint,' he said, 'and if I get the horrors and eggs and bacon I will raise Cain.'

'You can't,' I said, 'he's been dead about three thousand years.'

'Oh,' said the Captain, 'I only just heard about it. I'll give you a golden guinea for a noggin, Jim.'

JIM:	Why do you drink it?
CAPTAIN:	It gets me there.
JIM:	Where is there?
CAPTAIN:	Here.
JIM:	Here? But you're always here.
CAPTAIN:	Yes. See? It works!
JIM:	It doesn't take you somewhere else.
CAPTAIN:	This is somewhere else.
JIM:	Were you Flint's cabin boy?
CAPTAIN:	Yes. One morning I said, 'I've brought your breakfast up.' He said, 'Serves you right for eating it. Ha, ha.'
JIM:	Was he cruel?
CAPTAIN:	If you misbehaved he'd bury you up to your neck in shit.
JIM:	Did he shoot anyone?
CAPTAIN:	Yes. He shot the ship's cat every day until it ran out of lives.
JIM:	Did he make many enemies?
CAPTAIN:	He didn't make 'em; they was already there.
JIM:	Did you battle with the French?
CAPTAIN:	Oh, yes I did; I threatened a French sailor with my cutlass. He jumped overboard, he started to drown. 'Help, help,' he shouted, 'I can't swim.' 'Look,' I said, 'I can't play the fiddle but I don't shout about it.'
JIM:	What was your happiest moment?
CAPTAIN:	Ah! I can't remember her name.
JIM:	Have you shot anybody?
CAPTAIN:	Yes, anybody!
JIM:	What was your mother's name?
CAPTAIN:	Richard, she was a man.
JIM:	How did he give birth to you?
CAPTAIN:	With great difficulty.

'I want none of your money, Captain,' said I, 'but what you owe my father who is upstairs dying on his deathbed. I'll get you one glass, and no more.'

When I brought it to him, he seized it greedily, and drank. It ran out the other end.

'Ah, ay,' said he, 'that's some better. And now, matey, did that doctor say how long I was to lie here in this old berth?'

'At least a week,' I said.

'A week! I can't do that: they'd have the black spot on me by then.'

'What is a black spot? Is it an accident?'

Grasping my shoulder he struggled until he got into a sitting position, and then fell back again.

'That doctor's done me. Jim,' he said at length, five feet eleven inches, 'you saw that seafaring man today?'

'Black Dog?' I asked.

Bow wow! Bow wow!

GROUCHO: Is that Black Dog?

'Now, if I can't get away they will tip me the black spot. Mind you, it's my old sea-chest they're after. That and this 'ere treasure map.'

He produced an oilskin packet. It contained a tattered old map which he carefully unfolded. It was alarmingly brittle and encrusted with sea salt, sand, seagull shit and bits of Jaffa Cake. Someone had marked an 'X' where the treasure lay. The seagull had marked most everything else.

'But what is the black spot, Captain?' I asked.

'That's a summons, mate. It means your time is up.'

'When is your time up?' I said.

GROUCHO: I'd say any minute now!

'But keep your weather-eye open, Jim.'

But as things fell out, my poor father, who still lay dying upstairs on his deathbed, died.

The Captain got downstairs next morning on a stretcher. He had his rum bum baccy, eggs and bacon. The night before the funeral of my father who now lay dead on his deathbed upstairs, the Captain was as drunk as ever; it was shocking in a house of mourning to hear him singing:

All the nice girls like a candle,
All the nice girls like a wick.

He was breathing hard and fast, like a man on a steep mountain. When he was drunk he had an alarming way of drawing his cutlass and he swung it around his head taking one of his ears off. Once he cut off the arm of an innocent bystander.

So things passed until the day of the funeral of my father who now lay dead in his coffin. I was full of sad thoughts about his coffin which was drawing slowly along the road. Suddenly I saw someone else drawing slowly along the road. He was blind and he tapped with a white stick; he was hunched as if with age or weakness, and wore a huge old tattered sea cloak. You could see his arse through his trousers. He stopped, raising his voice.

'Will some kind friend help a poor blind man who has lost the precious sight of his eyes in the defence of his country? Where or in what part of this country he may now be?'

'You are at the "Admiral Benbow" Inn, Black Hill Cove, my good man,' said I.

'I hear a voice,' said he. 'Will you give me your hand?'

I held out my hand, and the horrible creature gripped it in a moment like a vice.

'Now, boy,' he said, 'take me to the Captain.'

'Sir,' said I, 'I dare not.'

'Oh,' he sneered, 'take me in straight, or I'll crush your balls.'

And he gave them a wrench that made me cry out. 'OOWWWwwww!'

'Sir,' I said, 'he sits with a drawn cutlass, but his pistol is real.'

'Come, now, march,' interrupted he. 'Lead me to him and when in view cry out, "Here's a friend for you, Bill." If you don't I'll do this . . .' and with that he did the Highland Fling so terribly that I fainted.

As I opened the parlour door, I cried out, 'Here's a friend for you, Bill.'

The poor Captain raised his eyes, and at one look the rum went out of him and left him staring. The expression on his face was of terror, mortal sickness – malaria, swamp fever, Yellow Jack and mumps.

'Now, Bill, sit where you are,' said the beggar.

The Captain's finger stirred and the blind man heard it. I saw him pass something from the hollow of the hand that held his stick into the palm of the Captain's, which closed upon it instantly.

'That's done,' said the blind man; and with accuracy and nimbleness, skipped out of the parlour and fell on his face in the road. I could hear his stick go tap-tap-tapping into the distance.

The rum started coming out of the Captain, he stood swaying for a moment, and then with a peculiar sound, Gaglipough!, he fell his whole height, five feet eleven inches, face-foremost on the floor. Alas, my dead father didn't know that now lying dead on the floor was the Captain. He had been struck dead by thundering apoplexy. It was a rare disease only caught from kangaroos. Of late I had begun to pity him, but as I saw him dead, I burst into a great flood of tears, and I had to swim for it.

4. THE SEA-CHEST

I lost no time, of course, in telling my mother all that I knew, while she wasn't sleep-walking. The neighbourhood, to our ears, seemed haunted by approaching footsteps; and what with the dead body of the Captain on the parlour floor, and the thought of that detestable blind beggar ready to return, there were moments when I jumped out of my skin in terror and then went back into it again. Something must speedily be done. It occurred to us to go forth together and seek help in the neighbouring hamlet. We ran out at once into the gathering evening; all the while the Captain lay dead on the floor.

Bow wow! Bow wow!

GROUCHO: Whose dog is that?

The hamlet lay not many hundred yards away on the other side of the next cove. We were not many minutes on the road, though we sometimes stopped and I laid hold of my mother and harkened. But there was nothing but the low wash of the ripples and the croaking of the crows in the wood, that and the National Lottery on TV.

It was already candle-light when we reached the hamlet, and I shall never forget how much I was cheered to see the yellow shine in doors and windows. 'Three cheers,' I said, 'for the yellow shine in the doors and windows.' You would have thought men would have been ashamed of themselves not to help us. Not one man would return with us to the 'Admiral Benbow' to stand guard. For that matter, anyone who knew of the terrible Captain, it was enough to frighten them to death. In fact, one of them who knew the Captain was so frightened he dropped dead from fright.

'If none of you will accompany us, we will go back the way we came.' All they would do was to give me a loaded pistol, lest we were attacked.

My heart was beating finely when we two set forth in the cold night upon this dangerous venture. We could neither see nor hear anything to decrease our terrors, till, to our huge relief, the door of the 'Admiral Benbow' had closed behind us.

I slipped the bolt at once, and we stood and panted in the dark, alone in the house with the dead Captain's body on the floor.

'Draw down the blind, Jim,' said mother. 'Now we have to get the key of his chest.'

I felt in his pocket; sure enough it wasn't there.

'Perhaps it's round his neck,' said mother. I tore open his shirt and sure enough it wasn't there either. Finally we found it already in the lock. She turned the key. The lock played a little tune, it had been made in Japan.

There was nothing to be seen on the top. We came across a canvas bag that gave forth at a touch the jingle of gold coins. 'Gold!' I said in an excited voice.

'I'll show these rogues that I'm an honest woman. Hold my bag,' said my mother. And she began to count over the amount of the Captain's score.

We were about half way through when I suddenly heard a sound that brought my heart into my mouth and out onto the floor. I put my hand on her hand. 'What is it?' said mother. 'It's my hand,' I said. I heard the tap-tap-tapping of the blind man's stick. It drew nearer and nearer, then it struck sharp on the inn door. We could hear the handle being turned, rattling the lock, then a long silence. At last the tapping recommenced, and to our joy it drew slowly away.

'Mother,' said I, 'take the whole lot and let's be going.' I was sure the bolted door would bring a hornet's nest about us.

'I'll take what I have,' she said, jumping to her feet.

'And I'll take this to square the account,' said I, picking up the oilskin packet from the sea-chest. The next moment we were groping each other in the fog.

'My dear,' said my mother suddenly, 'take the money and run on. I am going to faint.'

This was certainly the end for both of us, I thought. How I cursed the cowardice of the neighbours; how I blamed my poor mother for her honesty while the Captain was laying dead upon the floor. I managed to drag my mother down to the bank at the roadside, but it was early closing so we couldn't cash the cheque. So there we had to stay – my mother almost entirely exposed, you could see it all, and both of us within earshot of the inn. Thank heaven nobody tried to shoot at our ears!

GROUCHO: I must be in this story again soon.
Bow wow! Bow wow!
GROUCHO: It's that dog again – who owns him?

5. THE LAST OF THE BLIND MAN

I crept along to the inn again. I sheltered my head behind a bush of broom, or a broom of bush. I saw my enemies arrive, seven or eight of them, running hard, their feet beating out of time. It was exactly four-thirty. One of them was the blind beggar. The others weren't.

'Down with the door!' he cried. 'Down with Saddam!'

They rushed at it and went straight through and out of the back. The blind man again cried out, his voice sounding louder and higher, as if he was afire with eagerness and rage.

'In, in, in!' he shouted, and cursed them for their delay.

'Bill's dead!'

Yes indeed, the Captain lay dead on the floor. But the blind man swore at them again for their delay.

'Search him, some of you shirking lubbers, and the rest of you aloft and get his sea-chest.'

'They've been before us, Pew. Someone's turned the chest out alow and aloft.'

'Is it there?' roared Pew.

'Is what there?'

'Oh, anything,' said Pew.

'Flint's fist I mean,' he cried.

'There's no Flint's fist up here,' said the man.

'You below there, is anything on Bill?' cried the blind man.

Another man below began to search the Captain's body.

'I'm sorry, Bill's been overhauled . . . and he's running beautifully.'

'It's those people of the inn – it's that boy. I wish I had put his eyes out!' cried the blind man, Pew. 'Scatter, lads, and find that treasure map.'

There followed a great to-do through all our old inn, the pounding of heavy feet in the search of the treasure map. The buccaneers heard the sound of approaching horses. At last a gallant band of men coming to our aid.

'We left it too late, lads,' said one of the cowards.

The men scattered at the approaching horses' hooves, hives and heeves. Pew stood his ground and was trampled to death and lay dead in the ditch while the Captain lay dead on the floor. I hailed the riders.

'Pew is dead,' I said, 'in the ditch and the Captain is dead on the floor.'

Back at the 'Admiral Benbow' the house was in a state of smash; all the furniture had been thrown down in their furious search for the treasure map.

'What were they after?' said Mr Dance, one of the horsemen.

'Well to tell you the truth, I should like to get it put in safety. I think this is a treasure map. I thought Dr Livesey might like to see it,' I said.

'Perfectly right,' he interrupted. 'I might as well ride there.'

'Dogger,' said Mr Dance, 'take this lad.'

I mounted holding on to Dogger's belt. We struck out making for Dr Livesey's house. Blind Pew was dead in the ditch and the Captain still dead on the floor.

GROUCHO: Two for the price of one! Wait until their relatives get the news. Now read on. By the way, does anybody know whose dog that is?

6. THE CAPTAIN'S PAPERS

We drew up before Dr Livesey's door. I jumped down and knocked. The door was opened by a maid.

'Is Dr Livesey in?' I asked.

'No, he's gone to the Hall to dine.'

I did not remount but ran to the lodge gates. We were led down a passage to a great library, where the squire and Dr Livesey sat beside a bright fire. The horses ruined the carpet.

I had never seen the Squire Trelawney before. He had a very worn face. He must have travelled mostly on his face.

'Dance, you are a bold fellow for riding down that black, atrocious miscreant,' said the squire. 'As a magistrate I regard it as an act of violence for which you could be tried and hung.'

'And so, Jim,' said the doctor, 'you have the thing that they were after, have you?'

'Yes sir,' said I, and gave him the oilskin packet.

The doctor took it, his fingers itching to open it.

'Squire,' said he, 'Hawkins will sleep at my house. I suppose he can sup here.'

A big pigeon pie was brought in and put on a sidetable. It flew away.

'You have heard of this Flint I suppose?' asked Dr Livesey.

'Heard of him!' cried the squire. 'He was the bloodthirstiest buccaneer that sailed. He could never drink enough of it.'

'Now Jim,' said the doctor, 'we'll open the packet.'

The doctor cut the stitches with his medical scissors. It contained a book and a sealed paper.

'First of all we'll try the book,' said the doctor.

We tried it and there was nothing in it.

Finally the treasure map. The doctor opened the seals, out fell the same shit caked, Jaffa Caked map I had seen in the 'Admiral Benbow'. Further on it was written: 'Bulk of treasure here . . . The bar silver is in the north cache.

'The gold is easy found in the sand hill, N. point of north inlet cape, bearing E.'

'Treasure!' said Dr Livesey, and fainted.

'Tomorrow I start for Bristol,' the squire announced. 'In two weeks we'll have the best of ships, and the choicest crew in England. Hawkins shall come as cabin-boy.'

'Trelawney,' said the doctor, 'I'll go with you. There's only one man I'm afraid of.'

'And who's that?' cried the squire. 'Name the dog.'

GROUCHO: Never mind that, whose dog is he?

'You,' replied the doctor; 'for you cannot hold your tongue.'

'Yes I can,' said Trelawney, grasping hold of his tongue between his finger and thumb.

Bow wow! Bow wow!

GROUCHO: There it goes again! Whose dog is it?

PART TWO
The Sea Cook

7. I GO TO BRISTOL

No longer than the squire imagined ere we were ready for the sea. The doctor had to go to London to his practice. He had to practise until he got it right. We brooded by the hour over the treasure map. When we could brood no longer we put a hen over it.

So the weeks passed away as did my Auntie Florence. The following letter arrived.

'Old Anchor Inn, Bristol, March 1, 17–'

'Dear Livesey. –

'The ship is bought and fitted. Her name is the HISPANIOLA.

'By chance I was standing on the dock, when by chance I fell in talk with a fellow. I found he was an old sailor, he smelt of rum bum and baccy and kept a public house. Long John Silver was his name. He had lost his leg and never found it.

'Through him we discovered a crew. In a few days we had a company of the toughest old salts. Those we didn't like we threw over the side.

JOHN TRELAWNEY

'P.S. Give my regards to Jim's mother. Is his father still dead?'

The next morning I arrived at the 'Admiral Benbow'. I found my mother in good spirits, my father lay no longer on his deathbed nor was the Captain lying on the floor. They had buried them both before they went off. Night passed and the next morning I said goodbye to my mother.

The mail picked us up about dusk and at dawn put us down on the dock side at Bristol.

Mr Trelawney had taken up his residence on the docks.

JIM:	Squire, are you a farmer?
TRELAWNEY:	That I am, Jim.
JIM:	What do you have on the farm?
TRELAWNEY:	Oh everything – cows, sheep.
JIM:	Do you send them for slaughter?
TRELAWNEY:	Yes, you have to before you can eat 'em.
JIM:	Do you have any pets?
TRELAWNEY:	Yes, I've a three-legged dog. His name is Rover but when he barks he falls over.

That night we were all aboard. We pulled up the anchor and put out to sea for sea trials. The trials involved a murderer, two arsonists and a sheep dog.

Squire Trelawney was walking the deck in a capital imitation of a sailor's walk, one step forward and three back. Some of his own servants had joined the crew, all under the command of our good ship's captain, Captain Smollett.

'So here we are,' said the squire, and so we were here.

'Soon,' I cried, 'It will be the treasure. In fact, quite soon.' It was good to know that quite soon we would find the treasure.

GROUCHO: It's taking a long time for them to get to me.
Q: Yes, you're playing the waiting game.
GROUCHO: Oh? I wondered what I was doing. What are *you* doing?
Q: I'm waiting in the wings.
GROUCHO: If I had wings I'd fly away over you and let you have it.
Q: You mean you'd shit on me?
GROUCHO: Oh you're lightning quick, you must have a high IQ.
Q: What's a IQ?
GROUCHO: Obviously I was mistaken.
Q: You are a difficult man with whom to get on. Apparently you don't get on with women either.
GROUCHO: With them I try to get off. Did you know there were no dry cleaners in Peru?

8. AT THE SIGN OF THE 'SPY-GLASS'

Out of a side room in The 'Spy-Glass' inn came the proprietor, Long John Silver. His left leg was cut off at the hip, and under the left shoulder he carried a crutch. On his right shoulder he had a parrot that blasphemed. 'Fuck all of you,' it screamed.

'Mr Silver,' I said, holding my hand out 'My hand,' I said.

'So it is,' said Silver.

GROUCHO: Yes, he's got another one just like that.

'You must be Jim Hawkins,' said Silver.

'Yes, I am Jim Hawkins.'

'Now, Jim, have you ever clapped eyes on Black Dog?'

'Yes, sir.'

Just then one of the customers at the far side rose suddenly and made for the door.

'Oh,' I cried, 'stop him! It's Black Dog!'

'I don't care two coppers who he is,' cried Silver, 'but he hasn't paid his score. Harry, run and catch him.'

'Get the bastard!' shrieked the parrot.

One of the others leaped up, and started in pursuit.

'If he were Admiral Hawke he shall pay his score,' cried Silver. 'Who did you say he was?' he asked. 'Black what?'

'Black Dog, wot Churchill had,' I said. 'Has Mr Trelawney not told you of the buccaneers? He was one of them.'

'Wot, Churchill?'

'No, Black Dog.'

Standing by was Seaman Morgan. 'Now, Morgan,' said Long John, very sternly, 'I seen you talkin' with the rogue but you never clapped your eyes on that Black – Black Dog before, did you?'

'Not I, sir,' said Morgan, with a salute, poking his eye out.

'You didn't know his name, did you?'

'No, sir.'

'If you had been mixed up with the likes of him, you would never put another foot in my house. What was he saying to you?'

'Well we were a-talkin' about a recipe for curried cat,' answered Morgan.

'And now,' said Silver, 'let's see – Black Dog? Yes, I've seen the swab. I've seen him come here with a blind beggar with a face like a dog's bum with a hat on.'

'That he did,' said I. 'His name was Pew.'

'Pew!' he said. 'That was his name for certain.'

Then of a sudden he stopped and his jaw dropped. It hit the floor with a clack. He began to laugh and that so heartily, though I did not see the joke, because it wasn't funny.

The squire and Dr Livesey sat together and finished off a side of beef on the bone – and were seriously ill.

'Well, squire,' said Dr Livesey, 'I don't put much faith in your discoveries, as a general thing; but I will say this, John Silver suits me. He will make a fine ship's cook, and he has no regard for buccaneers.'

GROUCHO: The fool!

9. POWDER AND ARMS

'Now Jim,' said the doctor, 'you can go for a good sleep for the night in your hammock.' We were well out to sea, at least six feet from the quayside. The mate, Mr Arrow, was a brown old sailor with earrings in his ears and a terrible squint; he kept walking into the mast. I soon observed that things were not good between Mr Trelawney and the captain.

'Captain Smollett, sir, axing to speak with you,' said Mr Arrow.

'Alright axe! Show him in!'

'Well, Captain Smollett, I hope all is shipshape?'

'Well,' said the captain, 'I had better speak plain.'

'Yes. I understand plain fluently.'

'I don't like this cruise; I don't like the men; and I don't like my officers. That's short and sweet.'

GROUCHO: So you don't like officers that are short and sweet?

'Then why don't you get off?' said Livesey.

'I would get off but I'd only drown. You see, I can't swim.'

'Well,' said Trelawney, 'I can't play the violin, but I don't tell everybody about it. Perhaps sir, you may not like your employer either?'

But here Dr Livesey cut in.

'Stay for a bit,' said he, 'stay for a bit.'

GROUCHO: I'll stay for a bit. Where is she?

'You don't, you say, like this cruise?' said Trelawney.

'Alright then, I don't say I say it,' said the captain. 'So far I find that every man before the mast knows more than I do. I don't call that fair!'

'No,' said Dr Livesey, 'I don't.'

'I have learned that we are going after treasure. Treasure is very ticklish,' said the captain.

'Then why aren't you laughing?' said Trelawney.

'It is a way of speaking,' said the captain.

'Yes, that is a way of speaking,' said Trelawney.

'I don't like treasure voyages on any account.'

'That is all clear,' replied Dr Livesey. 'Now, next you say you don't like the crew?'

'Yes, next I was going to say I don't like the crew,' said the captain. 'How did you know?'

'What about Mr Arrow?' said Trelawney.

'He's a good seaman when he's not walking into the mast.'

'Any more?' he asked.

'One more,' said the captain. 'There's been too much blabbing already.'

'Far too much,' agreed the doctor. 'It's everywhere. There's blabbing all over the deck.'

'The hands know about the treasure, so does that bloody parrot,' said the captain and he continued, 'I don't know who has this map; but I make it a point, it shall be kept secret even from me and Mr Arrow. Otherwise I would ask you to let me resign.'

'And where would you go?'

'Overboard even though I can't swim,' said the captain.

'Well,' said Trelawney, 'I can't play the violin, but I don't tell everybody about it.'

As a magistrate, he knew there was no legal limit on the number of times you could use the same joke in one book.

'I wish,' said the captain 'to make a garrison of the stern part of the ship, manned with my friend's people and provided with all the arms and powder on board.'

'In other words you fear a mutiny,' said the doctor.

GROUCHO: Doesn't anybody get on with anybody on this ship?
JIM: The voyage is fraught with danger.

GROUCHO:	It's worse, they've all got the clap.
JIM:	Even Mr Arrow?
GROUCHO:	Him especially. He didn't get that squint from walking into the mast, you know.
JIM:	Unknown to the crew the captain has piles.
GROUCHO:	I thought he said he had them taken away.
JIM:	Where to?
GROUCHO:	Somerset I think.
JIM:	Yes, that's a good place for piles.
GROUCHO:	How long were you in the King's Navy, Captain?
CAPTAIN:	About six feet two inches.
GROUCHO:	That's tall for a sailor.
CAPTAIN:	Yes, it's also tall for a dwarf.

We were all hard at work, changing the powder and the berths, when the last man or two, and Long John along with them, came on board in a shore-boat.

The cook came up the side like a monkey, it was a brilliant disguise.

'My orders!' said the captain shortly. 'You may go below, my man. Hands will want supper.'

'Ay, ay, sir,' answered the cook; touching his forelock, he disappeared at once in the direction of his galley.

GROUCHO:	What's this with the one-legged guy?
JIM:	He wasn't always one-legged.
GROUCHO:	I was going to say, shouldn't he have another?
JIM:	Yes.
GROUCHO:	What happened to it? Did he sell it?
JIM:	It was blown off by a cannon ball.
GROUCHO:	Did he get compensation? He could have made a lot of money.
JIM:	It was in a war.
GROUCHO:	Then he should sue the opposition.
JIM:	It was a war against the French.
GROUCHO:	Then he could get it in francs – all he needs is a good solicitor.

'You, ship's boy,' Captain Smollett cried. 'Off with you to the cook and get some work.'

I went below and Silver was bending over a saucepan of brown bubbling stuff.

JIM:	Is that an Irish stew, John?
SILVER:	That's the current opinion, lad.
JIM:	Have you had turkey for Christmas?
SILVER:	No I had my brother and sister for dinner.
JIM:	Did they taste nice?
SILVER:	Delicious.
JIM:	You are a strange man, John.
SILVER:	I used to be a strange woman till I had the operation.

JIM:	Are you English?
SILVER:	No, Mum and Dad were Irish tinkers.
JIM:	What do tinkers do?
SILVER:	They mend people's broken kettles. If they weren't broken, they'd break them for them first.
JIM:	Didn't the owners complain?
SILVER:	No, it was too late. The country is full of broken kettles, Jim.
JIM:	The Irish are supposed to be hot-headed.
GROUCHO:	Oh, yes. I felt an Irishman's head once and it was very hot.
JIM:	Groucho, where did you come from?
GROUCHO:	A long line of Jews . . . that'll be another $380, please.
JIM:	You make a good living.
GROUCHO:	You call this living? Dogs have a better life than us.
JIM:	A dog's life?
GROUCHO:	Yes.

Bow wow! Bow wow!

GROUCHO:	Whose dog is that?

Bow wow! Bow wow!

GROUCHO:	You see? There it goes again. Wait a minute, it might be worse than I think. It could be *two* dogs; that or it's one dog barking twice, or two dogs barking once.
JIM:	How can a man think like that?
GROUCHO:	By living with gorillas.
JIM.	You've lived with gorillas?
GROUCHO:	How do you think I can think like that?

10. THE VOYAGE

All that night we were in a great bustle getting stowed into place.

GROUCHO: Look boy, I don't want to be stowed into place – it's undignified.

'Now, Barbecue, tip us a stave,' cried one voice. ['Stave' = Middle Ages English for joke.]

'Ay, ay, mates,' said Long John, who was standing by; with his crutch under his arm, he looked deformed. 'What do you call a two foot tall Irishman? A knee Mick! Ha! Ha! Ha! Ha!'

That night as I dreamed in my hammock one end collapsed and I was knocked unconscious. I saw stars and a nursing sister from Catford.

Mr Arrow turned out far worse than the captain had hoped. He began to appear on deck with hazy eyes, red cheeks, stuttering tongue, sick down his shirt and marks of drunkenness. Sometimes for a day or two he would appear sober. We could never make out where he got the drink. One dark night, with a head sea, he disappeared overboard and was seen no more.

'Overboard!' said the captain. 'Well, gentlemen, that saves the trouble of putting him in irons.'

Actually Arrow swam ashore, won the National Lottery and married the Spice Girls, one at a time.

But there we were, without a mate; and we had to advance one of the men. The boatswain, Job Anderson, was the likeliest man. He had followed the sea all his life. Mr Trelawney had also followed the sea, but only until he caught up with it. And the coxswain, Israel Hands, was a careful, wily, old, experienced rum bum and baccy seaman.

JIM:	Israel – how did you get that name?
ISRAEL:	I'm Jewish.
JIM:	You aren't allowed pork, are you?
ISRAEL:	No. You know what a Jewish dilemma is Jim?
JIM:	No.
ISRAEL:	Pork chops at half-price, ha ha.
JIM:	Were you circumcised?
ISRAEL:	They *had* to, it was all hanging down. When the Rabbi weighed it, it was ten-and-a-half pounds!
JIM:	Captain Smollett says your wife was in prison.
ISRAEL:	She was on the game.
JIM:	Game? What game?
ISRAEL:	Well, let's just say it wasn't tennis, Jim.

So we just said 'It wasn't tennis, Jim.'

JIM:	Why, Hands, do you get so drunk?
ISRAEL:	To forget.
JIM:	Forget? Forget what?
ISRAEL:	Buckingham Palace.
JIM:	Why? Why Buckingham Palace?
ISRAEL:	I dunno. I forgot.

Israel Hands, was a great confidant of Long John Silver, so the mention of his name leads me on to speak of our ship's cook, Barbecue, as the men called him.

JIM:	Silver, how old are you?
SILVER:	See that oak tree?
JIM:	That's three hundred years old. You're not three hundred years old.
GROUCHO:	Not yet, Jim.
JIM:	What's an oak tree doing in the middle of the Atlantic?
GROUCHO:	Looks like the breast stroke to me.
JIM:	Did you serve aboard a ship?
SILVER:	*HMS Warspite* – she was a good ship.
GROUCHO:	With a *slight* tendency to sink.
JIM:	Did you sail the seven seas?
GROUCHO:	Oh more than seven – eight, nine, ten seas and seventeen oceans and twenty-eight rivers. Then he ran out of water.
JIM:	Did you ever sink an enemy ship?

SILVER:	Yes, the *HMS Albion*.
JIM:	That's a British ship!
SILVER:	I wondered why they shot the captain.
JIM:	Did you meet any pirates?
SILVER:	Yes I met one in Clapham High Street.
GROUCHO:	You must have been in great danger in Clapham High Street.
JIM:	Tell me, Silver, how many brothers and sisters do you have?
SILVER:	At the last count eleven sisters and seventeen brothers.
GROUCHO:	What other hobbies has your father got?

Aboard ship he carried his crutch by a lanyard round his neck, to have both hands as free as possible to strangle people. It was something to see him wedge the foot of the crutch against a bulk-head, and propped against it, yielding to every movement of the ship, get on with his cooking like someone safe ashore.

'He's no common man,' said the coxswain to me. 'He's brave – a lion's nothing alongside Long John. Once he was confronted by a lion and he knocked it to the ground. He was fined thirty shillings by the RSPCA for cruelty to animals, but he loves his parrot.'

'Cap'n Flint I calls my parrot, after the famous buccaneer.'

And the parrot would say, with great rapidity, 'Pieces of eight! pieces of eight! pieces of eight,' till you wondered that it was not out of breath, or till John threw his handkerchief over the cage. 'Take that bloody cloth off my cage!' screamed the parrot.

'Arrh, she's lovely she is,' the cook would say, and give her some sugar, and then the bird would peck at the bars and swear straight on. 'Fuck you and the crew,' cried the parrot.

'There,' said Silver, 'Here's this poor old innocent bird o' mine swearing blue fire.'

'Fuck all of you,' cried the parrot.

In the meantime, the squire and Captain Smollett were still on distant terms with each another – about a mile; the squire despised the captain. The captain, for his part, never spoke. As for the ship, he had taken a downright fancy to her. 'I have taken a downright fancy to her,' said the captain.

At this the squire would turn away and march up and down the deck, chin in air.

'A trifle more of that man,' he would say, 'and I will explode.' He had a trifle more of that man and he exploded.

11. WHAT I HEARD IN THE APPLE BARREL

A barrel of apples had been put on deck for anybody to help himself. After sundown it occurred to me that I should like an apple. Alas, there was only one left so I dived in. I was sitting in the bottom of the barrel eating the apple when a man began to speak. It was Silver's voice, he was encouraging a mutiny. Therefore, I would not have shown myself for all the world.

To my horror Silver seemed to be in league with this mutinous crew and planned eventually to take over the *Hispaniola* and look for the treasure. He ended by saying, 'I claim Trelawney. I'll wring his calf's head off his body with these hands. Now lad, get me an apple to wet my pipe.'

My heart skipped a beat and my liver, kidneys and spleen danced a sailor's hornpipe.

'Oh don't you go sucking up apples, John. Let's go and have a rum.'

Never was I so relieved. It took half the night to clear it up.

Just then I looked up. It was night and the moon shone directly above me. Then the voice of the lookout shouted, 'Land ho!'

12. COUNCIL OF WAR

'And now, men,' said the captain, when all the crew was sheeted home, 'has any one of you ever seen that land ahead?'

'I have, sir,' said Silver, 'many a time. I have watered there, mostly against a tree.'

'I have a chart here,' says Captain Smollett. 'See if that's the place.'

Long John's eyes burned in his head and set fire to his hair. 'Ay, here it is: "Capt. Kidd's Anchorage." '

'Thank you, my man,' says Captain Smollett. 'I would like you later on to give us a hand.'

'Doctor,' I said, 'let me speak to you in the cabin. I have terrible news.'

'My lads,' said Captain Smollett, 'I've a word to say to you. I have to tell every man who has done his duty, alow and aloft, as I never ask to see it done better. And if you think as I do, you'll give a good sea-cheer.'

A cheer followed. It rang out so full and hearty I could hardly believe these same men were plotting for our blood.

'One more cheer for Cap'n Smollett,' cried Long John.

GROUCHO: Grovelling little bastard.

I went below and found the captain, the doctor and the squire. The captain was smoking with his wig on his lap which he set on fire. When he put it on it was still smoking. Quickly I told them all of the cook's intention to kill us all, take charge of the *Hispaniola* and find the treasure.

'Now, Captain,' said the squire, 'you were right, and I was wrong. I own myself an ass.'

GROUCHO: I wonder where he stables it?

'Captain,' said the doctor, 'Silver is a very remarkable man.'

'He'd look remarkably well hanging from a yard-arm, sir.'

GROUCHO: How can you look well hanging
            from the yard-arm? Well hung, perhaps . . .

'Now if it comes to blows some fine day we can count on your own home servants, Mr Trelawney?' returned the captain.

'Yes,' said the squire, 'as upon myself.'

'Three,' reckoned the captain, 'and seven counting Jim Hawkins here.'

GROUCHO: Three plus Jim is seven? I'm glad you're not my accountant.

'Well, gentlemen,' said the captain, 'the best that I can say is not much.' So he said 'not much'. 'Hawkins, I put prodigious faith in you,' added the squire.

It was indeed through me that safety came. There were only seven out of the twenty-six on whom we could rely; so that the grown men on our side were six to their nineteen. They gave me a pistol which I swallowed for safety.

GROUCHO: Is this a first or second-class ship?
JIM: This is not a passenger ship.
GROUCHO: Then how do you make money?
JIM: We sell pianos.
GROUCHO: I know a wonderful pianist. She can't read music, so she reads the
            New York Daily Herald. Mainly the gossip column. She once played an
            entire concerto about Jean Harlow sleeping with Douglas Fairbanks.
            A man can't do much when he's sleeping.
JIM: My mother can't sleep. She's a somnambulist, she walks in her sleep.
GROUCHO: Where to?
JIM: My father's bed, mostly. Until he died in it.
GROUCHO: So where does she walk to now?
JIM: France.
GROUCHO: France? She'd have to swim.
JIM: No, she takes the ferry.
GROUCHO: Does she speak French?
JIM: She speaks a smattering.
GROUCHO: I wish I could speak a smattering, I'd go there.
CAPTAIN: Who is this strange man?
JIM: He says he's Groucho Marx.
CAPTAIN: What are you doing on my ship?
GROUCHO: I'm not doing anything on your ship. If I did I'd clean it up.
CAPTAIN: Look, will you help us fight the mutineers by stopping them?
GROUCHO: So I go up to them and say 'Stop!' Then what?
CAPTAIN: You shoot them.
GROUCHO: Can't we shoot them first *then* say stop after?
CAPTAIN: That will be too late.
GROUCHO: Too late? It's only three o'clock.

CAPTAIN: Three o'clock? That reminds me I must put my watch back.
GROUCHO: I'm not putting my watch back. I haven't finished paying for it yet.
CAPTAIN: Have you ever fired a musket?
GROUCHO: No, but I fired my secretary.

PART THREE
My Shore Adventure

13. HOW I BEGAN MY SHORE ADVENTURE

The appearance of the island when I came on deck next morning was altogether changed. Although the breeze had now utterly failed, we had made a great deal of way during the night, and were now lying becalmed about half a mile to the south-east of the low eastern coast. Grey-coloured woods covered a large part of the surface. This even tint was indeed broken up by streaks of yellow sandbreak in the lower lands, and by many tall trees of the pine family, out-topping the others – some singly, some in clumps; but the general colouring was uniform and sad.

The hills ran up clear above the vegetation in spires of naked rock. All were strangely shaped, and the Spy-glass, which was by three or four hundred feet the tallest on the island, was likewise the strangest in configuration, running up sheer from almost every side, and then suddenly cut off at the top like a pedestal to put a statue on.

GROUCHO: Oh God! No more boring descriptive writing, Jim. You're just holding up the book. What I want to know is what's holding *me* up.

The *Hispaniola* was rolling under in the ocean swell.

GROUCHO: My God, here he goes again!

I was a good enough sailor but this standing still and being rolled about like a bottle was a thing I never learned to stand without a qualm. Suddenly I had a qualm. The sun was very hot so we didn't touch it.

'There's a strong scour with the ebb,' said Silver, and sure enough there was a strong scour with the ebb.

The plunge of our anchor sent up clouds of birds, so the crew shot them down; but in less than a minute they were up again, whereupon they were all shot down again. Before the crew could murder the entire nesting population of the island, the captain allowed them to go ashore and I volunteered for one of the boats. Anderson was in command of my boat and instead of keeping the crew in order he grumbled.

'Well fuck,' he said, 'this is not forever.'

GROUCHO: No, but it's getting on that way.

If the conduct of the men had been alarming below decks, it became truly threatening when they assembled to board the boats. They lay about the deck growling together in talk. The slightest order was received with black looks, sometimes red, sometimes green.

'My lads,' said the captain, 'we've had a hot day. A turn ashore'll hurt nobody – the boats are still in the water; you can take the gigs, and as many as please can go ashore. I'll fire a gun half an hour before sundown. Hawkins, you will stay on board the *Hispaniola*.'

So I was to remain behind and watched as the shore party made their preparations. At last the party was made up. Some used lipstick, powder and rouge and they looked beautiful. Six were to stay on board, the remainder were to embark with Silver. Then it was that an idea came into my head. In a jiffy I had slipped over the side, and curled up in the foresheets of the nearest boat.

Bow wow! Bow wow!

GROUCHO: For God's sake, whose dog is that?

No one took notice of me, only the bow oar saying, 'Is that you, Jim? Keep your head down.' But Silver, from the other boat, looked sharply over and called out to know if that were me and yes it were me.

The crews raced for the beach; the bow had struck among the shore-side trees and I had caught a branch and swung myself out, and plunged into the nearest thicket, while Silver and the rest were still a hundred yards behind.

'Jim, Jim!' I heard him shouting.

I ran straight before my nose, and my nose led me to where I was now, here. And that's exactly where I was, *here*.

GROUCHO: Here is not a bad place to be – I mean you could be there and then where would you be?
JIM: Here.
GROUCHO: Like I said, here is a good place to be.
JIM: How did you get here?
GROUCHO: I followed you and found myself here.
JIM: What do you hope to do?
GROUCHO: Nothing, so it shouldn't take long.
JIM: You're a very hard man to understand.
GROUCHO: Okay, I'll try talking slower, but that will cost me, you know.
Bow wow! Grr! Bow wow!
GROUCHO: Will somebody shut that dog up!

14. THE FIRST BLOW

I had crossed a marshy tract full of willows, bulrushes, and odd, outlandish, swampy trees; and I had now come out upon the skirts of an open piece of undulating, sandy country, about a mile long, dotted with a few pines, and a great number of contorted trees, not unlike the oak in growth, but pale in the foliage, like willows. On the far side of the open stood one of the hills, with two quaint, craggy peaks, shining vividly in the sun.

GROUCHO: I keep telling you – no more descriptive stuff; we'll never finish this job.

I turned hither and thither, hather and thather, and found myself going backwards among the undergrowth. Then I came to a long thicket of these oak-like things – I heard afterwards that they were called trees. All at once there began to be a bustle among the bulrushes; a wild duck flew up with a quack.

GROUCHO: That's quite normal for a duck.

Soon I heard the very distant and low tones of a human voice, I now recognised the voice as Silver's, now and again interrupted by the others. By the sound they must have been talking earnestly, and almost fiercely. At last the speakers seemed to have paused but the birds themselves began to grow more quiet; they were frightened to fly any more with the trigger-happy crew around.

Crawling on all-fours, I came into a little green dell. There I saw Long John Silver and another member of the crew come face to face.

'Silver,' said the other man, 'you're brave or I'm mistook. Will you tell me you'll let yourself be led away by this kind of messy swabs? As sure as God sees me, I'd sooner lose my hand. If I turn again my dooty –'

Far out in the marsh there arose a sound like a cry of anger then a shot followed by a long drawn-out scream ... 'Arghaaraaagagggggggghhhh-hhhawwwwww!'

GROUCHO: Obviously he took a long time to die.

'John,' said the sailor, stretching out his hand till it reached Silver.
'Hands off!' cried Silver.
Sure enough, his hands came off.
'Hands off, if you like, John Silver,' said the other. 'But in heaven's name, tell me what was that?'
'That, Tom?' returned Silver, 'I reckon that'll be Alan.'
'Alan!' Tom cried. 'John Silver, long you've been a mate of mine but if I die like a dog ...'

GROUCHO: Are you the one that keeps barking?

'You've killed Alan. Kill me, too, if you can. But I defies you.' So he defied him. With that, the brave fellow turned his back and set off walking to the beach. Silver whipped the crutch out of his armpit, and sent that missile hurtling through the air. Thud!! It struck poor Tom with a stunning violence right between the shoulders. He gave a sort of gasp and fell.

Tom lay motionless upon the sward; but the murderer minded him not a whit.

'I mind not a whit,' he said hopping whitlessly over to retrieve his deadly crutch.

Now Silver put his hand into his pocket, brought out a whistle, and blew upon it several blasts. Was it half time between us? Should we change ends? He had already slain two honest people; would I come next?

GROUCHO: I'd say yes, but it's fifty–fifty.

I ran as I never ran before, sideways. As I ran fear grew and grew upon me, until it turned into a kind of frenzy, a kind of frenzy – a frinzy! Would not the first of them wring my neck like a chicken's?

GROUCHO: Yes.

It was all over, I thought. Goodbye to the *Hispaniola*. There was nothing left for me but death by starvation or death at the hands of the mutineers.

GROUCHO: That's sensible thinking.

A fresh sound brought me to a standstill.
Bow wow! Bow wow! It was a dog.

GROUCHO: Yes, but whose dog is it?

15. THE MAN OF THE ISLAND

A figure appeared. What it was, whether bear or man or monkey, I could in no wise tell. It seemed dark and ragged; more I knew not. But instantly the figure reappeared, and began to head me off. From trunk to trunk the creature flitted like a deer, running manlike on two legs, but unlike any man that I had ever seen. Yet a man it was. It put the shits up me. But the mere fact he was a man had somewhat reassured me. I walked briskly towards him.

As soon as I began to move in his direction, he reappeared and threw himself on his knees. His clothes were in tatters!

'Who are you?' I said.

GROUCHO: Whoever he is he needs a good tailor.

'Ben Gunn,' he answered. His voice sounded hoarse and awkward like his balls had just dropped. 'I haven't spoke with a Christian these three years.'

'Three years!' I cried, 'Why not? Were you shipwrecked?'

'Nay mate,' said he, 'marooned. Marooned three years agone,' he continued, 'and lived on goats since then, and berries and hamburgers and chips. You mightn't happen to have a piece of cheese about you now?'

'Do you know, for once I haven't. I've got a Swiss Army jack-knife.'

[Ben Gunn seeing Groucho –]
BEN: Who are you?
GROUCHO: If only I knew.
BEN: Are you from the moon?
GROUCHO: The nearest I got to the moon was Brooklyn. Who is this, Jim?
JIM: Ben Gunn.

BEN:	And I'm a silly bugger.
GROUCHO:	Someone has to be one, unfortunately it happens to be you.
BEN:	So would you be if you'd been marooned three years.
GROUCHO:	Oh, my nose bleeds for you.
BEN:	Look, I don't like you.
JIM:	He means well.
GROUCHO:	So did Hitler.

'Now you,' he cried, 'what do you call yourself?'

'I call myself Jim Hawkins,' I said.

'Jim Hawkins?' said he. 'You've got a good memory for names. I tell you something, Jim. I am rich, rich I tell you. I am rich! I am rich!'

JIM:	You don't look rich to me. You look pretty skint.
BEN:	Do I? Have pity on a poor old bugger.
JIM:	All right – so you're a poor old bugger. You say you haven't spoke to a Christian for three years, why?
BEN:	There ain't any on the island. Sometimes cannibals landed on the island.
JIM:	Why didn't you talk to them?
BEN:	They didn't speak English; apart from that they'd chop yer balls off and eat you. They crapped on the beach and I trod in it. You could smell me for bloody miles.
JIM:	I still can.
BEN:	That's not the shit, that's me.
JIM:	So if you're rich, I'd guess you know where the treasure is – where is it?

His laughing brought on a terrible fit of coughing, combined with intermittent letting off at the back. I waited for it to stop but it didn't. He walked backwards into the woods and then he walked forwards out of it.

'Now, Jim, you tell me true; that ain't Flint's ship?' he asked.

'All right, it ain't Flint's ship. Flint is dead,' I said.

'How do you know?'

'They buried him. Someone else took his place.'

'Not a man – with one – leg?' he gasped.

'Silver?' I asked.

'No, wooden,' says he.

'He's the cook; now, the ringleader too.'

'Where do you come in all this?' he said.

I told him the whole story of the voyage and the predicament in which we found ourselves.

'Ay, but you see,' returned Ben Gunn, 'what I mean is, would your Captain be likely to come down to the toon of, say, one hundred thousand pounds in treasure?'

'I'm sure he would,' said I. 'As it was, all hands were to share.'

'And a passage home?' said Ben.

'Why yes,' I cried.

'Let me tell you,' he said, 'I was here when Flint buried the treasure. He killed six of his crew. I came back on another ship and we sighted the islands. "Boys," said I, "here's Flint's treasure island; let's find it." Twelve days they looked for it and every day worse than the next. Finally they said, "As for you, Benjamin Gunn, here's a musket, and a spade. You can stay here, and find Flint's money for yourself."

'Well, Jim, three years have I been here, and not a bite of Christian diet from that day to this. But now, you look at me. Do I look like a man before the mast?'

'Not at the moment, right now you're a man before the tree.'

'Then,' he continued, 'you'll say this: Gunn-is-a-good-man-and-he-puts-a-precious-sight-more-confidence-in-a-gen'leman-born-than-in-these-gen'le-men-of-fortune,-having-been-one-hisself.'

'I don't understand one bloody word that you've been saying. How am I to get back on board?'

'Ah,' said he, 'well, there's my boat, that I made with my two hands. I keep her under the white rock. If the worst come to the worst, we might try that.'

Just then, although the sun had still an hour or two to run, all the echoes of the island awoke and bellowed to the thunder of a cannon.

'They have begun to fight!' I cried. 'Follow me, follow me!'

I began to run towards the anchorage. The marooned man in his goatskin trotted easily and lightly.

'Left, left,' says he. 'Keep to your left, Jim!'

So he kept talking as I ran. The cannon-shot was followed by a volley of small arms. Another pause, and then, not a quarter of a mile in front of me, I beheld the Union Jack flutter in the air above a stockade.

16. NARRATIVE CONTINUED BY THE DOCTOR: HOW THE SHIP WAS ABANDONED

SHIP'S LOG

May 4, 17–

Hunter, one of the Squire's men, Doctor and the Captain took jolly-boat to island. Found stockade whilst ashore. We heard a shot and death cry. Was it Jim Hawkins? Would he live to be 17 . . . or 18, 21 or 57?

Returned to ship. Held crew at gun point. Loaded jolly-boat with supplies and ammunition.

On deck Squire and Captain confronted mutineers.

'Mr Hands,' shouted the Captain, 'There's two of us with a brace of pistols each!'

'Oh Christ,' said Hands.

'If any of you move that man is dead.'

'Which man is that?' said Hands.

Each hoping that 'that man' was one of the others, the mutineers rushed and hid below.

Signed: Smollett
Captain RN

It was about half-past-one – three bells in the sea phrase – that the two boats with the mutineers went ashore from the *Hispaniola*. The captain, the squire, and I were talking matters over in the cabin. Had there been a breath of wind we should have fallen on the six mutineers left. Down came Hunter with the news that Jim Hawkins had slipped into a boat and was gone ashore with the rest.

[Hunter – Doctor – Captain (on board ship)]

DOCTOR: Jim Hawkins – gone ashore? Did he swim?

HUNTER: No. Somehow he smuggled himself on one of the boats.

DOCTOR: Good God! What was the boy thinking of?

HUNTER: Well sir, he was actually thinking of his mother sleep-walking.

DOCTOR: Does she walk far?

HUNTER: He said on one night she ended up at the Naval Barracks in Portsmouth.

DOCTOR: What in God's name was she doing?

HUNTER: Looking for a sailor – when she met one, she said, 'Hello sailor.'

DOCTOR: That poor Jim, that poor boy, he's only sixteen.

HUNTER: We all were once.

DOCTOR: Yes, we can only be sixteen once. God, what am I saying?

HUNTER: Can't you remember? You were saying we can only be sixteen once.

DOCTOR: Yes, of course, now I remember.

HUNTER: Look sir, I'll take a telescope and scan the island.

[Hunter, through his telescope, spotted Jim hiding in the bushes.]

CAPTAIN: I wonder what Jim's game is?

HUNTER: I think it's football, sir.

There came a ringing cry of a man at the point of death.

'Good God,' said the Doctor, 'Jim Hawkins is gone! He will never be 17 . . . or 18, 21 or 57!'

The squire was sitting down, white as a sheet, thinking of the harm he had led us to.

SQUIRE: I was just thinking of the harm I had led you to.

DOCTOR: You shouldn't blame yourself. We'll do that.

We had no time to lose. I told my plan to the captain, and between us we settled on the details. We put Redruth, a loyal man, in the gallery with a musket. Hunter and I loaded the jolly-boat with supplies. By this time, tumbling things in as they came, we had the jolly-boat loaded as much as we dared. Joyce, another of those loyal to us, and I got out through the stern-port, the man Gray made up the last of our number and we made for shore as fast as we could row.

The little gallipot of a boat was gravely overloaded with grown men, and three of them over six feet high. Add to that powder, pork and provisions. Several times we shipped water and the tails of my coat were soaking wet before we had gone a hundred yards. The captain made us trim the boat, and we got her to lie a little more evenly. All the same, we were afraid to breathe.

'I cannot keep her head for the stockade, sir,' said I to the Captain. 'The tide keeps washing her down. Could you pull a little longer?'

'Not without swamping the boat,' said he.

'We'll never get ashore at this rate,' I said.

'The current's less a'ready, sir,' said Gray. 'You can ease her off a bit.'

'Thank you, my man,' said I, quite as if nothing had happened, and indeed it hadn't.

Suddenly the captain spoke up again. I thought his voice was a little changed.

'The ship's gun,' said he.

'I have thought of that,' said I. 'They could never get the gun ashore, and if they did, they could never haul it through the woods.'

'Look astern, doctor,' replied the captain.

There, to our horror, were the rogues we had left on board busy getting off her jacket, as they called the stout tarpaulin cover under which the cannon was stowed. Not only that, but the round-shot and the powder for the gun had been left behind and it would be all put into the possession of the ones aboard. But the worst of it was, that with the course I now held, we turned our broadside instead of our stern to the *Hispaniola* and offered a target like a barn door.

'Who's the best shot?' asked the captain.

'Mr Trelawney,' said I.

'Mr Trelawney, will you please pick me off one of these men, sir? Hands, if possible,' said the captain. 'Now easy with that gun, sir, or you'll swamp the boat.'

The squire raised his gun and we leaned over to the other side to keep the balance. They had the gun slewed round and Hands, who was at the muzzle with the rammer, was, in consequence, the most exposed. Just as Trelawney fired, he stooped, the ball whistled over him, and it was one of the others who fell.

The cry he gave was echoed by his companions on board and by a great number of voices from the shore. Looking in that direction I saw other pirates trooping out and tumbling into their places in the boats.

'Here come the gigs, sir,' said I, 'most likely going round by shore to cut us off.'

'They'll have a hot run, sir,' returned the captain. 'It's not them I mind; it's the round shot. When you see the match, we'll hold water. You hold yours and I'll hold mine. If I dared,' said the captain, 'I'd stop and pick off another man.'

Where the ball passed, not one of us knew precisely; but it must have been over our heads and the wind of it may have contributed to our disaster. Our boat sank by the stern, quite gently, in three feet of water, leaving the captain and myself, facing each other, on our feet, with wet bollocks. We waded ashore, so far in safety, to the stockade. We landed all the stores.

No sooner was everything ashore than we set to provision the stockade. We all made the first journey, heavily laden, and tossed our stores over the palisade. Then, leaving Joyce to stand guard, we returned to the jolly-boat and loaded ourselves once more. We proceeded till the whole cargo was bestowed, and then Hunter and Joyce took up their position in the stockade.

The mutineers had the advantage of numbers but we had the advantage of arms and the bonus ball of 8.

17. NARRATIVE CONTINUED BY THE DOCTOR: END OF FIRST DAY'S FIGHTING

SHIP'S LOG

May 6, 17–

Flew Union Jack above stockade. Attacked by mutineers, after sharp encounter mutineers fled leaving one of them dead. Alas, Seaman Tom Redruth mortally wounded.

May 7, 17–

Ship's cannon opened fire but the ball whistling over was behind us. We served breakfast. Took up positions at loop holes in stockade. Bombardment continued all day without harm. Made midday meal – ham, bread and some wine. Guard stood to all night calling the hours.

May 8, 17–

Flew Union Jack above stockade. Attacked by mutineers. After sharp encounter mutineers fled.

Signed: Smollett
Captain RN

Just then, with a roar and a whistle, a round-shot passed high above the roof of the log-house and plumped far beyond us in the wood.

'Oho!' cried the captain. 'Blaze away! You've little enough powder already, my lads.'

All through the evening they kept thundering away. Ball after ball flew or fell short, or kicked up the sand in the enclosure; but they had to fire so high that the shot fell dead and buried itself in the soft sand.

'There is one thing good about all this,' observed the captain; 'the wood in front of us is likely clear.'

The captain sat down to his log, and here is the beginning of the entry:

'Alexander Smollett, master; David Livesey, ship's doctor; Abraham Gray, carpenter's mate; John Trelawney, owner; John Hunter and Richard Joyce, owner's servants, landsmen – being all that is left faithful of the ship's company – with stores for ten days at short rations, came ashore this day, and flew British colours in the stockade in Treasure Island. Thomas Redruth, owner's servant, landsman, shot by the mutineers.'

And at the same time I was wondering over poor Jim Hawkins' fate.

A hail on the land side.

'Somebody hailing us,' said Hunter, who was on guard.

'Doctor! Squire! Captain! Hullo, Hunter, is that you?' came the cries.

And I ran to the door in time to see Jim Hawkins, safe and sound, come climbing over the stockade. He told of a strange man called Gunn, who claimed he had found the treasure.

18. NARRATIVE RESUMED BY JIM HAWKINS: THE GARRISON IN THE STOCKADE

As soon as Ben Gunn saw Union Jack colours, he came to a halt; he was colour blind and didn't know he was white. He stopped me by the arm, and sat down.

'Now,' said he, 'there's your friends, sure enough.' He went on, 'Why, in a place like this, where nobody puts in but gen'lemen of fortune, Silver would fly the Jolly Roger. No; that's your friends. There's been blows, too, and I reckon your friends has had the best of it.'

GROUCHO: This guy still here?
JIM: Yes. He knows where the treasure is!
GROUCHO: I'm very pleased to meet you. You'll make a great film.
Bow wow! Bow wow!
GROUCHO: Who owns that bloody dog?
BEN: A film? – I might be dead by then.
GROUCHO: That's the right answer. You go to the top of the class and jump off.
BEN: What are you torkin' about?

GROUCHO:	I'm talking about five words a second. Any faster and I'd blow the budget.
BEN:	Are you mad?
GROUCHO:	Only on Thursdays starting at midday.
BEN:	You should be put away.
GROUCHO:	I am put away, it just happens to be here.
JIM:	Groucho, I must hurry on and join my friends.
GROUCHO:	Why? Are they coming apart?

'Now,' said Ben, 'when I'm wanted you know where to find me, Jim, just where you found me today. And him that comes is to have a white thing in his hand: and he's to come alone. Oh! and you'll say this: "Ben Gunn," says you, "has reasons of his own." '

The *Hispaniola* still lay where she had anchored; but, sure enough, there was the Jolly Roger – flying from her peak. At length I thought I must return to the stockade. I skirted among the woods until I had regained the shore side of the island and was soon welcomed back by the faithful party.

The cold evening breeze whistled through every chink of the crude building, and up my trouser legs agitating my swonnicles. Sand in our eyes, sand in our teeth, sand up our backsides, and when we shit it was like concrete.

Gray, the new man, had his face tied up in a bandage for a cut he had got from the mutineers; and poor old Tom Redruth, still unburied, lay along the wall stiff and stark, under the Union Jack.

'Is this Ben Gunn a man?' asked Captain Smollett.

'That or he's queer,' I said.

'Three years on a desert island would turn anybody queer,' said the Squire.

'Was it cheese you said he had a fancy for – no rum bum or baccy?' the Captain enquired.

'Yes, sir, cheese,' I answered.

'Well, Jim,' says he, 'I don't have any cheese, but I've got a Swiss Army jack-knife.'

Before supper we buried old Tom and stood round him for a while bareheaded in the breeze. A good deal of firewood had been got in. Then, when we had eaten our pork, and each had a good stiff glass of brandy, the three chiefs got together to discuss our prospects.

It appeared they were at their wits' end what to do. We would be starved into surrender long before help came. But our best hope was to kill off the buccaneers. From nineteen they were already reduced to fifteen, two others were wounded, and one at least – the man shot beside the gun – severely wounded, if he were not dead. Every time we had a crack at them, we were to take care saving our own lives.

'So,' added the captain, 'if we are not all shot down first, they'll be glad to be packing in the schooner, and they can get to buccaneering again.'

I was dead tired, as you may fancy; and when I got to sleep, which was not till after a great deal of tossing, I slept like a log during which some silly bugger threw me on the fire.

'Flag of truce!' I heard someone say; and then, immediately after, with a cry of surprise. 'Silver himself!'

19. SILVER'S EMBASSY

SHIP'S LOG

May 9, 17–

Today Silver approached with Flag of Truce. With caution we allowed him into the stockade.

Signed: Smollett
Captain RN

Sure enough, there were two men just outside the stockade, one of them waving a dirty white cloth. 'It needs to be washed in Rinso,' cried the captain. The other, no less a person than Silver himself, was standing placidly by. Both waded knee-deep in a low, white, evil-smelling vapour. The island was plainly a damp, feverish, unhealthy spot.

'Don't go near them,' said the doctor, 'or we shall get damp, feverish and unhealthy in this spot.'

'Keep indoors, men,' said the captain. 'Ten to one this is a trick.'

'Who goes? Stand, or we fire!'

With that we shot off a musket.

'Flag of truce,' screamed Silver, as he ducked.

'And what do you want with your flag of truce?' cried the captain.

'Cap'n Silver, sir, to come on board and make terms,' he shouted.

'Cap'n Silver? Don't know him. Who's he?' cried the captain. And we could hear him adding to himself: 'Cap'n is he? My heart, and here's promotion.'

'Me, sir. These poor lads have chosen me cap'n after your desertion, sir,' – laying a particular emphasis upon the word 'desertion'. 'We're willing to submit, if we can come to terms, and no bones about it. All I ask is your word, Cap'n Smollett, to let me safe and sound out of this here stockade, and one minute to get out o' shot before a gun is fired.'

'My man,' said Captain Smollett, 'I have not the slightest desire to talk to you. You can come, that's all. If there's any treachery, it'll be on your side, and the Lord help you.'

'Why,' said Silver, 'there you all are together like a happy family, in a manner of speaking.'

'Yes, that's a manner of speaking,' said the captain. 'If you have anything to say, say it.'

'It,' said Silver.

The two men sat silently smoking for quite a while. They stood silently smoking for quite a while.

'Look, why don't we sit silently smoking for quite a while?' said the captain.

Occasionally Silver spat. Something would hit the ground that looked like a raw egg.

'Now,' said Silver. 'Give us the chart to get the treasure by.'

Captain Smollett rose from his seat. 'Is that all?' he asked.

Silver's face was a picture called *Titanic*; his eyes started in his head with wrath. He shook the fire out of his pipe.

'Give me a hand up!' he cried.

'Not I,' returned the captain.

'Who'll give me a hand up?' he roared.

'I'll give you a foot up,' said the captain, kicking him up the arse.

Growling the foulest imprecations, Silver crawled along the sand until he could hoist himself upon his crutch. Then he spat into the captain's eye, temporarily blinding it. Nobody at that time knew of a terrible earthquake in Italy, a whole village destroyed, 170 people killed, thousands injured.

20. THE ATTACK

As soon as his spit-laden eye cleared Captain Smollett spoke.

'I have nothing further to say,' he said.

'Then let us use sign language,' said Silver.

The captain stuck up two fingers.

'What's that mean?' said Silver.

'In sign language it means "bugger off".'

'Well, before I bugger off,' said Silver, 'I want that treasure map.'

'First,' said the captain, 'give me your crutch.'

'But it's my only visible means of support,' said Silver.

Captain Smollett snatched the crutch from under his arm and shouted, 'Timber!'

Silver fell slowly sideways and crashed to the ground.

'I'll get you for this,' roared Silver.

'Oh?' said Smollett. 'What will you get me? How about a nice vintage red wine?'

'I'll give you vintage red wine,' snarled Silver.

'Look, Silver, I'll give you your crutch back if you get me a bottle of vintage French wine.'

With his crutch back Silver set off to find a bottle of vintage French wine. He returned to the stockade and reported to the captain.

'Captain, I've searched the island and do you think I could find a bottle of vintage French wine?'

The captain put one hand to his forehead and the other over his heart, and ran out of hands.

'For God's sake tell me if you found a bottle of vintage French wine.'

Smollett staggered back, forwards and sideways and snatched Silver's crutch. 'Timber!' he yelled.

Silver fell slowly sideways and crashed to the ground. 'I'll get you a vintage bottle of red wine for this.'

'I don't believe you any more,' said Smollett. 'I'll give your crutch back if you'll come back one by one, clapped in irons, to be taken back to England to face trial and then hung.'

Silver agreed but had no intention of coming back one by one, to be taken back to England, face trial, and then hung.

Bow wow! Bow wow! Woof woof!

'That must be somebody's dog,' said Silver.

GROUCHO: That's what I keep saying.

'Ah, you never were a good judge of men,' said Trelawney.

GROUCHO: What about women?

'Silver and his men could attack us at any time,' said the captain.

'What time is that?' said Hawkins.

GROUCHO: Midnight would be good for them.

'Hear that? Before the hour's out we shall be boarded. We're outnumbered, I needn't tell you that, but we fight in shelter; and I've no manner of doubt that we can drub them, if we choose.'

'Hawkins hasn't had his breakfast. Hawkins, help yourself, and back to your post to eat it,' continued Captain Smollett.

So I went back and ate my post.

'Doctor, you take the door but don't expose yourself in case there are ladies present. Hunter, take the loophole on the east side; Joyce you stand by the west side; Trelawney, you're the best shot, you guard Windsor Castle.

'Men,' said the captain.

'He means us,' said Hunter.

'Men, we are outnumbered ten to one.'

'Ten to one?' said Trelawney. 'I'll take those odds.'

'Toss out the fire,' said the captain, 'we don't want to be hindered by smoke.'

The iron fire basket was carried out bodily by Trelawney setting himself on fire. We put it out pouring bottles of vintage French red wine over him.

'Stop pouring!' shouted Trelawney, 'I can't swim.'

'Look,' said Captain Smollett, 'I can't play the violin, but I don't tell everybody.'

An hour passed away but fortunately none of us. Some seconds passed, till suddenly Joyce whipped up his musket and fired. The report had scarcely died away when there was a scattering volley, shot behind shot, like a string of geese, from every side of the enclosure. Several bullets struck the log house.

'Did you hit your man?' asked the captain.

'No.'

'Load his gun, Hawkins. How many should you say there were on your side, doctor?'

'I know precisely,' said Dr Livesey. 'Three shots were fired on this side. I saw the three flashes – two close together – one farther to the west.'

'Three!' repeated the captain. 'And how many on yours, Mr Trelawney?'

Before he could answer, suddenly, with a loud huzza, a little crowd of pirates leaped from the woods on the north side, and ran straight to the stockade. At the same moment, the fire was once more opened from the woods, and a rifle-ball sang through the doorway and knocked the doctor's musket into bits. Carefully he put it together with UHU.

The boarders swarmed over the fence like monkeys. Squire and Gray fired again and yet again; three men fell, one forwards into the enclosure, two back on the outside. But of these, one was evidently more frightened than hurt, for he was on his feet again in a crack, and instantly disappeared among the trees. The doctor continued to mend his musket.

Two had bitten the dust, one had fled, four had made good their footing inside our defences; while from the shelter of the woods seven or eight men, each evidently supplied with several muskets, kept up a hot, though useless, fire on the log-house.

The four who had boarded made straight before them for the building, shouting as they ran, and the men among the trees shouted back to encourage them. In a moment, the four pirates were upon us.

The head of Job Anderson, the boatswain, appeared at the middle loophole. God knows how he managed it!

'At 'em, all hands – all hands!' roared the captain in a voice like thunder.

At the same moment, another pirate grasped Hunter's musket by the muzzle. 'Ahhhh!' he screamed, 'that's bloody hot.' Meanwhile a third, running unharmed all round the house, appeared suddenly in the doorway, and fell with his cutlass on the doctor. The doctor had nearly mended his musket.

'Out lads, out, and fight 'em in the open! Cutlasses!' cried the captain.

'Round the house, lads! round the house!' cried the captain; so we started to run round the house. I perceived a change in his voice, his balls must have dropped.

Next moment I was face-to-face with Anderson. He roared aloud, and his cutlass went up above his head; flashing down he cut his toe off. I had not time to be afraid, but, as the blow still hung impending, leaped in a trice upon one side, and missing my foot in the soft sand, rolled headlong down the slope.

And yet, in this breath of time, the fight was over, and the victory was ours, just as the doctor had mended his musket.

Gray, following close behind me, had cut down the big boatswain ere he had time to recover from his lost blow. Another had been shot at a loophole in the very act of firing into the house, and now lay in agony, the pistol still smoking in his hand. A third, as I had seen, the doctor disposed of at a blow. Of the four who had scaled the palisade, one only remained unaccounted for, and he, having left his cutlass on the field, was now clambering out again with the fear of death upon him.

'Fire – fire from the house!' cried the doctor. 'And you, lads, back into cover.'

In three seconds nothing remained of the attacking party but the five who had fallen, four on the inside, and one on the outside, of the palisade. The doctor and Gray and I ran full speed for shelter, went past it and had to come back again.

We saw at a glance the price we had paid for victory. It had cost us twenty-two pounds eight shillings. Hunter lay beside his loophole, stunned; Joyce by his shot through the head, never to move again; while right in the centre, the squire was supporting the captain, one as pale as the other.

'The captain's wounded,' said Mr Trelawney.

'Have they run?' asked Captain Smollett.

'All that could, you may be bound,' returned the doctor; 'but there's five of them will never run again.'

GROUCHO: Can I come out now?
JIM: You cowardly swine.
GROUCHO.   Yes, that's what they all are saying. Listen!
Bow wow! Bow wow!
GROUCHO: See? He's still at it!

PART FOUR
My Sea Adventure

21. HOW I BEGAN MY SEA ADVENTURE

There was no return of the mutineers. 'They have had their rations for today,' said Smollett. Out of the eight men who had fallen in the action, only three still breathed. Of these, two were as good as dead (as *good* as?); the third died under the doctor's knife, he stuck it in his heart. Hunter never recovered consciousness. He lingered all day and died, so I ate his dinner.

My own accidental cut across the knuckles was a fleabite. Dr Livesey patched it up with plaster, it set hard and I never used them again.

As for the captain, he was wounded but not badly. The wound had only displaced some muscles in his calf. He was sure to recover but he must not move his leg, swim, play rugby, hockey, or ride a bike. After dinner the squire and the doctor sat by the captain's side in consultation. Suddenly the doctor put a cake on his head, then a hot dinner over it, then his hat on and two pistols in his sock, put the map in his pocket and left the stockade. The swine! Supposing one of us gets ill?

Gray took his pipe out of his mouth. 'Where in the name of Davy Jones is he going?'

'I think in the name of Davy Jones he's going to find Ben Gunn.'

I laid hold of a brace of pistols, and as I already had a powder-horn and bullets, I felt myself well supplied with arms. I stopped; an idea came into my head. I was to go down the sandy spit, find the white rock and ascertain where Ben Gunn had hidden his boat.

The scheme I had in my head was to board the *Hispaniola*, cut her loose and guide her to the shore beyond sight of the mutineers. Then Captain Smollett and his crew could board it and sail for England. Through the bushes I observed Silver and his cut-throat gang. Suddenly his parrot began to scream, 'Old Flint the bastard is dead.' Then he whistled 'God Save the King' during which the mutineers respectfully stood to attention but I don't think they meant it.

The white rock was visible a mile away. If it had been invisible I would never have found it. Crawling on hands and knees I finally reached it. If I had stood up and walked I would have got there quicker.

By the rock was Ben Gunn's boat, well, not a boat but a coracle. It was made from goats' skin. I carried it to the water's edge, floated it, jumped in and went straight through the bottom. I quickly patched it using a Singer Sewing Machine which luckily I had found on the beach. The coracle was a perfect craft for someone of my height and weight, inside leg and shoe size.

Down I sat to wait for darkness, and made a hearty meal of biscuit.

22. THE EBB-TIDE RUNS

I am very sure I never should have made the ship at all but for the tide. The tide was still sweeping me down; and there lay the *Hispaniola* right in the fairway, hardly to be missed.

Soon I was alongside her hawser, and had laid hold. The hawser was as taut as a starling's bum. One cut with my sea-gulley, and the *Hispaniola* would go humming down the tide in the right direction for me. It occurred to me that a taut hawser, when cut, would suddenly become as dangerous as a kicking horse, a blow to the jaw, a club on the head, being run over by a fire-engine, stamped on by an elephant and, oh, numerous other things too terrible to be listed.

Just then a strong wind blew down at sea level. I felt the hawser slacken. I opened my gulley and cut strand after strand, after strand, after strand. Finally the vessel only swung by two.

All this time I heard the sound of loud voices from the aft cabin. One was Israel Hands and one wasn't. It was O'Brien. Both were pissed out of their heads. Even as I was listening one, with a drunken cry, opened the stern window and threw up all over me.

At last the hawser fell slack again and with my teeth and gulley I cut the last fibres. At the same time the schooner began to turn upon her heel, spinning slowly, end for end, across the current. Soon the ship was nose on for the shore in the direction of the stockade. I came across a rope hanging overboard, grasping it, I hauled myself up to the aft window. There I saw Hands and O'Brien locked together in a deadly wrestle, each one at the other's throat, sometimes at each other's nose, sometimes at each other's chin – it was terrible. A sudden lurch and I fell back into the coracle

I opened my eyes at once. All round me were little ripples, coming over with a sharp, bristling sound. The *Hispaniola*, a few yards in whose wake I was still being whirled along, seemed to stagger in her course, and I saw her spars toss a little. As I looked longer, I made sure she also was steering to the shore.

At that time I did not know there had been terrible fires in Java burning down homes; 21 died.

23. THE CRUISE OF THE CORACLE

I was now gaining rapidly on the schooner; I could see the brass glisten on the tiller as it banged about; and still no soul appeared upon her decks. I could not choose but suppose she was deserted. If not, the men were lying drunk below, where I might batten them down.

Then of a sudden the ship came swooping down. The bowsprit was over my head. It was also over my body. With one hand I caught the jib-boom, while my foot was lodged between the stay and the brace; and as I clung there a dull blow told me the ship had struck the coracle; that's what the dull blow told me. Suddenly I knew then I was left without retreat on the *Hispaniola*.

24. I STRIKE THE JOLLY ROGER

The main-boom swung inboard, catching me on the back of my head. I saw stars and a hot dog vendor from Lewisham. There were two watchmen. O'Brien lay dead on his back, as stiff as a handspike, with the arms stretched out like those of a crucifix, and his teeth showing through his open lips; Israel Hands was propped against the bollards.

While I was thus looking and wondering, in a calm moment, Israel Hands turned partly round and, with a low moan, writhed himself back to the position in which I had seen him first. The moan, which told of pain and deadly weakness, and the way in which his jaw hung open, went right to my heart. But when I remembered the talk I had overheard from the apple barrel, all pity left me.

JIM:	Hands! You've had it!
HANDS:	No I haven't, I been at sea six weeks.
JIM:	Doing what?
HANDS:	Killing O'Brien, ha, ha!
JIM:	Why did you kill him?
GROUCHO:	He wouldn't stop telling him Irish jokes.
HANDS:	I'd heard them all before.
JIM:	Groucho! Where did you come from?
GROUCHO:	I keep asking myself that.
HANDS:	Don't let Jim kill me.
GROUCHO:	Do you intend to kill him?
JIM:	No.
GROUCHO:	How's that for service?
HANDS:	God bless you, sir.
GROUCHO:	I've never been called sir before, it's usually been 'Hey you, shit face!'

'Are you alive, Hands?' I said. He and his blood-covered body answered 'Yes,' and collapsed with effort.

I asked him if he would like to dance the tango. Sportingly he said 'No.'

GROUCHO: Oh, don't be a spoil sport.

He drummed up enough strength to say 'Brandy'. Shopping around I found a bottle of it in Harrod's Wine Department. He must have drunk a gill before he took the bottle from his mouth – it was trickling out the back.

'Aye,' said he, 'by thunder, but I wanted some o' that! Where do 'ee come from?'

GROUCHO:	I keep asking myself that.
JIM:	He's a murderer, Groucho.
GROUCHO:	A solicitor needs him.
JIM:	You mean he needs a solicitor.
GROUCHO:	No, the solicitor needs him, he's got to make a living.

'I've come to take possession of the ship,' I said. Next I ran down the Jolly Roger, and hoisted the Union Jack. 'God save the King,' I said.

'Fuck the King,' said Hands.

'Look,' he said, so I looked. 'You'll be wanting to go ashore,' he said.

'Yes,' I said. 'But I'm not going back to Captain Flint's anchorage. I mean to take her to North Inlet and beach her.'

He nodded. 'Aye, get me more brandy and I'll teach you how to steer the ship.'

So I gave him some brandy and he taught me how to steer the ship. In three minutes I had the *Hispaniola* sailing before the wind. I lashed the tiller, went below and got a soft silk handkerchief of my mother's that she gave me when she wasn't sleep walking. I bound Hands' wounds.

'God bless 'ee,' said Hands, so God blessed me.

After he had a swig of brandy he began to pick up. First he picked up some rubbish on the deck. Then he picked up a copy of *Newsweek*. Yet his eyes followed me around the deck and then they rolled back to him. He gave me a comfortable smile, but he was filled with treachery and rum bum and baccy.

25. ISRAEL HANDS

'This 'ere is an unlucky ship, Jim. We've tried the National Lottery five times but won bugger all,' he said.

He drank some more brandy. By now he was really pissed. He staggered into the mast and lay unconscious; flies settled on his face and crapped on him. I continued to steer the ship. He came to.

'Ah, O'Brien,' he slurred, ' 'ee's dead.'

GROUCHO: That or he's a brilliant actor.

'Yes, he's in another world,' I said, 'and watching us.'

GROUCHO: God, he must have wonderful eyesight.

'Look, Captain,' said Hands. 'Could you get me some wine? The brandy is doin' me.'

For some reason he wanted me below deck. 'Wine?' I said. 'What would you like? A Chablis or a Mouton Rothschild?'

'Yes' he said.

I scuttled below. I mounted the forecastle and popped my head out of the fore companion. He had got possession of a blood-stained knife, then hid it on his person. I returned on deck with a bottle of wine. I felt sure I could trust him on one point – we both wanted the ship beached. Hands had adopted his original position, his head hung down as if he were too weak to move.

GROUCHO: Look out, Jim, he's acting!

Hands snatched the bottle, knocked the neck off and drained it. 'Here, cut me a chunk off this stick of tobacco.' So I cut him a chunk off his stick of tobacco.
'Now look 'ere,' said Hands.

GROUCHO: Yes, Jim, look here. There's a nice bit to beach the ship in.

'Starboard a little – steady – starboard – starboard – starboard a little – steady!' He issued commands which I breathlessly obeyed. All of a sudden he cried, 'Now, my hearty, luff!' And I put the helm hard over; the *Hispaniola* went hard on to the sandy beach.
Perhaps I had heard a creak or seen his shadow moving with the tail of my eye.

GROUCHO: Your eye's got a tail? So's my dog but it's the other end.

Suddenly the *Hispaniola* struck, staggered, ground for an instant in the sand. We almost rolled together into the scuppers, Groucho, Hands and I. Hands jumped to his feet.

GROUCHO: Look out, Jim, he's got a duck!

Sure enough, there was Hands half-way towards me with the dirk in his hand.

GROUCHO: A dirk? Don't you mean a duck?
JIM: No, Groucho, you can't be stabbed with a duck.
GROUCHO: Are you sure, Jim? A friend took me to a restaurant once and I got stuck with the bill!

Hands raised the duck over his head and lunged at me. I leapt sideways, drew a pistol from my pocket and, as he stabbed at me with his duck, I pulled the trigger. The hammer fell, there followed no flash – it was useless with sea water. He continued to threaten me with his duck. Quick as thought I sprang into the mizzen shrouds, rattled up hand-over-hand, and did not draw a breath till I was seated on the cross-trees.
The duck had struck not half a foot below me. Below me Hands climbed with his mouth open; I threw a musket ball in it; it went right through him. I lost no time in re-priming my pistols, and pointing them at him I said, 'One more step, Hands, and I'll blow your brains out!'

GROUCHO: No, he hasn't got any.

'Jim,' said Hands, 'I reckon we're fouled, you and me, and we'll have to sign articles.'

I listened to his words with a smile.

Suddenly with the speed of light, back went his right hand over his shoulder, something sang like an arrow through the air, I felt a blow then a sharp pang. I was pinned by the shoulder by the duck. Both my pistols went off and fell from my hands. They did not fall alone; with a choked cry Hands fell from the shrouds and plunged into the sea.

GROUCHO: He's fallen into the water.

Hands: Help! Help! I can't swim!

GROUCHO: Listen, I can't play the violin but I don't shout about it. See if this will help.

So saying, Groucho threw a cannon ball on him. He sank without trace. He was dead, wounded, shot, stabbed and drowned.

26. 'PIECES OF EIGHT'

My first thought was to pluck forth the duck that pinned me to the mast. I threw some duck food on the deck and he immediately flew down, ate it and died. It was poisoned.

GROUCHO: Jim? You've poisoned the duck. Wait until the RSPCA hear of this.

I threw O'Brien over the side. The Irishman had never been taught to drown, so Groucho threw another cannon ball on him.

'I'd better be getting ashore and back to the stockade,' I said.

I looked over the side; the water looked shallow. I jumped in; the water was up to my waist. At last I was off the sea, nor had I returned empty handed. There lay the *Hispaniola* ready for our own men to board again. I became aware of a red glow against the sky.

GROUCHO: I, myself, have nothing against the sky. It's never done me and my family any harm.

Suddenly right in front of me a glow appeared on the trees. It was red and hot as if it was the embers of a bonfire smouldering. For the life of me I could not think what it was. It was the embers of a bonfire smouldering. Suddenly a brightness fell on me. Of course, it was the moon.

GROUCHO: One day man will walk on it.

JIM: I don't believe you.

GROUCHO: I knew I'd have trouble convincing you.

At last I came to the stockade itself. As I drew nearer, I heard a heartening sound; it was Captain Smollett and his crew snoring. Well, one or some of his crew.

GROUCHO: It's just as well not to blame everybody. Some may not be snoring and are innocent!

With my arms before me I walked forward steadily. I should lie down on my own place and enjoy their faces when they found me in the morning. My foot struck something – it was a sleeper's leg. And a shrill voice in the darkness, 'Pieces of eight! Fuck!' It was Silver's parrot.

I had no time to recover. The sleepers awoke. With a mighty oath a voice shouted, 'Who the fuck is that?' It was Silver.

I turned to run straight into the arms of a mutineer.

'Bring a torch, Dick,' said Silver.

And one of the men left the log-house and presently returned with a lighted brand.

GROUCHO: Watch out Jim, they're going to set fire to you!

PART FIVE
Captain Silver

27. IN THE ENEMY'S CAMP

I realised the mutineers were in possession of the stockade and me.

GROUCHO: But is it insured against Fire, Floods or Earthquakes?

Six was all that was left of them. One lay on his bed, a blood-stained bandage round his head which told that he had recently been wounded, and still more recently dressed.

The parrot sat on Long John's shoulder which was covered in parrot's crap. He himself looked paler and more stern. Was it the parrot's crap?

'Now Jim,' said Silver, 'as you are here, I'll give you a piece of my mind.'

I took it and thanked him for it.

'What has happened to all my friends?'

'You can't go back to your lot,' said Silver. 'They won't 'ave you and the doctor's dead against you. "Ungrateful scamp" is what he said.'

Thank heaven my friends were still alive, but incensed at my 'desertion'.

'Lad,' said Silver, 'no one's a-pressing you.'

Sure enough, none of them were a-pressing me.

'I've a right to know where my friends are.'

'Wot's wot?' snarled one of the mutineers. 'You'd be a lucky one as knowed that.'

'Well, I am lucky,' I said, 'so I knowed that.'

'Batten down your hatches,' said Silver to the mutineer.

'Fuck you, Silver,' he said.

'And fuck you, too,' said Silver.

GROUCHO: What a witty tongue he has.

'Yesterday,' said Silver, 'love was such an easy game to play. Yes, yesterday Dr Livesey came down with a flag of truce. "Captain Silver," he said, "You've sold out. The ship's gone." We looked out, and there, sure enough, was the ship, gone!

' "Well," says the doctor, "let's bargain."

' "How many are you?" says I.

' "Four," says he, "and one of us wounded. As for that lad, we don't know where he is!" '

'Is that all?' I asked.

'Yes, that's all you are to hear,' said Silver.

'I have a thing or two to tell you,' I said.

'Yes, tell me a thing or two,' said Silver.

'Well, the schooner, I cut her loose, and I . . .' I said, thumping my chest, giving me a fit of coughing. 'I, what was I saying?'

'You were saying you cut her loose,' said Silver, handing me a cough sweet.

'Yes, then I killed the men you left aboard. You'll never never find the ship. Now, Mr Silver, I take it you will tell the doctor my story?'

'All right,' said Silver, 'you little bastard.'

'That little bastard,' said Morgan who knowed Black Dog!' And he sprang up, drawing his duck.

Silver sprang to his feet – in his case, his foot. 'Who are you, Morgan! Don't you cross me.'

Morgan, a religious man, crossed himself.

GROUCHO: Why not? He's crossed everybody else.

A hoarse murmur came from the others.

'Morgan's right,' said one, two and three. 'The lad's not one of us and neither's anyone that stands with him!'

'Well,' snarled Silver, 'I'm ready. Take a cutlass him that dares.'

Not a man stirred, not a man answered.

GROUCHO: You've given them the shits.

'That's your sort, is it?' Silver took his pipe from his mouth and spat at what looked like a bowl of porridge hiding on the floor. 'Well, you're a gay lot,' said Silver.

GROUCHO: Thanks for the warning.

They, for their part, moved to the end of the stockade.

GROUCHO: Not much of a part.

A low hiss emanated from them. I thought one of them had a puncture. Occasionally they would look at Silver.

'Wot are you saying?' said Silver, spitting high in the air, landing it on a mutineer's head.

'You dirty bastard,' he shouted.

'Pipe up. Let's hear wot you got to say.'

'We haven't said anything, we've only been hissing,' they said.

'Ax yer pardon?' said one.

'All right, ax,' said Silver.

'I ax yer pardon,' said one. 'Accepting you for to be captain I claim my right to step outside for a council.' So saying, they all stepped outside for a council.

The sea cook instantly removed his pipe from his mouth.

GROUCHO: It'd been in worse places.

'Did you see that, Jim?' said Silver.

'Yes, you removed your pipe from your mouth,' I said.

'Now look you here, Jim Hawkins,' said the sea cook.

So I looked here.

GROUCHO: Can you see anything there?

'You're within a plank of death,' said Silver. 'They're going to throw me off.'

GROUCHO: Will it be Beachy Head or the GPO Tower?

'But you stand by me, Hawkins, and I'll stand by you,' said Silver.
'You mean all is lost?' I asked.
'Aye, by gum I do,' he answered. 'Understand me, Jim, I've a head on my shoulders,' said Silver.

GROUCHO: It's a good place for it.

Silver drew some cognac from the cask and poured it into a bicycle, which he drank through the handle-bar, then rode it round the stockade stopping now and then to take a sip from the handle-bar.

GROUCHO: You shouldn't drink and drive.

Silver shook his great shaggy head, like a man who looks forward to the worst. The very worst is death.

28. THE BLACK SPOT AGAIN

The council of mutineers lasted a long time.

GROUCHO: A year to be exact.

They were collected in a group; one held a light, another held a tree, and another held a cow. He also held a bible. The party moved towards us.
'Here they come,' said I, and here they came.
'Let 'em come,' said Silver. 'I've still got a shot in my locker.'
'What good is that?' I said.
'I don't rightly know,' said Silver.
Five of the mutineers approached, one holding his closed hand in front of him.
'You can't fool us,' said a mutineer.

GROUCHO: Why not? I've fooled everybody else.

'Hand it over, lubber,' said Silver, taking another sip from the handle-bar.
The mutineer passed something to Silver.
'The black spot, ha, ha,' said Silver. 'This black spot 'as been cut from the Holy Bible. What fool's cut a Holy Bible?'
'Ah there,' said Morgan. 'Wot did I say? No good'll come o' that.'
'Well, you've fixed it now,' continued Silver. 'What bloody fool cut the Holy Bible?'

'It was Dick,' said one.

'Dick was it?' said Silver. 'He's seen his slice of luck go.'

There a long man with yellow eyes spoke. 'Belay that talk, Silver. We tipped you the black spot, ha ha. See what's written on the back.'

Silver read it. ' "Book of Kings, Chapter I, verse 17. And lo Christ went unto Galilee and a great crowd gathered." '

GROUCHO: Anyone sad enough to have looked up that quote and found it's wrong – get a life!

'Below that, Silver,' said yellow eyes.

Silver read, 'Step down.'

'Come now, Silver,' said George, 'You're a funny man.'

GROUCHO: Yes, tell 'em a joke.

Silver rode his bicycle round the mutineers, occasionally taking a drink from the handle-bar.

'Look, just dismount from that bicycle and help us vote.'

'Listen,' said Silver, 'I'm still your captain till you outs with your grievances; till then I shall continue to ride my bike and drink from the handle-bar.'

'You let the enemy out of this 'ere stockade for nothing. Then there's this 'ere boy,' said George.

'Is that all?' said Silver.

'Enough, too,' said George, doing a back somersault, landing on his feet. 'We'll all swing for your bungling.'

'Who forced my hand to be captain? Who tipped me the black spot, ha, ha cut from the Holy Bible with Book of Kings written on the back?'

'Go on, John,' said Morgan doing a back somersault landing on his feet. 'Speak up to the others.'

'Maybe,' said Silver, refilling his bike with cognac, 'you don't count for nothing, a *real* doctor come to see you every day – you John, with your head broke – or George Merry, with ague shakes, and you, Morgan, with swollen balls and the shits, all for free.

'And as for the boy, we will be glad we got a hostage when the time comes,' said Silver.

And he cast down a paper that I immediately recognised as the treasure map. Why the doctor had given it to him was more than I could understand. The mutineers leaped upon it like a cat upon an elephant (mouse?). And by the oaths and childish laughter you would have thought not only were they fingering the very gold, but were at sea with it, in safety.

Suddenly they stopped. They were not fingering the gold, they were not at sea in safety; no, they were all still stuck in the stockade with Silver riding his bike around them.

'Oh, let's have a go, Silver,' said Morgan.

'Just this once,' said Silver.

One by one the mutineers took turns to ride and drink from the handle-bar, finally all falling into a drunken sleep.

It was long ere I closed my eyes that night. Before I did, I thought of my mother sleep walking and wondered where she was. [That night she had reached Billingsgate Fish Market.]

Silver himself slept peacefully and snored aloud. My heart was sore for him, wicked as he was, to think of his perils ahead, and – the gibbet that awaited him.

GROUCHO: Oh, an unhappy ending. Stay asleep, Silver; when you wake you'll be hung.

29. ON PAROLE

I was awakened by a gentle kick to my head by Morgan. I could see the semi-sober sentinel shake himself together; he fell in bits on the floor. Remembering his duty he called out the time, 'One o'clock and all's well.' He was seven hours late.

'Stockade ahoy!' said a hearty voice.

'Here's the doctor,' said Silver from his bed. 'He must have come here in the dark. His face is covered in bruises through walking into trees.

'You, Doctor, top of the morning to you,' said Silver from his bed.

'George, shake yourself, help the doctor over the ship's side,' said Silver.

'Don't let that smelly bugger touch me, I don't want to catch it,' said the doctor.

'We've quite a surprise for you,' said Silver rising from his bed. 'We've a little stranger here, a noo lodger rent free.'

'Rent free?' said the doctor. 'You're a fool.' The doctor paused. 'Wait, you don't mean – Jim Hawkins?'

'I *do* mean Jim Hawkins,' said Silver moving towards the doctor and colliding with him.

The doctor seemed stunned by the news which had been broadcast that night by the BBC overseas programme.

'Is he safe?' said the doctor.

'Alive and well,' said Silver.

'Well, well,' said the doctor, 'Duty first. Let's overhaul these patients of yours.'

He proceeded towards the 'Sick Bay'. He went among them as though it was a visit to a quiet English family.

'Ah, you're doing well, John,' he said to the bandaged head. 'If ever a person had a close shave it was you.'

'Yes, it *was* me,' said John.

'Your head must be hard as iron,' said the doctor.

'Yes, it is,' said John.

'Well, you, George, you're a terrible colour. Your liver must be upside down.'

'It is, sir,' said George.

'Ah, Morgan, you've got swollen testicles.'

'No sir, I've got swollen balls.'

'That as well?' said the doctor. 'Well every day dip them in cold water three times a day. You've got varicocele.'

'What's that?' said Morgan.

'Swollen Balls,' said the doctor.

'Got the shits as well,' said Morgan.

'Have you any porridge?' said the doctor. 'Eat a big bowl every morning.'

'So I dips me balls in cold water three times a day, and eat porridge every morning?' said Morgan.

GROUCHO: You've something to look forward to.

'Dick don't feel well,' said Silver.

'I can give you some pills for that,' the doctor replied.

'No, I mean him,' said Silver, pointing to Dick. 'He don't feel well.'

'Doesn't he?' said the doctor. 'Well, step up, lad, let me see your tongue. God, this tongue is enough to frighten the French fleet. No, I'm afraid he must be put to bed. He has Swamp Fever; give him these tablets morning and night.'

The news seemed to alarm the mutineers.

'Is it contagious?' said one.

'Very,' said the doctor, putting his medicines back in his bag.

'Dick is sick,' said Morgan, ' 'cause he spoiled his Bible.'

'Nonsense,' said the doctor. 'It's not knowing honest air from poison. Camp in a bog, did he? Silver, you don't seem to have a notion of the rules of health. Before long you'll all die of swamp fever, typhus, plague, chilblains and piles. Can I now speak to the boy?'

Silver turned to Hawkins. 'Hawkins, will you give me your word of honour not to slip your cable?'

I gave readily the pledge.

'Then, Doctor,' said Silver. 'Step outside. I'll bring the boy to you.'

We advanced to where the doctor awaited. 'You'll make a note, Doctor, that I saved this boy's life.'

The doctor jotted down in a note book, 'Remember Silver saved boy's life. Pick up dry cleaning. Buy milk.'

The doctor nodded his head but it didn't fall off.

'Jim, you're not afraid?' said the doctor.

'Doctor, spare me. I blame myself for my situation. I'd been dead by now if it hadn't been for Silver. What I fear is torture.'

'Yes,' said the doctor, 'I've made a note of it.'

'Jim,' said the doctor, 'I can't stand this – let's run for it.'

'No, I've given my word,' I said.

'I know, I know,' he cried. 'We can't help that. Let's run for it like antelopes.'

'I can't run for it like antelopes. I gave my word, but if they torture me I won't tell where the ship is. It lies in the North Inlet on the Southern beach.'

'The ship?' exclaimed the doctor.

Rapidly I described my adventures.

'It's you that saved our lives, Jim. Silver,' he cried as the cook drew near, 'don't be in a great hurry to find that treasure.'

'Why sir, I do my possible, which that ain't.'

The doctor didn't understand that, neither did I.

'I'll give you hope, Silver,' said the doctor. 'If you get alive out of this wolf-trap,' said the doctor, 'I'll do my best to save you.'

Silver didn't know he was in a wolf-trap, but he was grateful.

'You couldn't say more if you were my own mother.'

'Silver, I am not your mother. My advice is, keep the boy close beside you and if you need help, shout halloo. Good-bye, Jim,' he said, and he turned and walked into a tree.

Bow wow, Grrr, Woof woof!

GROUCHO: My God, he's getting more confident.

30. THE TREASURE HUNT – FLINT'S POINTER

'Jim,' said Silver, 'if I saved your life, you saved mine, I'll not forget it.'

Yes, he would not forget it, he said so.

'Now, we're going on this treasure hunt. You and me must stick close, back to back.'

GROUCHO: You won't get very far in that position.

'We'll find the treasure and we'll save our necks.'

GROUCHO: Only your necks? Not much to look forward to, eh?

A mutineer called us saying breakfast was ready. It was roast turkey, shot in the bush.

GROUCHO: What a terrible death.

'I've just eaten three times more than I couldn't eat,' said Silver, swallowing the parson's nose.

GROUCHO: My man, what has the parson got to say about this?

JIM:	Listen, it wasn't the parson's, it was the turkey's.
GROUCHO:	Oh? What's a turkey doing with a parson's nose? Hasn't he got one of his own?
JIM:	Please go away, Groucho, and die.
GROUCHO:	I'll have to think about that. Now whose dog is this?

Bow wow! Bow wow!

GROUCHO:	Believe me, you'll miss me.

A mutineer was throwing masses of food away on the fire as though there was no tomorrow.

GROUCHO: Yes, there is a tomorrow, just you wait and see!

'Aye mates,' said Silver, 'Lucky you 'as me to think for you with this here head. Sure enough they got the ship, but once we hit the treasure, we'll find it.'

No wonder the men were in good humour. I was terribly cast down.

GROUCHO: Cheer up, Jim, let me terribly cast you up.

Silver still had a foot in either camp.

GROUCHO: And that's no mean feat with only one foot!

'If the mutineers do attack us, there's Silver, a cripple, and only me, a boy,' I said.

GROUCHO: I'll give a hundred to one you'll lose.

We made a strange group of people, all but me armed to the teeth.

GROUCHO: Why do people want to arm their teeth?

Silver had four pistols – one in front, one at the back, one in his sock and one under his hat. 'Let 'em come one come all,' he growled.

At his waist Silver had a cutlass. His parrot was still on his shoulder, ankle deep in parrot shit, still talking. 'Avast ye lubbers, get below!!!'

GROUCHO: Don't get below him, he'll shit all over you.

With a rope around my waist, I followed after Silver who held the loose end in his teeth.

I gave the rope a sharp pull and out shot Silver's teeth.

'Dwon't byou bever bdo bthat bagain,' he mumbled.

GROUCHO: Give him his teeth back or he'll never talk again.

Silver returned his dentures back, but wait! His face had gone a funny shape.

GROUCHO: My God, he's put them in upside down!

Silver reversed his teeth and his face fell back into place.

So we all set out for the treasure, even the fellow with the bandaged head and the one with the shits and the swollen balls, and struggled one after another to the beach. We jumped on the long-boat and soon we were pulling out to sea, heading for the point near the treasure.

GROUCHO: You men don't mind me travelling as a stowaway? Are these the first class planks?

We pulled easily by Silver's directions with Groucho hanging on behind. We consulted the map:

TALL TREE. SPYGLASS HILL BEING A POINTER TO N. OF NE. SKELETON ISLAND ESE., AND BY E. TEN FEET.

GROUCHO: Who's got ten feet? He could make a fortune in the circus. Does he have an agent?

'We'll only find this spot,' said Silver, 'by reading the compass.'

GROUCHO: I only read the *Sun* for its page three boobs.

After a long passage, we landed at our chosen place. We began to ascend the slope towards a plateau. At the first onset, heavy, heavy, miry ground, matted, marshy vegetation, snakes, lions, tigers and gorillas delayed our progress.

GROUCHO: Don't forget the quicksands, which I am in at the moment.

'Stay there,' said Silver. 'We'll collect you on the way back.'

GROUCHO: Wait! I might have disappeared by then!

We had gone half a mile when the man farthest away began to shout in terror. The reason was he was standing over a skeleton.
' 'ee's dead,' said Morgan. 'But what sort of way is that for bones to lie? T'aint natural.'
Indeed at a glance the man lay perfectly straight, his hands raised above his head like a direction pointing directly ahead.
'I've taken a notion into my old numbskull,' observed Silver.
The body pointed straight in the direction and the compass pointed ESE and by E.
'I thought so,' said Silver. 'This 'ere is a pointer. Right up there is a line for the pole star and the jolly dollars!'
'This skeleton was Allardyce, he owed me money,' said Morgan.

GROUCHO: Looks like you won't get it back. Does anyone know if dry cleaning takes out quicksand stains?

'He stole my duck and he was killed by Flint,' said Morgan.
'Come, come,' said Silver, 'stow this talk. Flint's dead. Let's head for the treasure.'

The mention of Flint had an effect on the mutineers. They spoke with bated breath. The terror of Flint grew on them.

GROUCHO: If it grew on me I'd chop it off.

31. THE TREASURE HUNT – THE VOICE AMONG THE TREES

'I don't feel sharp,' said Morgan. 'Thinking of Flint gives me the shits.'

GROUCHO: Then don't you come near me.

All of a sudden a ghostly voice came from the middle of the trees.

Fifteen men on the dead man's chest –
Yo-ho-ho, and a bottle of rum!

'It's Flint, by –!' cried Merry.
Yes, it was Flint, by –!
The song stopped as suddenly as it began.
'Darby M'Graw,' it wailed, 'Darby M'Graw, Darby M'Graw.'
'That's Flint all right,' said Merry. 'Let's all fuck off.'
'Thems was 'is last words,' said Morgan, 'Let's fuck off.'
Dick had his bible out and read ' "And Jesus walketh on the water." '
'Bollocks,' said Morgan, ' 'ee would 'ave drowned!'
'Shipmates!' shouted Silver, 'I'm here to get that treasure. I never was feared of Flint. There's seven hundred thousand pounds not a hundred yards from here! That weren't Flint's voice, it had an echo now. Spirits don't have an echo. By the power!' shouted Silver, 'It were Ben Gunn, the silly bugger.'
'Why, nobody minds Ben Gunn; he's a silly bugger,' said Morgan.
Suddenly the mutineers' spirits had returned. They put their tools on their shoulders and set forth again.

GROUCHO: Tools on their shoulders? They must be deformed.

Merry walked first with Silver's compass.
Dick alone clutched his bible, looked around him with fearful glances; Silver even joked him on his precautions.
'Who makes all the ice cream in Israel? Walls of Jericho! Ha-ha!'
But Dick was not comforted; it was plain he was falling sick. His temperature was growing higher; finally he started to smoulder, then burst into flames and fell to the ground. There was no water so they all urinated on him to put it out.
The first of the trees reached proved the wrong one; 'Fuck,' said Morgan. So was the second; again 'Fuck,' said Morgan. The third tree rose two

hundred feet in the air – how it got up there we never knew. But it was not that that impressed them, it was the knowledge that seven hundred thousand pounds lay in its shadow.

Silver hobbled on his crutch; he cursed when flies in swarms settled on his nose. It was hard to keep up with the rapid pace of the treasure-hunters, who were moving at fifty miles per hour. Dick was lying on the ground a smouldering mound stinking of piss.

Bow wow! Bow wow!

GROUCHO: Good God, he's *still* here!

We were now at the margin of the thicket.

'Huzza, mates, all together!' shouted Morgan; and the foremost broke into a run, the foremost arrived first.

And suddenly, not ten yards further, a low cry arose. Silver doubled forward.

Before us was a great excavation, not very recent, for the sides had fallen in and grass had started to grow on the bottom.

GROUCHO: Grass is growing on whose bottom?

In this was the shaft of a pick broken in two, and the boards of several packing cases strewn around and an old hamburger and chips. One of these boards had been branded with a hot iron; on it was the word *Walrus* – the name of Flint's ship.

All was clear. The treasure had been found and rifled; the seven hundred thousand pounds were gone. They all said 'Fuck!'

GROUCHO: Look on the bright side, boys. You can get unemployment benefit.

32. THE FALL OF A CHIEFTAIN

Each of these six men was as though he had been struck. With Silver the blow passed instantly.

'Jim, take that and stand by for trouble.'

So saying he passed me three pistols from under his hat. At the same time he began retreating until he had put the hollow between us and the mutineers. He looked at me as if to say, 'Here is a tight corner.'

GROUCHO: Right now you're five hundred to one.

The mutineers, with oaths and cries, leaped into the pit to dig with their fingers, throwing aside boards as they did. One ate the old hamburger and chips. Morgan found a piece of gold; he held it up with a stream of 'Fucking hell! What the fuck is this?'

'Two bloody guineas!' roared Merry. 'That's your seven hundred thousands is it, Silver?'

'No it isn't,' said Silver, 'it's two bloody guineas.'

'You're the man for bargains, are you?'

GROUCHO: Yes, he shopped modestly and only went to auctions.

'Mates, I tell you,' screamed Merry, 'I tell you now – that man there knew it all along. I look on the face of him and you'll see it wrote there.'

Sure enough, written on Silver's forehead was 'That man there knew it all along.' By this time everyone was in Merry's favour. They began to scramble out of the excavation, but on the opposite side. Well, there we stood, two on one side, five on the other.

At last Merry seemed to think a speech might help. He cleared his throat, it landed on the other side. 'Ladies and Gentlemen, unaccustomed as I am to public speaking,' he began. 'Men,' he said raising a cutlass in his hand, 'follow –'

Just then, crack! crack! crack! Three musket shots flashed out of the thicket.

Groucho: It's the Twelfth Cavalry

Merry tumbled head first into the pit; the man with the bandaged head spun round, dead.

The remaining mutineers fled in the direction of away. Before you could wink, we were joined by the doctor, Gray and Ben Gunn, the silly bugger.

'Forward!' said the doctor, 'we must head them off before they reach their long-boat.'

We set off at a pace of fifty miles an hour. Silver followed us at the lesser speed of forty; oh, the agony that he went through till the muscles of his chest were fit to burst; in fact the muscles of his chest did burst and he came out. It took him ages to scoop himself back in again and rebutton his doublet after which a shrill little voice could be heard from inside screaming, 'Pieces of eight! Fuck you!' He was already thirty yards behind us and on the verge of collapse.

'Doctor,' he called, 'I'm on the verge of collapse; there's no hurry.'

Sure enough, we were between the mutineers and their boat so we sat down to catch our breath. Mind you, you can catch your breath standing up but we were doing it further down.

Long John joined us. 'Thank 'ee doctor; you came in the nick-o-tine. So it's you, Ben Gunn the silly bugger.'

'Yes, I'm Ben Gunn,' said the marooned 'silly bugger'.

'Ben Gunn, you silly bugger, you had the treasure all the time!'

Ben Gunn, the silly bugger, had found the treasure and carted it back to his cave. It took him two years to do it.

'Yes, I went all around the island. I took it to my cave, but I couldn't find anywhere to spend it!'

Silver laughed. 'Ha ha, don't worry, we'll find somewhere.'

We found the mutineers' boat and smashed it into teeny-weeny pieces.

'Ah,' said Silver, 'it was fortunate for me I had Jim Hawkins here. You would let old John be cut to bits, and never give it a thought, Doctor.'

'No,' said the doctor, 'even if you were cut to teeny-weeny bits.'

GROUCHO: Using a scalpel, I presume?

We all made for Ben Gunn, the silly bugger's cave. The squire met us. At Long John's salute, he flushed. Someone had pulled his chain.

'John Silver,' he said, 'you're a prodigious cook, villain, imposter, thief, murderer, mimic and a bank manager, sir.'

GROUCHO: Making seven all together.

'Thank you for me being all those,' said Silver.

After a long walk we entered the cave; before a big fire lay Captain Smollett and in the far corner a great heap of silver doubloons and quadrilaterals of solid bars of gold. At the sight of it the doctor fainted.

'It's too much for him, but it's not too much for me,' said Silver excitedly.

Little did we know that at that moment there were terrible floods in Bangladesh with 32 drowned.

'Now you, John Silver,' said the captain, 'what brings you here, man?'

'I was carried here by Ben Gunn,' returned Silver.

'God forgive you for being a scoundrel,' said the captain. So God forgave Silver for being a scoundrel.

What a supper we had that night. Long John roasted a whole goat, with vegetables grown by Ben Gunn, that and a bottle of old wine from the *Hispaniola*. Never, I'm sure, were people happier, especially those poor people in Bangladesh.

33. AND LAST

Next morning, we fell to work carrying the mass of heavy gold bars to the *Hispaniola*. It ruptured poor Ben Gunn and Silver. Instead I sorted out the silver doubloons, accidently slipping some into my pockets. When they asked me what the bulge was I said it was a rupture caused when sorting doubloons. There were strange Oriental coins stamped with what looked like wisps of string or bits of spiders' webs. In the end I realised they *were* wisps of string and bits of spiders' webs.

So far no sign of the three mutineers.

'You don't expect them to put signs up showing where they are?' said the captain.

'It would be very useful if they did, sir,' said Silver.

At last – one night the doctor, Silver and I were strolling on the hill when from the thick darkness came a terrible noise between shrieking and howling, a sort of 'shrieowling'.

'Tis the mutineers,' said the doctor. 'They sound as if they've got rabies!'

'But there are no mad dogs on the island,' I said.

GROUCHO: Yes there is. There's one that keeps going 'Bow wow! Bow wow!'

Silver, I should say, was allowed his entire liberty, though they all treated him like a dog. They threw his food on the floor.

'I suppose,' said the doctor, 'you could hardly ask me to call you human?'

'No, sir, Long John Silver will do,' said Silver.

'If I was sure those three we heard were raving, I'm almost certain that two of them have the fever, either malaria, typhus or clap. I must leave this camp and, whatever the risk, it is my duty to attend them,' said the doctor.

He went, treated them and gave them medicine. They beat the shit out of him and sent him back. The doctor returned in a sorry state and said, 'I made a mistake.'

'I'm sorry to see you like this,' said Silver.

'You're sorry!' said the doctor.

'Those men down there don't keep their word,' said Silver.

Bow wow! Bow wow!

GROUCHO: Whose dog is that?
BEN GUNN: It's mine.
GROUCHO: Can't you keep him quiet?

That was the last word we had of the pirates. It was decided we must leave the island. We weighed the anchor, which was all we could manage, and stood out of North Inlet. Birds flew up and we shot them. We saw the colours still flying above the stockade.

The three mutineers must have been watching us; there we saw all three of them kneeling on a beach, their arms raised in supplication. It went to our hearts, all except Silver; it went to his liver. 'Fuck 'em,' he said. Seeing us sail away, one of them leapt to his feet shouldering a musket and sent a shot whistling over Ben Gunn's head. Ben Gunn lay flat on the deck.

'Am I safe?' he asked.

'Only if you stay there,' said Silver, as another shot flew past his ear.

'I hope you all bloody starve to death,' he shouted at them.

They did.

Faintly from the shore came, 'Fuck you, Silver!'

Soon the island was lost in the mist. We were short of men on board, so everyone had to bear a hand. I bore my hand, I used it every day. We had set course for home, which was England, God save the King, but God help the people.

LOG OF *HISPANIOLA*

August 6, 17–
Heavy seas and wind, crew washed overboard.

August 7, 17–
Crew washed back on again.

August 8, 17–
Silver shot albatross. Immediately ship began to sink. Silver resuscitated the albatross. Ship immediately stopped sinking.

August 9, 17–
Captain down again. Ben Gunn up.

August 10, 17–
Capetown
Docked. Entire crew went ashore, stayed there a week in a brothel. Most of them came back with it.

August 17, 17–
Doctor injecting all with the clap with mercury. In hot weather some become seventeen feet tall.

August 18, 17–
Once more set sail for England. Realised we were going in the opposite direction.

August 20, 17–
Still going in wrong direction. Told captain. Re-set sail for England.

September 3, 17–
Heavy storm. Crew washed overboard again.

September 5, 17–
Crew washed back on again.

September 16, 17–
Ran onto submerged rocks.

September 17, 17–
Ran off submerged rocks onto rocks behind us.

September 20, 17–
Captain's fiftieth birthday. We gave him a gift-wrapped anchor. He threw it overboard. Brought ship to a halt. Pulled anchor up. Ship on way again. Ship's rudder jammed. Ship going round in circles.

September 21, 17–
Ship still going in circles.

September 22, 17–
Captain says he's getting giddy.

September 23, 17–
Captain still giddy.

September 24, 17–
Silver lowered down the stern, straightens rudder but gets stuck between it and the ship.

September 25, 17–
Lower Jim Hawkins to help Silver. He comes up but Hawkins is stuck down.

September 26, 17–
Hawkins still stuck down. We lower food to him. He sends back empty plate and asks for more. Instead we heave him up to eat it.

September 27, 17–
Ship going straight, which is more than can be said about the crew.

September 29, 17–
Lightning storm, a fire appears in the rigging. 'My God,' said Silver, ' that's Saint Elmo's fire.' 'What's he want do that for?' said Ben.

October 23, 17–
Home. Finally we reached Bristol. Five men only of those who had sailed returned with us. Drink and the devil had done for the rest. We were not quite as that other hell ship they sang about.

With one man of her crew alive,
What put to sea with seventy-five.

All of us had an ample share of the treasure. Some used it wisely, wild nights with women; others foolishly. Captain Smollett retired after wild nights with women. Gray saved his Navy money, and spent it on wild nights and women. Ben Gunn, he got a thousand pounds, spent it in three weeks and started begging, he was still a silly bugger. Silver disappeared clean out of our lives. I believe he ended up with Deptford Flo, stump rot, the clap and his parrot. With my money I cured my mother of sleep-walking. Sometimes I sit up in bed and I hear the surf booming on that island and hear Silver's parrot's sharp voice, 'Pieces of eight, pieces of eight!'
Bow wow! Bow wow!